VICIOUS
A FLAWED SERIES
BOOK 3

AURYN HADLEY

KITTY COX

SPOTTED HORSE PRODUCTIONS

Vicious is a work of fiction. Names, characters, places, brands, media, and incidents are either the product of the author's imagination or are used fictitiously. Any resemblance to actual events, locales, or persons, living or dead, is entirely coincidental.

The author acknowledges the trademarked status and trademark owners of various products referenced in this work of fiction, which have been used without permission. The publication/ use of these trademarks is not authorized, associated with, or sponsored by the trademark owners.

Copyright © 2023 by Auryn Hadley / Kitty Cox

All Rights Reserved. In accordance with the U.S. Copyright Act of 1976, the scanning, uploading, and electronic sharing of any part of this book without the permission of the publisher and the copyright owner constitute unlawful piracy and theft of the author's intellectual property. Thank you for your support of the author's rights.

Cover Art by DAZED designs

Edited by Sarah Williams

DEDICATION

This book is for anyone who's been knocked down and pulled themselves back up. It's also for the ones who offered a helping hand when it wasn't really their problem. Sometimes shit is hard, and no one should be expected to always do it on their own.

When you feel alone, just know you're not. We see you. We are cheering you on. You are a hero to us, even if we don't know about your struggles.

Auryn Hadley

Kitty Cox

SENSITIVITY WARNING & LIFELINES

SENSITIVITY WARNING: Discussions of off-screen suicide, rape and assault, bullying, cyber harassment, violence, and more.

National Sexual Assault Hotline - RAINN (Rape, Abuse & Incest National Network) is the nation's largest anti-sexual violence organization.

Anyone affected by sexual assault, whether it happened to you or someone you care about, can find support on the National Sexual Assault Hotline. You can also visit **online.rainn.org** to receive support via confidential online chat.
1-800-656-HOPE (4673)

The 988 Suicide & Crisis Hotline is a national network of local

SENSITIVITY WARNING & LIFELINES

crisis centers that provides free and confidential emotional support to people in suicidal crisis or emotional distress 24 hours a day, 7 days a week in the United States.
Dial - 988 or
Text **STRENGTH** to 741741
(988lifeline.org)

National Suicide Prevention Lifeline - If you or someone you know is struggling with drug/alcohol addiction or having thoughts of suicide, please reach out to
1-800-273-8255
(suicidepreventionlifeline.org)

Trevor Project - If you are a young person in crisis, feeling suicidal, or in need of a safe and judgment-free place to talk, call the TrevorLifeline now at
1-866-488-7386
or over text message:
Text **START** to **678678**.

The **Trevor Project** (thetrevorproject.org) is an American non-profit organization focused on suicide prevention among lesbian, gay, bisexual, transgender, queer, and questioning youth.

Trans Lifeline's Hotline (translifeline.org/hotline) is a peer

SENSITIVITY WARNING & LIFELINES

support phone service run by trans people for our trans and questioning peers. We believe that some of the best support that trans people can receive is from trans community members with shared lived experience.

AUTHOR'S NOTE

Some events in *A Flawed Series* overlap those of *Gamer Girls* and *Shades of Trouble*. Many details mentioned within will allow the reader to understand what happened, but for those of you who want the in depth details, you will find them in the *Gamer Girls* and *Shades of Trouble* series.

Spoiler Alert - each series has spoilers for the other.

CHAPTER 1

CADE

I could barely see as I turned into the drive. Everything was blurry from the tears welling up, but I knew the Andrews farm like the back of my hand now. Slowly, so as not to spook any horses, I idled my Impala towards that grassy spot we all used to park.

Then I shut it off. What I couldn't do was breathe. My throat was so damned tight, and it hurt. Fuck, if I was honest, everything hurt. Still, I needed to get my shit together. If I was going to ask for a favor, then I needed enough control over myself to suck up my damned pride and just *ask*.

After wiping my face dry, I pushed open the heavy steel door, listening to it creak, and climbed out. On auto-pilot, my feet turned for the backyard. There, a massive grey mongrel was wiggling excitedly to see me, and it helped more than anything.

"Hey, Quake," I tried, but my voice was rough from the abuse to my throat.

When the poor excuse of a guard-dog woofed excitedly at the

attention, I opened the gate and went in, aiming for the main door - but I wasn't the only one who heard him. From the building I'd always thought of as a garage or shop, Riley walked out. There was a soft little smile on her face, right up until her eyes landed on me.

"Knock!" she screamed, hurrying towards me.

No, she was running. I'd never seen this woman lose her cool before, but she rounded the edge of the yard and rushed right up to me, dropping something along her way. That, more than anything else, proved how focused she was on me.

"Knock!" she yelled again before palming the side of my face and making me look at her. "Oh, shit, Cade. What the fuck happened?"

"I, uh..." I had to pause for a little cough. "Um, Dad found out."

Everything about her changed in that instant. The softness began to solidify. Her eyes narrowed and her body grew stiff. Her touch was still gentle, but the whirlwind of a woman before me had just turned into a fucking tornado.

"Inside," she ordered. "Fuck, I'm assuming he kicked you out too?"

"I kinda ran," I admitted. "That's what Jericho said to do, but her mom's home this weekend because she got busted for fighting at school, and I can't go over there, so I was hoping that maybe it would be ok if I just crashed here for the weekend until I can figure something out?"

Damn, that actually didn't sound too bad. Surely she'd say yes. She had to, because if Riley wouldn't let me crash here, I had no fucking clue where I'd be living.

But the woman had me walking, heading for the door. "Your father hit you like this?" she asked again.

Which was when I looked down. Ok, I was more of a mess than I'd realized. My shirt was torn at the waist. How, I had no clue. It wasn't bad, but still obvious. Then there was the dirt on my shoulder and jeans from when I'd been on the ground. Oh, and that was blood on my arm. Probably a scratch, because it wasn't much.

"Um..." I nodded. I didn't want to say yes.

I didn't want to admit how bad it had been. I really didn't want to utter the words that might make me crack. Right now, I was holding it together with sheer determination, but just thinking about this? No, it was too much. Too heavy. Too fucking terrifying, because I wasn't supposed to be fucking homeless! I was supposed to be ok until I graduated.

Damn it, my eyes were getting blurry again. Not that it mattered, because Riley led me into her house and right to the living room no one ever seemed to use. There, she eased me down onto a couch.

"Ok," she said, crouching before me. "We can move the nursery into Kitty's room if we have to. I mean, if Knock's not sure about you staying in his room. We'll get a real bed for you, but I have supplies to make you comfortable until then." Then she caressed the back of my head, jerking her hand away when she hit a lump Dad had left me. "Don't worry, Cade. You're home now. We got you."

Then Knock said gently, "Welcome to the Andrews Clan. And Riley, he can stay with me."

"Then we'll worry about the bedroom if you two break up," she decided, glancing back to look at him. "Because we don't leave anyone behind."

"Teamwork's overpowered," he agreed.

But damn, my throat was getting tighter. Still, I had to say it. I just had to. "Death over Dishonor, right?"

Knock nodded. "Yeah, and you're going to need some of Riley's good drugs."

"Did you grab my bridle?" she asked him. "I don't have many

harness bridles in yearling size, and we both know Quake would eat it, but better a bridle than a friend."

Knock just held up a tangle of leather. "Will trade for drugging my boyfriend."

"Deal," she agreed, pushing to her feet to snatch the leather from his hands and head up the hall.

Then Knock immediately took the spot beside me. "What the fuck, babe?"

"Dylan told my dad," I admitted. Then I cleared my throat, trying to push back both the emotions and the damage. "Dad came home early. I, um, kinda confirmed it. Knock, I can't go back."

"It's ok," he promised. "I have a pretty nice room, and I'm willing to share."

I just jiggled my head. It was supposed to be a nod, but I was a complete mess right now. Still, there was one more thing I needed to know.

"What kind of drugs?" I asked.

"Riley gets tossed off a horse a few times a year," he explained. "Now that she's not broke, she goes to the doctor to make sure she didn't hurt anything too badly - mostly her head. Well, they always give her pain meds. She takes one, hates how it fucks with her thinking, and stops. So she's got a lot of it stored up in the medicine cabinet."

"Oh." Ok, that made sense. It also sounded like Riley.

However, when the woman in question came back, she was on the phone. "...Yep. And Knock's room, it sounds like. Yeah." Then she jerked her chin at me. "What did you bring with you, Cade?"

My mouth opened, flopped a few times, and then I just shook my head. I had nothing. Fuck! Not even clean clothes! The only thing I'd made it out of that place with was my car and what I was wearing. Thankfully, I hadn't taken my wallet out of my pocket or I'd have lost that too!

"Not even a go bag," she told her phone. "Yeah. I think that needs to be tonight. Mhm. Full bitch-mode, babe. No one messes with my family." She chuckled softly. "Stray number two. Ok, fine! Three. Sue me. See you in a bit."

"Logan," Knock explained. "Means she's got a plan."

"I kinda don't," I told him. "I just... Jeri told me to run, and that was all I could think. Dad tried to choke me out, but I got his hand off me - "

"This?" Knock asked, gently tracing a line on the side of my throat.

"I don't know," I mumbled. "Maybe?"

He nodded, looking so damned calm when I was in the process of shattering completely. Those dark brown eyes of his just found mine, held them, and then he smiled softly.

"It's going to be ok," he promised. "One way or another, we'll make sure of it."

"But how?" I asked.

He shrugged. "You might have to clean the barn some more."

Which made me chuckle. "I actually like cleaning the barn. It's peaceful."

"Deal!" Riley said as she made her way out of the kitchen.

Damn, that woman was all over the place, and she was zooming more than I was used to. I turned, trying to see where she was going next, but grunted when I found something else that hurt. Knock just caught my chin and turned me back so I was facing him.

"Don't worry about her," he said gently. "Also, don't try to stop her. She's got an idea, and she's working on it. We don't ask until she gives us our assignments."

"Because of me?"

"Yeah," he agreed. "She called you family. See, my big sister has a bad habit of picking up strays and building her family around them. Started with Kitty. Shit, if I'm honest, it started with her parents picking her up."

"Not sure that counts," I pointed out.

"Does to her." He shrugged. "She was adopted into this place, Cade. Not born. Adopted. Then came Kitty. There were some horses and dogs in the middle, then Quake, then me, and now you. Logan wasn't a stray, though. He was the one smart enough to see what she hides under all her anger and determination, realize it was something he couldn't live without, and make sure he was worthwhile."

"So how do I make sure I'm worthwhile?"

"You cleaned the barn," Riley said as she hurried from the stairs back into the kitchen. "You also rode the horse." Her voice came to me from the other side of the wall. "Mostly, it was that you didn't pick on Zoe for being a horse girl. You gave her a reason to be proud of it, and you didn't pick on the ones who like them." Then she came back with a glass of water and a pair of pills. "Take these. Do not try to refuse."

"Yes, ma'am." I accepted the pills with one hand and the water with the other.

They were oval, white, and I had no clue how hard they'd hit, but Riley said to take them, so I took them. When I was done, Knock took the glass and set it on the table beside him. Riley was already off again.

"He needs to learn how to play Eternal Combat!" she yelled from a back room. "Don't care if he's red or blue, but he will *not* play for yellow!"

"Play yellow," Knock told me. "She'll love it."

"What color do you play?" I asked, barely knowing the game.

Mostly, I knew it was how this household made most of their money. Not in that game necessarily, but by being professional gamers, and this one helped them prepare for their tournaments. I also knew they were friends with the co-owner of the company who made it. First-person shooters, however, weren't exactly my best genre. I wasn't bad, but I certainly wasn't good.

"I play for blue," Knock said. "My outfit is called Paradox, and you'll love them. Cool guys. Pretty sure I can get you an invite too."

"Know the guild leader that well?" I was trying to make it a joke, but it didn't come out sounding like I wanted.

Knock just gestured to the area of the house where Riley had last been. "Yep. You do too. It's also an *outfit*." He gave me a weak smile. "Feeling better yet?"

"Yes and no," I admitted. "I just..." A heavy breath fell from my lungs. "I don't know what happened. I don't know what I'm supposed to be doing. I..." When I tried to inhale, it trembled. "My dad..."

"I know," he promised, leaning in to wrap his arms around me. "Fuck, trust me. I know. And you feel so lost because those people are supposed to be your parents. Home is supposed to be safe, but it never really was. You tried to change yourself, be something else, but you just couldn't, and they saw the real you and rejected it, and it hits you in a way you can't put words to."

I tried to resist. I wanted to be strong. I didn't want to turn into a mess in front of this guy. I wanted him to think I was strong, sexy, and that I had my shit together, but this? The feel of his comfort, the soothing sound of his voice, and the complete understanding?

My arms went around his back and my face found that spot between his shoulder and his neck. That trembling breath stuttered a little more, and my eyes decided to just fucking betray me. They didn't leak. They ran.

"I didn't mean to," I mumbled against him. "I tried to wait. I tried so hard to push everything away. I didn't have friends. I didn't hang out with anyone. I played games. That was all I had, just playing Flawed. I didn't even talk to the one person I enjoyed seeing the most because I was trying so hard to just *wait*. And then she moved here. Jericho moved here, changed my life, and made me think it was ok to be me - and now I've lost everything!"

"No," he promised. "No, Cade. We're going to make sure you're ok." He kissed the top of my head. "I'm going to take care of you." And his hands moved gently over my back, comforting me in a way I hadn't known I needed. "Right now, all you need to do is break, babe. I got you. We all have you. It's ok to fall down this time, because we're all here to pick you up. That's what real friends do."

So I gave up trying to be tough. Fuck it. I let myself cry.

CHAPTER 2

KNOCK

While Riley stole Cade away to get him cleaned up and in a shirt that wasn't torn, I sent a text to Ripper and Zoe. I almost sent one to Jeri as well, but paused. She'd taken the news of that girl at school dying a little too hard. I knew brittle when I saw it, and the last thing I needed was to make it worse, so I called Hottie.

He was confused at first. Clearly, she hadn't filled him in yet, but she would. I knew she would. He also promised they were on the way, which was what I needed right now. Cade needed backup. More than that, he needed to know we weren't leaving him because of something we'd already accepted.

It sounded stupid when put like that, but I understood the feeling. His own father had just kicked him out. He'd be waiting for everyone else to reject him right now. I had, when it had happened to me. Instead, I'd been accepted and it had changed my life, so this was my best attempt to pay it forward.

First came Zoe. Evidently she'd picked up Ripper, because the pair came inside with Quake bounding beside them. I was just about to explain what was going on when Cade came out of the bathroom. The shirt he was wearing was a little loose. One of Logan's, I thought. It also didn't matter. The way Cade looked at his friends standing beside me proved I was right. He was too tense.

"You look like shit," Ripper said, crossing the distance before even Zoe could.

Then he wrapped Cade up in a hug. I saw Cade wince, proving he'd been hit pretty hard, but he didn't pull away. It also took him a little too long to figure out what to do. Slowly, almost timidly, his arms lifted to wrap about Ripper's back.

"Dad hit me," he breathed.

Ripper just held him a little longer. "I'm so sorry," he breathed. "I'm so, so sorry."

But Zoe had her hand up, holding it over her mouth. "Ripper, bring him over here. He needs to sit. He has to hurt. Has anyone made coffee for him yet?"

From the kitchen, Riley called out, "Making it now!"

"I just don't know what to do now," Cade said as Ripper guided him back to the couch. Slowly - looking like he hurt all over - he sat beside me. "Did you tell them?"

"I figured you might need some reassurance," I explained, hoping I hadn't fucked up. "Together, maybe we can - "

The opening of the door made me pause and look up as Jericho and Hottie hurried in - but Jeri was carrying a box. It wasn't that big, but it looked like mail or something? There were those papers on the outside, at least.

Her eyes landed on Cade and she paused. For once, she didn't rush in. Instead, she looked down at her box, back to Cade, and then the box again.

"I know, we never use the living room," Zoe said, waving her and Hottie further in.

Jeri turned to put the box down, but paused again. It was almost as if she had something precious in there, but what?

"What's in the box?" I asked.

And that was what made her finally set it down on the closest table. "Nothing. It can wait." And then she hurried over to Cade. "I'm so glad you ran." And she threw herself against his chest, slamming into him in the hardest hug yet.

"Oww," he groaned, hugging her back. "Shit, Jeri. Easy. I'm still healing from the first beatdown, and Dad wasn't exactly gentle."

She let go and knelt before him. "He fucking hit you?"

"Yeah. Dylan told him we got in that fight at school because I was kissing some guy. Dad said he'd beat it out of me, so I ran. Just like you said, I ran, but I know your mom is home this weekend - "

"Will be," Hottie corrected. "Her flight hasn't landed yet."

"Yeah, but that's why I came here," Cade went on. "And Dad didn't want to let me leave. He..." His swallowing was loud. "Um, I told him I'm bi."

"Good," Jeri said. "Fuck him if he doesn't like it."

"Not how that works," I told her.

"Yes, Knock, it fucking well is!" she snarled, but the anger was too much. Too pointed. "If someone doesn't like what we do, then fuck them! If they think bullying or hitting or trying to change someone will help? If they think they can make us bend until we break, we will fucking well find a way to *prove them wrong!*"

"Jeri..." Hottie breathed.

And she snapped her mouth shut on whatever part of that rant would come next, but I'd seen it. This wasn't just about Cade. This was bigger, deeper, and building up inside her. Those words had been but the smallest crack, and I had a feeling too many more would shatter her.

Because I'd seen this before. I remembered my friend Rhaven

backed into a corner with her deepest, darkest secret being held over her head. Like Jeri, she'd tried so hard to be tough about it, but it had looked the same way: fragile.

"It's ok," I assured her. "He's going to be fine."

"But where are you going to stay?" Jeri asked Cade.

"Here!" Riley yelled from the kitchen again. "We've got room."

We really didn't. In truth, this house was about to crack at the seams with people, animals, and a lack of space. She was also right, because we made it work. Somehow, all of us found a way to make our close proximity into a benefit instead of an annoyance.

But I'd only been dating him for a bit. Shit, he wasn't even officially out of the closet! Boyfriend was still a term I was trying to get used to, and now he was moving in with me. Not just under the same roof, but into my room, sharing my bed, and waking up beside me every single morning.

It was great. It was amazing. The reason why sucked, and that in itself made all of this more scary. What if he came out and some other guy at school caught his eye? What if we couldn't share a space without fighting?

No. I wouldn't think like that. He needed me - well, us - so he got all of us.

"Ok," Riley said as she came back into the living room somehow balancing a few too many cups in her hands. "Coffee for everyone. Pick a color, grab it, and do not drop it."

One by one, we all took our cups. Pink for Jeri. Purple for Ripper. Red for Zoe. Blue was mine and Cade went for the orange. That left yellow and green for Riley and Hottie. Smugly, she passed over the yellow one, keeping the green for herself.

"Looks like I need to buy some more travel mugs," she said, moving to my other side to claim a seat of her own. "Ok, so the plan - "

Quake cut her off as he began barking like an idiot. Riley just sighed and set her cup down, clearly intending to get to her feet, but the door opened before her butt left the cushion. Logan stormed in.

"Quake, hush. I wasn't going that fast," he told the dog. Then his eyes turned to Cade. "Welcome home, little brother. I hear we have shit to do."

"We do?" Cade asked.

"As I was about to say..." Riley tried.

Logan just waved her down, then began peeling off his suit coat. "You are eighteen. Your father not only evicted you from your home without the necessary warning time, he also assaulted you. That's not legal, Cade. From the sounds of it, you have nothing. The Silk shirt looks good on you, though. I'll ask Chance to send a few more."

Cade just looked down at his shirt. "She said this is yours."

"Mhm," Logan agreed. "Which means you don't have one of your own. We're about to change that. You feeling good enough for one more push?"

"Where are we going?" Jericho asked.

Logan laughed once, dryly. "You? Nowhere." Then he looked at Hottie. "How do you feel about lending us those muscles?"

"More than willing," Hottie assured him. "What am I lifting?"

"Holding back," Logan corrected. "Q, I need a few business cards. Cade, you're going to get only what you need. Preferably clothes and little else."

"Computer," I pointed out. "He won't want to leave that."

"Did your father buy the computer, or did you?" Logan asked Cade.

"A bit of both," he admitted.

"Take the main box. Leave the monitor, peripherals, and everything else. The hard drive is the main goal, but we don't want to waste time pulling it. Q, babe?"

"Tools," she said, getting up and hurrying to the bedroom. "You need to change, Void."

"No," he assured her, "I don't. Right now, I'm going to be as legal as I need to, because *no one* fucks with us and gets away with it." Then his eyes moved to me. "And the little bitch who did this?"

"Wasn't a bitch," Zoe pointed out. "It was Dylan."

"I know," Logan assured her, "and yes, he's a little bitch. Ruin him, Knock. This crossed a line."

"Working on it," I promised. "You want me to go with?"

"You handle the house," Logan said. "I think taking you there would incite worse. Hottie and I..." He turned to look at the man in question. "Do you have a better name?"

"Grayson," he offered.

"Hot," Ripper suggested. "Hurts my pride a bit less to call him Hot, short for HotShot."

"Ok," Logan said, clearly still going. "Hot and I will make sure Mr. Bradford can't lay hands on Cade. If he does, we will press charges for assault. It won't go far, but the police intervention will give us the time for Cade to get what he needs from the house."

Hottie chuckled. "Sounds like you've done this before."

"Terrorizing people is my day job," Logan explained. "Kicking their asses is my preferred one. But no. I just had a little chat with my dad on the way home, so I got a few extra tips and tricks. Trust me, I learned from the best."

Hottie just nodded. "Gonna trust you."

But Jericho hadn't said a thing. That wasn't normal. When I glanced over, she was looking at that box again, which made me think it was important. Possibly something she didn't want Cade to know? Well, if that was the case, I'd ask once they were gone. Hopefully it would keep me from freaking out while waiting for them to get back.

Then Riley stormed back into the room. This time, her synthetic dreads were pulled back in a massive ponytail. That was her work hairstyle. She pressed a handful of business cards into Logan's hand and held up a set of keys.

"We're taking the truck," she announced. "And Hottie? If that fucker makes it past you, I'm going to put my fist in his face. That's assault too, and I don't want to get arrested, so don't let it happen, ok?"

"And what am I doing?" Cade asked.

Logan just smiled at him. "You're going to let us carry you for as long as you need, because that's how teamwork becomes overpowered. The first step is going back to your place, scaring the shit out of your father with your new-found power and prestige. When I tell you to, you will get only what you own or need. Clothes - all of them." He paused. "Q?"

"Garbage bags," she told him, holding up a roll. "Unlike you, I'm used to moving fast."

He nodded. "Clean, dirty, or whatever, Cade. We'll sort it out later. Any gifts or mementos. All the things you would not want to lose if that place burns down, because as of tonight, it may as well be gone to you. That bridge is burned. You will never need to go back. I swear I will make sure of it."

Cade just nodded slowly. "I don't know how to thank you," he breathed.

Which was when Logan finally moved closer and gently rubbed the guy's shoulder. "This, Cade, is how a family really works. Doesn't matter if we share DNA. Doesn't matter if we're officially related. Family are the ones who have your back." Then he turned to look across the room at everyone here. "And I think you have a pretty big one. Let us help. That's how you thank us, because it makes us feel less helpless."

CHAPTER 3

HOTSHOT

The truck was big. Big enough that the back seats had more than enough leg room. Surprisingly, it wasn't Logan who drove, but Riley - and that woman handled this thing like it was an extension of herself. Beside me, Cade stared quietly out the window. In front of me, Riley and Logan were talking softly, probably making plans.

I was just trying to keep my shit together. This was now. This mattered. Jeri would be ok with the rest of Ruin, because those people would take care of her. I tried to make myself believe that, but I felt like I was abandoning her when she needed me most. Shit, if I was honest with myself, I felt like I was barely able to focus.

That girl was my whole world. Ever since my fiancée had died, Jeri had become my lifeline. Before that, she'd been the closest thing to family I had. This mess with Cade sucked, though. It had to be handled, because it was real. He was real. This was the here and now.

But that box was too heavy.

I couldn't even convince myself to say what was really in it. Proof. That was what I'd go with. It was a good enough word, because the proof was in there. Proof of things so horrible, my mind tried to shy away from them, but this? It was a fucking good way to distract me.

Cade needed me, and I needed to keep putting one foot in front of the other. That was what Jeri had told me so long ago. So long as we kept progressing, kept going forward, then we would eventually wade through the shit life kept dumping on us. It wasn't fair Cade had to go through this, but Amber? That poor girl...

Nope. Not right now. I wrenched my mind back to the present just as Cade told Riley to turn up a driveway. The house wasn't at all what I'd been expecting, though. It was grey. A sad color that would've made me think of snow clouds back when I lived in Colorado. Too blue to be called anything but cold, but not blue enough to break free of the boring shade of grey. A few pieces of the siding were missing, chipped away from age and weather. Beneath, green-and-white striated patterns were visible, clearly another layer of crap that cold color was hiding.

Then there was the roof. It was a darker grey, but in so many different shades. A patch here was darker than the rest. One over there was lighter. It looked like someone had just said it was good enough, which told me all I needed to know about Cade's father.

The moment we parked, all of us climbed out. The four of us grouped up in front of the truck; Logan made a "wait" gesture, then headed for the door. I shifted to follow, but Riley grabbed my arm, holding me back.

"Let him do his thing first," she told me.

Naturally, Logan didn't even make it to the door before Cade's father stormed out, holding a shotgun. I tensed, but Riley's hand just held me in place. Glancing over, I saw she had one on Cade's arm too. The most impressive thing, however, was Logan.

The man climbed the stairs, holding out a business card. "Mr. Bradford?" he asked, completely ignoring the gun. "My name is Logan Weiss, Attorney at Law. I'm here representing Cade Bradford in an unauthorized eviction. We would like to settle this amicably and out of court, so - "

"That's not my son!" the man snapped.

"Didn't say he was," Logan assured him. "And yet, there is plenty of documented proof that Cade lived here until this afternoon. I was unable to find a notice of eviction filed with the county. That, Mr. Bradford, is a complication. Like I was about to say, our settlement is to have one hour to remove Cade's belongings, limited to clothing, mementos, and one computer case. If you agree to this, then we will refrain from filing for civil action."

"You think talking all fancy to me is going to make me give in?" the man asked, hefting his shotgun like he wanted to make sure Logan saw it. "Boy, I know how to deal with your type."

"Yes, sir," Logan agreed. "I'm sure you do. I also happen to know that Brian Sanders with the Sanger Police Department was notified we were coming to make an offer. If you would like to kick us off your property, we will go - and then be forced to settle this in court. According to Cade's knowledge, your financial situation might make that more complicated for you."

"You sayin' I'm poor?"

"Sir," Logan told him, "I'm saying I'm a very good attorney, and I will make sure you're poor by the time I'm done. *Or* you can simply let the boy get his things. Two options. Your choice. I get paid either way."

Yeah, but I was pretty sure Cade hadn't told Logan half that shit. Granted, just looking at this place, a few of those guesses were pretty easy to make. Besides, no one could really afford a lengthy court battle. That was part of what made them so terrifying.

So, while we watched, Cade's father debated his options. He glared at Logan, aware the man wasn't intimidated by his gun at all, then finally sighed. In that moment, I knew we'd won. A second later, Cade's father stepped aside and gestured for Logan to go in.

"After you, Mr. Bradford," Logan told him, glancing back to catch Riley's eye.

"Now is when you get to be a wall," she told me. "Cade, you stick with me."

Together, we headed inside. I went first, finding Logan only a few paces away, passing Mr. Bradford a business card. Cade turned Riley up a hall and the pair quickly disappeared, so I moved to Logan's side.

"And who the fuck are you?" the old man snapped.

Logan answered while I was still trying to think of a proper response. "This is Grayson. He's operating as security for me today. So long as you make no move to assault my client, Grayson will simply stand here quietly. If you try to do so much as touch Cade, Grayson will throw you to the ground while we wait for the police to handle the assault charges."

"You one of those queers?" he asked next, sneering at me.

I glanced at Logan, who answered again. "Grayson's sexuality isn't applicable, sir."

"Well, that's why I kicked that boy out. He tell you that? He fucked some little boy!" Mr. Bradford huffed as if that was the most disgusting thing he could imagine. "Admitted it, too! Not even fucking ashamed, and I did everything to raise him up right!"

"I understand," Logan told him.

"No, I don't think you fuckin' do!" Mr. Bradford snarled as he set his shotgun down by the corner of a plaid recliner - still within reach. "I didn't produce no fucking faggot! That boy can't be mine! I'm not giving him shit."

"He's only collecting his own things," Logan assured him. "Clothes you can't wear, items he earned on his own, and gifts."

"I paid for all that shit, so fuck him! Let him see how hard this world is when he fucks around like this. Time for him to find out what shit I really do for him."

Which was when Riley emerged from the hall carrying an overloaded garbage bag. I wanted to offer to help, but she had it. I also didn't trust this fucker not to go after Cade again.

"What's that?" Mr. Bradford demanded, pointing at the bag.

"Clothes," Riley said without stopping.

He just turned to glare at Logan next. "This one of those 'woke' things? You helping because you're one of those social justice warriors? Don't you realize boys his age just want to fuck something, and a goddamned pita pocket will do? He ain't gay! He's confused. He needs to see the world is hard, and his dick isn't supposed to be making his decisions for him!"

"That," Logan said, "is not my responsibility, sir. I'm only here to enforce a settlement for an illegal eviction. Nothing more, nothing less."

Jesus christ, how could this man be so calm with what this fucker was saying? I wanted to punch the asshole just on principle. If that made me some social justice warrior, then so be it. I didn't give a shit what someone called helping a friend. This didn't have a damned thing to do with politics or anything else - except the young man who'd somehow become one of my friends.

Because if this was what Cade had been listening to his whole life? That would hurt. It was the sort of crap that wore down someone's soul, breaking them slowly from the inside out. I might not know Cade that well, but I knew enough. He was a good man. He was working hard to become a better one. More than all of that, he treated Jeri good.

And to me, *that* was the only thing that mattered.

Yeah, maybe he and I were supposed to be competing for her attention. We really weren't. He had his place in her life and I had mine. Whose dick went in her next didn't really change any of that. It also didn't make fucking her more important than the one thing it seemed all of us were actually chasing: her heart.

I had it, though. I wasn't sure I had the slice I wanted. No, "slice" was the wrong way to think about it. Style? Fuck, I didn't know. What mattered was that she loved me. As a friend, as more, it didn't matter, because I'd take it. I was pretty sure she also felt something for Cade - and Knock, and Ripper. She wasn't quite ready to admit it, but she showed it in her little ways.

Things like the smile she gave them, the way she relaxed when they were around, and how hard she was willing to fight for all of them, even Zoe. Those four were her "crew," as she called it. They meant something to her, and for too long, the only stability in her life had been me.

I should've been jealous. Ok, if I was honest, I was, a bit. I could also see how much better she was doing with them. The friends she'd made here were changing her life for the better, and how could I resent that? How could I try to keep her from them? What kind of partner would I be for her if I got in their way?

But Cade's father wasn't nearly done with his rant. When Riley came back in, he rounded on her, looking like he was about to get in her face. Without thinking, I moved to put myself between them, more than willing to do exactly what Logan had suggested: put this prick on the floor.

"You some queer too?" he demanded.

Riley smiled at him in that polite-but-forced way, and just kept going.

So Mr. Bradford snapped at Logan again. "I warned Cade not to go down this path, you know. I made it damned clear what would happen if he did."

"I'm only here because you didn't file an eviction notice," Logan said again.

"This is my fucking house!" the man roared.

"The State of Texas still has laws," Logan pointed out so very calmly.

"And that little shit is no son of mine! I disown him. Fuck, I have a feeling he weren't never mine. No son of mine would be a damned queer. He'd be a real man! He'd be after girls, not pathetic little boys! And if I see Cade again, I will make sure he can't fucking embarrass me." Then he raised his voice. "You hear that, Cade? If I ever see you - don't fucking care where - I will kill you! I will make sure people know I didn't do this to you. I will not let your sick perversions ruin my good name!"

Holy fuck. The only reason I was able to stand so calmly was because I was reeling inside. This was what Cade had been afraid of? This was what his dad thought was ok to say in front of how many witnesses?

No.

Because maybe Ruin had been making miracles happen with Jeri's recovery from her trauma, but that? It made up my mind for me. This was Cade's trauma, and it was playing out in real time. This was going to live in the back of his mind for years. *This* was something he'd need help with.

And he was my partner. That came before all else. To me, it was enough of a reason to make sure he always had someone he could talk to, because when I'd been his age, the guys in our game had been there for me. I would make damned sure he didn't have to cope with this on his own.

Mr. Bradford continued to rant. Logan continued to give him calm, legally intimidating answers, and I stood there making plans. Load after load of stuff was carried to the truck by Riley, and from the speed of her trips, it was clear Cade wasn't fucking around in his room.

And then, it was over. Carrying his computer case and a handful of cables, Riley escorted him through the living room, keeping herself between the boy and his father. Not once did Cade bother looking over.

"We're done," Riley declared just as they walked through the door.

So Logan offered Mr. Bradford his hand. "Thank you for your cooperation, sir. You should receive a notice in the mail next week regarding the termination of your familial status."

"My fuckin' what?" he asked.

For the first time, Logan smiled, and the look was far from kind. "Making it legal that you are not his father. That means you will not be responsible for anything in his future, he will be ineligible to inherit from you, and you will have no rights to him as a family member, including but not limited to hospital visitation, tax credits, and emergency notifications."

"Good."

So Logan gestured to the door. "After you, Grayson."

I headed that way, ready for anything to go down once our back was turned, but it didn't. Logan and I both made it to the truck and climbed in. Riley already had it started and was backing up the drive before either of us was belted in.

"Get it all?" Logan asked.

"Yep," Riley said.

Me? I just looked over at Cade and clasped his shoulder gently. "So you know, that took balls. I couldn't have done it, and I respect you a hell of a lot more after seeing your reality." Then I rubbed. "Takes one hell of a good man to live his truth when it feels like the world is kicking him every step of the way. Never again, Cade. Be you. Be as bi as you want, or weak - or strong. I don't care. To me, you look like a damned good man regardless."

Cade just leaned forward and pressed his face into his hands.

He nodded, refusing to lower his arms, but he didn't say a thing. It wasn't until I heard the first gasp that I realized he was crying.

"Shit, c'mere," I told him, pulling him against my side in a hug. "We're partners, Cade. My shoulder is yours anytime you need it."

"I need it," he mumbled, twisting to hug me. "I also really needed to hear that."

CHAPTER 4

JERICHO

When they left, Knock squeezed Cade's hand gently, but that was it. Silence filled the room as Riley, Logan, Hottie, and Cade headed out. We heard the diesel engine start up, then the truck pulled out. Knock leaned to look through the window, watching, and eventually pushed to his feet.

"Ok," he said, heading over to the box I'd brought. "Downstairs?"

"Yes!" Zoe agreed.

"I got that," I quickly said, snatching the cardboard box before he could.

That earned me a look of concern from Ripper, but only for a moment. The group of us headed downstairs, coffees in hand, and claimed our usual places. Once again, I had this box on my lap and I didn't really know what to do with it.

"What's in the box?" Knock asked.

My mouth immediately went dry. "Uh......" And my eyes jumped over to Zoe.

"Cade?" she asked.

I shook my head. "Amber."

That made the room grow heavier as everyone stopped moving. I could feel their eyes on me. I could hear the comforting hum of the computers running smoothly. My breath came faster, though. I'd seen what was in here. I'd watched the video. She'd asked for *my* fucking help, and now I needed to tell my friends what I knew.

"It's..." Again, words failed me.

Seeing Zoe sitting there, looking so completely normal, was killing me. This could've been her. But if I said something, how would she take it? Would I undo all the progress she'd made over the last few months? Would I be hurting her the way she'd said I might hurt the guys?

Why did it have to be so fucking difficult? Why couldn't I just drop the truth out without needing to fucking *feel* something about it? I hadn't even known this girl, but the visions in my mind? Yeah, they all looked like either Nina or my father. They kept opening their eyes. They were begging, and there were bruises down the sides of their faces.

"What's in the box, Jeri?" Knock asked again gently - and yet there was something commanding in his voice. A calm reassurance that he was taking charge, along with the responsibility.

I still couldn't tear my eyes away from Zoe. Her bright red hair was pinned up today with curls dangling down her back. They were a little limp from a whole day at school, but still cute. Her perfectly red lips matched, but the scowl on her face didn't feel right.

"I don't want to tell you," I admitted.

"Why?" Zoe asked. "Jeri, what's in there?"

"It's from Amber," I told her. "Her phone. There are videos and... things."

Zoe's eyes narrowed. "What aren't you saying?"

"She was raped," Ripper guessed.

The look I gave him would've killed a lesser man. "Ripper!"

Zoe just huffed, holding up a hand to let her best friend know she had this. "Ok, so she was raped. Why don't you want to tell me?"

"Because what if this is too much?" I demanded. "What if this hurts you, Zoe?"

"Well, it sure as hell isn't going to feel *good*!" she shot back. "Jeri, just fucking spill it. We're all here. We can all handle this, can't we?"

I shoved to my feet. "I'm trying to think of you. Don't you get that? You're the one who told me to stop and fucking *think* about how someone else might feel. To not just barrel in and drop shit out there like facts, because someone might get their feelings hurt. Well, what if that someone is *you*?"

"And you showed me how to be stronger!" Zoe yelled, matching my tone. "You're the one who made me realize I'm not helpless. You're the one who showed me how to stop being a fucking victim and *do* something about this. Well, you know what? I can't fucking do anything if you're cutting me out." She slashed her hand through the air. "I can't be a part of Ruin if you keep everything from me, because 'oh no, poor Zoe might be triggered!'"

"So I'm supposed to just rub salt in the wounds instead?" I demanded. "No! I'm trying to protect you, don't you get that?"

"*And I don't need to be protected*!" Like me, she pushed to her feet, but her words came out so hard she was leaning with them. "I get to protect people too, Jericho. I get to be a hero too! So he fucking raped me? So fucking what? This?" She gestured to her body. "This is mine, and I fucking take it back. I'm done being scared. I'm *done* being weak. I'm fucking done being anyone's bitch but my own! So stop fucking shutting me out!"

"She killed herself!" I roared.

Zoe paused, her eyes going wide. "Oh, shit. Oh, Jeri, it's not my trigger you're worried about..." And she hurried to cross the distance between us, hugging my shoulders just as hard as she could. "It's yours."

"No," I tried to say, but my voice cracked. "Zoe, they had a video. Stephanie told her about the blackmail videos because she tried to apologize for sleeping with John, so Amber went looking, and she found one of her. They all raped her. She wasn't even conscious, and..."

"Shh..." Zoe breathed, sliding her hand up and down my back. "I'm not dead. I have friends who helped me, Jeri. Amber didn't."

"It's worse than that," I admitted.

"How can it be worse?" Ripper asked.

But Knock had already moved to get the box. The top was just pushed down, not folded closed or anything. Reaching inside, he lifted up the little white stick.

"Shit."

"Oh my god," Zoe breathed. "She was pregnant?"

"Why not just get an abortion?" Knock asked.

"Texas," Zoe told him.

"And her parents," I said. "And there's more. So much more, but I barely got the chance to look in there before Hottie said we had to come here, and I just..."

"Can't," Zoe finished for me. "You can't do all of this and hold yourself together."

So Ripper gestured for Knock to move the box away. "Which means we deal with that later. Look, I don't mean to sound like an asshole or anything, but Amber? We can't help her anymore. Right now, Cade is the one who needs us, and he's still here. We can do something to make this better for him."

"Monday," Knock decided, setting the box behind his monitor on his desk. "This will all keep until then. For now, we need to deal with one thing at a time."

"But - " I tried.

He just gave me a soft, knowing look. "It'll keep, Jeri. But if you think this isn't tearing Cade up? Yeah, I have bad news. This is just as bad for a guy like him. His entire world just got turned upside down, and he's going to blame himself - or maybe us. We're the ones who encouraged him to come out a bit. We're the ones who pushed back against Dylan and that fucking video he was holding over Cade's head. And now? The only one hurting because of it is Cade."

"I'm kinda hurting for him," Ripper said. "Man, seeing him like that? His dad beat the *fuck* out of him!"

"Tried to kill him," I corrected.

"But now he's ok," Knock said. "Riley's moving him in, so he's going to be fine. Logan will find a way to make sure his dad can't fuck with him. It's what they do, and Kitty will work out a wage for him to earn something for helping out around here."

"What about you?" Zoe asked.

Knock slowly sat back down in his own chair, making the rest of us do the same. "Huh?" he asked.

"How are you doing with this?" Zoe rephrased. "I mean, you have to be freaking at least a little, right?"

"Is it too fast for you?" I asked, because that would've been my problem.

Knock just ducked his head and shoved his hand into his blue hair, letting out a heavy sigh. "I don't know."

"Not good enough, man," Ripper told him. "It's us. C'mon. Talk it out, right? That's what we do?"

Knock chuckled once, but it was weak. "Um, I'm kinda freaking out a bit. I mean, I was in the barn, picking up horse shit, when Riley started screaming my name. I thought she must be hurt bad, so I came running. I rounded the corner in time to see her best small bridle in the middle of the back yard - and Quake will chew the shit out of those things - but she was leading Cade inside. I just..."

"Freaked," Zoe offered.

"Yeah," he agreed, sounding almost defeated. "I kept thinking about all the shit, you know? Not just ours, either. I mean, like my gamer friends. Doxxing and death threats, puppies carved up on doorsteps, horses getting hurt, and more." He let go of his hair to scrub at his face. "I was so sure I couldn't fix it this time, because it's going to happen, and it's Cade. I mean, I really..." He looked up, his deep brown eyes landing on me.

"Really what?" I asked.

"Care," he breathed.

Because that was the one thing I had trouble with. Caring meant losing people. I was getting better, and damned if I didn't care about these people more than I had anyone in years. I fucking *cared*, and it scared the shit out of me, but seeing the look in Knock's eyes made me realize that maybe I wasn't the only one worried about it.

"But he's going to be ok, right?" I asked. "I mean, if he's living with you, then it's basically unlimited sex?"

Knock jerked his chin at me. "That what you and Hottie are doing every night?"

"Well, no, but - "

"That!" he said, flailing a hand at me. "There's more to it than fucking. I mean, shit, never mind the fucking. Getting that right? And now I have to figure out if I brush my teeth before I say anything to him in the morning, or is it just kissing with morning breath that's gross? Like, what's the line, and what if I fuck it all up because I don't know it? Not like I can just ask Riley now, because Cade will hear, and then I'll look even more pathetic!"

The strangest thing was how this little insight into Knock's thoughts was helping me more than I wanted to admit. They were the same sorts of things I worried about! Normal things, maybe? I didn't know, because people didn't just talk like this, but we did. I could also help him out a little.

"Fuck morning breath," I told him. "If you're sticking your dick in his ass - or vice versa - and willing to play in shit, then a little bad breath is nothing. Besides, fuck that. If he doesn't like it, he can get out of bed first. And you know what else works?"

"Not at all," he assured me.

"Talking."

Knock groaned. "Kinda what we're doing, isn't it?"

"To him, dumbass," Ripper said. "Like, ask him if he's got a problem with something. Maybe he does. Maybe he's never thought about it. Either way, it sure as shit won't hurt."

"But I'm fucking living with my boyfriend!" Knock huffed. "Like, *bam*. One second, we're figuring it out, and the next he's living with me, and I've never *really* had anyone spend the whole fucking night but Tiffany! And trust me, she does not count. I mean, Cade stayed over that once, but we were out all night trying to find the routers, and by the time we got back, we just crashed. Never mind that he'd just been beat up - the *first* time! - so nothing happened. I mean, we just slept for a bit, and then he left, so it's not like a real sleepover!"

"But are you opposed?" Zoe asked.

And the smallest, cutest smile touched Knock's lips. "No."

"Then it's ok," she told him. "Be friends first. I mean, I think Jeri's onto something with that, because it's working with me and Jinxy. Be friends, and you get that trust. You figure out how to disagree and make up. You find ways to talk about it. You have more than just sex, and I mean, if the sex is good, then that's just a bonus, right?"

"Icing on the cake," I told him. "And you can start the 'doesn't have to be every night' thing tonight. I have a feeling Cade will hurt too bad to be up for it."

"Spoil him," Ripper suggested. "I dunno, like a bubble bath and movies together. Not sure if guys would be into that, but it's what I'd do for a girl."

I glanced over and caught his eye. "Yeah?"

"Hush," he teased. "I mean to make her feel better."

Zoe just poked him in the ribs. "You're not really making that sound worse, just so you know. Still kinda sweet and romantic." Then she looked over at me. "And I'm not mad at you, Jeri. I didn't mean to yell at you like that."

"Yes, you did," I told her. "You were also right. I was so worried about hurting you I didn't realize how hard this is for me."

"Are you going to be ok?" Ripper asked.

I nodded. "I'll make sure of it."

"Not what I asked."

So I leaned back in the chair and sighed. "No, you said the right thing. We can't help Amber anymore. She's gone. Cade's still here, and I..."

"We won't lose him," Ripper swore. "Knock will make sure he knows he's loved. We will too." Then he leaned over his knees. "Whatever type of love you want to call that, Jeri, but it's ok. We are friends. That's our bond. All of us make each other stronger which makes our polycule unbreakable."

"And I love you," Zoe told me. "I love you as my female best friend, because it's ok. We got this, right?"

I nodded quickly. "Yeah. I'll make sure of it. Damn, Zoe, I love you too."

And the guys relaxed, soft smiles taking over their faces.

CHAPTER 5

CADE

I had control of myself by the time we got back. Immediately, the entire herd of people there began moving. Some grabbed garbage bags. Others took items that hadn't fit in anything. Like a chain of human labor, a line headed to the truck and then downstairs, dumping everything I owned in a row along the walls of the game room.

After that, things began to slow down. Jeri's mom called, wanting to know where the hell she was. She and Hot left because of it. Ripper and Zoe stayed long enough to make sure I knew that if I needed *anything*, they were here for me. Then they bounced.

Riley gave me a quick tour of the parts of the house I'd never needed before - like the laundry room and upstairs bedrooms - then she and Logan vanished. Kitty made a point of coming downstairs, hugging me hard, and calling me her little brother. Next, she looked at Knock, rubbed his shoulder proudly, and headed back upstairs. I could hear the television playing in the living room, but that was it.

We were alone.

"Which one of these has your clean clothes?" Knock asked, gesturing to the bags.

Tossing my hands up in defeat, I headed over to check. "Everything has been moved around so much, I honestly don't know," I admitted.

"Just need something for tonight and tomorrow," he assured me. "We'll go through this a little at a time."

"Yeah, but - " I snapped my mouth shut.

"Ask," he encouraged.

"Where is my shit going?" I asked.

Knock glanced up and smiled. "Our room. I'm gonna talk to Riley about furniture. We've got wall space, but not drawer space. The closet can hold a shit ton, but underwear doesn't really hang well."

I chuckled softly, because he was right. It was also the best I had. I felt like my head was still spinning, and only half of that was from the drugs Riley had given me. When she'd called it the good stuff, she hadn't been kidding!

Once I found a bag with clean stuff, Knock carried that into his room and started digging. He found a t-shirt I liked, a pair of jeans with a rip in the knee I'd worn a few times, and then a pair of red briefs. Those made him smile. The shirt and jeans, he put on top of his low dresser. The underwear? He took those with him as he left his room without an explanation.

"I'll be right back," he said.

Ok. Great. But what was I supposed to do until then? Because coming over after school was one thing. Just acting like I lived here? That felt strange. Foreign, maybe? I wasn't sure, but the casual way Knock's entire family acted about me moving in helped a bit.

Still, I'd lived in the same house with my dad for as long as I could remember. When a storm came through, I'd patched the roof. When the fence fell down, I'd put it back up. I *knew* that place. I'd put hours of my life into it.

This? It wasn't where I fit. Downstairs was like some cyber cafe. Upstairs was a rather respectable home with curtains and everything. Fuck, there were plants up there! Not a lot, but just little signs of a woman or two in the house. Things that made me feel brutish and just, well, out of place.

Then Knock came back. "Shoes off," he ordered. "Socks too."

Confused, I obeyed. "Why?"

"Because when Logan suggested doubling the size of the house, he asked Riley what things she always wished she could have but had never been able to afford. Then, he put them in." He held out his hand in an offer. "And my big sister is nothing if not amazingly practical."

Which certainly did not answer the question, and yet I wound my fingers between his and let him guide me out of his room and across the game room. At the back, the door to the bathroom was wide open. The lights inside were on, but dimmer than usual, and I could hear the sound of water running.

Then he led me inside. Against the side was the biggest bathtub I had ever seen in my life. Directly across from it was a massive walk-in shower. I'd sorta seen these before, when I stopped to take a piss, but watching the water slowly but surely fill that tub? I realized more than one person could fit in it.

"A bath?" I asked.

"It has everything to ease the aches of getting your ass kicked by a draft horse," he explained. "Also, the water pressure is good enough that the shower works at the same time. So, here's your choice. Do you want a minute alone to process, or would you rather have some help cleaning the sand from your hair?"

"Help," I decided, without giving myself time to think about it.

Because my instinct was to insist I was ok, say I could do it on my own, and try to prove I was tough. The reality was very, very different. He was offering me something I'd never really had in my life with no strings attached: kindness, compassion, and gentleness.

He shut and locked the door. I stripped out of my clothes, pausing when I needed help with my shirt. Fuck, my arms were killing me! The pants were easy. Getting into the tub wasn't, but Knock was right there to hold me steady when my legs wanted to give out.

Then I lowered myself into the amazingly warm water. Not hot. Not tepid. This was perfect, and yet the scrapes and scratches across my body still stung. The water taking the pressure of my weight made it worth it.

Knock crawled in beside me a second later. I wanted to look at his dick. Fuck. I definitely had, but hopefully not in a bad way. I was just feeling so strung out and unable to keep up, so my only option was to give in. If I fucked up, I'd apologize and hope that was good enough.

Then Knock scooted around behind me. "Lean back. Let's at least get the sand out of your hair."

"Babe, I'm worthless," I told him even as I leaned back.

He smiled down at me. "I've had those drugs before, so I know. You're also going to sleep so hard tonight, but it does help."

He gently began massaging my head while it was in the water. My knees were only bent a bit, and the water was still flowing, still filling this pool-sized container. Ok, it wasn't quite that big, but damn. This was one hell of a tub.

"They fuck in here, don't they?" I asked.

"Oh, probably," he said. "In truth, they fuck just about everywhere. Riley and Logan definitely have a healthy sex life, but the best part is they want others to do the same. No shame, no pressure. That sort of thing."

"And Kitty?" I asked.

"Kitty has triggers. Bad ones. When she was a little kid, she watched her father kill her mother. When she got older, boys at school treated her like shit. They acted like being a foster kid made her something to use up and throw away. Now, she wants nothing to do with relationships."

"Sounds familiar," I mumbled, thinking of Jeri.

"Same idea," he agreed, "but different reasons. Kitty's scared of the relationship itself. Jeri's scared of caring, because everyone she loves is ripped away from her." Then he tapped, encouraging me to sit up. "But what about you, Cade? I'm sure your mind is just chaos right now, so talk to me?"

I eased my head out of the water with my back to him. "I feel like the matrix glitched," I tried to explain. "One minute, we were all worried about Alpha Team and blackmail videos, then Amber was dead, and when I got home, my dad tried to kill me."

"How bad was it?" he asked as he carefully lathered up my hair.

Holy shit, that felt good. I was also pretty sure I wouldn't have been able to do it myself. My left arm did not want to lift that high. My right was aching pretty good, but that seemed to just be muscles. My back was killing me, though, and every movement I made sent this dull sensation up my spine that would probably suck without these drugs.

"He choked me," I answered, trying to keep it to just the facts. "Cornered me against the wall and was going to choke me out. I'm stronger than him, though. I pulled his hand off, but my fucking voice hurts."

"You have a pretty good bruise starting."

Not surprising. "And he hit me in the back when I had to stop and unlock the door. A few more times when I was outside. I mean, I hit him too, but yeah. I dunno. Like, I've never seen him like that before - and he'd been drinking."

"And down to rinse," Knock said as his hands moved to support my back. "But don't worry. You'll never have to see him again. Not unless you want to."

"What if I don't?" I asked, looking up at his bare, wet chest while he worked all the suds from my hair.

"Then you don't."

"No," I groaned, sitting up so I could shift around and face him. "Knock, what does it mean if I don't want to see my own dad again?"

He slid over to a corner and caught my side, pulling me closer so my back was against his chest. His arms went around my body, hugging me from behind, and we both could stretch our legs out. What I didn't expect was for his mouth to be so close to my ear.

"I was so scared to call my parents," he said softly. "They kicked me out, and I crashed with a friend for one night because I had plane tickets to go to a gamer tournament. I was trying to figure out how to get to the airport, but his mom thought I was trying to get to some family who'd give me a place, so she drove me. I just didn't know it was true."

He leaned in to kiss the side of my neck and kept going. "When Riley found out, there was no question about it. She told me I had a home, just like she did you. Thing was, Logan had his own apartment and more space back then. Well, that was great, but in order to move, I had to get my records, right? That required calling my folks because I wasn't eighteen. Fuck, and just thinking about it made me want to curl into a ball. Not even seeing them, Cade. Just talking to them on the phone!"

"Yeah," I breathed, because that was how seeing my father made me feel.

"So she did it." He pressed the side of his head against mine. "And trust me, the Riley you've seen so far has *nothing* on her when she's in a mood. If my dad tried to talk smack to her, she would've put him in his place. But you know what?"

I twisted back to see him. "What?"

"I haven't spoken to them since. Not once. No social media, no emails, no phone calls. I also haven't missed them at all. I thought I would. I was so sure leaving it all behind would be hard, that the transition to this life would be too much, but it wasn't. Sure, I fumbled. Yeah, I had some moments where I just needed silence and to breathe, but they gave it - and I will do the same for you."

So I turned on my side, floating halfway in order to hug his waist. "And us?" I asked.

"Just like Hot and Jeri," he assured me. "We're going to figure it out while sharing a space, right? And when it gets hard, we're going to yell, throw things, and then talk. If we can't talk, we'll go to one of them and ask for more help."

It hurt to hug him tighter, yet I had to. This new world he was talking about sounded amazing. More than that, it sounded *possible*. It sounded like it was up to me, and this wonderful, sexy, and compassionate man was offering it all up on a silver platter.

"What's the catch?" I asked.

He lifted a dripping hand to smooth my hair back from my face. "Would you believe me if I told you there's no catch? I like you, Cade. I..."

I nodded. "More than like," I said softly.

"Definitely more," he agreed. "I just really want this to work. I've never had anyone stay the night like that. Never just, um..."

"As your boyfriend," I realized.

"Yeah."

"And now I'm moving in." I let my eyes close. "I can crash on the couch, you know."

"But I don't want you to," he swore. "That's the craziest part of this. When Riley said you'd move in, I felt this rush. This excitement. Not because of what happened, but because it meant you wouldn't have to go home again."

Which was enough to make my eyes jump open. "Yeah?" And I pushed myself back to sitting.

"Yeah," he breathed. "We're still chasing Jeri, and we're not leaving our polycule, but maybe curling up against you to fall asleep might be ok?"

I answered him the only way I knew how. Leaning in, I pressed my mouth to his and kissed. Slow, lazy, intoxicated kisses that he returned. Calm ones that explored. Our mouths moved, caressing each other and pushing the horror of the day just a little further away, right up until the overflow drain began gurgling.

"Shit," Knock breathed, pulling away so he could shut off the water. "Don't want to flood the basement again."

"Again?" I asked.

Which made him shrug deviously. "Evidently, good sex is the best excuse for not shutting off the water. We should try it sometime. I mean, when you aren't more green and blue than anything else."

"Mm, but these colors are working for me," I teased.

He just pulled me back against his chest. "They are. Now relax for a moment, Cade. I'm not going anywhere. I'm also really good at listening to anything my boyfriend wants to talk about."

"Yeah?" I asked. "Know anything about cars?"

"No, but I learn fast."

Which made me smile. "Yeah, babe. You really do. Thank you. I needed you today, and you were there. Here. Whatever."

"Always," he swore. "I'll pick you up every time you need it, because I think you'd do the same for me."

So I laced my fingers with his across my stomach. "Yeah, I would." And for the first time today, I actually smiled. A true, honest one. "Always, Knock. I really fucking hope that's a promise I can keep too, because you deserve nothing less."

"Keep that up," he warned, "and I'll have a much better word than like."

Which convinced me that today might not be the worst day of my life. Maybe, just maybe, it was the start of a new chapter. At least I really fucking hoped so.

CHAPTER 6

JERICHO

The whole drive home from Knock's place, I felt like I'd forgotten something. That stupid box had become some kind of pacifier for me. Without it, my anxiety was off the charts, refusing to acknowledge this could wait until Monday. It could. Knock was right. Now if only my brain would agree!

But seeing Mom's car parked in the driveway pushed all of that from my mind. She'd been frantic to come home and find the house empty. Considering she was only here this weekend because I'd gotten into a fight at school - and out of it thanks to Logan's legal intervention - I had a feeling this was going to be bad.

"I'm going to get so grounded," I told Hottie as I climbed out of his car.

He huffed at that. "We were just talking to Knock's family like she wanted. Add in some gay bashing for why you got in a fight."

Yeah, ok, that was a good idea. It also wasn't what was really bothering me. Sure, Mom's anger was the most obvious part, but beneath that was this subtle awareness that things between Hottie and me had changed this semester. A lot. He was no longer just my safe "big brother." He was my partner, and Mom would *not* be ok with that.

"And us?" I asked as I made my way around the front of his car.

"Just like old times," he assured me. "Good friends, Jeri. I mean, that's what you prefer to call it, right?"

I nodded, but hated it. Still, as we headed into the house, his words worked. The plan made sense. Five years of being "just friends" with Hottie had built habits I was still clinging to. Little things that worked with "more than friends," but would keep me from making this awkward.

Although I barely opened the front door before Mom demanded, "Where have you been, young lady?"

"Uh..." I paused in the foyer, trying to locate where her voice had come from.

Hottie stepped in behind me, closing the door. "We went to see that other boy's family," he explained, heading straight for the kitchen.

That was where Mom was. I wanted to say she was hiding, but far from it. She was cooking, and from the stuff strewn across the countertop, it was a frantic or manic sort of thing.

"What are you making?" I asked, intending to put away the things she wouldn't be using.

"Burritos," she said.

Nodding slowly, I grabbed the syrup and eggs. "Cool."

"Don't take that tone with me!" she snapped, turning to give me that maternal look which meant I was in deep trouble. "And leave the syrup. I need that."

"No," Hottie told her, jerking his head at me to show I could keep going. "Mom, you're making bean burritos. No syrup with it."

"I was going to do scrambled eggs on the side," she told him. "I know you like those, Drake. A little syrup on top, right? See, I might work a lot, but I didn't forget."

"No, you didn't," he agreed, clasping her arm gently, completely accepting that she thought he was my dead brother. "Thanks, Mom, but burritos are fine."

"I just..." She set down the spatula and turned to face the pair of us. "Do you know how scared I was when I got home and both of you were gone?" Her gaze landed on Hottie. "Your sister isn't old enough to hang around with you and your friends - and you don't need to be getting her in trouble!"

"We went to find out what happened at her school," he said gently.

I had no clue how he could be so careful with my mom's mind. He never snapped at her - even when I would've. He didn't try to correct her. He just rolled with her latest delusion and tried to guide her back towards reality.

Mom looked at him for much too long, and then recognition lit up her face. "The fight!" Immediately, she turned to me. "And? I want to know what you were thinking, Jericho."

"Um..." I glanced at Hottie, who nodded encouragingly. "Well, these guys are gay, right?" I did not want to get into the nuances of their sexuality, so gay worked. "And they were kissing, so these bullies went after them."

"And how did *you* end up in the middle of that?" Hottie got her glare next. "Is this a gang thing? I *told* you to stay away from those types of kids. They will only get you in trouble - or worse, killed!"

"It's not a gang," Hottie assured her. "Remember, we moved to Texas to get away from all that."

"Oh." Mom licked at her lips. "Right. A nice, small town." She nodded. "Sorry. I just worry. I'm so scared something's going to happen to you, Drake."

"I know you are," he assured her. "But Jeri's a good kid. She's even making better grades."

"Which does not excuse fighting," Mom grumbled. "Drake, when I left, I made it clear you're supposed to keep her in line. No skipping school. No fighting. No breaking the rules or she'll have to go live with her aunt and uncle. If you can't accept the responsibilities of taking care of your sister, then we'll make sure she's in a place where she can't get in trouble."

"Mom..." I tried.

Hottie lifted a hand subtly in my direction. "And I told you I've got this, Mom. She's fine. Sometimes, she's going to get sick, or have cramps, or need to stay home. I'm not going to let her mess up her education, but I'm trying to do what you would, ok? And this time, I think she was right."

"To get in a fight?"

He nodded. "She stood up for someone getting bullied. Mom, one of these bullies beat up his girlfriend. The same girl died by suicide. It's a mess, and these boys are *bad*. All Jeri did was protect these two boys who needed her help."

"Because they're gay," she said, sounding like she was still trying to understand the lie we were weaving.

"And one of those boys just got kicked out of his house because the bullies outed him," Hottie went on. "His dad beat the crap out of him and tossed him out. See, sometimes bullying hurts in ways we don't expect, and Jeri understands that. She also didn't hit the guy first."

Mom turned her eyes on me. "What happened?"

"Uh, Dylan hit me hard enough to knock me down," I explained. "My brother -" Because I couldn't handle calling Hottie Drake. "- taught me enough that I knew I had to get up, but Dylan kept coming and he wouldn't stop, so I hit back."

"And why did this boy hit you in the first place?" Mom wanted to know

I grimaced. "Um, because I called him a few names so he'd leave my friends alone. They've been picking on Zoe too."

And Amber, but Mom wouldn't know about her. Mom wouldn't even care about her. The fact that Mom was actually keeping up with this one fight was a little impressive, but I had to remember that in her mind, I was still thirteen years old, not eighteen.

"I still don't think you should be able to fight at school and not get punished," Mom said, sounding like she was coming to a decision. "No. You're going to spend the weekend here. No friends. I'm going to need you both to prove you really can handle this arrangement. I know me leaving for work is hard on you both, but I expect Drake to keep an eye on you, Jericho." Her next words were pointed. "Not spend all his time hanging out with those friends of his."

"Don't even talk to them anymore," Hottie promised. "I've just been playing games and going to work, Mom. Pretty boring stuff. Jeri's even been doing her homework."

Ok, I really hadn't been. For a couple of weeks, I'd managed, but that was about it. Since then, I'd let it slide. My grades were ok, though. Not great, but good enough. I just didn't know how anyone would expect me to worry about homework with all the rest of the crap going on at school!

Never mind that we still needed to find those blackmail videos. Tiffany and her friends might be free of their control, but if that asshole realized I'd lied to him? Yeah, nothing would stop him from making this worse. Amber's death proved it!

Because they didn't care. The Alpha Team - as they called themselves - thought they were above such things as consequences. Dylan had all but said that to my face! His father would be pissed, so no one would mess with him, and things like that. I had a feeling the four others he called friends felt just about the same.

But Amber was still dead. Suicide, she'd said in her video. To me, it might as well be murder. She hadn't died because she'd wanted to. She'd died because those fuckers had destroyed her, making her think she'd had no other options.

She'd been wrong, but also alone. She hadn't had anyone to jump in and help the way I would've if she'd just *said something*. Fuck, to help the way Hottie was right now by pretending to be Drake. Even worse, I had a feeling where there was one - Amber - there had to be more.

More girls the Alpha Team had hurt. More kids at school who were teetering on that edge. More disgusting things those boys had done that we hadn't found yet. More evil to fight.

Because thinking of them as evil let me believe good had a chance of winning. Good always defeated evil, didn't it? That was how the world was supposed to be balanced, damn it!

It wasn't.

Bad things happened to good people. Shit came out of the blue. Assholes had no guilt about it, money made power, and I had this impressive ability to always end up in the middle of it. Yeah, probably because Mom was only around a few weekends here and there, leaving me mostly to raise myself.

While my mind had gone off on a tangent, Hottie had taken over handling dinner. He now had the spatula, but Mom was hovering, asking questions about how school was going for him. Grabbing the syrup and eggs again, I continued on my mission to put away the excess crap Mom had scattered all over, listening the whole time.

"Yeah, I don't have any classes this semester," Hottie explained. "Next fall, I'm going to college in the next town over. Close, Mom."

"But how did you do that without graduating?" Mom asked.

His shoulders slumped a little more. "It's a special program. I got my grades up and took extras. Graduation is this May, so you can come to that?"

"Oh, so you still get to do that?"

"Mhm," he agreed - but it was my graduation he was talking about, not his. "That's why I can look after Jeri. I leave for work about a half hour before she goes to school. Now, if you'd like, you can call the school on Monday and have them contact me when she gets sick or something?"

"I don't want to put too much on you, honey," Mom insisted.

He smiled at her. "And I don't want you to feel like you have to fly back when I really do have this. It's ok, Mom. Jeri's pretty good. I mean, most of the time. Well, when she's not having one of her tantrums, but I kinda like that girl."

"And dating?" Mom asked. "Have you met someone yet?"

Hottie just chuckled. "Yeah, um, maybe? I don't know. Working on something, at least. Don't jinx it, ok?"

"Ok," Mom agreed while I kept cleaning. Then she turned, and it was as if she'd just realized I was right in front of her this whole time. "Oh, Jericho, thank you. I didn't realize you were helping out."

"Getting good at that," I told her.

Mom pulled me in for a side hug. "I'm proud of you, you know. You're getting to be a very responsible young lady. High school should be easy for you. Just remember to keep your grades up, ok?"

"Promise."

But inside, I was breaking a little more. With "Drake" here, she barely even remembered I existed. With "Drake" around, my issues suddenly became unimportant. With "Drake" alive again - in her mind - she got a moment of the life she should've had, and I couldn't even hate her for it. I wanted my brother back too, but every so often, Mom's brain allowed her to have him.

So I kept cleaning, refusing to scream out loud like I wanted to. I longed to tell her I was here - right fucking here! - but I knew it wouldn't help. Mom didn't love me less. She simply wanted her son back. The problem was that I did too.

I wanted *everyone* to stop dying.

CHAPTER 7

HOTSHOT

Dinner was tense. Jeri smiled at all the right places and didn't complain, but I could see the pain on her face. Worse, Melissa fawned all over me, convinced I was her dead son. Yeah, this happened often enough that I was used to it, but when Jeri was in the room, it hurt a lot worse.

The shittiest part was that this woman was the closest thing to a mother I'd ever had. She wasn't ok. She might never be ok. Yet even as broken and traumatized as she was, she'd still been there for me in ways none of my foster parents ever had been.

I had no problem calling her "Mom." I did that even when she remembered who I was. Now, with things between me and Jeri being a lot more than simple friends, I preferred to think of her as more of a mother-in-law, just because it was less creepy, but it only helped so much.

Because I was faking this.

Yeah, I was damned good at faking it. I had years of experience under my belt. I'd faked being tough when I'd been weak. I'd faked confidence when I was insecure. My entire life had been one moment of putting on the right mask at the right time to make it through the latest bullshit after another. Sure, most of that had been foster families. Onc kid accused me of stealing his game, so I had to make sure I was faultless. Things like that.

And then there'd been Nina.

Losing her had ripped me apart. Jeri and Jinxy were the only ones who knew how bad, though. For everyone else, I'd been "ok." It had been easier than listening to the awkward apologies and condolences. It had given me space in my mind to adjust to being alone all over again. To listen to the apartment creak as the building settled. To hear the ice maker running. To have no one else alive living in my home with me.

Now there was Jeri. That night, as I laid in my bed trying to convince myself to sleep, I listened to her winding down. The fall of water in the shower made it clear she was washing her hair. The sound of her drawers opening in her room as she got dressed was soft. Even the shifting of her bed as she climbed into it was audible with my door slightly open.

Those were the sounds I missed so much. The ones that proved someone in the house was alive. Slowly, however, they began to fade. The house got quiet. The traffic in our safe little neighborhood died completely. I still laid there, staring at the sliver of less intense darkness where my door wasn't all the way closed, waiting - hoping - to hear her roll over in her bed.

To be alive.

I didn't know the girl who'd died by suicide. I also didn't need to. I could imagine what her family and friends were going through right now, trying to understand why she'd given in. I knew that pain so intensely, but this time it wasn't Nina I was thinking about - it was Jeri.

Losing Nina had hurt in a way I'd never imagined was possible. Finding her in the bathroom had been a nightmare I'd fought against ever since. And yes, I'd researched why people made that decision, desperately hoping some understanding of *why* could dull the pain a little, but it hadn't.

It had just made me more paranoid. Anyone, at any time, could leave me. So many had, in one way or another. First, it had been Drake. Losing him had rocked my world. The guy had been my only friend. The one person who I'd thought couldn't leave me - until he had.

Foster parents had come and gone in the middle. Foster siblings too. Then Nina. Now I was paranoid about Jericho. She really was all I had left. Well, Jinxy, but that was different. Our friendship was easier, less desperate. Less *necessary*.

Not that I didn't think of Jinxy as a brother in some ways. It was more that we could go for weeks without talking and I was fine with it. Jericho was different. She'd taken up my waking thoughts since Drake had died. First, it had been my paranoia that she'd get lost in the shuffle. Then it had been me trying to figure out how to *be* a big brother so I could help her out.

Now, it was different. I shouldn't have slept with her. I *should* have kept my damned hands to myself, but this thing between us was working. After that wild, passionate morning, we'd fallen into this casual comfort that words simply couldn't describe.

Maybe I was replacing Nina with her? I didn't think so, since the two women were nothing alike. Nina had been so kind and considerate. She'd been gentle on the outside with this core of steel that had allowed me to believe she was unbreakable. Jeri was a forest fire. She burned hot - *always*.

Safe was not a concept Jericho understood. Not physically, not emotionally, and not even mentally. She was all-in, all the time. The girl was a complete and total disaster waiting to happen, but for the right reasons. Usually for someone else.

So when her room grew too quiet for too long, I couldn't help myself. Even knowing Mom was asleep downstairs, I still got up and snuck across the hall. Jeri's room was dark. I could see her little body curled up at the edge of her bed.

As silently as I could, I made my way around to the other side and slipped under the covers. Immediately, she scooted back, pressing her body into mine. I shoved an arm under her neck. The other went around her waist. Then I hugged, holding her close so I could breathe in the smell of her.

Shampoo, fresh sheets, and the scent that was just her. I couldn't get enough of it. This was what I thought about when she wasn't around. The smell of my girl in my arms had some primal place in my mind. Something that spoke to all of my deepest, darkest fears and pushed them away.

"Hottie?" she asked.

"Shh," I breathed. "You're supposed to be asleep."

Instead, she turned in my arms to face me. "I can't. I keep thinking about Amber."

"Yeah," I said gently. "I keep thinking about you."

Even in the darkness, I could see her brow furrow as she took my words wrong. "No, listen," she insisted. "Tiffany and her friends? They're in the same boat. I lied. I told Dylan we had a video, and he backed off, but we don't. There's no video, yet I think Amber might have something. I think that's why she sent me the box."

I nodded, accepting that. "Ok, but what about you?"

"Huh?"

"You," I insisted. "Jeri, how much can you take before you break? I saw you fucking crying this afternoon. You don't even cry at funerals!"

"Shh," she hissed, reminding me to keep my voice down. "Mom would freak if she caught you in my bed."

"And I'd tell her we're talking."

Ok, and it definitely wouldn't go over well, and probably would send Melissa into another of her episodes, but that was beside the point. I just wanted to make Jeri feel like someone had control over something in her life. If that meant I had to figure out how to be the responsible one, then I would do it. Hell, I *had* been doing it. That was why the pair of us worked.

"Jeri," I tried when she kept looking at me, "I can't lose you."

"I'm not going anywhere," she promised.

"No, listen," I begged. "Nina said the same thing, and then she did. This girl, Amber?" She nodded, so I kept going. "What do you want to bet she told someone the same thing? Maybe even you or Tiffany? I don't want to hear that. I don't want you to make me feel better. I just..."

She palmed the side of my face. "You can't leave me either, Grayson."

Fuck. My throat went tight and my heart took off. Not because of my name, but rather it was the soft, calm, mature way she said that. This girl wasn't old enough to realize how shitty the world could be, and yet she'd had a front row seat to it for her entire life. She knew, probably better than me, and still she said that so easily, diving right into my greatest fear.

"I can't lose anyone else," I said, the words too soft to have true sound.

She pushed closer, somehow tucking her head under my neck so she could wrap her arms around my back. "But we will. Someone always dies, Hottie. The goal is to make sure it's not us. Even better, we need to stop the villains before they can take another, right?"

"This isn't a game," I chided. "They aren't villains."

"But they are!" she insisted. "They have to be! That's the only way any of this makes sense, don't you see? They're the villains. How else can they refuse to see the pain and suffering they're causing? If they aren't villains, then what are they?"

"Spoiled, pampered, privileged boys," I told her. "They're the kind of guys who've never had a hardship in their lives, and their parents' money, prestige, or power has removed every possible hurdle. They're *normal*, Jeri, and that's the worst part about all of this. They're just fucking boys, doing stupid boy shit, and not caring about who they hurt in the process."

"Which sounds an awful lot like a villain to me," she countered. "And heroes destroy villains. They don't ignore it. They don't say they're too busy." Her voice cracked slightly. "They don't spend time worrying about partners or boyfriends, polycules, and lovers when people are hurting!"

"No, no, no," I begged, knowing where she was going with this. She was trying to blame herself for actually living her life. "Jeri, heroes also take care of themselves. They can't save anyone if they're broken too. Those friends of yours? They've helped you heal, and the more you heal, the stronger you are."

"No," she whispered, pulling back to look at my face. "I'm not. The more I care about them, the more I'll hurt when something happens to them - and it will. That's just math, Hottie. When it was just you and me, we were ok, right?"

"And you weren't as happy," I reminded her. "Jeri, I *need* you to be happy. That's the part you're missing. I'm not ok with you stumbling along as a shell of yourself. That's what you did after Russel died. You faked it, and I let you, because I understood, but I shouldn't have."

"Yeah, but - "

"No," I said, cutting her off. "Listen, baby girl. I need you to be ok. I really fucking *need* you to be happy. I need you to do stupid teenage shit like cut class and spend time with those guys. I need to hear you giggling with Zoe about whatever shit you girls are into this week. *I* need that, because it reminds me that you want to live. It pushes back my fears of losing you."

"But I won't..." she tried.

I leaned in to kiss her brow. "But you might." Then I hugged her again. "We all could. That's the problem with desperation and anguish. We can't stop them. Happiness can, but we're just people, Jeri. Alone, we don't have the tools to fight back. That's what those bonds are for. They're a thing to hold on to when the world is trying to pull you apart. They're a tether to keep you in place when shit shoves you down. I need you to love those people, because it makes me feel like you're finally safe."

"Oh." And she reached up to gently wipe her thumb across my cheek. "But I need to fix this."

"Then we'll fix it," I swore. "But maybe we can find a way to fix it without destroying ourselves in the process? Because, if you haven't figured it out, I do love you. I love you in a way I can't even wrap my mind around. I love you like family, like a friend, and like a woman who fits so perfectly in my life. I *love* you, Jericho, and I don't know who I'd be without you, so will you please do this one thing for me?"

"Have other boyfriends?" she asked, the confusion audible.

I nodded. "And girlfriends. Well, just friends. With benefits or without. I mean, I'd be thrilled if you felt comfortable enough to call someone your boyfriend, but I get it. I really do. For you, that's a big step. For me, this is one."

"Which this?" she asked.

I smiled softly. "Letting you see my demons. I'm supposed to be the one slaying yours, you know."

"But that's not how partners work."

I smiled sadly. "No, it's not, so I'm trying. I'd just really like it if you gave me this one thing. Don't stop living, baby girl. Don't destroy yourself to become a hero. Fall in love instead. Find a reason to feel things even stronger, and then unleash all of that on the ones who deserve your wrath, and I will be standing beside you every step of the way."

She licked her lips, watching my face intently. "What if something happens to one of them, though?"

"But if you love them, they'll have something to hold on to too."

"Nina had you!" she hissed.

Which felt like a punch in the gut, but I understood. I knew she had to say it, because I couldn't stop thinking it. That was the one flaw in my big "plan," if this could even be called that. More like wishful thinking.

"Nina thought she had to be strong." I sighed and rolled onto my back. "She didn't want to bother me. She downplayed the problems so I wouldn't see her as some weak and needy girl. She isolated herself, Jeri. Even from me, in a way. Sure, she lived with me, and I never realized how bad the shit she was dealing with was because there's more than one way to be alone." Then I looked over. "And I see you doing the same thing. You try so hard to be strong for us that you don't realize it's scaring the shit out of me."

So she rolled into the crook of my arm. "I feel like I'm cursed. I feel like this shit follows me around, and I'm scared to get close to anyone but you, because you can understand. I know it's stupid, but it just feels like getting too close to anyone dooms them, and I don't want to be the bad luck charm."

"But they're already close to you," I countered.

She nodded. "And I try not to think about it."

"So how do we fix this?" I asked.

She lifted her eyes to mine. "Can we kill Dylan?"

I laughed once. "Sadly, no. That's kinda illegal."

"So is hacking," she pointed out.

"Different level of illegal."

She sighed dramatically, but then wrapped her arm around my waist and hugged. "I feel like the world has thrown us girls out with the trash, Hottie. I feel like I'm the only one who sees it. It's like, they're all so well trained to just accept that they have to be nice, and polite, and ladylike - even as the boys are walking all over them. They fight with each other because that's easier than pushing back against what's really bothering them, and I just don't fucking know how to fix it!"

"So how do I keep that from ripping you apart the way Nina was?"

She shifted a bit, curling her lower arm up against her chest. "I don't know."

"Me either," I agreed, "which is why I can't sleep. One day, this rage inside you is going to make you feel the same way Nina did. You'll be so sure there's no other way out, and that fighting isn't helping. When that happens, I'll be alone, and then I'll do the same."

For a little too long, she laid beside me, just breathing. "Hottie?" she asked.

"Yeah, baby girl?"

"There's nothing I can say to make that fear go away, is there." It wasn't a question.

I still answered. "Not really. Seeing you happy helps more than anything else. It's why I'm not jealous of those guys. They make you live, and *that* is all I want. I'll be second, or fifteenth, or even two hundredth if it means you're still living and being happy."

She nodded. "How can I do that without being paranoid someone else is going to die because I didn't stop the villains?"

"Maybe we worry less about the deaths, and more about the end results?" I offered. "We focus on making sure these boys pay, and pay dearly. We fucking stop them, Jeri. And if a few more people die along the way, it's not our fault. It's what villains do. It's the shitty nature of not knowing what the fuck they're doing that makes it hard to stop them. We accept we're not the bad guys. We're also not gods, knowing everything all the time. We can only do what we can do."

"And maybe we learn more?" she asked.

"I can do that," I agreed.

So she shifted again, sliding a little lower just to drape her leg over mine as she got into position to actually sleep. "The heroes have to fail before they can win," she said softly.

"Are you sure we're actually the heroes?" I asked.

Which made her grow still. For a little too long, she said nothing. I glanced down, wondering if she'd fallen asleep on me, but her eyes were open and staring at the far wall. Something was going on in her mind, so I waited.

Finally, she said, "That's the part I've been missing. We're not the heroes. We aren't the good guys. We're the ones with no rules to hold us back."

"Jeri..."

So she looked up at me. "We don't save people. We stop the assholes. Saving is someone else's job. Ours is to fuck shit up. If we save a few along the way, then great, but we are not the good guys, Hottie. We're the villains' nightmare." She laughed once, then snuggled her head into my chest. "And that's why I'm going to be ok with not obsessing over this. The good guys can save the damsels. My job is to destroy the bad ones. Nothing more. Nothing less. And maybe a few breaks will help me figure out new ways to do that, so I don't need to obsess over defeating the assholes, right?"

And it felt like a band across my heart had just released. "Thank you," I breathed.

"Help me?" she asked. "Because that sounds good, but it won't be easy."

"And yet you're already doing it," I assured her. "Trust me, you're damned good at fucking shit up - and making it work. Look at your little polycule thing. Oh, and the word you're looking for, baby girl, is vigilante."

"I prefer nightmare," she assured me. "But this is me trying, Hottie."

"Yeah, and this is me letting you in," I admitted. "Because we're going to figure out how to fight the demons. Both the ones in our heads and the ones in the real world."

"Vigilantes," she mumbled. "Mm. Ruin. I like that better. We're the Ruin."

"Yeah, we are."

CHAPTER 8

JINXY

The game was oddly silent all night. I hadn't realized how big of an impact Jericho and her guys had on the guild's regular Discord chatter until none of them were there. Worse, Zoe was gone as well. So were all the members of Ruin - except me.

When Hot had said he had to go because of a family emergency, I'd assumed he meant Jeri's mom was home. I'd heard all about the fight they'd gotten in. Zoe hadn't left out any details. Hot had explained how her mom was pissed about it. Not unreasonably so, but the kind of anger that came from a woman who'd raised her kids in an inner-city school sort of pissed. The type that was supposed to keep her kids safe.

And now, Saturday morning, I still hadn't heard a thing. I was starting to panic. This was why I hated being up in Colorado all alone. When it had been me and Hot, it hadn't sucked as much. Jeri's friends had popped in often enough to keep me updated, but not anymore.

Nope, real-life stuff had started intruding. The kind that had the FBI arresting Zoe's rapist in the middle of a pep rally at school. The kind of real that had Hot forgetting I didn't have a fucking clue half the time, and never popping into Discord to give me a head's up. The kind that had me pulling out my fucking hair!

So I sent off a text to Zoe, hoping it wasn't too early there, since she was an hour ahead of me.

> **Shawn:**
> Hey, just making sure everything's ok. Last I heard there was a family emergency, and now everyone's gone quiet.

Then I waited. I was hoping for a read notice, or maybe even those three dots that would show she was typing. Instead, my phone rang in my hands. I may have yelped in surprise, and I fumbled the damned thing a few times, but since it didn't hit the ground, I technically hadn't dropped it.

"Yeah?" I answered desperately.

"Hey," Zoe said, her voice adorably rough like she'd been sleeping.

"You ok?" I asked.

"Mm..." She shifted, making the sounds travel across the phone. "Just woke up. Heard your text. Thought this was easier."

Damn, I liked the idea of her talking to me before she was even out of bed. I adored the way she sounded so lazy and relaxed. I had a feeling it looked really good on her too, with that red hair a complete mess and her lips all puffy from sleep.

"So everything's ok down there in Texas?" I asked.

"Huh? No." Then she inhaled. Sniffed, maybe? "No one told you about Cade?"

"What about Cade? The last I heard we were working on

finding blackmail videos, all of you got into a fight, and Jeri was worried her mom would be pissed."

"Oh." There was more rustling. "Ok, um, yesterday sucked."

Which told me basically jack and shit. "And?" I pressed.

"Hang on!" she laughed. "Shawn, I'm trying to sit up so my brain will wake up. No, wait. I have to pee. Just sit here."

And then she was gone. No, she didn't hang up, but I heard her walking across the room before a door closed. The little minx had just left her phone on the bed, hadn't she? Of course she had. Granted, thinking before a morning piss was pretty much impossible for me, so I couldn't really blame her.

But it didn't stop my paranoia from spiraling out of control. Yesterday sucked? There was something about Cade? Jeri's mom was supposed to be home, which explained why she and Hot had been MIA, but not everyone else!

Fuck, not even Knock had been in-game. Then again, he probably had another one of his big tournaments coming up, so he might be playing the other. Considering it was his paycheck, I couldn't even be annoyed about it. But Zoe's version of things not being ok and mine weren't necessarily the same. For all I knew, those boys who called themselves Alpha Team had gone after my girl again.

Just as I was ready to lose my mind, she was back. "Ok," Zoe said. "So, here's the fast update. John is one of Dylan's friends. He beat up his girlfriend, Amber. That's what started the fight on Wednesday."

"I knew that," I promised.

"Well, Amber killed herself, and they announced it at school yesterday. Ok, they said she had died, not how. We were all freaking out over that, but it gets worse."

"How the fuck does it get worse than that?" Because suicide? Shit, no wonder I hadn't heard from Hot and Jeri. "How's Hot?" I asked.

"He seemed ok," she admitted. "Not great, but ok. Jeri's a fucking mess, though. I guess Amber sent her a package before she did it? I don't know. We all agreed to set that aside until Monday."

"Zoe," I breathed. "No, baby. Listen to me. Hot's fiancée died by suicide. Jeri's dad too. This isn't ok. It's going to be fucking with them bad."

"I know!" she insisted. "But Cade got kicked out, and that has to come first."

The air refused to enter my lungs. It felt like I'd been kicked repeatedly in the chest, just one after the other. My mind could barely keep up with everything she was saying, but the fact that Zoe sounded ok was enough to let me finally catch my breath.

"What happened?" I managed to get out.

"Dylan told Cade's dad that Cade is gay," she explained. "Cade hadn't been home long when his dad came home and tried to beat him to death. Shit, Jinxy. He looked bad, too. And that was after he cleaned himself up a bit! Like, there's this mark across his neck. His father tried to strangle him, and it's not a light one. I just..." She pulled in a deep breath. "I can't imagine. My parents are jerks sometimes, you know? Like, they've been so worried about me going places and just being a normal teen now. It's all about what Evan did, and how I need to be careful and shit. Annoying, right? But compared to Cade's dad?"

"Not even the same," I agreed. "No, I get ya. What's he going to do?"

"Move in with Knock," she said. "Well, Riley and Logan took over, so he has a place. They even grabbed Hottie and headed to Cade's dad's place to pick up his stuff. Logan went into his attorney mode, scared the shit out of the guy, and Cade got enough of his stuff that it's not a big loss."

"Still has to suck," I reminded her.

"Yeah," she agreed. "Ripper and I were up all night talking

about how we can help him. Unfortunately, we just don't know how. Knock's family is going to make sure he's ok, and Ripper says we can't make him feel like a pussy by babying him too much, so I dunno how to help."

"Give him a hug," I suggested. "Tell him you're still his friend. Right now, those are the things he's going to want, since his parents just cut him from their life. I mean, it makes you feel like your entire foundation - everything that made you into who you are - is a lie."

"I can do those things," she promised. "It's also just his dad. I don't know if he's told his mother."

"Probably doesn't want to," I realized. "Not if moving in with her means he'll leave everything there."

"Yeah," she muttered. "And sounds like he isn't close with her."

"What about you?" I asked next. "Did you know that girl?"

She made a little noise like she was mulling my question over. "I knew who she was. Shit, everyone did. Amber Callihan was the valedictorian. We all knew she would be since, like, fifth grade. She was one of those, you know? The perfect type."

"Which usually means high pressure at home," I countered.

"Yeah..." She sighed. "Well, Jeri has - had - this box of stuff. In it was a pregnancy test. She said Amber was raped. I don't really know anything else, or how Jeri knows all of this, but it sounds bad."

"But how are *you* doing?" I asked again. "Zoe, I know this will be hard on Jeri and Hot. I'm guessing it won't exactly be easy on you."

She was silent for just a little too long. "I don't know," she finally admitted. "It's different."

"Different how?" I pressed.

"It's not me!"

"And?"

She grumbled under her breath. "I don't know. All I can tell you is that I'm done being the victim. I mean, when Knock asked Jeri about the box? Yeah, she didn't want to say anything because it was about rape. I mean, how many times have my friends tried to not tell me things, or to keep it from me lately? And there she was, right in front of me, trying to hide it when she was holding the damned thing!"

"Because we're all worried about you too," I reminded her.

"And I'm *fine*!" she snapped.

"Are you?"

She inhaled to say something, and then just pushed her breath back out. "No..."

"And that's ok," I promised.

"But it's kinda not," she said. "Jinxy, I don't want to hold everything up. I don't want them to have to pick their words carefully around me. I don't want to be reminded of what happened and how I can't get over it as fast as I wanted. I don't want to be broken!"

"No one does, but we all are." I bent over my knees and shoved a hand through my hair. "Baby, every person in the world has a little bit of broken to them. I mean, that's why Flawed appeals to us, right? We're finally in a place where we're not alone. That game is the one thing that stands up and admits that being perfect is a damned lie, and then makes it cool to accept that we're not."

"Yeah..."

"So stop trying to be perfect, and start trying to work with the flaw you got. Make it a strength, Zoe. Just like in the game. So you're triggered by stuff, right? Shit, I know I am."

"What triggers you?" she asked.

I chuckled softly. "Getting cut out. Feeling like I'm on the outside."

"Oh, Shawn..." she breathed, realizing that was exactly what they'd done to me last night. "I'm so sorry! I didn't know!"

"And I hadn't told you," I admitted. "That means it's not your fault."

"Can I ask why?"

Yeah, that was a little harder. "Um, because when I was young, I got busted. See, I used to live in Texas. I'd just learned how to run a few scripts, right? Not real good hacking, but enough. And then I hacked into someone's phone to help a friend. Oh, I got busted too. Charges pressed and the whole thing. But the part most don't realize is that getting arrested at that age? It's fucking horrifying."

"I can imagine."

I nodded, even though she couldn't see. "So I went to juvie. I got put in an orange jumpsuit and then into a cell. My parents didn't call. They didn't try to get me an attorney. Nope, the state did that. And then Gran showed up. Seems one of the guards at the place had looked into my arrest and realized I was just trying to help. He recommended me to the Southwind program, and Gran was there to pick me up."

"And your parents?" she asked.

"They didn't want a thing to do with me," I admitted. "Which, I'm sad to say, is more common than you'd think. For most of us at Southwind, our parents were overwhelmed with kids they couldn't afford, handle, or understand. Once someone else took charge, they got the break they'd been hoping for."

"Your grandmother," she realized.

"Gran," I corrected. "She was certainly not my grandmother. More like a mom, and her partner filled the role of that vodka aunt, you know? Always encouraging us to bend the rules a little, think outside the box, and try harder. Bea taught us there's a difference between 'good' and 'successful.' Gran taught us how to succeed using Bea's cheat codes. She showed us we didn't need to break the rules. We needed to rewrite them to fit us, then convince everyone else they'd always been that way."

"So a pretty good childhood?" she asked.

I chuckled, because it had been. "Yeah. I mean, for the most part, it was. Except for that time when I was in juvie. Shit, I've never been that scared, and I know it's nothing for most people, but I was a scrawny, nerdy little dork boy, Zoe."

"Helpless," she realized.

"Yeah, which is why I hate feeling like I don't know how to help."

"Me too," she agreed. "Shawn, I'm not freaked out that rape happens. I'm not even triggered by the thought that other people are raped, or that these assholes have done horrible things. I already know they have. The part that makes me feel like I want to run and never stop? It's that. It's feeling like I'm helpless all over again. Like I'm not going to be good enough or strong enough, or brave enough to step up when someone *else* needs me."

"You will," I promised. "You're too damned strong to do anything else. And maybe you'll need to hold my hand - or Ripper's - but you'll still stand there, lifting your chin, and saying 'you have to come through me first.'"

"Yeah," she said. "I like that."

"That," I told her, "is how I see you. Not the girl in the pictures you send me, Zoe. I see that defiance, and I like it. Even when it trembles, I like it."

"So, maybe I'll make sure to update you on what's going on, and you can remind me I'm still strong even when I'm quaking in my boots?"

"Deal," I said a little too quickly. "Mostly because it means I might get to hear your voice every night now."

She giggled. "It's possible. I mean, I'm getting pretty good at talking."

"And that," I said, "is a bigger step than you know. It means you're going to be ok, Zoe."

"My version of ok," she corrected.

Yeah, but I had a better point. "Isn't that the only one that matters?"

"Huh." She paused. "Yeah. I think it just might be."

CHAPTER 9

JERICHO

I spent all day thinking about what Hottie had said to me last night. In the darkness of my room, it had all been so clear. His words had made so much sense. The feeling of him showing me his own weaknesses was indescribable, bringing us closer in a way I hadn't expected.

But that was the thing. I liked being closer with him. I knew he understood me. I knew he would be ok, because the "worst" had already happened when he'd lost Nina, right? That meant he'd survived my supposed curse. He had to be the exception to the rule that seemed to be my bad luck.

The others couldn't say the same. Zoe had been raped, though. Wasn't that enough? How much did someone need to suffer in order to be safe from this *thing* that kept striking the people around me?

Not that I really believed there was a thing. I also knew most people didn't have this much shit dropped on them. While normal lives might not look like something on TV, they also were nothing at all like mine - and that was the problem. I had no other way to explain the never-ending pile of horrors that kept happening except to call it a curse.

I also didn't believe in that shit. I wasn't superstitious. I knew this was nothing more than a shitty roll of the proverbial dice. Things happened, those things had consequences, and the consequences piled up, right? But the Kings of Gaming had killed Nina, targeting her for writing articles about gaming. Dylan and his friends were members of the Kings of Gaming. My friends were trying to stop them.

And that chain right there was what freaked me the fuck out. Things happened. In this case, the Kings of Gaming. Those things had consequences, like Zoe's rape and Amber's death. It was time for the consequences to start piling up, and the last thing I wanted was for my friends to become part of the body count.

So while Mom tried her hardest to have a nice weekend at home with her "son" and daughter, I fretted about all of this. Knock would go after KoG, with or without me. They'd already attacked his family. He was invested and not about to stop. Cade would probably help him, since Riley, Logan, and Kitty had accepted him into the family. That put him in almost the same position as Knock, right?

Zoe had her own reason to hate them. Evan had abused her because she was a gamer girl. No, I couldn't prove that yet, but all signs were sure pointing that way. That meant KoG had already hit her once, and she deserved the chance to hit back.

Then there was Ripper. He didn't really have any skin in this game. Then again, Zoe had been his best friend since they were little. He loved that girl the way I loved the guys in my guild. He was brave, strong, and had already proven he was resilient.

I just wasn't sure if all that meant they were safe. So when Mom finally called it a night, I headed upstairs to do the same - and my mind kept obsessing over this. The line of shit was already in motion. My friends were already targets. Dylan and his stupid-ass Alpha Team wouldn't just leave them alone because I refused to care about them. It was stupid to even think that way.

But I felt it.

The dumb part of my mind was insistent that not caring would keep them from getting hurt. It said that if I pulled away, they'd be safe. It said this was all my fault - always my fault - so I had to tackle it on my own or others would end up like Amber. Others I cared about, because caring was a weakness. Caring was how I got hurt. Caring was the one thing I wasn't allowed to do anymore.

And that voice wouldn't shut up.

So I got up and walked across the hall. Hottie was lying on top of his blankets in the dark. He looked over as the door opened, then shifted to pull the blankets back. I crawled under them, he did the same, and we met in the middle of his bed.

"I was trying to stay in my room tonight," he whispered.

I nodded to show I heard, but I had bigger problems. "I know it's not a real curse, but I feel like I can't care about them or something bad will happen."

"Not how it works," he assured me.

"No, listen," I insisted. "Just listen for a sec, Hottie?"

"Ok," he relented. "I'm listening."

"It's not real. I *know* that. I *feel* like I need to pull away to save them. I *know* it won't help. I *feel* like it's my fault if they get hurt." I pulled in a breath, trying to make the chaos in my head make sense. "I'm not stupid. I know this is all bullshit, but it's also KoG. They targeted Nina. Zoe's a gamer who's a girl. Knock is already fighting, and now Cade will too. Ripper will protect Zoe - "

"And you," he added.

I nodded again, knowing he was right. "So they're already in danger, right? It's not me. It's KoG. It's Alpha Team. It's the villains, because I really don't have a better word than that."

"Then 'villains' works," he assured me.

"But you want me to be happy so you can be ok. Believe it or not, I really do want to be happy, Hottie. I *like* the time I spend with my friends. I really like all of this, and I like my friends. Together and as individuals, but is that ok? Is liking too much? What if it's more than like? Can I stop that?"

"Do you - "

I pressed a finger over his lips. "You're listening, remember? Because I've never lost anyone who's just a friend like that. It's always been family. It's people I love in one way or another. So I made sure I didn't let myself care that much, but what if I do? What if I already care, and I'm just using other words so it doesn't overwhelm me? What if KoG doesn't give a shit about my feelings and fucks them up anyway? Would it hurt me any less?"

He rolled onto his side so we were facing each other. "Am I still listening?"

"No, I don't think so," I mumbled.

And he smiled. "So, what I'm hearing is that maybe you're starting to fall for these guys - or at least *really* like them - and you're trying to figure out how to balance that?"

"No," I groaned. "Hottie, I'm saying I love you, but it's not a shield. If something happened to you, I already love you. I love you so much, I don't know how I'd survive without you, and I can't take that back. It also won't stop KoG from hurting you." I licked my lips as my mouth went dry. "And the same is true for them."

"But Zoe would be there for you," he countered. "Jinxy too. I have a feeling Knock, Cade, and Ripper would jump in without slowing down. They'd hold you up for as long as you needed."

I nodded. "And if it was Ripper who died?"

"Then the rest of us will carry you," he promised.

"I'm still scared," I told him, "but I'm trying, Hottie. I'm trying to figure this out."

He gently swept my hair back from my face. "Because I asked you to?"

I grumbled and rolled my head, showing he wasn't quite right. "Because you brought it up and I've been thinking about it. You need me to be happy, right? So I want to be happy to help you, but what makes me happy? Well, my friends do, but getting close makes me scared, and scared isn't happy, so how do I balance that?"

"Jeri, you don't have to do something just because I ask you to."

"I know," I promised. "It's just that I think you might be right this time, and I don't know who else to ask but you. I mean, does calling someone my best friend put a target on them? Well, that's stupid if this curse isn't real, but then why does it *feel* like it would?"

"That's a trauma response," he explained. "It's the lizard part of your brain searching for some correlation to latch on to in an attempt to survive a hostile world. It sends out panic signals when patterns start to repeat, and your pattern is based on people you loved, so your emotional closeness is what triggers it."

I nodded. "Ok, and I'm going to guess the only way to stop that is to ignore the lizard and do something anyway?"

"Yeah, that's pretty much what my therapist said. Not in those words, but the basic idea."

"Then be my boyfriend?" I asked.

His eyes widened but he said nothing. Instead, he scanned my face, looking like he was waiting for the punchline of the joke or something. I wanted to explain, but my mind had just stalled out. I'd actually asked that. I meant it. It all made sense to me, but I had no clue how to get him to understand why this was what I needed.

"Boyfriend?" he finally asked.

I jiggled my head quickly, because he could laugh it off. "You want me to take a risk so I'll get better, right? Well, this is my risk. I figure that since you want it, then you're risking yourself - which is fucking stupid, and I know it, but just go with me here?"

"I'm following so far," he promised.

"So, maybe I can do the boyfriend thing, and since you're already safe, I can figure out how to be a girlfriend, and then maybe I can, I dunno, like go from partners to boyfriends too? I kinda still want to be partners, just because I like Zoe and Jinxy in our polycule, but that's not the point."

"Then what's the point?"

I took a deep breath, then paused. Shit. I wasn't sure what the point was. Well, I felt it, but words were hard. This wasn't the kind of conversation I was used to. I knew all the ways to say no, to push people away, but not the ones to say yes - or even please.

So I rambled. "I love you, Hottie. I always have, in one way or another. You're also supposed to be safe. You're my rock, the thing that keeps me stable when everything goes to shit, and I'm supposed to be yours. I mean, isn't that what a relationship is supposed to be? We help each other, hold each other up, and we don't need to be little icons of boyfriend and girlfriend. We can just be two people who care about each other, who are willing to let the other all the way in, and..." I had to pause so I could swallow. "Maybe I can learn how to fall all the way in love if you'll show me?"

"I don't need that word from you," he said gently. "Baby girl, call me whatever you want."

"I want to try calling you my boyfriend, because I need you to help me get over this fear. I just don't want to be some little Barbie doll who's expected to suddenly be a perfect little accessory to your life. I want to be a partner. I want the kind of 'girlfriend' role Nina had. The kind I know you can make work, so I'm asking *you*, Grayson. I want to be your girlfriend, because someone has to be first, and you won't ever leave me."

"No, I won't," he swore, reaching up to cup my face. "And yeah, I'll be your boyfriend. Jeri, I will be anything you want me to be, but I have one condition."

"Ok?"

"Never," he said, his voice turning rough, verging on a growl, "give in to make me happy. Never stop burning as brightly as you do. Never stop fighting the things that piss you off - even if that's me. Do not become perfect for me. Don't change yourself to make me happy, because you already make me happy, you hear me? I will be your boyfriend, baby girl, so long as you promise you will never become my pretty little bitch."

"I swear on Drake's grave," I breathed.

And he kissed me, hard, rolling me onto my back in the process. "Equals," he said. "Fumbling, fucked up, and willing to figure it out."

I pulled him closer. "Yeah. I like that 'fucked up' part." Then I pulled at his shirt.

CHAPTER 10

JERICHO

I got Hottie's shirt over his head, then pushed at the waistband of the soft pants he was sleeping in. Lying over me like he was, he had to balance as he reached back to help. That allowed me to steal one more kiss before he gave in, flopping onto his back so he could get himself naked.

Yeah, I didn't waste any time removing my own clothes. My shirt came off, my panties were next. I was still working my last leg free when I began crawling towards him for one more kiss, because this was my boyfriend. Hottie. The man I'd been crushing on for as long as I could remember, the guy who'd been my best friend through all of that, and now the man who was my partner in all things.

I wanted to make this official.

He met me halfway, kissing my lips so hard, even as one hand found the back of my neck and the other landed on my waist. When I kept crawling, he guided me closer, but what he didn't do was lie back. Instead, he pulled away just enough to look right in my eyes.

"Your mom is downstairs," he whispered.

"Don't care," I assured him as I straddled his lap.

But his hands prevented me from lowering myself onto him. "Baby girl, if we get caught like this, a whole lot will change, and not in good ways."

I just smiled and relaxed my legs, sliding downwards. "Then don't get caught, Grayson."

A smile flickered over his lips. "Condom, Jericho."

I leaned forward to kiss him again. "You have exactly ten seconds to deal with that before I lose patience."

So he leaned back and stretched. "The benefits of youth, huh?" he asked as he fumbled open his nightstand's drawer. "Ready to go with a stiff breeze? One day, baby girl, I'm going to teach you all about foreplay."

Then he relaxed, a little packet now in his hands. Without shame, the man tore it open and rolled the thing on. I was kneeling there, only inches out of the way, watching. I liked the way his dick strained against the constraint, the tendons in the backs of his hands as he got it on, and how casually he handled the whole thing.

Because sex with everyone else had always been frantic. Maybe that was teenage hormones, or maybe it was me. I honestly didn't know, but something about the way Hottie handled this made it feel different. Less like he was a thing that would vanish if I didn't use him up fast enough, and more...

More like a man I could love completely.

Shit, that was the difference. The condom wasn't about him. It was about me. It was his way of taking care of me, just like how he'd gone down on me that first time. It was a subtle way for him to show he cared for more than just the pleasure he got from my body. He wanted me - all of me - and not just for right now.

The thought hit me like a ton of bricks, and the only way I could deal with it was to kiss him again. Not hard, though. No, this was soft and full of feeling. I allowed myself to experience his lips as they pressed against mine, to enjoy the motion of his tongue in my mouth, and to explore with my hands. I held him, savoring his muscles flexing under my palms as he did the same back.

"Hottie?" I breathed.

"Yeah, baby girl?"

I palmed the side of his face. "I've never made love before."

He paused. Shit, *I* paused. For a moment, there in the darkness of his room, lit only by the ambient glow of the streetlights through his curtains, we looked at each other. Not timidly, either. We both looked, and it felt like he saw me. All of me. Every flaw, every strength, and all of my fears laid out to be picked through.

Then he smiled softly. "Then make love to me."

Those words made me feel like he'd picked them all - each and every broken piece that fit together to make me, he'd accepted. He was also giving me the power to put them together however I wanted, because I was not his trophy. I wasn't his possession. Just like he'd said a moment ago, I was his equal. His partner.

So I lowered myself down. Slowly, I could feel myself stretching around him as he filled me. Beneath me, with his back to the pillows, Hottie's eyes slipped closed and he inhaled. It was a soft sound, but I loved it.

Shit, I loved him. Not like. Not trusted. Yeah, all of those were included, but they weren't nearly strong enough for the way I felt as I pushed my *boyfriend* into my body. This man was a part of me. Maybe it was comfortable, but was that a bad thing? Did we have to be wild and stupid for our love to mean something?

Or was this more? This calm, quiet need that existed between us was what made me feel safe. This man, with his perfect body and gorgeous face, was more than his looks. He was my world. He was my safe place. He was the safety net that allowed me to be brave, and as my weight reached his hips, I understood the difference between fucking and making love.

Fucking was for me.

Making love was for him.

So I moved, rolling my hips as I lifted back up just a bit. His eyes jumped open and both of his hands found my waist. That look was a good one for him. I did it again, loving how his eyes held mine, but I wanted to give him so much more.

So I leaned in and kissed him. The rhythm of our bodies was slow, but that made every motion even more important. The bed didn't creak, but our breath was getting faster. Subtle, deep sounds kept getting trapped in his throat. They weren't quite moans, but they really wanted to be.

And they were for me. The man I loved was giving himself to me, letting me lead, and it was amazing. I clasped the back of his neck, using that hold for balance as I pumped myself onto him, but I needed another taste of his lips, his neck, and even his shoulder. My mouth wandered as my body moved, but so did his.

Those hands on my waist moved higher. His thumbs found my breasts, teasing the nipples. The gasps of his breath each time I pushed down onto him were so sensual, and my own little inhales mixed with them perfectly. My eyes alternated between being closed - so I could focus on every touch, every sensation - or open so I could see him.

This beautiful, amazing man was mine. I loved him. It was ok to love him. It had to be, because I already did, and I couldn't stop it. I loved the way he listened, the way he pushed me, and this. Every single touch on my body felt so good, but it was more than mere contact.

It felt like emotion turned physical. This time, being with him was intense in a whole different way. Our bodies moved slowly, leaving time for kisses, touches, and more. Neither of us talked. There was nothing to say, but so much to feel.

The way his fingers gripped me hard was erotic. He wasn't scared of hurting me. The light brush of his lips against my neck was a tease. The swirling of his thumbs over my nipples and the slick hardness of him filling me repeatedly had my nerves on fire. I wanted to moan. I longed to whimper with pleasure.

I just breathed. Hard, forceful pants when I pressed him deeper inside me. Slow, deep inhales as I fought to hold back my own sounds. I breathed, needing nothing but to be a little closer to my boyfriend. Wanting to prove I was tearing down all the walls I'd erected between my heart and his.

I let him in. Into my body, into my mind, and into my heart. I gave in, stopped fighting, and just loved him. Leaning my head back, I sank down again, loving how well we fit together - and his mouth claimed my breast. He sucked. I pumped. Our bodies moved together in perfect harmony even as the pleasure built inside me, pushing against all those restraints I'd tried to make.

And it was more than I could take. I gasped, a hint of my voice wrapped around the sound, and he kissed me. His hands kept me moving, rocking me onto his body, taking over as my legs began to tremble. This was partnership. This was love. This, more than anything else, was surrender, and it felt so fucking good.

So I let go.

The orgasm took me even as Hottie drank in my sounds, muffling them with his kisses. Again, then again, he pumped me onto him, riding me through the sensation until he couldn't take anymore. So much pleasure. So much desire. My mind could barely comprehend it all, until Hottie gasped and froze. His groan was deep and barely audible as he found his own release.

Pushing out my breath, I leaned forward to throw my arms around his neck, needing something to hold onto. His moved around my back, hugging my chest against his. Together, entwined, we both just breathed. I could feel his heart crashing against my body, and my own pulse matched.

"I love you," I breathed in his ear.

His arms tightened around me. "I wanted to wait, you know." Slowly, he let me go and leaned back so I could climb off. "I thought that after you graduated from high school, or maybe college... I dunno. Just later. After you'd had the chance to figure out who you are and what you want, so I wouldn't be one of those assholes who tried to take advantage of you."

I moved to lay on the bed beside him. "But you don't."

"But I could," he countered, even as he removed the condom and climbed out of bed. Heading across the room for the trashcan in the corner, he said, "If I tried to push you to be something, Jeri, we both know you'd try. You'd believe me when I said it was a good idea. See, that's what scares the shit out of me."

"That you care about me?" I asked, not quite following.

He came back to bed and slid beside me. "No, that a woman as vivacious as you could be broken by a man. That I could be that man, even if I didn't mean to. That no matter how much you say you're one of the guys, never learned how to be a girl, or anything else, you're still vulnerable to that."

"But *you* wouldn't," I countered.

He shrugged. "Not intentionally. Doesn't mean I won't by accident. That's why I'm saying something. Jericho, I do not love you because you're easy. I don't love you because you're beautiful - even though I think you are. I don't love you because you're what I expect. I love you because you are strong enough to stand behind your convictions, screaming them at the top of your lungs and punching the shit out of anyone who disagrees."

"Yeah?" I asked, kinda liking how that felt.

He nodded slowly. "Yeah. I love that you're willing to listen and consider it when I tell you what I need, but also to think about what you need, and to figure out a way to still be true to yourself." Then he cupped the side of my face, tilting my head so we were eye-to-eye. "I also love that I'm your boyfriend now."

"My first."

"I know." Then he kissed me again. Gently. Softly. Tenderly even. "Trust me, I know, and I'm going to do my best to make sure I don't let you down."

"Me too," I promised.

"Mm, but I want you to let me down, challenge me, and force me to become a better man."

"Then maybe you'll do the same for me?" I asked. "I mean, equality and all."

"I swear on Drake's grave," he breathed. "And you cannot sleep here tonight. I wish you could, but that would not end well."

So I kissed him again. "I need a stuffed animal, Hottie. Something to curl up with that smells like you."

"Means I'd have to sleep with it first," he teased.

So I tapped his nose and then rolled for the edge of the bed. "See, now you're getting it."

He chuckled. "Jeri?"

I paused and looked over. Hottie ran his eyes over me, taking his time about it. Slowly a smile began to curl his mouth.

"You are beautiful, you know. Fuck, you had to grow up into a knockout. The kind of woman I can't resist." Then his smile faltered, but his eyes didn't leave. "Better than Nina, just so you know."

"Different," I corrected. "And I'm not jealous of her, Hottie. I loved her too, you know."

"Yeah." He sighed. "I think that's why I can do this. Now go to your own room. I need to snore after that."

I pulled on my shirt before figuring out which way out my panties went. "I have a feeling you'll curl up against me in about an hour, huh?"

He just murmured. "Bed, baby girl. We're being good. We're also keeping this whole girlfriend-boyfriend thing from your mom."

"So long as she's calling you Drake, we definitely are," I agreed, turning for the door. But I paused with my hand on the knob. "Hottie? I do, you know. Love you, I mean."

"I know," he promised. "You showed me."

As I left his room, I had a smile on my face. I couldn't even explain why that felt so good, but it did. He knew I loved him. I was getting this right.

I also wouldn't let anything take him from me. Not any of them.

CHAPTER 11

RIPPER

For a weekend that had started out insane, it had been impressively quiet. Zoe and I talked. She talked to Jinxy. Evidently, Jinxy talked to Hot at some point on Saturday, but only to check in - but I hadn't heard anything from Knock or Cade. Text messages to them had been replied to with simple emojis, but little else.

So, on Sunday morning, I decided to take matters into my own hands. After begging out of church, I convinced my old truck to start up one more time, and headed to their place. The thing wasn't happy with me lately. Ok, mostly it was the weather. Texas winters had given way to spring warmth, which made my truck limp and thump in a way that gas engines weren't really supposed to.

But it got me there, just like it always did. Pulling into the drive, it coughed a few times, making me beg it not to backfire, and then I found a place to park. When I turned the key to kill the engine, it huffed a few more times, just to let me know it was not happy about this.

Yeah, if that didn't announce my arrival, nothing would. Needless to say, when I climbed out, I wasn't shocked at all to see Quake wagging excitedly at the fence. Since he was outside, that meant someone had to be up.

"Hey, bud," I told the dog. "Who's a good boy?"

Well, he was, of course, and his body wiggled even more to prove it. I chuckled, because a dog that size should not be that cute, and yet he always managed. As I headed towards the gate, he followed, huffing in his excited way.

"You know you're supposed to sleep in on Sundays, right?"

Cade's voice made me jerk to a stop, because it hadn't come from the direction I'd been expecting. Turning, I found him leaning against the open barn entrance with a funny-looking rake in his hand. Never mind the bruises on his face, arms, and that dark line around his throat.

"Holy shit," I breathed, changing direction to head right for him. "You look like hell."

"Feel pretty good, though," he promised, leaning back to put his rake inside the barn. "And so you know, your truck is trying to die on you."

"Yeah..." I flapped a hand in the direction of the old thing. "One day, it'll strand me on the side of the road, but today was not that day."

He chuckled and pushed away from the wall. "Well, since the herd is in there eating, I have some time. I also learned something really cool since I moved in." Then he clasped my shoulder and turned me back towards my truck. "See the building that looks like a garage and no one ever uses?"

"Yeah?"

"It's a carriage house, and there are two massive horse carriages in there," he explained, steering me straight towards it.

"Riley also has a rather impressive set of tools to work on the things. Her dad's stuff, she said. Automotive tools, for the most part, some power tools, and basically anything a good farm needs."

"Ok?" I still wasn't sure where he was going with this.

Then he looked over and smiled at me. "And I know how to fix your truck."

"I just... Cade, I came by to make sure you're ok!"

He rubbed my back, but the curl on his lips stayed. "Ripper, this is just me proving I am. Pretty sure Knock's still out, Riley definitely is, but Logan and Kitty are up. I handled the feeding this morning, so it's not like I'm about to go back to sleep."

"Well, yeah, but..."

My words died as he opened a normal-looking door and we stepped into the carriage house from the back. Most people would call a building like this a shop. It was bigger than a two-car garage, but there were definitely two vehicles taking up space in it. One was a beautiful carriage fit for a princess. It had the whole convertible top and everything.

The other looked more like the ones I saw in Budweiser ads. It was big. Wooden poles stuck off the fronts, which I was pretty sure was where the horses went, but damn. I'd never seen anything like this up close.

"Why doesn't she do anything with these?" I asked.

"Because Deviant Games doesn't need wagons," he explained. "Yep, I got the primer on the farm yesterday. And yes, I had to sign a non-disclosure agreement since I now work here."

"And the gas station?" I asked.

"Called and quit," he explained. "Dad knew about that; Riley didn't want me to take the risk of him showing up, so yeah. I'm a full-time shit shoveler for Andrews Shires now. My boyfriend is a co-owner."

As he spoke, he was rummaging through one of those big metal toolboxes. The kind that had drawers and was as tall as I was. When he had what he wanted, he gestured for me to head back out, clasping the necessary tools in one hand.

"Go pop the hood on that thing?" he asked.

Yep, at this point, I was just along for the ride, it seemed. So while Cade went to the front of my truck, I got in the cab, found the lever to release the hood, and made sure the emergency brake was fully engaged. By the time I made it back around to the front, Cade was already leaning into the engine.

"You know I didn't intend for you to work on my truck, right?" I asked.

He shrugged. "I like working on cars. I enjoy the whole mechanical aspect. If this does that, then something else works." And he'd already zeroed in on a piece of the engine.

I had no clue what anything under the hood did. Not my area of interest, but Cade looked comfortable with all the grease-coated metal. The same guy who struggled with coding clearly had an affinity for the old-school kind of hardware. But that still wasn't why I was here.

"So how are you doing?" I asked, moving to lean beside him. "No bullshit, man. How are you handling what all happened?"

He grimaced as he worked a nut free, then sighed. "I don't know. They make it easy, though. Like, this whole house is fucking insane. We all take turns with meals, doing what we can and learning more. We all take turns with cleaning rooms. We all step up and help, but there's no list or anything."

"Doesn't really tell me about you," I pointed out.

"Kinda does," he said. "See, that's the thing. I got babied that first day. Yesterday, they started to nudge me into helping. Today, I got up and fed the horses." Then he looked over. "Ripper, I feel like I fucking *belong*. Not like I'm crashing here, or getting in the way. They just made space for me in the middle. Not the edge - the fucking middle!"

"And Knock?" I asked, remembering he'd been a little nervous about Cade moving in.

Cade chuckled. "Um, yeah. It's good."

"So lots of fucking?" I teased.

His hands stilled. "That's the thing. No. Lots of talking. Plenty of kissing. Shared showers and shit like that, but I kinda get Jeri and Hot now. We talk. We're figuring it out, and putting it all out there, which is fucking weird as hell."

"Is it, though?"

He gave up on the truck so he could turn and lean his back against the front of it. "This is." Then he set his wrench on the bumper. "Not in a bad way. It's just..."

I turned to match him. "Safe?" I suggested.

"More like mature," he corrected. "Knock's not like most guys." Then he groaned. "Shit, that damned line. What I mean is that he spends all night with gamers in their late twenties to early thirties - and he fucking fits in. That's what he thinks of as normal. This high school shit? Being all fucked up about knowing what we want? That's not what they do."

"Yeah, but I'm pretty sure you're his first boyfriend."

He nodded. "So he talks it out. That's what works for Riley and Logan, so he does the same. And when he tries, it makes it easier for me to try. So yeah, um, we kinda agreed to move slow. Like, we're sharing a bed and all, but we agreed we don't want to feel like we have to be down to fuck all the time. We can do a little of this, or maybe some of that, and just let it be enough."

"So, hand jobs?" I joked, bumping his shoulder.

Cade hung his head. "Actually? Yeah." When he glanced at me, his face was a little redder than normal. "And my dad isn't around to get pissed about it. I don't have this fear in the back of my head that he's going to find out, because he already did."

"So, relief?" I guessed.

"Maybe?"

"Or is it more that all of this is new?" I tried next.

Cade shook his head at that. "No."

"Talk to me?" I begged, because I was actually worried about him.

I knew all of this had to be a lot. Shit, if it had happened to me, I would not be this chill only a few days later. I also knew Cade was damned good at acting like things were no big deal when they really were.

"Look," I tried next, "I'm not trying to talk you out of staying here. I'm also just going to throw it out there that my parents mentioned that if you need a place, they'll make one for you. We got a spare room and all, so you aren't stuck here with nowhere to go."

"You told your parents?" he asked.

I nodded. "Yeah. They called your dad a few names. I also told them I wouldn't say why he kicked you out, but they guessed. They said your dad has a reputation, so I corrected from gay to bi. I hope that's not out of line?"

"No," he assured me. "I just..."

"You haven't figured out you can come out yet," I realized. "You've been hiding it so long that it's second nature." I reached over to clasp his shoulder. "Do you even want to? I mean, being able to and wanting to aren't the same thing, right?"

"I don't know," he admitted. "Ripper, I haven't gotten there yet. I'm still..." He gestured to the property around us. "I know what's in the carriage house. I can feed a herd of Shires on my own, without help. I'm sharing a bed with my boyfriend, and no one thinks that's weird. I'm good, but I still feel like I'm going to wake up."

"I am *not* pressuring you," I swore. "I'm just making sure my best friend is ok, and the only way I know how to be a best friend is with Zoe."

He flashed me an impish little smirk. "I'll take it. I kinda like your version of a best friend. I mean, you drove all the way over here?"

"Because you both were giving me fucking one-icon answers!" I shot back.

He laughed. "We were gaming. Shit, and that's another thing I have to get used to. This house? Fuck, they take that shit seriously. First-person shooters are nothing like MMOs. Blink and you're dead, and usually it's Logan who killed me."

"Not Riley?"

"I'm in Riley's outfit now." He bumped my shoulder this time. "It's not a guild. It's an outfit. So far, I've been allowed to hang out with this one guy's girlfriend. She's also new, so they've been training us how to not die. Not that it helps much, but it's intense. And to everyone in there, it's work."

"So you gonna go pro?" I asked.

"Fuck no," he assured me. "Nope. That world is even crazier than ours, but it's fun to peek in and watch for a bit. I kinda want to see one of their tournaments, and I guess there's one in Dallas at the end of the month."

"That," I agreed, "would be fun. Get to see Knock all fancy and shit?"

"I know, right?" he asked before turning back to my truck. Then, "Ripper? How am I going to explain the bruises at school?"

"Your dad is an abusive alcoholic," I told him. "This was the last straw, so you left. You're eighteen and he can't stop you."

"But won't people wonder why he hit me?"

Which meant Cade wasn't ready to come out yet. If he was worried about that, then he was still processing, and this was definitely going to take some time. Damn, I could only imagine how scary it must be.

But what I said was, "Nah. I think the alcoholic part makes up for that. Besides, most people know you're all into Jeri, and I'm sure she will make a fuss over you in the morning."

"What if I want to come out?" he asked next.

"Then think about it," I told him. "Cade, this is high school. People are going to try to tear you down for anything they can. Decide if this is something you even want to bother with, because it doesn't matter to us. We love you for being you."

He stared at my engine for a while, and then reached into his pocket. Pulling out his keys, he passed those to me.

"Take my car home today. I'll get a ride to school with Knock, and that should give me time to fix your truck."

I blinked hard, not sure where that had come from. "Um, ok? I don't... Cade?"

Then he turned and hugged me. "I love you too, man."

And that was when I finally understood. I'd said we all loved him for being him. Here, in the point of his life that should be a low one, he was currently on top of the world, and this was how he was trying to give back. He also didn't know how to say it, so he was doing instead.

"You don't have to fix my truck," I said as I hugged back. "All I need is for you to be my friend, Cade."

"But I can do this," he promised, pulling away. "You've done so much, and this is something I can do." Letting out a sigh, he shoved back his unruly hair. "Let me? I don't want to be carried, man. I don't want to be the one always getting rescued. I want to help too, and this is what I can do."

So I nodded. "Ok, but just know that you do a hell of a lot more than you think. That, Cade, is why we all jumped in. You do a shit ton for us. You just don't realize it because you're actually a good guy."

"Yeah, but I feel like everyone dropped everything for me."

"We did," I admitted. "Kinda like you did for Zoe. Like Jeri does for all of us. That's why we work."

"I still want to fix your truck," he mumbled.

So I lifted his keys. "I'm going to drive this too fast."

"The tires break free easily," he said before turning back to my truck. "And you need all new filters, new spark plugs, and at least an oil change. After that, I'll tune it up a bit, and this baby will purr like a kitten."

"It'll still be an old piece of shit truck," I reminded him.

"Nope," he said. "This, Ripper, is a classic. You're looking at it wrong, so you aren't seeing the best parts."

I huffed out a laugh and nodded. "Kinda like all of us, huh?"

"Yep. Exactly. That's why we all make such good partners." And the look he gave me made it clear he mostly meant me and him.

CHAPTER 12

JERICHO

Mom left late Sunday. Not once did she figure out that Hottie wasn't Drake. The entire weekend, she'd been plunged right back into the "good ol' days." So, when she headed back to work, it was almost a relief, even if I hated myself for thinking like that.

Mom didn't mean to be a mess. Then again, neither did I. That was why I wanted Hottie to be my boyfriend. Most girls I knew would've wanted it for other reasons, like bragging rights, to think they had a stronger relationship with him, or things like that. Not me. I knew words and feelings didn't always match up.

And that was kinda my problem.

Because all weekend, I'd been feeling things. Lots of things. Things that were so fucking obvious I couldn't really ignore them anymore. Things that scared the shit out of me.

Amber's videos were one. Cade getting kicked out was another. Worse, seeing the bruises on him? Never mind the warm feeling I got when I saw all of my guys working together. None of this was detached or "safe." It was all invested, and that little paranoid voice in the back of my head said it was a problem.

But Hottie was my boyfriend now, and he still loved me, so I was ok. This was all ok. I might be a train wreck mentally, but I was still chugging along. And yet, as I drove myself to school Monday morning, I decided I wasn't going to tell anyone about my new status update.

Not yet. Not because I didn't want them to know. Not exactly because of that, at least. It was more that I needed time to get used to this. I had a boyfriend. My paranoia said this was just asking for something bad to happen. I was tempting the fates, or some shit.

So for now, this was my secret. If Zoe could keep her thing with Jinxy to herself for a little while, then there was nothing wrong with me doing the same. Besides, we were all supposed to be worried about Cade first, right?

Yet when I got to the table, Cade and Knock weren't there. Ripper was, and he had a little smile on his face. Beside him, Zoe was rolling her eyes at whatever he'd been talking about. The moment I was close enough, she decided to drag me into it.

"If a guy lets you drive his car, it means he has a crush, right?" she asked.

"Uh, yeah," I said, claiming the spot on Ripper's other side. "Why?"

She tapped Ripper's leg with her foot. "Because someone's driving that hot rod today."

"It's an Impala," Ripper said, and it sounded like it wasn't the first time. "I only have it because Cade has a ride with Knock."

"Uh-huh..." I was grinning, because this was too good to pass up. "Jealous?"

"Nope." And he leaned into me. "Because my partner's working on my truck for me."

"See!" Zoe said. "It's clearly a thing."

"A cute thing," I told Ripper. "Like a bromance or something?"

"Just to be clear," Ripper said, "I'm trying to get in your pants, not -"

But the sounds around us changed. Mostly, that was from the table of gamers beside us, but it wasn't only them. Together, the three of us turned to look in time to see Knock and Cade making their way over. Yeah, it didn't take much to figure out what had everyone talking.

Cade looked like shit. The bruises were obvious. The mark on his throat stood out even at a distance. There was no hiding the fact that he'd gotten his ass kicked by someone. The question was which story we were going with.

"What the fuck?" Carson, one of the gamers, asked as Cade and Knock got closer.

"Dad," Cade explained. "He's drinking again, so I found a new place to stay."

Carson's eyes jumped to Knock. "Yours?"

"Yep," Knock said.

Carson just nodded. "Good. Thought it might've been the Reapers. You know, since they're suspended."

"Until tomorrow," a dark-haired girl added. "Dylan and his friends all got the max suspension for that fight with your crew, Knock."

"Trust me, I know, Marissa," Knock said, giving her a weak smile.

But they didn't stop. Those two kept walking until they reached the table we now called ours. They also didn't touch. Shoulder to shoulder, they looked just like most guys walking the same direction, but I knew better. I had a feeling Knock really wanted to wrap his arm around Cade's back in support, and I wouldn't be shocked if Cade kinda wanted to lean into him - because I would've.

"So," I said when they were closer, "do Zoe and I need to pull out some makeup tricks?"

"I got the goods," Zoe offered, reaching back for her purse.

Cade waved her down. "Enough people have seen me already. No sense hiding it. I'm just going with the fact that my dad's a drunk who fell off the wagon, and I'm not staying there and dealing with it after this."

Not that he was bi. Not that he and Knock were together. Yep, I heard that loud and clear.

"But how are you?" I asked.

He shrugged. "A lot better than I expected. What about you, Jeri? I saw the box."

"Didn't dig into it," Knock promised. "Figured that's for tonight."

"After school?" Zoe suggested. "I mean, I think we're all curious."

"And scared to see what's in there," Ripper added.

Cade was still looking at me, ignoring all the rest of that. "What about you, Jeri?"

I pulled in a breath, intending to assure him I was fine, but those words just didn't want to come out. I technically was fine. I also really wasn't. I had this surface level of fine that allowed me to keep going, but was it just a mask? Because something had changed with Amber's death, and I had a funny feeling that something was me.

"I don't know," I admitted.

Knock jerked his chin at me. "What does that mean? Say it in more words?"

"Um..." Yeah, easier said than done. "Amber dying really got to me, guys. I'm not gonna lie. I'm shook, and I feel like it's my fault. I am also more worried about making sure nothing happens to Cade, because - " And I snapped my mouth shut.

"Because bad things happen when you care," Knock finished for me.

I just nodded, even if it was more like jiggling my head. "And now look at him!"

"I'm fine," Cade promised as he came closer to cup the side of my face. "Bruises, Jeri. Knock made sure everything is working out."

"And is it?"

He nodded. "Yeah. We're good. I even like my new home. Don't tell Zoe, but I'm kinda working on being a horse girl."

"You're not a girl," Zoe groaned. "But I'll let you be a horse girl with me anyway."

He smiled at her, which reassured me more than anything else. He did it so easily and honestly, not like it was forced. Cade really was ok, at least mentally. I had a feeling it wasn't that simple, but Knock said when he'd gotten kicked out, it had ended up being a good thing, so hopefully the same was now true for Cade.

"What about you, Zoe?" Cade asked next. "I heard what Amber sent. How are you coping?"

"I'm ok," Zoe promised, but then she paused. "No. I'm pissed, stressed, and wanting to *do* something about it. Guys, I know rape happens, but that? I dunno, it's a lot."

"You have no idea," I grumbled.

"How much did you watch?" Ripper asked.

"Just like a video and a half," I admitted. "There's a lot on there."

"We all watch it together," Knock decided. "Anyone who needs to tap out does. No harm, no foul. No need for any of us to tackle this on our own, right?"

"Think it's going to be that bad?" Ripper asked.

"Yeah," Knock admitted, "I kinda do. I know exactly what happens when KoG members fuck with women."

"And speaking of that," I said, "we still have videos to worry about."

"That's what we're talking about," Zoe said.

I shook my head. "Tiffany's. Look, I got Dylan to back off with a lie. I mean, I didn't intend to lie. I assumed someone had a video of us at his party, when he drugged us. But whatever I said hit him hard. Harder than it should've, so I kinda rolled with it, and now we're bluffing."

"And," Cade added, "Dylan will figure that out. When he does..." He pointed at his own face. "He's already proven he'll follow through on his threats."

"Shit," Zoe breathed.

"So get Jinxy back on board with tracking down cloud storage," I told her. "I'll have Hottie help him. I mean, I feel like it's been an eternity since we were focused on that, but it really hasn't been."

"About four days," Knock said. "But you're right. We need a plan."

"And we need to see what Amber sent," Ripper said. "I have a bad feeling that's going to change our plan."

"There's a USB drive," I warned them.

"Yeah," Ripper muttered. "Kinda proves my point."

"So," Knock said, taking over. "Right now, our goal is to make it through today. Cade's going to be getting a lot of attention because of his pretty colors. The Alpha Team isn't here, so we get a breather on that. Once school's out, we hit my place and make this happen?"

"Should I call Hottie?" I asked.

"Yeah," Knock said. "If you think he can take it?"

I grimaced. "Suicide's his button."

"Let him decide," Zoe told me. "Tell him what we're doing, and let him know he can come or not, depending on what he feels is best for him."

I nodded. "Ok. And then?"

"Nope," Knock said. "We're not worrying about that. Right now, the plan is for the here and now. The rest will be decided once we get there. Little steps, Jericho. Tackle what we can handle."

I reached out and caught his hand. "You trying to say I'm working on spiraling?"

"I'm doing my best to keep you from it," he admitted.

Then Zoe reached behind Ripper to clasp my shoulder. "Jeri, it's ok for this to be hard. It's sure as shit not supposed to be easy."

"And we shouldn't be dealing with it," I reminded her. "We're supposed to be worried about *high school*."

"This," Cade said, "*is* high school. This is what incels, assholes, and abusive parents do. We're not on some chick-flick channel's after-school program. This, Jeri, is the ugly part of growing up, and you know what?"

"What?" I asked, ready for the worst.

"We're what makes it better. Us being here for each other. Us being here for those who don't have anyone. We are the light at the end of the tunnel, because for some of us, there isn't one at home. See, that's why I'm ok today. Not because this shit..." And he gestured to his throat. "...doesn't hurt. It's because I know you'll go full bitch on anyone who has a problem with it."

"We all will," Ripper promised.

Cade just smiled at him. "Yeah? And you wonder why I said I'll fix your truck."

"Totally a bromance thing," Zoe fake-whispered at me.

"Crush," I whispered back.

Knock chuckled, but Cade just rolled his eyes. "It's a partnership thing, ladies. This is what friends do. And in case you forgot, Jeri made it clear that's what we are, right? We're close friends."

"Very close," Knock agreed.

"Very," Ripper said, glancing at me.

"Nope," Zoe said. "Feeling left out over here. No closeness at all. No one's letting me drive their hot rod."

"Impala," Ripper moaned.

So I tapped Zoe's leg. "Bet Jinxy would."

"Jinxy doesn't have an Impala," Zoe pointed out. "Like, a real, old-school hot rod! How am I supposed to experience the joys of life if I've never driven something like that?"

"Ask your partner if you can drive his car?" I suggested.

Zoe just looked over at Cade. "Hey, sweetie?"

"It is *not* a crush thing," he told her before she could even get going. "Not even close. But - and I'm saying this where everyone can hear - if you promise you won't wreck it, you can drive the hot rod."

"Yes!" Zoe said, pumping her fist. "This means Cade and I have a bromance too!"

"Partners," he countered. "Did you forget the gay cowboy detectives in love?"

She just smiled at him. "I like horse girls better, and we still get hats."

"I'm fucking buying you a hat if you keep this up," Cade warned.

And yet, their playful banter was helping. That heavy feeling in my chest was finally letting go. All we had to do was make it through a day of school, and then we'd finally know what Amber had sent me.

The big question was whether she'd tell us why.

CHAPTER 13

JERICHO

For me, the day was pretty boring. Dylan, John, Wade, Landon, and Parker were all missing. There was no one in the halls to avoid or brace for. Like always, my classes were dull. Unfortunately, that made the day feel like it was dragging on, because I knew what we had to do this evening.

For Cade, however, it wasn't as much fun. At lunch, he told us about how all of his teachers had pulled him aside to ask if he needed help. Each time, he'd given the same story about his father being an alcoholic. It was true, to a point, and that he'd already moved out meant the teachers left him alone.

But when lunch was over and I was heading to my fourth-period class, Tiffany decided to fall in beside me. I was braced for her to ask about their videos again, because I had no news. Instead, she decided to surprise me.

"Want to tell me what really happened to Cade?" she asked.

I dropped my head and groaned. "His dad got pissed."

"Uh huh. And?"

I looked over and met her eyes. "Because Dylan made sure of it."

That was all she needed to hear. Tiffany grabbed my arm and pushed me to the right, aiming for one of the many girls' bathrooms. I didn't even try to resist. Clearly, these were her safe spaces. Or at least a space where she could talk without fearing the Alpha Team listening in - even if they weren't here today.

But when she marched us towards the sinks, she called out, "Anyone in here needs to get the fuck out!"

"Peeing!" a girl called from one of the stalls.

"Do it faster!" Tiffany snapped, her bitch-mode turned up to max.

"Hey," I chided her. "Lay off. This falls under that bullying thing. You are not some queen bee to tell others how to deal with their bladders, Tiff!"

"Yeah, but I also don't want some freshman listening in and spilling my secrets all over school."

The toilet flushed, and then the door opened. "Sophomore," the girl said as she walked out, heading for the sinks.

There, she proceeded to clean her hands purposefully. The kind of washing that was intentionally slow. I couldn't help myself. I laughed.

"You asked for that," I told Tiffany. "Now you get to deal with it."

The sophomore flashed me a smile. "See, Jericho gets it." Then she grabbed a paper towel, dried her hands, and left.

I just gaped after her, flicking a finger in her direction. "How does she know my name?"

"Pink dreadlocks?" Tiffany suggested. "You do sort of stand out."

"Yeah, ok." Then I turned to lean against a dry sink. "So, what did you want?"

Tiffany paused to look at the bathroom stalls, making sure all the doors were open before answering. "What the fuck happened with Cade?" she demanded.

"Dylan outed him to his dad," I explained. "Cade went home Friday, then his dad showed up and lost it. Beat the shit out of him. Thankfully, Cade ran to Knock's place. Well, Knock's family got his stuff, and now he's living there."

"And they're still..." She let the sentence trail off, almost like she didn't want to say the words out loud.

"It's good," I promised. "They're figuring it out, but in a good way."

She nodded. "Ok." Then she pushed out a heavy breath. "At church, I heard Amber killed herself. A bunch of people were talking about it. Her parents are trying to make it sound like an accident - probably because they don't want to accept it."

"Yeah," I breathed. "And she sent me her phone."

"What?!"

I nodded slowly. "Yeah. Um, we haven't really gotten into that yet because of Cade."

Tiffany just waved that away. "So she really killed herself? Why?"

I licked my lips. "Because she was pregnant."

"Fuck..." Tiffany groaned. "She said they had a video."

I nodded slowly. "Yeah, and on her phone, she left me a video explaining how she doesn't remember any of it." I had to pause so I could swallow. "Tiff, she says they all took a turn."

Before my eyes, Tiffany's shoulders slumped. Her body deflated. It was as if the pride that kept this girl going was leaking out. Worse, I knew that feeling. It was the kick in the gut that couldn't be stopped. Shit, it couldn't even be seen coming!

"How?" Tiffany asked, her voice too soft.

"They drugged Zoe," I offered. "I don't know yet. We haven't looked at the videos she left us."

"Wait," she begged, lifting a hand. "Us? Videos? Go back, Jericho."

"When I got home on Friday," I said, "there was a box that had been mailed to me. It was from Amber. It had her phone, the passcode, a pregnancy test, and a USB drive. I watched one video. The one on the main screen named 'Watch Me.' I was working on the next when shit blew up with Cade, so we put Amber's stuff on hold."

"Ok." She nodded as if trying to rattle all of that into place. "And now Cade's ok, right?"

"Right."

"But Amber was raped, probably drugged, and pregnant?"

Again, I said, "Right."

"And there's a video of it," she finished.

I just reached up to scrub at my face. "Yeah. It seems these guys really like their fucking videos. I mean, why?" Under my breath, I grumbled in frustration. "That just seems like it's too big of a risk to me. I mean, for some fucking points on the KoG forums? To gain internet clout with incel fucknuts? Why would they risk getting caught like that for something so stupid?!"

"The points are probably the least of their worries," she pointed out. "Jeri, these guys are entitled little pricks. They liked making us miserable. Fucking *liked* it! Making the videos just lets them relive it."

"I don't think so," I countered. "I mean, when Zoe went to the cops, the police said they couldn't do shit because she nodded. Consent, they said, even though she was visibly fucked-up. Like, too fucked-up to *give* consent."

"And my friends said the same," Tiffany reminded me. "They all agreed, and their videos all made that clear."

"Because they fucked up somewhere," I mumbled, turning to pace the length of the bathroom. "That's got to be it. The videos aren't for their kink. It's their own proof because they fucked up once. Someone, somewhere, has something on them. They abused some girl, and she made them realize they need to video the consent so they won't get arrested!"

Tiffany groaned. "Which is why y'all were asking about their exes."

"Yeah," I admitted. "But who? When? And most importantly, what the fuck can we do if we find her?"

"No," Tiffany said, catching my arm to stop my pacing. "Jeri, you're missing the most obvious problem."

"Which is?"

"My friends." She paused until she had my complete attention. "Natalie, Stephanie, Breanna, and Yvette. They all have videos. They all fucking consented. They don't like talking about them, so I only know the most basic shit, but think about it! Zoe was drugged. Amber was probably drugged. What about my girls? Were my friends drugged too?"

"They're serial rapists," I breathed.

Tiffany nodded. "Yeah, so what are we going to do about it?"

"By 'we,' you mean me, right?"

She huffed out something like a laugh. "No, I actually meant we. I mean, I can ask the girls, and push them to see what happened. I dunno, maybe they have something that can help you find more shit?"

"But what shit?" I asked. "The cops already made it clear they won't do anything with proof of consent in the videos! It's like, if we girls fuck, we're assumed to be guilty. And the things they told Zoe? Like the fucker made it clear she'd get dragged through the mud if she actually wanted to press charges. But if no one presses charges, then what?"

"Dylan and his friends get away with it scot-free," Tiffany replied. "Yeah. That's what they're counting on. No one can touch them. No one will fuck with their families. They think they're above the rules because they always have been!"

"And that's bullshit!" I snapped. "It's so much fucking bullshit, but we're stuck, Tiff."

"You, like, all of you?"

I nodded. "We can't find the storage. There's a million places to keep things on the internet. After Evan got arrested, the rest cleaned up their phones and computers. The videos just aren't there. Worse, they aren't looking at them. There's no trail on the web - or their computers - for us to follow to find them. And even if we did, getting into the storage site? I mean, hacking Google isn't exactly easy."

"Shit," she breathed. "Ok, so how do I help?"

"You?" I laughed once. "No offense, but you're not exactly a geek."

"Maybe not," she agreed, "but I do know the people you're talking about. There has to be something I can do."

I just lifted my hands and let them fall back to my sides. "I don't know."

"Ok..." Tiffany pulled in a hard breath. "So we start with me asking my friends what really happened. That'll take a while, because I can't exactly do it in a group."

"And I'm going to be looking through what Amber left this evening," I admitted. "Maybe she'll have a break in the case."

"Is that what we're calling it?" Tiffany asked.

"It's the best I have," I admitted. "And I know finding and removing those blackmail videos is important to you - "

"Not as important as keeping my friends safe," she assured me. "If the guys are raping girls, then this is worse than I imagined. They didn't all get suckered into a little orgy. They were tricked into it!"

"But is that rape?" I asked. "Tiff, they agreed. They thought it would be fun. I mean, those guys are hot. They're popular. The chance to do something like that? I think a lot of us would say yes."

"Yeah, but they didn't agree to having it used against them later!"

"And that's not the same as rape!" I shot back.

She just set her jaw and lifted her chin. "It should be. Abusing someone with sex is still abuse, Jericho. I don't care if it meets the legal definition. I don't give a flying fuck if the cops will do a damned thing about it. Those guys crossed a line when they blackmailed my friends, and I'm going to make them pay."

"We both are," I swore. "One way or another."

"So let me help!" she insisted.

I just lifted my hands, relenting. "Ok! I don't know how, since most of what we're doing is online."

"Yeah, but I have some pull in places you don't," she countered. "The guys come back to school tomorrow, and I have a feeling they're going to be pissed, so let's make it even worse for them?"

"We can't out Cade," I told her.

She shook her head. "This isn't about that."

"Kinda is." I sighed. "Tiff, all of this is about those assholes making it clear they can do what they want, to anyone they want, and not get in shit for it. Cade falls into that category. Dylan dragged him through shit for years because of a video. Then he did the same thing to your friends. He fucking drugged both of us! We thought he was dealing, but - "

"Oh, fuck," she mumbled, moving to look into the mirror. "Shit, Jeri. He's not dealing the ketamine. He's *using* it."

"Yeah," I agreed. "That's sure what it sounds like. And Amber said there are more videos. I'm kinda hoping Amber's wrong and they're your friends."

"Huh?"

"She said it wasn't you or your friends," I admitted. "On her video. She said that. But if she's right..." I didn't want to think about the implications of that.

"It's not them."

"You sure?"

She shook her head. "No. Fuck, right about now, I'm not sure of anything, but I'm willing to bet the smartest girl in school knows - knew - what she was talking about. Jeri, those 'other videos' won't be my friends. Amber knew about my friends. Not exactly what the videos were of, just that the guys had something to use on them. That's how I got her to tell me about hers."

"And she would've checked," I groaned. "Fuck. Means Zoe isn't the only one."

"Yeah, and it means something else too." She clasped the edge of the sink before her. "The closer we get, the more desperate Dylan and the guys will become. They're already raping us, Jeri. How far will they go if we push them into a corner?"

I just looked over at her. "It's a risk I'm willing to take."

"Yeah," she agreed, "me too. I'm fucking tired of feeling like I'm helpless."

"And I'm tired of not stopping it." I nodded decisively. "So let's keep the others out of this."

She scoffed. "Sure. Sounds good. But we both know that won't work. Dylan will hit whoever he thinks is weakest. John's going to be rocked after losing Amber, but the others?"

"Yeah, but Dylan's pretty much the ringleader," I pointed out.

"He likes to think he is," she corrected. "Wade doesn't agree. Landon and Parker are opportunists. They just want the sick fun, I bet. But Wade's the problem. If he sees Dylan slipping, he will take advantage of it. I'm scared that means one of us will end up the victim."

"I'm good with that," I assured her.

"No, you idiot," she snapped. "Not you and me. One of ours. Zoe. Natalie. Yvette. One of our *friends!*"

"So we do this quietly," I decided. "They think we have a video that could ruin them. We don't. We still let them think that and go on our merry way, right? Just pretend like everything is good."

"While trying to dig up as much dirt as possible," she agreed. "Someone knows something. I'll figure it out."

"And when they fuck up online, I'll be there," I promised. "Because I'm fucking tired of losing."

"Aren't we all," she agreed.

CHAPTER 14

RIPPER

After school, I headed home, got some cash from my dad for the work on my truck, then headed over to Zoe's house to pick her up. Cade's Impala took up most of the driveway when I parked it, but the look on Zoe's face as I got out and handed her the keys? Yeah, so worth it.

"No wrecking the hot rod," I warned her.

She just grinned. Ok, and then she took almost five minutes to get the seat close enough for her short legs to touch the pedals, but that was cute too. When she finally got the car started and backing down the driveway, she looked happier than she had in *months*.

"Oh, it's a beast!" she giggled before pushing the gas just a little too hard.

The tires chirped as they tried to spin, but she let up too fast. Shoving a hand over my face, I shook my head, then decided that wasn't enough. I needed to hold on to something with this crazy girl behind the wheel!

"Please don't kill me?" I begged.

She just scoffed. "I'm a good driver."

She actually was. Zoe didn't take risks because she'd had to work so long and so hard to save up enough for her car. Her family was barely scraping by. Sure, they had enough, but just barely. To Zoe, that meant the things she did have were a little more valuable because of it.

Plus, what we were about to do wouldn't be easy. We all knew that, and yet it felt almost like we were all trying our hardest to ignore it. If letting Zoe drive Cade's Impala too fast helped, then I'd be a willing sacrifice.

"So, did Cade say your truck was done?" she asked.

I nodded, even though she never took her eyes off the road. "Yeah. Evidently, it just needed some normal care. Dad gave me some cash to pay him back for the parts."

"Oh..." Her lips curled one more time. "So now he's buying you presents! Total crush, Elliot." Then she grunted. "Ripper! Damn it. I'm going to get it right."

"My name is still Elliot," I assured her.

"But everyone calls you Ripper," she countered. "And it works for you. I like Ripper better, but Elliot's a habit."

"So should I start calling you Roux?"

She made a face and shook her head. "Nah. I actually like my name. I just couldn't get anything else in the games."

Which was fair. "And it's not a crush," I assured her. "Just my male best friend."

"Yeah?" She giggled. "So, maybe unrequited?"

"He's bi, Zoe, not desperate!"

"So Jeri's desperate?"

I was losing this debate and I knew it. "That's not what I meant."

She just pressed her lips together, her brow furrowing as she drove. "Look. You're cute, Rip. Sorry. Don't mean to make it weird, but you are. Jeri agrees with me. The glasses. The dimples. It's all cute. The kind of cute that girls like. Now, considering Cade and Knock like guys too, and this is a whole open mess of fucking around..."

"I'm not fucking a guy," I grumbled.

"But what if it is a crush?" she asked. "Have you even considered that?"

"I'm still straight, Zoe!"

"But you could kiss him once..."

I leaned my head back and sighed. "So you're going to kiss Jeri?"

She shook her head. "Nah. Patriarchy or something. Um, sexist male ideas? I dunno. Help me out with a good feminist excuse here?"

"Maybe you're straight?" I offered. "Maybe, just maybe, she doesn't do it for you? Kinda like Cade doesn't do it for me. He's a friend, Zoe, and I have few enough of those that I'm perfectly happy with a little kindness between friends."

"But Jeri's love life would be a LOT more fun if you and they and she were all in a big ol' puppy pile in bed." She paused at a stop sign and glanced over. "You know they had a threesome, right?"

"I do," I promised. "I also know I can't compete with that, so I'm not even trying. Never mind how I'd probably have a panic attack with that many people seeing me naked. Zoe, I have fucking stretch marks, ok? Not exactly the sort of sex appeal Jeri can get."

"And yet she still keeps you around." She accelerated onto the main road to Knock's place, using just a little too much gas. "Mm, momma loves this car!"

"What about you and Cade?" I asked, deciding to change the subject away from me.

"I'm not fucking anyone," she assured me.

"Ok, but kissing isn't fucking," I pointed out. "Or cuddling, or flirting, or any of that. Besides, you two seem to get along really well. Maybe the crush he has is on you?"

She blew that off. "Nah. Cade is way too into Jeri and Knock. Besides, I'm with Jinxy."

"Still an open thing," I said.

"And I'm not about to steal my other bestie's guys!"

"Jeri doesn't get jealous like that," I reminded her. "She actually prefers the mess because it makes her feel less isolated and vulnerable."

"And I'm not ready!" she finally snapped.

"That," I told her, "is a good answer. But so you know, you *do* flirt with Cade."

"Because he knows I'm not serious," she explained. "I made sure of it. I talked to him, Rip. He's kinda like my shield, and flirting with me is kinda like his. It makes us both feel a little more normal, you know? And since we know it won't go anywhere, it's, I dunno, like practice."

"Does Jinxy know?" I asked.

She shrugged. "Not exactly."

"Think you should tell him?"

"Not with his Gran being so sick." She bit her lower lip. "Um, but I probably should, huh?"

"You and he need to talk about what you're doing," I told her. "Zoe, we're about to look at some horrific shit. Shit that might just trigger the fuck out of you. What happens if you can't talk to him for a few days? Or if you can't handle flirting with him? Or, shit, I dunno. Anything!"

"He kinda knows," she mumbled.

"About?"

She made a gesture with her hand, waving it vaguely. "About everything. About how hard it is. I dunno, about how friends is different from lovers, and touching is something I'm hyper-aware of, you know?"

"I do," I promised. "And I'm sorry I wasn't there for you."

"But I didn't tell you," she insisted. "So you know, I didn't tell you for a reason - because I didn't want to think about it. I wasn't ready for anything to change, because it did, Ripper. It all changed once I said it out loud. It also got better, but that doesn't mean it's easy! I mean, sure, I don't have to hide when things feel weird, but I also feel like a pussy because I can't just be like Jeri."

"And Jeri melted down over Amber's suicide," I reminded her. "She has her own triggers."

"Do you?"

The car slowed as Zoe neared the entrance to Knock's ranch. That gave me a little time to think about the question. Did I? Yeah, kinda, but not like Zoe and Jeri did.

"It's different," I said as she limped the car up the drive. "I feel like a failure. I feel like I'm not man enough, or strong enough, or good enough for the people I care about. Every time someone calls me a loser, reminds me I'm fat, or anything else, it hits me."

She parked beside my truck and turned the car off. "That's definitely a trigger, Rip. It counts."

"Is this a case of collecting them all?" I joked.

She just shook her head. "No, but it means you can understand. It means we can understand you. I kinda think it's why Ruin works, because we're all flawed, you know?"

"And we're not alone," I said, finishing the game's tagline. "Yeah. I just didn't expect it to carry over to real life."

So Zoe tossed me the keys. "But it did, and now you get to tell your male partner that you brought his baby back. I'm still rooting for a kiss!"

The little wench climbed out, giggling at me. Huffing like I was annoyed - I really wasn't - I exited the car on my side, and the pair of us headed for the yard. This time, Quake wasn't around. From the other cars in the yard, I knew we weren't the first here, so the pair of us headed inside.

And stepped into chaos.

"You can have the upstairs," Riley was yelling. "The rest of us need to get our game on!"

"No!" Knock came storming up the stairs, spotted us, and smiled. "Hey, guys. Everyone else is downstairs." Then he stormed into the kitchen. "This is Ruin shit, Riley. It comes before your kill to death ratio."

"And do you know how quick the Dallas convention will be on us?" Riley asked. "If you want to keep your sponsorships, you need to make sure you aren't taken out in the first round."

"I need to fucking take out the bad guys first!" Knock yelled. "Get that through your fucking head, Q. The farm is safe. The horses are fine. Dez isn't going to cancel your fucking contract because you have a bad game. This? *Women are being raped!*"

Riley came around the corner. "What?"

Knock pushed out a breath. "Yeah. We need the game room for a few hours. You can have it all night."

"I'll stay up with you," Logan promised. "I'll push back my schedule at work."

Riley merely closed the distance to Knock and cupped the back of the guy's head. "How do I help?"

"You let me do what I need to do. This is KoG, Riley. Maybe they're low-level, but if this is what the low fucking levels do? I mean, Quake sucked. What they did to the horses wasn't cool, but it didn't really hurt them. This?"

Then Riley looked over at Zoe. "And you're ok with this?"

"I'm done being a victim," she swore.

Riley just nodded. "Doesn't mean the trauma's done with you."

"And she can tap out anytime," I added. "No one is required to stay. We won't make anyone do this, but we all felt that together, it might be easier."

"Ok," Riley said. "I'd offer to make dinner, but I'm going to guess food is out?"

"Definitely," I muttered.

Knock just pointed at me. "What Ripper said. Q, this ties in, ok? I know it does. I'm just not sure how. That's why I have to do this. That's why Cyn's been helping me learn."

"Ok," she said again. "Just be careful?"

He laughed once. "As careful as you'd be."

"Yeah, good point," Riley said. "Gonna make a wild guess the group of you don't want any help, right?"

"We'll call if we need it," Knock promised. Then he jerked his head at the stairs again. "Sorry, you two. Normal family drama."

Which made Riley laugh as she turned back for the kitchen. "And most people would call us dysfunctional."

"But we're the most functional form of dysfunction there is," Knock teased. "It's why we work."

I had to give it to him, he had a point there. This house was complete chaos, but it always seemed to work. There was just this feeling of happiness in it, even when they were screaming at each other. It was an understanding I'd never seen anywhere else, almost like they'd found a way to be ok with each other's rage, hurt, and everything else.

They'd found a way to be true to themselves, I realized as I made my way down the stairs behind Zoe and Knock. That was why it worked. There weren't rules about when they could feel something, or how they should feel it. They were just open. They dumped it all out there, and didn't take offense.

Kinda like Ruin.

So as I reached the basement, I looked over to find Cade. "Hey," I told him. "Brought your baby back. Let your other girl drive it too."

VICIOUS

"Nice," he said, holding up his hands when I lifted the keys. I tossed them over, so he nudged a set on the desk beside him. "And your truck is purring like a kitten now. I may have gone around the block."

"Block?" Jeri asked from the other side. "What do you call a block around here?"

Knock made a big circle over his head. "Pretty much half of Sanger."

So I closed the distance to Cade and dug into my pocket. "Pretty sure this should cover the parts and your work."

Cade just wrapped my fingers around it, refusing to take the cash. "It's Knock you need to ask about that."

"You weren't supposed to tell," Knock said.

"And I'm not taking money for something you paid for," Cade countered.

Knock sighed. "Ripper, it's fine. I got to see my boyfriend doing something he loved. Let's call it even?"

"Yeah, but - "

"I make almost eighty thousand a year," Knock broke in. "Not quite six figures, but close enough. Call it taking one for the team?"

So I shoved the money back into my pocket, headed over to Knock, and kissed him soundly on the cheek. Behind me, Zoe squealed with laughter. Before me, Knock looked completely confused, and his face was quickly turning red.

"I mean, if you're buying me things, it's a crush, right?" I joked. "So the least I can do is kiss you for it."

In the corner, Hot just groaned. "That is not how this works, guys. Not at all."

"Shut it!" Zoe told him. "I need some guy-on-guy action, and this is the only chance I'm going to get."

So Knock turned, crossed the room and kissed the shit out of

Cade right in front of all of us. For a split-second, Cade froze in confusion, and then he kissed back.

Damn. Ok. Well, that wasn't really my kink, but those two looked good together. Comfortable. Happy, even. Wait, that was why I was smiling, even as my eyes tried to look at anything but them. It was because they were happy. We - all of us - were happy.

And that wasn't going to last very long.

CHAPTER 15

ZOE

Ok, seeing Cade and Knock kiss like that was hot. I kinda liked how easy it was for them, unlike earlier in the year. Now, those two were comfortable with each other, and that made their little relationship a whole lot sexier to me.

Sorta like Jeri and Hottie over in the corner. They had this grace between them that was hard to explain. Sure, comfortable worked with them too, but it was different from Knock and Cade. Jeri and Hottie were calm, with this deep understanding of the other that just showed in their little glances.

Ripper hadn't gotten there with anyone yet. Well, me, but he and I most definitely would not be fucking again. That had been a one-time deal, and it had been pretty weird. Safe, sure. Experimental, definitely. Repeatable? Not at all.

Or maybe that was me? I didn't know, and it really didn't matter. He was into Jeri, and she was into him. The pair were cute together, but I had a feeling that until Ripper got over his own insecurities, he wouldn't find that deep understanding the others had, and I hated the idea of him being a third wheel.

Sadly, our little fun could only put off our reason for being here so long. Eventually, Knock pulled out Amber's phone, unlocked it with a code on a pink Post-It Note, and then plugged it into a computer. Naturally, he picked the one with the biggest screen.

"I'm downloading this all onto the hard drive," he explained. "If nothing else, it gives us another copy."

"Put it on the Squirrel," Hottie suggested.

Knock nodded. "Yeah, but we're also going to need Jeri to explain some of this to us."

"I think we should do the videos first," I said, working hard to keep my voice from sounding as freaked out as I felt.

"Why?" Cade asked.

I pushed out a breath. "Because isn't that how Amber found it? She saw the videos and then she made the stuff for us."

"For Jeri," Hottie corrected. "She specifically said it was for Jericho."

And across the room, Jeri's face was getting pale. "She said I was the one who could help."

"It's ok," Ripper said, heading to her just to kneel in front of her chair. "She didn't know the pressure she was putting on you."

And Jeri threw her arms around his neck. Beside her, Hottie gently rubbed her back, almost as if he didn't know what else to do. Because he didn't! Shit. I was an idiot. This was hard for him too. His fiancée had died by suicide! Fuck!

"We need rules," I decided, speaking up before I knew what I was about to say.

"Like?" Knock asked.

I just shook my head. "Triggers. Freaking out."

"Stop," Cade said. "Pause, hold up, or even wait. Fuck, running for the stairs. I think any of that works."

Reaching into the box, Knock pulled out the USB drive next. "So, vote. USB or phone first?"

"The USB has the videos," Jeri explained. "The phone is Amber."

"USB," I voted.

Jeri grunted thoughtfully. "Yeah, let's do the hard part first."

"I think we should do the phone," Knock said.

"I don't want to do the phone," Hottie admitted.

"No vote," Cade announced. "I think they're both going to suck."

"So USB it is," Knock said, plugging the stick into the same computer as the phone.

A few clicks of the mouse pulled up the drive, showing four different videos, along with some Word documents and a few photos. Letting go of Ripper, Jeri leaned forward to look.

"What's the picture?"

Knock clicked to open that up, and the screen filled with a bulleted list. Some items on it had a line through them, struck out. Most, if I was honest. The first one I saw that didn't have a line through it made my stomach turn.

- make her puke on my dick.

Yeah, no. That was the sort of thing these guys *wanted*? What the actual fuck? But beside me, Cade was mumbling the list to himself, not saying enough for it to be out loud, but clearly showing his distaste in the process.

"This is what gets them off?" he asked. "Fuck, that's like a checklist of the worst porn shit out there!"

"Cum on her face," Knock said. "Anal, plug all holes... Shit." He moistened his lips quickly. "Is this some kind of point rating for KoG, or a personal fantasy list?"

"No way to know," Hottie said. "I mean, half that shit is what most guys joke about, so maybe both? What bothers me more is the ones with the strikeout text."

"Means they were done," Jeri said softly. "So let's see the first video and compare?"

"This," Knock grumbled under his breath, "is not porn. It's nothing like porn."

And then he opened the first video: Amber. Before he even clicked play, my insides were twisting, but I pulled in a deep breath, reminding myself I could do this. I was not a victim. I was a motherfucking threat! That meant I had to push through this, right?

And then the image started moving. Amber was thrown onto the bed, but she didn't move. No, wait. She blinked! Her head sorta moved up and down like she was trying to nod. And yet, her eyes weren't focused at all. My gaze locked on her face as darkness began to claim the edges of my vision.

Things were happening, but I couldn't handle that. All I could see was the slackness of Amber's expression. Her eyes weren't quite open. They also weren't exactly closed. They did move, and so did her mouth, but she wasn't there. If she was conscious at all, I'd be surprised.

But the Alpha Team didn't care. I watched as her face shifted, her hair completely disheveled against the side of it. The girl looked dead, and now she was. She was fucking dead, but no one seemed to care! No, not dead.

Drugged.

A flash of a body over me smothered everything else. My lungs forgot how to work. I blinked hard, pushing those memories away, but it didn't help. I was supposed to watch this. I had to fucking *help*! I needed to prove I was a part of this team, but then it happened again.

The feel of warm breath.

The sounds of laughter.

It wasn't even the view. It was the sounds, the memories - and it wasn't stopping. My guts twisted harder, proving I was not ok, so

I tried to focus on breathing. Clenching my eyes closed should've helped. I could no longer see Amber's face - instead, I saw Evan's.

That night. It was a blur. It was a confused jumble of pieces that had never fit together, and yet I couldn't make them go away. I heard Dylan laugh, but I had no idea if that was in my mind or on the computer because I could still feel that breath.

Hot. Heavy. I couldn't move away from it.

It was all I knew, and the sight of Amber like that was too much. Shoving to my feet, I begged them, "Stop? Please, just pause it?"

"Zoe?" Ripper asked, partially standing as if ready to rush to me.

But I lifted both hands, holding him off. "I thought I could do this, y'all. I wanted to help."

"It's ok," Jeri assured me. "Zoe, you don't need to see this."

I nodded, the movement some trembling thing that was good enough. "I, um..."

"I'll go with you," Cade offered.

I pressed my hands at him this time. "No. Stay. No offense, but I just want some fresh air and no guys."

"Take Quake," Knock said. "And Zoe? If you need anything..."

I shook my head at him, slapped my leg to get the dog's attention, and then rushed up the stairs. Ok, I probably should've said thank you or something, but I couldn't. Fuck, I could barely breathe. I kept seeing Evan. Just one little moment, not even two whole seconds, but it was the thing that was replaying in my mind over and over with each step.

Thankfully, Quake followed. When I reached the main floor, I turned for the backyard, not caring about the sounds of Riley and Logan in the kitchen. I didn't want help. I certainly didn't want anyone to fucking *touch* me. I just needed air. Lots of air. Wide open air!

So I barreled through the back door with Knock's dog on my

heels. As soon as I was outside, my lungs could fill again, so I sucked in the biggest, sweetest breath I could. Then I gently closed the door behind me, but Quake took off.

"Hey, buddy!" Kitty said as she came in the backyard gate. "Who are you..." Her words fell silent but her feet began to move faster. "Zoe?"

"Hey," I mumbled, mostly because that was the best I could do.

"Sit," she ordered, pointing at the edge of the porch. "You look ready to pass out. What happened?"

Fuck. This was exactly what I didn't want. Still, I took her advice and sat. "We're trying to go through the stuff a dead girl from school sent Jeri. Kitty, it's rape videos."

My voice was strained. Weak. High. I could hear it. It sounded like I was whimpering, and I fucking hated it. I also couldn't quite make it stop!

"Shit..." she said, dragging the word out as she lowered her heavily pregnant body down beside me. "Breathe," she ordered. "Big breath in."

I inhaled, aware of the concern on her face.

Kitty smiled encouragingly. "Now push it all out slowly. There you go. Now in again?"

"I'm ok," I promised before inhaling a second time.

She just gave my arm a sympathetic rub. "Yeah, but you look like shit. This, Zoe, is what a panic attack feels like. Is your chest hurting?"

I nodded.

"And you feel like your lungs won't fill all the way?"

I nodded again, even as I pushed the air out.

So she lifted her hand, encouraging me to breathe while she talked. "Lightheadedness, an urge to go somewhere, or do something. There's a million symptoms, but it's panic. It's what happens when someone with trauma gets triggered, hun." Her hand moved down, saying I should exhale. "And it's ok. Trust me,

I've done this enough. Shit, when I found out I was pregnant, I had one. More when I was your age. And seeing that? I bet it brought back some memories, huh?"

"I just get this flash of him over me," I admitted.

"Keep breathing," she ordered. "Zoe, it's ok. It's normal. This does not make you weak, or useless, or anything else. Know how I know that? Because I used to feel the same way, and Riley proved me wrong. This is a sign of your strength, ok? This shows you took something most people couldn't handle, and you're still powering through it like a badass."

Which made my breath hitch in the middle. "Amber killed herself."

"I heard," she assured me. "Well, that a girl at school died, I mean. I'm assuming that's the same one?"

I murmured an affirmative sound. "She was pregnant, and they raped her, then she sent Jeri some videos before she killed herself. Including her rape video - which they're looking at downstairs because Amber asked Jeri for help."

"Fuck." Kitty reached down to rub her belly. "Yeah. This isn't something someone should be forced into. This..." She glanced down. "He should be a miracle, not a manacle. And a child from rape?"

"Her boyfriend would've made her marry him," I explained. "John wanted a nice little traditional housewife type. Amber was the valedictorian, though. She didn't want to be a stay-at-home mom. I mean, she never talked like she did, at any rate!"

"And you?" Kitty asked.

I opened my mouth and paused. Why was talking about Amber so much easier than talking about myself? Never mind that I didn't know how to answer that! So I decided to go with something easier.

"What do you mean?"

"What do you want to be when you grow up?" Kitty asked. "I'm not talking about a job, either. I'm talking about your life. I'm talking about the big picture, Zoe."

"I want to be strong," I said softly.

Because that was all I really wanted. I was so tired of feeling like those guys had kicked my legs out from under me when they weren't even here. I was so fucking *sick* of letting them control me in any way. I was done with the freakouts and fears. I just wanted to be strong. I wanted to kick ass. I wanted to be the kind of woman who could push through all of it and save others!

"So you want to feel nothing?" Kitty asked. "I mean, that's one way of being strong. If nothing hurts, then nothing can stop you."

"No!"

She smiled. "Then what kind of strong do you want to be?"

"I want to help others," I insisted. "I want to keep this shit from happening to anyone else!"

"An activist," she said, rephrasing that. "A good goal, but it's not easy. It means staring straight into your own personal abyss over and over, but you want to know something?"

"Sure."

"It does get easier," she promised. "Each time the abyss looks back, you see little weaknesses in it. Each time you stare it down, you realize it can't touch you anymore. Now, that doesn't mean you won't break, but here's the thing." She leaned back and looked out at the pastures spreading out in the distance. "When you know that pain, it's easier to help others. When you've been there - or close to there - you understand a little more what they need."

"Were you... raped?" Then I groaned. "Sorry. You don't have to tell me."

"I wasn't," Kitty said. "No, I just had a boyfriend film us without me knowing, and then he put my sex tape up everywhere. That was when I was not much older than you, Zoe. I wanted to die. I was so sure I couldn't survive the shame, the harassment, or the teasing of the other students - but Riley was there. Mom and Dad were there. They reminded me it wasn't *my* shame I was feeling. It was his. Some asshole was trying to make me feel bad for doing the same thing he had. The only reason it was working was because I was a girl, but being a girl doesn't make us weak."

"It kinda feels like it does."

She shook her head. "Nope. It makes us care. Don't confuse the two things. Feel what you need to feel, Zoe. Curl up in a ball and cry your eyes out because you can. *Feel* it. Process it. Accept that this happened, and it's one ugly step on the crooked and broken road we call life. Not all of them are as bad. Most of those steps are beautiful, amazing things." Then she looked over. "And when the next girl is sitting on your porch, looking as pale as a sheet, you will know what she needs better than someone who hasn't been there. You will be able to turn all of that pain into a weapon to protect her."

"Yeah," I said, swallowing as my throat tried to tighten up. "I kinda like that."

Then she reached over and rubbed my shoulder. "And I have all night if you want to unload. Sitting here as the sun sets is also a good option. We get some amazing ones just over the big pasture." She pointed to show where she meant.

"Can I play it by ear?" I asked.

She nodded. "Yep. I mean, not like my pregnant ass is getting up any time soon."

And I could finally laugh. It was weak and broken, but also real. "Hey, Kitty? Thanks. I kinda like that idea, you know?"

"Which?"

"That maybe my pain can become my superpower."

"It can, but only if you stop feeling shame. Shame is giving *them* power. Take it back, Zoe. This isn't on you. It's on them. Feel rage. Feel sorrow. Feel anything you want except that."

I pulled in a deep breath and looked at the dozen black horses against the quickly greening grass. Out here, there was a peace that simply didn't exist in town. It was quiet. It was natural. It was honest in a way that was hard to explain. It made my answer easier than I expected.

"Determination," I said. "I don't care how many times they knock me down. I will not stay there."

"That's my girl," Kitty praised.

CHAPTER 16

JERICHO

Zoe left the room in a rush, and we all watched her go. A silence descended on all of us. After much too long, I realized what she'd said. No guys. That meant everyone else. That did not include me.

"Should I go after her?" I asked.

"I don't think so," Ripper said. "Jeri, I think she honestly wanted to be alone."

But Knock had his phone out. "I'm also telling Riley to keep an eye on her. I mean, if she's outside with Quake, she'll feel like she has solitude, but it doesn't mean we won't know if she breaks down."

"Respecting her space and watching over," Hottie said. "Yeah. Probably the best call." Then he sighed. "We shouldn't have let her watch."

"So, you're going to tap out for the suicide part?" Cade asked.

Hottie opened his mouth to snap something back, and then slowly shut it. Again, he sighed. "Point made. I want to say no.

Mostly because I don't know this girl. I have never met her, wasn't friends with her, and I know it happens. That doesn't mean she won't do or say something that won't get me."

I reached over to rub his knee. "You good?"

"Yeah," he muttered. "Start the video, Knock. Might as well get this over with."

Knock pressed play. The video was horrific. There was no other word to describe it besides that. Nothing about this was sexy. It wasn't appealing. Even if I didn't know the story behind it, this still wouldn't have been some kind of turn on. Like Knock had said, this was not porn.

No, this was vile. I had a million other words that would work almost as well: disgusting, abusive, abhorrent, and so on. As the clip played, I ran through them in my mind like a mantra. Everything these guys did made me hate them a little more. Worse, they didn't even try to hide their faces.

Those fuckers were proud of this. They even laughed. The five of them fucking *laughed* as they abused Amber, like it was some kind of a game to them. I wasn't sure if they were drunk, stoned, or simply that completely evil. I also didn't care.

I was going to make them pay. Somehow, we'd find something in all of this to use against them. We fucking had to!

After Amber's video came another. Just like with Amber, the girl was clearly on something. The one after that was fucked-up, but not comatose. It was the fourth video when things changed.

This girl fought back. She pushed. She screamed. Around the room, we all winced with each sound she made, but we watched, looking for anything we could use to catch these assholes - because this was rape. All of this was, yet this video was the worst.

"Wait!" I gasped, sitting up.

Knock immediately paused the video.

"Go back?" I begged. "Play the start again?"

"You can really stomach seeing that shit again?" Ripper gasped.

"Not really, no," I promised.

Still, Knock restarted the video. The violence of the girl trying to push them off was different from all the rest. The look in her eyes was terrified, but determined. And then, I realized something else.

"Knock, play the first ten seconds of the others?" I begged.

He turned to give me a confused look, but did - and that was when I was sure. Over and over, the first three videos started the same way. The girl was clearly drugged - or fucked-up on something. Still, each one made a subtle little movement. Each one nodded her head.

But not the last one.

"Shit," I breathed.

"What?" Hottie demanded. "Jeri, what are you seeing?"

"Amber and the other two? They consent." I pointed at the screen. "Play it again, Knock?"

He did, and this time I shouted, "There!" when she did it. Amber's wasn't much, but it made her blink. The next girl was a little more obvious. The third one definitely nodded.

"Now the last one?" I asked.

Knock started it, and around me, the guys all groaned. From the first second of recording, this girl fought back. There was no nod. She fought, she screamed, but she wasn't strong enough. What happened after that made my stomach turn - and it seemed I wasn't the only one.

Ripper jumped up and hurried to the bathroom, pushing the door only mostly closed behind him. The sound of retching came right after. Knock went to pause the video, but Hottie told him to keep going. To let it play to the end.

The whole time, she was conscious. When Dylan had slipped something in my drink - or whichever of his friends had actually done it - I'd slowly lost the ability to control my body. I'd seen colors, and I knew I hadn't taken that much. I'd only had a few sips of my soda.

Zoe had said she saw things. According to Knock, ketamine was hallucinogenic. It was also a horse anesthetic. That was why I'd lost function. If they'd tried to do that to me, I wouldn't have been able to push or kick the way this girl was.

And she hadn't consented.

"That's it," I breathed as the video ended.

The toilet flushed, and then Ripper came out of the bathroom. "Her name is Marissa. She's a gamer."

"What?" Knock asked, looking at the screen again. "She's a blonde!"

"Marissa used to have long blonde hair," Ripper said. "She cut it this summer. Went full goth, wears masculine clothes." He paused to wipe at his chin. "Carson broke up with her because she cheated on him." Then he groaned. "Fuck! ...At some party."

"Shit," Knock breathed. "He told me she messed around with some popular guy at a party when they were together. That's why he kicked her out of his guild."

"Yeah, BAD," Ripper agreed. "I always thought she went on this butch kick because they broke up."

"But it was because she was raped," I said, putting the pieces together. "Hottie said it himself. They don't rape guys - so she wanted to look like a guy. Fuck!"

"Think she'd talk?" Cade asked.

No one in the room answered. We all just looked at each other. Yeah, but that wasn't even the most important part of this video. Nope, they'd missed it.

"Guys..." I said. "She didn't consent."

"None of them did!" Hottie snapped.

"No, fucking listen!" I snapped. "With the first three, the Alpha Team makes them nod. They clearly show something that could be argued as consent, right? But Marissa?" It felt wrong to give her a name. To make her a real person, not just a victim, but she deserved nothing less. "She fought."

"And?" Cade asked. "Spell it out, Jeri?"

"She wasn't drugged," I said. "She fought. They held her down. They had to fight her the whole time. She also didn't consent. We all know they repeat what works, so why is hers different from Amber's? Why isn't Marissa drugged and nodding like everyone else?"

"Oh shit," Knock breathed. "Because they fucked up once and learned from it?"

"Has to be," I said. "We've been looking for an ex. We knew they'd perfected blackmail a while ago with Cade. I think something about Marissa went wrong for them. Something about Marissa convinced them they needed the proof of consent to cover their asses."

"And we never knew she was a victim," Ripper said softly.

"Shit," I grumbled. "We didn't realize they were *raping* girls! We thought it was just Zoe. The rest were consensual, but we're fucking idiots. Why would they go that far with Zoe and no one else? This? They fucking think it's working for them!"

"Because it is!" Hottie snapped. "Don't you get that, Jeri? It *is* fucking working. If this girl cut her hair over the summer, then this video is from before that. These assholes have been doing this for an entire year - or damned close - without anyone even asking them what's going on."

"And when Zoe went to the cops," I realized, "that asshole was quick to point out her consent. Do you think more girls tried?"

"Shit," Cade breathed. "Jeri, do you think these girls even knew they were recorded? I mean, Zoe had a video, but they left it on her phone. Tiff's friends all had their videos waved in their face, but they said they'd agreed. This?"

"Amber said she hadn't seen it until she tried to break up with

John," I admitted. "But they keep using videos as blackmail, so maybe? I dunno. It could go either way."

"Which means we need to watch the videos on the phone," Knock said. "All of it, Jeri." He looked over at Hottie. "And it's not going to be easy."

"And then?" I asked.

"You're missing the biggest thing," Ripper said as he dropped down on the couch at the side of the room. "Jeri, you know how you told Dylan you had a video?"

"Uh, yeah?" Because that had been the bluff I'd used to get Tiffany free.

Ripper just gestured at the screen. "You now have four. You have videos of three drugged girls. One of them doesn't have consent. Amber just gave you the leverage to keep Tiffany and her friends out of the Alpha Team's clutches."

"It sounds so comic book when you say it like that," Knock mumbled.

"Or B-movie villain," Ripper said. "Yeah, I know, but it's still true. Those videos need to go on the Squirrel, because if Dylan needs proof, she needs access."

Which was when Hottie shoved to his feet. "Fuck!"

"What?" I asked, turning to face him.

"The goddamn Squirrel!" he said, referring to our locked-down server. "It's cloud storage, basically."

"Technically an FTP server," Knock corrected.

"Yeah, but listen to me," Hottie insisted. "We have one. They aren't hard to get. It's private, it's not on site, and it's fucking damned near impossible to get into, right?"

"Yeah..." Knock said.

"And where better to store all the dirty little videos you don't want the cops finding?" Hottie pressed. "The Squirrel. You said it yourself, the fucking FBI can't even find the thing. That's what we've been doing wrong. We're looking for them to log into

Google Drive, OneDrive, Dropbox, or whatever! They won't, because someone, somewhere, has a fucking server that's private!"

"But there would still be hints if they went there," I said.

"Sure," he agreed. "Browser history, cache, temp files. But clearing the history and the cache would remove those. Worse, most routers don't store outgoing destinations. In other words..."

"No trace," I realized.

He nodded. "Yeah, because they aren't using a storage service. They're using someone's server. I'm willing to bet it's someone with KoG."

"Fuck," I hissed.

"And likely on the dark web," Knock added. "Everyone had Tor on their desktops. Some on their phones. If they're accessing this server via the dark web..."

"We're fucked?" Cade guessed.

"Yeah," Hottie said. "So fucked. See, the shit on the dark web? It takes a special browser to see. It's all out there, but hidden. So, if you want to go someplace on the dark web, you'd best have the address."

"The numbers," Knock told Cade. "Not like a dot-com type."

"Gotcha," Cade said. "And somewhere out there is a server with the shit we need." Then he gestured to the monitor. "And this is our blackmail, right?"

"But it's not enough," I countered. "We can't get them to give up more by showing a few videos they're already trying to hide."

"Maybe not," Cade said, "but what we can do is keep them from doing anything else. We make it clear we have evidence to use against them. We let them know we'll escalate this, right?"

"To who?" I asked. "Cade, when Zoe showed the cop her video, they didn't fucking care!"

"It wasn't that bad," Zoe said from the top of the stairs. "He said he'd prosecute, Jeri." Pulling in a breath, she began to make her way down. "Are they still playing?"

Knock quickly closed the videos on the monitor. "No. You're good, Zoe."

Which was enough to let her come the rest of the way down. "The cop said he'd do something. He just made it clear that it wouldn't be easy. He said he'd tell my parents, and all I could think was how disappointed they'd be, but they weren't. And if we have to turn these in..."

"It's Marissa," Ripper told her.

"No..." Zoe breathed.

"And she's the one that didn't consent," I told her. "Zoe, she didn't nod and she wasn't drugged."

"Her hair is long and blonde too," Cade added. "So, like, July?"

"Was she the first?" Zoe asked.

I just shook my head. "No way to know. She does seem to be the one that made them alter their 'system,' though." Then I pointed at Ripper. "And he puked."

Zoe sucked in a breath and hurried over to him. "Oh my god, Elliot, are you ok?"

He grabbed her by the arms. "I'm fine. I just realized I knew her, felt like I did when you told us, and got sick. *I* am fine, Zoe. What about you?"

She nodded. "I'm going to be ok."

"Zoe..." he warned.

She just leaned into him, pressing her head into his chest. "I'm going to make sure I'm ok, Rip. Fucking these assholes up is going to help more than anything." Then she leaned back and looked over at Hottie. "And I think we get to tap you out for the next part. I'll watch and you get to enjoy the amazing sunset that's going on."

"Yeah," he said, pushing to his feet. "I actually think that's a good idea. And if anyone wants to join me halfway through, I'm fine with company."

CHAPTER 17

KNOCK

Amber had made all of her videos for Jeri. They were personable, almost like the girls had been friends, but they'd only ever talked that one time. Still, Amber made a good point. Jericho was the only one who'd consistently been able to get under Dylan's skin. She was always right there, getting in the way of his plans, and fucking him over as often as she could.

But listening to a girl explain why she felt she couldn't keep living? It wasn't easy. By the time we'd finished everything on her phone, all of us had cried at least a little. And trying to imagine her life? The way she'd been pushed to be this perfect little shell of a person to fulfill her parents' dreams?

That hit too close to home for me. Ripper and Zoe had cool parents who actually gave a shit about them. Before Riley had changed my life, I'd been on the same path as Amber, trying to do anything to get a little parental approval. Jeri's mom was absent more than present, and Cade's dad was a complete dick. Still, I was willing to bet those two felt the same.

That was the problem with parental pressure. Raising children didn't exactly come with a manual, as Kitty was more than willing to point out. And yet, parents seemed to forget just how eager they'd been to please their own mothers and fathers. They assumed that because they were looking at the relationship from the other side now, their actions were the right ones and would make us "good kids."

But here we were, fucked up.

We also didn't decide a damned thing after watching all of that. In truth, we needed time to process the horror. Zoe wanted to know about the rape videos. Hottie wanted to know about Amber's. That led to a bit of discussion, but it all felt so tentative, as if we were scared of crossing some kind of mental or moral line.

So Zoe called it a night. We'd seen what we'd come to see. Now we had to process it so we could actually do something about it. As my friends picked up their shit and headed out, Cade and I stayed, feeling the tension in the room refuse to ease at all.

"What now?" Cade finally asked when we were alone.

"Now," I told him, "I need to see what options we have." Pushing to my feet, I glanced over at him. "Is it going to piss you off if I say this guy is secretive?"

"So I should go feed the horses," Cade replied. "Nope, I'm good with that. One of your pro friends, huh?"

"Something like that," I agreed, reaching over to catch his hand and squeeze. "And this is harder for me than I expected."

"Us or the videos?"

"The videos," I quickly assured him. "It's too close to what they've been doing to the pros, Cade. Fuck, what they did to Kitty! No, they didn't rape her, but they tossed out her sex tape. One her ex used as revenge. If you think having a million incel fuckers see that doesn't feel about the same?"

"No kidding," he breathed. "But we shouldn't even have this shit. I mean, how much trouble are we in if we get busted?"

"That's part of what I want to find out," I assured him.

So Cade leaned in and kissed me hard before pressing his brow to mine. "I'm going to make sure Ripper stays with Zoe for a bit. We know Hot's with Jeri, and I don't think any of us need to be truly alone for a few hours at least."

"Thank you," I breathed.

He let me go and stepped back. "See, I'm still useful. I'll also tell the house we're done." Then the sexiest guy I knew turned and jogged up the stairs, giving me the privacy I really needed without being offended at all.

A glance at the clock showed it was late. Not too late, but pushing eleven here. Most of my friends called that "prime time," so I didn't feel any guilt at all when I scrolled through my contacts, found the one I wanted, and made the call.

"This had better be good," came the response after only one ring.

"Cyn, I need advice."

His response was the flick of a lighter, the sound distinctive over the phone. Then he inhaled. "On?"

"KoG," I told him.

"Fuck."

"I just want to make sure I'm not fucking things up," I quickly explained.

"No, it's not that," he promised. "Well, not that I don't trust you, Knock. It's that shit always comes in fucking threes. I'm..." He paused for a long moment. "...a little overwhelmed with shit. Fucking military LARPers thinking their dicks are bigger because they got guns."

"With KoG?" I asked, feeling my heart stall for a moment.

"No, my *other* job," he explained. "They're riled up tonight. So talk to me. Looks like I'm pulling an all-nighter."

"And Zara?" I asked.

"Stole my dog and went to bed already," he assured me. "So what do you have?"

I told him. Laying it all out there, hiding nothing about where and how we'd gotten everything, I told Cyn about all of it - including Cade. I told him about the girls, how I knew one, and reminded him of how the cops in town had refused to help Zoe. I even told him about the method I'd used to rip the info from Dylan's router, find the tablet that kept showing up, and that we were *still* waiting for it to turn on, hoping he had some suggestions. He didn't. And yep, I definitely told him about the fight and how Jeri had bluffed her ass off.

"Good news about that," Cyn told me. "She now has the video she bluffed about. Good news on your possession of it. Amber committed the theft of data, not you. This counts as her deathbed confession of a sort, so you need to preserve the chain of custody."

"What?" I asked. "Cyn, what I'm wanting you to tell me is how we use this shit to get these guys arrested."

"You don't."

"Let me spell this out for you," I snapped. "We have proof that five guys at school are serial rapists! Four videos, Cyn. Four girls, plus Zoe. There are five more who have blackmail sex videos made by these same fuckers! They are *abusing women*. They are all members of KoG, so we know where they got it. What I need you to tell me is where and who I give this shit to so it can get them to go away forever!"

"Well, let me spell this out for you," he drawled, pausing to suck a long drag off his smoke. "You have multiple videos of sex, sent to you by a girl who said her boyfriend cheated. You have no way of proving this wasn't role play. You do not have a victim willing to report her crime. You even said there's proof of supposed consent. That means you have jack and shit."

"But - "

"Shut up and fucking listen, Knock," he broke in. "This is why this case is so fucking hard. They're skirting the law, and the motherfucking laws don't understand how the internet works. It doesn't get anything virtual. This is the wild-fucking-west, which is why we *need* vigilantes like Ruin. So fucking ruin them and make this stick."

"How?" I asked.

"In order for there to be a crime," he explained, "you need proof. Not something you can claim is proof. Not something they could say is taken out of context. You need a victim, you need a crime, and you need a whole shit-ton of proof, which you just don't have."

"We have videos with their faces visible," I explained.

"And no way to prove the girl isn't pretending," he reminded me. "Knock, we live in a world where the jury is asked if any women have been a victim of sexual assault, but no men are asked if they've committed assault. We are talking about a justice system that will ask what she was wearing, why she was drinking, and not how many times she said 'no.'"

"That's not fucking fair!" I yelled into the phone.

He laughed once. "No shit. It's fucked up in so many ways, but that's the way it is. If we want to get these fuckers, we have to accept that this shit is going to suck. We're smarter, and we can trap these motherfuckers one way or another."

Pushing out a heavy breath, I headed into my room and closed the door behind me. "Cyn, one of the girls is a gamer. She was here the night of the shooting. I fucking know her."

"And you know Zoe too," he pointed out. "I know it sucks. Trust me, I fucking *know*. But if you want to make sure this case doesn't fall apart in court, then you need to get some damned proof. Not opinion. Not an accusation. You need at least one - and preferably all - of those girls to go to the cops. That's unlikely."

"And Amber's dead," I reminded him.

"Yeah, but there are three others. Zoe already tried to report. The real shit thing is that a victim of rape usually suffers a hell of a lot more for reporting it than her rapist would if - and I'd like to remind you that it's not likely - he's even convicted."

I knew he was right. Shit, I'd read enough of that online, heard it from Kitty and Riley, and had gotten the smallest glimpse with Zoe's situation. This shit wasn't fair. It certainly wasn't *right!* That didn't mean I was willing to just let it go. These guys would strike again, and Cyn sounded like he thought we might have a chance to stop them. A slim one, but slim still counted.

"Ok, and what else?" I asked.

"You need some way to show this was not a game. The girls were drugged intentionally rather than just partying too hard. The girls said no. The start of the encounter - and I don't mean the sexual one. I mean how she ended up in that room. The more violent, sadly, the easier it is to prosecute, and ketamine makes them very compliant."

"Jesus," I groaned. "So you're saying these guys are going to just get away with it?"

"So get them on something else," he growled, his anger the calm but deadly kind. "Just like we did that first fucker. Find out if the girls are eighteen. That's a good start."

"The ones we know are," I muttered.

He sighed. "Ok, so assault is another option. I'm not talking the sexual kind. I'm talking about the battery kind. Proof of violence will make a rape charge stick easier. Here's the downside. It can't be high school shit, because that gets wiped away as boys being boys, and fucking losers being lame. Wouldn't want to ruin anyone's life or anything, right?"

The sarcasm was dripping from his words. I could hear it, and while I didn't know what his childhood had been like, I was now willing to bet he had not been one of the popular guys.

"So I have to let someone else get hurt before we'll have enough to send these dicks away?" I couldn't believe that.

"Or find the proof that has to already be out there," he told me. "Someone has a video, if it was a party. Someone knows something. You just need a lead on which way to go. You are a fucking hacktivist group, so hack, Knock. Find their texts and see what they're saying when they think no one's looking."

"They fucking cleaned their machines when Evan got arrested," I said. "There's nothing there, Cyn."

"There's always something," he promised. "This is *our* internet, so use it. Get into their Ring doorbells. Get their home security cameras. I don't fucking care, but find what you need, and make these assholes pay."

"So you're not even going to offer to help?"

"I *can't*."

And that was what made me finally stop reacting and start thinking. "What do you mean? Is this crossing a line?"

"No, I'm fucking busy, Knock. Believe it or not, the FBI wants me doing a hell of a lot more than chasing ghosts on the web. They think cyber-crimes are victimless - unless there's a money trail - so they put me on something more important, and shit's going to hit the fan."

"How can I help?" I asked.

He paused to take a long drag. "Protect the girls, Knock. That's how. No one fucking steps up for them but us. Me, you, and a handful of other 'simps.' It's bullshit, but it's the right kind of bullshit."

"Yeah," I agreed. "And so you know, Jeri thinks these guys learned their system through trial and error."

"Makes sense," he agreed.

"Which means they fucked up," I pointed out. "Somewhere out there is a girl they raped who has something that can be used against them. Thing is, I think it's Marissa. She wasn't drugged.

Hers seems to be the oldest of the videos we got. We also know Amber downloaded these from John's KoG account, so looks like she pulled up his posts and went backwards."

"Five victims," he said.

"Four," I corrected.

"Zoe," he reminded me. "And you know Zoe's timeline. Put it together, Knock. Means you're going to have to ask real hard questions these girls aren't going to want to answer. They sure as shit aren't going to tell any of you boys, so figure it the fuck out. Jericho and Zoe are a bigger asset than you realize. So's Riley. Use them, because the only way for us to make your case is for you to get it fucking right."

"What counts as right?" I asked.

"The kind of shit that can't be thrown out," he told me.

"And hacking kinda fucks that all up."

"Nope." He chuckled. "Now, the seven of you might get a little probation, but if you find shit in the act of committing another crime - hacking - and turn it in, it's still admissible. Just means I can't help."

"And you're busy," I said, showing I'd actually been listening. "Ok, I'll see what I can do."

"Start with the girl," he told me. "Hell, all of them, if they'll talk. Right now, you got two. Zoe and the dead one. Her videos count, believe it or not. That's the start of a pattern, but not a solid one. Get three and it's easier. Every girl after makes it even easier. Get the girls to trust you, Knock - and then you do whatever it fucking takes to keep them safe."

"That's what I'm trying to do," I promised.

"And I've got your back," he assured me. "Might not look like it, but I will always have your back. Turn your little girlfriend loose, bro. Let her run wild, because she's the type who doesn't have a clue how to give up."

"The type who wins," I agreed.

CHAPTER 18

CADE

I wasn't sure what Knock's friend had told him, but it couldn't have been good. He was a little sullen for the rest of the night. Then again, we all were. Those videos we'd just watched hadn't been easy to sit through. Thinking about them only made it worse. *Talking* about them? Yeah, that wasn't exactly easy.

So the next day at school, the mood wasn't good. We all wanted to *do* something, but what was there to be done? Nothing, until we had a plan. Even worse, seeing Marissa sitting with the other gamers at the table beside us was a reminder of the horror we'd watched.

I felt like I should tell her what I'd seen – but would that make it worse? Never mind that I'd actually seen it. While I knew we *had* to watch, it still felt like I'd violated her in some way. She hadn't given me permission to see that. Amber had, so how pissed off would Marissa be when she found out about it?

And to top it all off, Dylan and the rest of Alpha Team were back from their suspension. At least on the upside, it didn't look like anyone wanted to be around them. Those five guys stood together with a rather noticeable gap between them and the rest of the student body. That was a little gratifying.

But at lunch, the five of us finally had the chance to talk without fear of being overheard. Naturally, it was Jericho who got right to the point.

"We know they've been doing this since at least July," she said, looking at each of us. "We also know those parties happened every other week."

"At least," Zoe said. "During the summer, they sometimes happened more often."

"Yeah, but how many times?" Jeri asked.

Like everyone else, I shrugged. "I don't know. A lot," I explained. "John always had alcohol and his parents were never around. It just made sense to hang out there when we could."

"Okay," Jeri said, "but think about it. That tablet turned on at the parties. Well, after them. Jinxy said it was uploading enough data to be multiple videos." Then she lowered her voice. "What if those were all rape videos?"

"Wait," Knock said. "You think they raped someone at every one of their parties?"

Jeri tilted her head to the side as if not quite saying yes, but implying it. "Pretty much. The ones where they didn't rape someone were probably the ones where they had their orgies with Tiffany's friends. But think about it. Guys, shouldn't those count as rape videos too? Those girls were intoxicated, pressured, and then put in a situation that wasn't quite what they consented to. To me – and I don't know about the rest of you – that counts as rape."

"I agree," Zoe said.

Beside her, Ripper was nodding. "From what I've heard, none of those girls were sober. So far as I care, that makes it rape."

"Which means," I said, "this is a bigger problem than we realized."

"They're fucking serial rapists," Jeri hissed. "How does it get any worse than that?"

"Because they've been doing it right in front of everyone, and none of us have cared," I told her. "*That's* the big problem. If they were serial killers, then the cops would be after them, looking for forensics, and doing whatever they do. But because this is rape, and this is high school, it's assumed to be a stupid mistake, going too far, or having 'a little too much fun.'"

"That doesn't exactly make it better," Ripper said.

I just groaned. "I know. That's kinda my point."

"So how many girls are we talking about?" Knock asked.

And that had all of us looking at each other blankly. In my head, I was trying to do the math. We knew about Tiffany's friends, which made four. If I added in Amber, that was five. Then there were the three other girls whose videos Amber had given us. That was eight. Including Zoe made that nine – and I knew they couldn't be the only ones.

"We know about nine," I said.

"What about that freshman who overdosed at the last party?" Zoe asked.

Jeri dropped her head and groaned. "Do we know if she was raped?"

"No," Zoe said, "but we know she went to the hospital because she overdosed on something – and we know it was bad. To me, that sounds like ketamine. I mean, doesn't that fit what they've been doing to everyone else?"

The sad thing was that yes, yes it did. From the looks on everyone's faces, we all knew it. The real question was what could we do about it? This wasn't the sort of thing we could just hack and figure out. Worse, if Hot was right and the videos were being stored on someone's private server, then we would never find them.

"Okay, so what do we do?" I asked, looking over at Knock.

"Shut up," Jeri snapped as her eyes jumped over my shoulder.

Confused, I turned to see what she was talking about just in time to find Dylan making a straight line to our table. Of course he was. I almost hoped he tried something else, because I would love to see him get expelled permanently.

"Cade!" Dylan called out, sounding like he was so happy to see me.

"Go to hell, Dylan," I told him.

Naturally, it couldn't be that easy. The guy kept coming like he assumed he was still the hottest shit at school. He wasn't. Jericho had made sure of it, but it seemed the king hadn't yet realized he was sliding off his throne.

"So," he said as he reached my side and clasped my shoulder. "I heard you had a rough weekend. I guess I should apologize or something, hm?"

Shrugging his hand off my shoulder, I pushed to my feet. Chest to chest, standing much too close, we faced off. I wanted to make sure this asshole knew I wasn't scared of him. Oh, he'd tried to ruin my life, but he'd made one major mistake. He'd forgotten I now had friends – the real kind.

"Were you disappointed to hear I didn't die?" I demanded. "Or was that how you tried to get over Amber?"

Dylan just lifted his hands and took half step back. "Hey, look, we're all sad about what happened to Amber."

"But are you really?" I asked. "You don't seem to be torn up or anything. How's John doing, anyway?"

That made Dylan clench his jaw. "Don't act like you give a shit."

I took a step closer to him, making it clear I was no longer willing to be intimidated. "Why the fuck did you even come over here? You could've stayed over at your table, but no. You came here, wanting something, so you might as well spell it out."

Standing this close, I could see Dylan's nostrils flare as he sucked in a breath. The guy was pissed. Most likely because I wasn't sitting down and shutting up like I always had. Yeah, but he'd brought it upon himself, hadn't he?

"I heard things got ugly between you and your dad," he said. "Like I said, I came over to make sure you're okay."

"Yeah, but that's not what you said, is it?" I pointed out. "You wanted to know if you should apologize." Then I smiled. "Don't worry. I'm doing just fine. How about you?"

Glaring at me, he ran his tongue over his teeth behind his lips. "I got suspended for three days. How the fuck do you think I'm doing? Do you have any idea how pissed off my dad is?" He looked over at Jeri. "Thought we were supposed to have some kind of truce, huh?"

"Our truce only has to do with videos," Jeri told him. "Believe it or not, I do not control the school."

So Dylan gestured at Knock. "No, but it seems he does."

"So you're pissed that I take care of my crew better than you take care of yours?" Knock asked.

And all of this was only making Dylan more pissed. The guy had his fists clenched at his sides, and he was breathing so hard his shoulders were heaving with it, but that seemed to be it. Granted, the teachers watching over the lunch room probably were holding him back a lot more than we were.

"I'm going to make all of you pay for what you've done," he warned. "You don't get to fuck with me and think I'll ignore it."

Jeri scoffed. Knock chuckled. Ripper shook his head and Zoe rolled her eyes. If that was supposed to have been some kind of big scary threat, then Dylan had just failed. Unfortunately, that made him even more pissed off.

"Don't think I'm done with you," he snapped at me next. "There is a hell of a lot that you wouldn't want to get out."

"Yeah, like what?" I asked.

"Like the fact that your dad isn't really an alcoholic."

All I could do was shake my head. "Dylan, he is. He's done the meetings and everything. Shit, that's why my mom divorced him. I mean, if that's the line you want to go with, then have fun with it."

"I mean for why you left!" Dylan snapped. "Or do you think your friends are going to look at you the same after they know?"

It took far too long for those words to make sense in my brain. My friends already knew, but Dylan assumed they didn't. I'd hidden my sexuality for so many years, doing everything to prove I wasn't into guys, so he just assumed I would keep on doing the same thing. He was also very, very wrong, and there was an easy way to show him.

I didn't give myself the chance to think about what I was doing. I refused to weigh the pros and cons of it. Suddenly, the repercussions no longer felt like they mattered. The only thing I gave a shit about was proving Dylan wrong yet again.

So I turned to Knock, clasped the side of his neck, and bent down to plant a deep kiss on him. There, in the middle of the cafeteria, with a few hundred students watching, I kissed my boyfriend without shame.

Our tongues met. He kissed back. I felt his hand sliding up the front of my chest, but I pushed everything else away. For this one moment, the only thing that was important was getting this right. So I kissed him hard, convincing myself this was not something to be ashamed of, and Knock matched me move for move.

In the distance, someone whistled. On the other side of the cafeteria, someone else cheered. Like that was some kind of sign, more and more people joined in. Clapping started. A few more whistles were added. I tried to ignore it, but the cacophony around us grew fast enough I couldn't help but pull away, because I was struggling not to laugh.

"And that," Jeri told Dylan, "is another way of saying fuck you."

"Yeah," Zoe said, pushing to her feet. "And so you know, Dylan, you don't get to fuck up someone's life and get away scot-free. That's not how the real world works."

Dylan just huffed out a laugh, and one that sounded disgusted. "And now everyone at school knows you're a homo," he told me.

I just lifted my hands in mock defeat. "Oh no, whatever will I do? The next thing you know, my dad might hear something about it. Maybe he'll beat the shit out of me. Maybe I'll get kicked out and have nowhere to live." Dropping my arms, I turned to face Dylan, ready for him to do anything. "Oh right, that already happened."

Which made Dylan smile. "Oh, so does that mean you're couch surfing now? Let me know when you want to sell the Impala. I'll offer you a good price."

"Yeah, I'm living with my boyfriend now. Don't worry. I'm doing just fine."

Which was when Jericho made a subtle little shooing motion. "Run away now, Dylan. You made your move, and you made a fool out of yourself. In case you haven't figured it out yet, we don't care what people at school think."

"Yeah, well, you seemed to care enough about what Tiffany and her friends thought."

"No," Jeri assured him. "I care about taking care of my friends. Just my friends. The thing you can't seem to wrap your mind around is that I keep getting more while you keep getting less. Oh, and tell John that if he hadn't passed his girl around..." She leaned forward and there was nothing but fury in her eyes. "...then she might still be alive. I also know they didn't all nod first."

Dylan's entire body stilled. For much too long, he did nothing but stare at her. I was pretty sure the guy's mind was whirling, trying to come up with some other way to explain what Jeri had just insinuated. Those smooth, subtle little words she just said all but told him that she was no longer bluffing about having a video. He could probably even guess which one she had – or ones.

"Fuck you," he snarled.

Then he turned and hurried away. Oh, it was a clear and obvious retreat. He wasn't running, but he might as well be, and to me it felt like a victory. At least until I sat back down in my chair.

Then Ripper leaned forward to rub my shoulder. "Well, I guess that's one way of coming out."

I just groaned. "Fuck."

Because that wasn't what I'd meant to do. All I'd wanted was to shut Dylan up, and now everyone knew. The entire school had just seen me kiss Knock. There was no way to take it back, but that was the strangest part of all.

I didn't want to. I didn't have to. I was bi, and for the first time in my life, I didn't have to be scared of it.

CHAPTER 19

KNOCK

When school was finally over, I headed to Cade's locker. Today, he'd driven us to school. It would be stupid for both of us to drive, and since he'd loaned his Impala to Ripper yesterday, this worked out. It also meant I needed him to give me a ride home.

He smiled as I walked up, but didn't have much to say. I didn't think anything of it at first. We both got what we needed for the night, put the rest of our stuff away, and then made our way outside. The walk to the parking lot was calm and comfortable - until someone spotted us.

"Cute couple!" the girl yelled.

Confused, I looked over, only to find her staring at us. Beside me, Cade still said nothing. Even worse, he wasn't blushing. The guy was simply staring at the concrete under his feet as we passed over it.

"Cade?" I asked, starting to worry.

"Mm?"

"You ok?"

He let out a heavy sigh, but by then we were at his car. The conversation paused as he unlocked my door, then headed around for his. I climbed in. A moment later, he did the same, then started the car. Putting it in reverse, he backed out of his parking space and aimed for the traffic heading off campus.

"Is this about that kiss at lunch?" I asked.

A little smile flickered over his lips, but it wasn't enough to reach his eyes. "Yeah. I mean, I kinda fucked that up."

"How so?"

"Didn't exactly think it through."

Not helping. None of this was helping. I'd been out at school for months now. I also remembered how fucking freaked out I'd been when I'd first started telling people, and for me, it had been easy. For him, this was different. He'd worked so hard, for so long, to make sure he was seen as nothing but straight.

And now it was different.

"Are you ok?" I asked next.

I watched as his throat bobbed when he swallowed. "Yes and no. Yes, I'm glad it's out there. I don't have to fucking tell people now, you know? Dylan can't use it as a threat." He laughed once. "Shit, more people have said they're happy for me, support me, are pro-gay, and such than I've even heard before."

"So what's going on in your head?" I begged.

He glanced over. "I'm out." And then his eyes were right back on the road.

But that didn't tell me a damned thing. "And?" I pressed. "Give me more?"

So he pushed out a heavy breath. "All my life, getting caught would fuck shit up. Dad would kill me. My friends would probably beat the shit out of me. If I dared to let myself be myself, my life would be ruined." His tongue darted out to moisten his lips. "And I'm still braced for that."

My next words were as gentle as I could make them. "But it doesn't matter anymore."

"I know," he quickly promised. "I really do know, and the Alpha Team already beat my ass. My dad already tried. It's out there. They all knew before today, but now everyone in school knows, and my brain keeps thinking it's going to be a problem when it isn't."

"But how do you feel about it?" I asked. "Because I can stay hands-off."

He just chuckled softly. "Knock, that's the part that has me quiet. All of my instincts are screaming that I can't do this, but my brain knows it's bullshit. I can. Fuck, I can be your boyfriend in public now. No one fucking cares. It's cool, it's allowed, and like half the school is happy for me."

"Uh huh," I said, nodding slowly because I was completely lost.

He just gave me another one of those quick glances, but this one came with a smile. "Imagine how you'd feel if your lottery ticket ended up being a winner. There would be a pause, because you couldn't believe it. A lull as you waited for the rest of the joke, right? Yeah. That's me. All fucking day long, that's been me."

"So used to losing that it's hard to accept things really can be this good," I rephrased. "Ok, yeah. *That* is a feeling I can relate to. Like when I moved in with Logan."

"And I just moved in with my boyfriend," he reminded me. "Just. It's like one amazing thing is tumbling over the other, and I keep waiting for the part that's going to suck. And in the middle of all of this, we're dealing with some fucking heavy shit, you know? I shouldn't be this damned happy, but I kinda am, and I keep feeling like I'm missing something because of it."

"But you're not," I promised.

"I just don't really know how to do us at school," he admitted.

"Us?"

He nodded. "Like, is holding your hand weird? We don't really hold hands. If I wrap an arm around you, is that too girly? Can I kiss you at your locker? Mine? That kind of stuff."

"I'm not really a hand-holder," I admitted. "More of a side hugger."

"Same," he agreed. "And the kissing?"

"I'm completely down for kissing," I promised.

Beside me, the guy was finally starting to look more comfortable. Less tense, at any rate. His mouth was also stuck in some kind of perpetual half-smile now. Whimsical was the word I wanted to give it, but I had a feeling Cade would prefer to describe it as dumbfounded.

"So you don't regret coming out at lunch today?" I asked. "Because we can walk that back, you know."

"How?" he asked. "Say it was a joke?" Another one of those glances. "No, I'm not doing that. I kissed you. I'm damned proud of my boyfriend. I don't give a shit if Dylan or his friends like me. I've already been thrown out of my dad's place, so I'm doing this. I mean, it may not be the same way you did it, but this is me coming out."

"With a bang," I teased. "Why am I not surprised?"

"Huh?"

I laughed. "Cade, you're a go big or go home kinda guy. You went big with coming out."

And that made him sigh, like the last of his tension had just evaporated. "Yeah?"

"Yeah," I assured him. "And I like that about you. Jeri calls it being hot shit. Now, keep in mind that her longest and closest friend named himself HotShot, and I think you'll figure out where she got the term. Me? I prefer to call it sexy."

"I like sexy," he admitted.

"Very sexy," I promised just as he slowed to turn into our drive. "Know what else I like?"

"Mm?"

"That when Dylan came to throw down, you stepped up." I reached over to rest my hand on his leg, just above his knee. "You pulled a Jericho, getting in his face and throwing him off before he could mess with Zoe."

"I was actually thinking more about Jeri," Cade said. "Knock, these videos are hitting her hard. I mean, Zoe too, but that makes sense. She'll also admit it. Jeri won't."

"Hottie gets her to talk," I assured him. "You know he does. And Ripper makes her feel safe. You and me? We get to be the front line for her."

"The tanks," he said, using the game term for the defensive role. "Yeah, but that's why I got up in his face. I figured Dylan wanted to start shit about him getting suspended. I knew seeing me would get him going on about how I'd been kicked out. That wouldn't leave him time to fuck with our girls."

"Our girls," I repeated. "Yep, you're broken."

"Hey, I like Zoe!"

I laughed. "I know. And for some strange reason, she seems to like you too. I also think you're good for her. She knows she can push limits with you a bit. Different ones with Ripper. I think it's helping her a lot more than we can understand."

He pulled up in his new parking space and stopped the car. After pulling out his keys, he paused to look at me. "She's kinda part of my thing today. I mean, the overthinking thing."

"How so?" I asked as I opened my door.

Matching me, he climbed out the other side, talking over the roof of the car. "Well, when we were watching those videos, she said she needed space with no guys, right?"

"Yeah?"

"And that's fucking huge for her," Cade explained as he grabbed his stuff from the back. "Knock, she's opening up. She's trusting. She's re-learning her boundaries with guys, and those guys are us. I mean, what she went through?"

"No shit," I agreed, grabbing my own bag.

And then the pair of us headed for the backyard. Cade was on a roll, though. "Well, the way I see it, having everyone at school know I'm bi? That's got to be like a millionth of the terror she had when everyone at school found out what Evan did to her, right?"

"Probably."

"But it's freaking me out," he explained. "This tiny little sliver of shit is making me overthink so fucking bad. Like, what did Zoe do? She smiled. She made friends with Jeri. She laughed with us, and just plowed through like her trauma was nothing, and here I am being this big ol' pussy about it."

"Pussies are tough," I joked, since that was something Kitty would say.

He laughed. "Ok, fair point. And I think an apt one this time too. All I'm saying is - "

But the moment he opened the back door, his words died off. Inside the house, Riley was moving. Worse, Logan and Kitty were both here, and it was much too early for either one to be home. People were yelling. Things were happening. There was too much, and even poor Quake was overwhelmed with it all.

The dog was sitting up against the side of the couch, looking at each person who passed him by. Nudging Cade, I got him the rest of the way in, then closed the door behind us, and tried to make sense of this mess. As Logan passed, he saw us and jerked his chin in greeting, but didn't slow down at all.

"Murder can't update PsychoDreads!" Logan yelled, listing off names of our gamer friends. "He's out of play."

"Fuck!" Riley bellowed. "Who has Psyc's number?"

"TeamSpeak!" Kitty called back.

"He's not fucking *on* TeamSpeak right now!" Riley yelled before zipping into the kitchen again. Then she took two steps back. "Knock!"

"What the actual fuck?" I asked her.

"Basement, both of you," she said. "I need all hands on deck."

"Ok?" I reached up to press Cade that way. "Any hints?"

The answer came from Kitty. "Shooting at UNY-N. Murder and Zara are both ok. Cyn's in the hospital. Two gunshot wounds, possible surgery, and reports are slow to come in."

"He went full fucking fed!" Riley called after me. "We need him down!"

"What?" Cade asked, looking over, clearly not understanding any of that.

"Riley!" I snapped. "Secrets!"

"And now is not the fucking time for them!" she snapped, trailing behind us down the stairs with three massive cups of coffee. "In the middle of the campus, fucking jarheaded bigots decided to off every Middle Eastern student there. It's all over the motherfucking news, Knock. I'm talking CNN and shit."

"Fuck," I breathed.

Cade's head was snapping from side to side. "Whose school?"

"University of New York, North Campus," Riley said, pressing a coffee into his hands. "The man you know as Cyn - which is short for Cynister - shot and killed at least four guys. Probably a lot more."

"Oh fuck," I groaned.

"He shot up a school?!" Cade gasped.

"No," she said, steering him to a chair. "He took out the shooters - just like he did here for Knock's party. Cade, Cynister's name is Special Agent Jason Raige."

"The hacker?" Cade asked, his eyes jumping to me.

I wobbled my head from side to side. "Yeah, more like a Cybersecurity Specialist with the FBI. Oh, and he's also a sniper. Yeah, and he's the lead on the KoG case."

Cade still looked like he wasn't quite getting it. "The guy who told us how to frame Evan?"

So Riley grabbed his face and made him look at her. "He's a

shitty fed. He's a fucking brilliant hacker. He's also my friend and he saved my life. I owe him everything, and I promised him I'd get his back if he ever needed it."

"And right now," Logan said as he made his way into the room, "he needs it. Cynister's so damned deep into the gaming scene to get intel for the KoG case that he might as well be undercover. The problem..." And he clicked at his computer, pulling up a website.

There, on the front page of the news, was a clear picture of Cynister being loaded into an ambulance. Clearly that had been taken by someone on site, not a journalist, but it was too much. Fuck!

"He's blown?" I asked.

"Not yet!" Kitty called down from the first floor. "The news is reporting him as only an 'agent on site.' We need it to stay that way."

"And to get his fucking face down," Riley added. "Gone. No trace."

"You still need to call Psyc," Logan reminded her. "I'll handle everyone in Executive Pain, and Ice is taking care of the gamers in Paradox. Someone has to make sure Murder's outfit knows."

"Right..." And Riley turned to run back up the stairs.

"A cop?" Cade breathed.

"An agent with the FBI," I corrected. "A friend. He's on our side, and he needs our damned help, Cade. He's trying to bring down all of KoG, not just the Alpha Team."

He nodded. "Ok. What do I do?"

I just grinned. "Wanna learn how to use some scripts? Because we need to find every fucking picture of this incident and make sure none of them are of him."

"I'm finding replacement options," Logan assured me.

"Then we got this," I said. "Just tell me he's ok?"

"Murder says he'll live," Logan promised. "The problem is that Murder now knows about his job."

"So I'm not the only one in the dark?" Cade asked.

"No..." I said, dragging out the word. "Everyone outside this house is." Then I looked over. "I mean everyone. Jeri can't know about this. No one in Ruin. Cyn's our secret weapon. He's also making sure we don't get busted for hacking."

"And," Logan added, "he's the one who'll take out these little pissant KoG boys here in town. Cade, this guy is our ace in the hole. We need to make sure we don't lose him."

Cade just smiled at his screen. "Yeah. There's the other shoe, and it still hasn't fucked up my day."

"Huh?" Logan asked.

Cade looked over at him. "I kinda came out at school today. Well, I kissed Knock at lunch and everyone saw, so yeah. I think that counts."

"Nice," Logan said, leaning back to offer his fist for a tap. "Proud of ya, and if anyone gives you shit, I'm pretty good at discrimination too."

Cade tapped his knuckles against Logan's. "How are you at hacking?"

"Shit," Logan admitted. "I do the legal stuff. You kids handle the law-breaking stuff. So, um, start breaking some petty laws, boys. Let's show them why no one should mess with gamers."

"With Ruin," Cade mumbled under his breath.

"With *our* internet," I added. "Because it's time for you to learn how to own this shit, Cade."

"Teach me, master," he joked.

I just nodded even as my hands were busy on my keyboard. "Patience, Padawan. One day, you too will be a Jedi."

CHAPTER 20

JERICHO

Knock and Cade were quiet all night. I had a feeling Cade was dealing with coming out like he had. We all knew it hadn't been planned, but it sure had worked. Even better, what I'd heard in the halls yesterday sounded like most people approved. Not that it would change anything if they didn't, but it would make life easier for Cade.

But Amber's death was quickly being forgotten by the student body. The poor girl hadn't really had any friends - which made me feel even worse for her. She'd kept to herself, except for dating John. There weren't any announcements about her funeral, memorial, or whatever her parents were doing, and no one was really talking about it.

That just made me think about it even more. The girl had given her life to escape her abuse, and no one seemed to fucking care! Well, I did. She'd exposed a whole mess of bullshit in the process, and the only thing she'd ever asked of me was to fix it. So here I was, trying to figure out how to do that.

It all came back to Marissa, though. That was why, the next morning, I headed straight for her. Like always, she was hanging out in the general vicinity of Carson and the guys from BAD. I knew she wasn't a member, but she hovered. Then again, most of the gamers at Sanger High did the same.

"Hey," I said when I got to their table. Then I thrust out my hand. "I'm Jericho. You're Marissa. We haven't really met."

She eyed my hand suspiciously. "Yeah. Ok." Then she accepted my hand and shook once. "Hi."

"Can we talk for a minute?" I tried, tilting my head to show I meant alone.

Her eyes narrowed, but she pushed away from the table, waving an arm in front of her like I should lead on. Yeah, not exactly a friendly invitation, but I was willing to take it. Then again, nothing about this girl was what I'd call welcoming.

She was about my height, but lean - the thin and willowy type who turned androgynous under her baggy pants and shirts. Her hair was short, cut like a guy's, and blue-black. Clearly dyed. She didn't wear makeup, didn't try to impress, and wore nothing on her that wasn't black.

I would've expected heavy eyeliner and lipstick from most goths. Marissa wasn't that type. If I was honest, she gave me more nonbinary vibes than anything else, but Knock said she was a girl, so I was going with it. However, the thing that kept tripping me up was that *this* girl looked nothing at all like the one in the video.

So once I got her far enough into the grass for no one to hear what we were talking about, I turned to face her. "Um, you know Dylan and his friends, right?"

"Everyone does."

Yeah, that wasn't giving me a lot to go on. "Ok. Um..." Shit, this wasn't easy. "Well, you heard about what Evan did to Zoe, right?"

Her jaw clenched. "Yeah, Jericho. Everyone did. The fucker

got arrested at a pep rally. Kinda like a front-row seat for the entire school."

"And I heard you were at Knock's place for his birthday?"

She crossed her arms over her chest, proving there was a hint of a figure under her clothes after all. "What the fuck do you want?" she demanded.

"Ok, look," I said. "There's this group called KoG, which stands for the Kings of - "

"Gaming," she finished for me. "Yeah, we know."

"They're the ones who shot up Knock's place."

She just scoffed. "In case you missed it, I've known him longer than you." Then she made a point of looking me over. "And before you came, I was getting to be pretty good friends with him. Now, he's cut all of us out."

"Thought you were still into Carson," I countered.

Before my eyes, she shut down. No, she didn't move, but the attitude on her face turned to nothing. Not rage, not fear, but a perfect mask of absolutely nothing at all. Damn it!

"Look," I tried next, "Dylan and his friends are all members of KoG. We're trying to prove it, and I think I need your help."

"How so?"

Make or break time. Fuck. I had a feeling this was going to go bad. Zoe should be here. She'd be better at this. Then again, I wouldn't make her do it. Nope. This was on me. As the only girl in Ruin who wouldn't be fighting through some kind of trauma to have this talk, I *needed* to figure out how to make this girl give me *something* we could use.

"So, we found out they were in KoG when Zoe was raped," I explained. "And she said they all laughed at her. That means they watched. Marissa, they need to pay for that. Somehow, someone needs to make sure of it, and in order to do that, we need to bust them on something. The problem is that Dylan hasn't committed any crimes against us."

"You just said he laughed at Zoe," she shot back.

"Which isn't illegal," I pointed out, making a face to show what I thought of that. "See the problem?"

"And what the fuck do you want from me?"

"Um..." Damn it. I had to 'fess up! "Well, you know about Amber, right?"

"Bitch offed herself."

Damn. That hurt to hear. I couldn't even imagine saying it with so little regard for the poor girl's suffering, but this wasn't the time to call her out.

"Marissa, she was pregnant. She tried to break up with John. He beat the shit out of her, then forced her to watch the video of them having their way with her."

"Figured she was a slut."

"She wasn't!" I snapped. "That's what I'm saying. She was raped and had no memory of it. They drugged her and raped her. All of them, don't you see?"

"Well, there's your crime," she told me, turning like she was about to head back.

So I grabbed her arm, preventing her from leaving. "And before she died, she sent me evidence. Videos. One of them was you."

The girl's entire body stilled. Her eyes hung on me. I swore her skin turned a few shades paler, but it was hard to tell. What she didn't do was gasp, react, or even widen her eyes.

"I don't know what you're talking about," she finally said.

"Look," I whispered, moving closer but refusing to release her arm. "That's why I wanted to do this with no one else around. Amber sent me some videos those guys have. One of them is you. The cops say there's no crime unless there's a victim. Amber's dead, so she can't report it."

"And you think I'm just going to go report a rape so you can get your kicks?" She huffed like I was an idiot. "How about no."

"Can you give me anything?" I asked. "I know it had to be last summer because your hair was long and blonde, but there has to be more."

"What?" she gasped.

So I kept going, hoping I could convince her to help. "They're raping girls, Marissa. It wasn't just you and Zoe. This is what they're doing! Over and over, they're picking a target and then destroying her life the same way they did to Zoe - and you. I want to make them pay for that. I want to fuck up their world, but I can't without help!"

Marissa's mouth was hanging open, then she slowly started to shake her head at me. "Do you just have some kind of bucket list for how to piss off everyone at school or something?" Then she yanked her arm free of my hand. "No, Jericho. I don't fucking know what you're thinking, but I want no part of this fucking stupid idea."

"But you were raped," I hissed.

"Keep your damned nose out of my life," she shot back, taking a step closer. "I don't know what kind of deep-fake bullshit you're trying to pull, but I'm fine. Don't you get that? I'm fucking fine! I'm going to stay fine, and if you start getting all up in my business, all you'll do is make me one of these targets you're talking about."

I couldn't believe what I was hearing. Ok, I knew she might not want to talk about it, and I wouldn't blame her for not wanting to report it, but this? She was completely shutting me down and acting like I was making all of this up.

"Can you give me anything?" I begged. "See, after you, they changed. They started drugging the girls. They recorded them consenting with a nod. Why? If I just had some idea why they started doing things differently, then maybe the cops would stop calling a nod 'consent' and writing off what happened to them."

"Them?"

I nodded. "Amber sent four videos. She was one."

"Yeah, sounds like something I really don't want to be a part of."

This time, when she turned, she pulled her arms away so I couldn't stop her. Then she walked back over to her friends. She didn't storm. She didn't run. She merely sauntered there like our chat had been no big deal at all.

And I wanted to scream.

Not at her, because she hadn't asked for any of this. Nope, this time I wanted to yell at myself, because I'd fucked that all up. Then again, how the hell was I supposed to tell someone I'd just seen a video of their deepest, darkest secret and *not* make it weird as fuck?

She should've hit me. Or spit on me. If the tables had been turned, I would've called her a liar and shoved her off. My next step would be to destroy her reputation so that if she did speak out, no one would believe her. If I was in Marissa's shoes, I'd probably be in full survival mode, ready to tear down the world to protect myself.

She wasn't. Sure, she was a bitch, but could I blame her? Nope. And yet, something she'd said was spinning around the back of my mind. Marissa had asked if I had a bucket list to piss off everyone at school.

Bucket list.

That was why it stuck! Fuck! Amber had sent us a picture of John's bucket list! Turning my feet towards my friends, I hurried that way, hoping this might get us something. When I got close enough, Cade tapped Ripper's shoulder, gesturing in my direction. As one, my friends all turned, nothing but concern on their face.

"How'd it go?" Zoe asked.

Which meant they'd seen who I was talking to. "Uh, bad," I admitted. "Pretty sure I just made another enemy at school, and she won't admit anything happened."

"Do you blame her?" Zoe asked.

"Not at all," I promised.

"And she won't start shit," Knock said. "Marissa is more defense and less offense. She'll cuss your ass out if you cross a line, but she won't retaliate the way you would, Jeri."

"She also has to know Jeri's right," Cade pointed out. "I mean, you told her about the video, right?"

"Yep." I sighed. "And she basically just ignored me saying anything about it and kept acting like I was the crazy one."

"Which means she isn't ready to talk," Ripper said. "Jeri, you can't make her."

"I wasn't trying!" I insisted. "I was just giving her the chance, and no, I don't blame her for being bitchy. I just..." Another sigh fell from my lips. "Guys, remember the list Amber included?"

"Yeah?" Knock said, clearly confused at my change in subject.

"It wasn't the whole list," I pointed out. "I mean, it was a file on his computer, so maybe it's still there?"

"Could be..." He was watching me like he expected something.

I just reached up to shove my hair back. "It's kinda all we have left. I dunno. I'm hoping that maybe it's still there, or it can give us a hint of what they're doing. I dunno, like a website, or something? I think I'm going to go hunting for it after school."

"Worth trying," Ripper agreed. "If nothing else, maybe we can get some idea of why they're doing this."

"Because they're sick fuckers?" Zoe offered.

Cade nodded in agreement. "I think that's why. I really think it's that simple for them. These guys can, so they do."

Leaning my head back, I groaned in frustration. "Yeah, but that won't help us figure out how to stop them. We need a lead. Right now, any lead will do. We can't find the videos, we can't find the storage, and we can't bust them without something."

"So we find something," Zoe said. "It's what you're good at, right, Jeri?"

All I could do was shrug. "I don't know anymore."

"Then get good at it," she told me. "Stop trying to do this right, and start trying to ruin them."

"And we," Cade said, "will do our best to brainstorm other options - because it sounds like we're fucking stuck."

"Yeah," I agreed. "We are. We also can't let them win."

CHAPTER 21

HOTSHOT

The moment I got home after work, I fired up my computer. Snooping through Alpha Team's stuff was a lot easier when those boys were still at school. Less chance of getting caught if they couldn't be online, right? Even better, when I logged into Discord, Jinxy was already there, loitering alone in "Damage Control."

"Hey, man," I said when I saw his name.

There was a rush of sounds, a thump, and then Jinxy replied, "Sorry, thought I was alone."

"Clearly," I laughed.

He just grunted, unimpressed. "At least I'm making progress, Hot."

Wait, that was news. "You are?"

"Don't get too excited," he warned me. "I've just been surfing the dark web, looking through the worst of the worst for ideas on where these boys might be hiding their videos. I've got three popular dark web storage sites."

"Yeah, but they're probably using a personal server," I pointed out. "Kinda like we are with the Squirrel."

"Dunno about that," he countered. "This is KoG we're talking about. There has to be thousands, maybe tens or hundreds of thousands of incel boys with videos and pictures. Even if the Alpha Team is storing their *own* copies on some private server, the KoG forums are going to need something bigger. Something that can host all their shit, keep it up, keep it hidden, and not get ripped down by the cops, because it's all basically proof of some crime."

"Which sounds like something in Russia," I grumbled.

His murmur proved he didn't disagree. "Yeah. And hard as fuck to get into. The guy running this show clearly knows his way around the internet."

I scrubbed at my face even as I leaned back in my chair. "Ok. So let's break this down. We have five guys who have been serially raping girls for around a year. I'm assuming they didn't start this summer, but just escalated to taking the videos around then."

"Can't do that," Jinxy told me. "It's entirely possible they got in over their heads the first time, realized they liked the rush, and kept going. Since they're all in deep, they all have nothing to lose, you know?"

"But the whole thing is just weird!" I insisted. "C'mon, Jinxy. Tell me you haven't thought that. We have six straight boys - if we include Evan - who get invested in gang-bangs?"

"And a few of them who have some serious homophobia," he reminded me. "Those videos Zoe gave me of the fight at school? Yeah, it was all homo this and homo that. To me, that sounds a whole lot like denial."

"Wade, right?"

"Yeah, that's what Zoe called him. Dylan's not any better." Jinxy huffed out a dry laugh. "Considering Dylan was blackmailing Cade about kissing a boy? Well, it's not a stretch to imagine he may have been curious about it himself. I mean, we all know most humans aren't completely straight or completely gay. Sexuality is on a spectrum."

"And there you go sounding smart again," I teased. "But play this out for me? We have a group of teen boys who may or may not be questioning their sexuality - "

"In a place where that's not done," he broke in. "Hot, I'm going to bet those boys have parents who would not be ok with the gay."

"Ok, fair point, but all of them?" I grunted. "No, there's no way they're all curious or questioning. Not even in the closet. I mean, that's just statistically impossible."

"Not all of them," Jinxy assured me. "One or two. The rest? I think they got indoctrinated with violent porn. I think the leaders of that group played up the subjugation of women. I think we have a whole lot going on with them. You know, something like five different reasons, since there are five boys."

Which was a fair point. "Probably some domestic abuse at home too," I said.

Jinxy hummed as he thought about that. "Think so?"

"Maybe not physical, but mental and emotional? Yeah." I pushed out a sigh. "It's that whole male power thing, Shawn. Dad is a badass, so his son has to struggle to impress him. Son has to be a man, has to make sure women know their place, and all that shit. They try to mimic their fathers, which is why it's typically a generational thing. And worse, what's the most common type of porn now? The violent stuff."

"No kidding," Jinxy agreed. "Choking and fake BDSM is all over the place."

"Along with 'plots' that encourage male dominance," I said. "It's all geared to a male audience, so it's all about male fantasies, right? And what's the most common male fantasy about sex? That she really wants it, so he gets to take it. In the real world, that's called rape."

"Ok, good point," Jinxy agreed. "So we have a group of boys with powerful fathers - or families - and this idea that they need to be larger than life. Alpha males, hence their name. They somehow stumble on assaulting a girl, realize how much of a rush that gives them, and get addicted?"

"It's probably a lot more complicated than that," I admitted, "but pretty much. I'm sure there's some showing off to each other, some proving they aren't virgins, or aren't pussies, or whatever it was at the time. I have a feeling the dominance over women wasn't the end goal initially, but it is now. Hell, wouldn't shock me at all if these boys can't get off anymore without the idea of violence."

"Didn't know you took psychology courses."

I laughed. "No, I watch serial killer shows on the TVs at work. The women who come to work out are into that shit. And sadly, none of this gets us closer to busting these assholes. I mean, we know about nine different girls, Jinxy. Nine. I have a feeling they aren't the only ones."

"Probably not," he agreed. "I'm just shocked no one has reported them yet."

"Most girls don't," I said. "And do you blame them? Look at the shit Zoe's been through! There's no reward for it. We've all seen it on the news. That guy behind the dumpster who got like ninety days? Yeah, big fucking whoop, right? The girl ruins her own life for a guy to get some probation. Doesn't even keep him away from her. It's probably a hell of a lot easier for most of these girls to simply keep it to themselves."

"Safer," he corrected. "Not easier. Safer. No bullying, no revenge, no questions from parents, repercussions on their reputations, or any of that. But how many are out there? We need something - anything! - and someone has to know."

"Sounds like an average of every other week since July," I said.

Jinxy made a small noise, proving he was distracted. Then, "Hot? That's like thirty weeks, give or take."

"Shit."

Because that meant we could have up to thirty victims. Even if we cut that in half, it was still fifteen. A lot, no matter how we looked at it. Worse, there was no way at all to know who. From the girls I'd already heard about, one thing was obvious. It wasn't like these guys were going after only the popular girls or only the ones who gamed. They were all over the place.

"We need to get on those damned forums," I grumbled under my breath.

"Which ones?"

"KoG's."

Jinxy scoffed. "Yeah, and we're supposed to leave those alone. That's what Knock said."

"But why?" I demanded. "Everything we have goes back there. Every single thing. Alpha Team is fucking with these girls for KoG forum points or some shit. They're posting these rapes, which means there's going to be a record. I also have a feeling it wouldn't be hard to figure out their usernames."

"Probably the same as their game names," Jinxy agreed. "Yeah, with ya there. But Knock said it has to do with the FBI."

"So?" I asked. "Look, if the FBI is trying to make a case, then they need to make a damned case. If we hack in, get proof of this shit, and turn it in, then what?"

"We go to jail for hacking," he said. "Bad plan, Hot."

I groaned because he was right. "Ok, but everything we need is on there. We also know they aren't exactly hiding it!"

"And it's KoG," he shot back. "If you go snooping, they aren't going to blame *you*. They're going to focus fire on Jeri. They're going to assume it's her, and then she'll get the same shit Nina did!"

"But Jeri can handle it," I said, trying hard to convince myself of that.

"Can she? Can she really?"

"I don't know," I mumbled, cracking much too easily. "She keeps telling me she can, and she acts like she can, but the idea freaks me the fuck out."

"Me too," he agreed. "At least Zoe's scared of them. Jeri's not. Shit, pretty sure she's not scared of anything."

"She's scared of losing," I explained. "She's scared of not saving someone and watching someone else die. She is terrified of being the reason why, and the only way to stop that - in her mind - is to fight harder, bigger, meaner, or something."

"That's our baby girl," Jinxy said, only partially sounding like he was joking. "But speaking of her, how are things with the two of you after the big bone-fest?"

I groaned. "It wasn't like that."

"Pretty sure it was," he taunted. "Oh, I'm pretty sure your brain shut right down and your dick woke all the way up. C'mon, man. You can't bullshit me on this. I've known you far too long."

"Well..." I said, dragging out the word. "I can say she's now my girlfriend."

Jinxy made some shocked sound that was almost like he was choking. "Wait. Like, officially? How the fuck did you convince her of that?"

"She convinced me," I explained. "I mean, the whole thing with this girl killing herself? Yeah, it shook me a bit. I find myself watching Jeri closer than ever before, making sure I can hear her moving at night, and shit like that. So, we talked about it, and about how I need her to be happy. Those guys make her happy, so I don't want her throwing herself all-in with this rape mess."

"Too late," he pointed out.

I murmured in agreement. "Yeah, but she's trying. No, she's

not going to get it right immediately, but she's actually trying to care about more than the next fight, you know?"

"You mean she's falling in love with those guys."

"I fucking hope so," I mumbled.

"Hot, that's not exactly normal," he countered. "Shit, you and Jeri? We've all known that was going to happen. I mean, eventually, one day, and all that shit, but the two of you are inseparable. So why are you trying to get her with these other boys?"

"Because it's what she really needs," I explained. "And you know what? When you love someone enough, that's all that matters. Jericho *needs* those guys. They're safe, they take care of her, they keep her from blindly doing what I suggest, and they balance her, me... Shit, all of this."

"Ok..."

I laughed, because it was clear he didn't understand at all. "She's learning how to be a person offline, Jinxy. Because of those guys, Jeri's figuring out she doesn't need to save everyone. I mean, I think I've kinda pointed her at payback instead of some kind of savior complex."

He made a little noise. "Which isn't really better."

"For her, it is. It's one step further from feeling like she's cursed. It's also one step closer to learning how to feel things, you know? To let down her emotional walls and make friends. To fucking fall in love! I mean, what eighteen-year-old girl is more worried about scoring a hookup than a romance?"

Unfortunately, Jinxy had an answer for that. "Uh, most of the asexuals and aromantics I know. I mean, are you sure Jeri's not just aromantic? She's clearly not asexual."

I murmured, thinking about that. "No, I'm not. I also know it doesn't matter. Even people who are aromantic need human contact, right? Friends, if nothing else. So what if she wants to keep it to her level? I think we're all good with that. It also doesn't stop anyone from feeling things, you know? And she really needs to learn how to feel things."

"She's not going to let herself do that until she's gotten her revenge," Jinxy warned.

"Which brings us right back to hacking into KoG," I pointed out. "Yeah. We're fucking stuck, we know everything we need is right there, and none of us really understand why the fuck we can't get in there."

"Or if we even can," Jinxy countered.

I just scoffed at that. "We can. Might not be easy, but you know we could."

"With a little breaking and entering, sure." He sighed. "Hot, bring it up, but don't get your hopes up, ok? Knock said the feds are all over that, and if you got busted and went to jail?"

"It'd be worth it," I grumbled.

"It would destroy her," he countered. "It would undo every single thing you want for her. That girl would break, so how about we don't try it. You, Grayson, are her rock. If you're gone, all that's left is a lost and scared little girl trying to cover it up with bravado."

"Yeah, and one with the skills to get herself in real trouble," I agreed. "Ok. But I'm not letting this go with some half-assed answer like we got last time."

"I'd expect nothing less," he agreed. "But you gotta trust your crew. The whole crew, Hot. Ask, but do not be the one to fuck this all up."

CHAPTER 22

JERICHO

I spent all day thinking about that one little phrase Marissa had accidentally used. She'd asked me about a bucket list. Now, I was pretty sure she had no idea John had one on his computer, but life had a funny way of working out like that. A random comment by a girl who didn't want to talk to me had reminded me of something I should've looked at days ago.

So the moment I got home from school, I jogged upstairs, tossed my bag in the corner of my room, and fired up my computer. We'd left hooks in all of Alpha Team's computers, which meant it would be easy to get back in. This should be simple.

While my computer booted up, I rolled my chair back to the window and looked over at John's house. They didn't have football practice after school anymore, and the guy was supposedly grieving the death of his girlfriend. Granted, I had my doubts about it, but that was the cynical side of me talking. And yet, when I looked, I didn't see his car in front of his house. That meant I had a little time.

Wheeling back to my computer, I quickly got to work. Step one was always to make sure I couldn't be seen. VPN, encryption, and Dez had given us this handy little toy to mask our connections even more. Like this, it only took a few clicks, and I was right where I needed to be.

But hacking someone's computer was more like looking through a thumb drive. Sure, I could see all the programs, images, and other stuff, but that didn't mean I could activate it the same way. I could add programs or remove them. What I couldn't do was open up a fucking KoG forum and log in!

So I searched for the bucket list. The picture Amber had given us only had half the list on it. It was a photo taken of his screen by a phone. That only told me so much, and while I knew this was a long shot, it was the only avenue I had to chase right now, so I chased it.

Surprisingly, the damned thing was actually named "BucketList." Copying that over to my computer, I dropped it in a safe sandbox so no attached viruses would corrupt my system, and then backed out of John's network. But just as I opened the file to see what was on it, I felt a presence hovering over me.

I looked up to find Hottie standing there. "Uh, hi," I said awkwardly.

"Whatcha doing?" he asked, with only a slight bit of snark in his tone.

"Checking that bucket list Amber found."

"Mhm. Why?"

I opened my mouth, but paused. Slowly, I turned my chair so I was facing him. "What?"

"Jeri, you just dove into that guy's system," he chided. "What happened to being careful?"

I huffed in frustration. "Oh, c'mon, Hottie. We both know

that's easy shit. Besides, he's not home yet. I didn't change anything. I just copied the bucket list so I could look at the part Amber didn't get a picture of."

"Why?" he pressed.

I pointed at the stool in front of my makeup mirror. "You might as well grab that and pull it closer." Then I turned back to my computer to see what - if anything - I'd found.

Yep, it was a list of sick and disturbing perversions. Too many things had a line through them, but not everything. I couldn't help but chuckle when I saw the one about sleeping with two girls at once. Of course he hadn't done that.

But the list had nothing except an insight into the sick way these guys thought. Snarling under my breath, I closed the document and moved it to the Squirrel. The whole time, Hottie sat beside me, his presence much too obvious.

"Well?" he asked.

"I'd hoped that maybe there would be some line about logging in, or maybe a website," I admitted. "I dunno, just something! Hottie, that's pretty much the last thing I had to look at, and I'd forgotten about it until someone used that phrase with me today at school."

"Which phrase?"

"Bucket list," I explained. "It was Marissa."

"You talked to Marissa?"

Which was when I realized I had to go back and explain. "Um, I tried to," I admitted. "I didn't do too good, and she wouldn't say shit. I told her I'd seen her video, and while she didn't exactly deny it, she also didn't confirm. Mostly she just avoided the entire subject, all but called me a bitch, and walked off. So, yeah. That was a bust."

He just ducked his head to rub at his brow. "Do you blame her?"

"She should report it!" I insisted.

"Would you?" he asked, looking up to meet my eyes. "And before you answer, I'd like to remind you how you reacted after getting drugged."

My shoulders slumped as I realized he was right. "I know," I told him. "Hottie, I really do, and I don't blame her for not wanting to talk about it or anything. It's just so damned frustrating, you know?"

"Not really."

"There are all these girls!" I groaned. "So many of them, and no one at all is willing to say she was raped. I mean, look at Tiffany's friends! They say it was consensual. I mean, maybe it was, but I'm starting to think it was more of a manipulation, which is basically rape! These guys have fucked over so many girls, and they're going to keep doing it because nothing we do matters!"

"That's not true," he tried.

"But it is!" I insisted. "Zoe tried to report it and the cop shoved it back in her face. Do you think it'd be different for anyone else? So even if they do try to report it, nothing's going to happen. If they don't report it, nothing happens. If they talk about it, they're sluts, or were asking for it, or some shit like that. If they don't, then they're not trying to stop them. And yeah, I'm frustrated no one's trying to stop them, but that doesn't mean I don't *get it*."

Slowly, Hottie nodded his head. "Ok. So what do we do now?"

"I don't fucking know!" I snapped. "And that's why I wanted to check the bucket list. I dunno. Like some last-ditch effort, you know?"

"Or maybe we need to look at hacking into KoG?" he offered.

That made me pause completely. "The forums?"

"We know Amber got her videos from there," he pointed out. "We know these guys all have accounts. We know there's proof on those forums, but we're not allowed to even try? I mean, why not?"

"Because we'd get busted by the FBI," I said. "It could compromise Destiny Pierce's case, and Knock said we shouldn't."

"Knock said." He lifted a brow, making sure I thought about that. "Maybe it's just me, but Knock's reasons are pretty flimsy. I want a little better explanation, don't you? Especially since we're fucking stuck."

"It's kinda the only option we have left, huh?"

He nodded. "And you know we could do it. You, me, and Jinxy? We could figure out a way to get in. Nothing is unhackable."

"But it sounds like KoG is pretty damned close."

Which only made Hottie smile. "Maybe to a brute-force crack, sure. There are a whole lot of other ways, but we've been avoiding them. Why can't we hack Dylan's email and get in that way? Reset a password or some shit? There has to be a way. Get John's first pet's name. It doesn't have to be brute force to get in, but we need to know why we're not supposed to be in there."

"You don't think Knock's hiding something, do you?" I asked.

He shrugged. "I'm sure he is. I'm sure we all are. That doesn't mean he's hiding something bad, though." Then he sighed. "All I'm saying is we can't just give up."

"Because they'll just rape another girl - or girls!" I agreed.

"No." He reached over to catch my hand. "Because this is KoG, Jeri. These boys may be little pieces of shit in the group, but they're still in the group. You're a gamer girl. So is Zoe."

"Yeah?"

"And KoG doesn't give up." He paused to lick his lips. "Look at what they did to Nina."

My mind immediately jumped to Zoe. She'd already been raped, but Hottie was right. This was KoG. They didn't stop. They didn't slow down. They also didn't forget. Once someone was a target, they stayed a target until they were dead.

"Shit," I breathed as the reality of this hit me. "And they have to know Zoe busted Evan. That would make them come after her, wouldn't it?"

"And you," he said.

I waved that off, because it was the least of my concerns. "Hottie, if they go after Zoe, I don't think she could take it. If they sent her the sorts of things they sent Nina? If they bullied her to death?" I could feel my pulse picking up at the thought. "I mean, do you think they're already planning something? Or would Dylan and his crew have to bitch about it first? Like, how the fuck does that work?"

"I don't know," he told me, "and I don't care. I don't want to see either one of you hurt, but Jeri? I'm worried about you too. Zoe's a smart girl. You know she'd speak up if they hit her. She'd tell Jinxy or Ripper, if nothing else. But you?"

"I'm fine," I promised.

So he caught the arms of my chair and pulled me closer to him - and further from my computer. "You are not fine," he told me. "Baby girl, you're spiraling. You're hyperfocusing. You're doing all the things you do, and you're not talking to me."

"I'm just trying to fix this!" I insisted.

He shook his head. "You can't."

"But someone has to!"

"No," he snapped. "You aren't the hero, Jericho. You don't live online. You are not going to backslide into your old habits because it's easier."

"I'm not."

"When was the last time you hung out with your friends to do something besides this bullshit?" he asked, gesturing to my computer.

I cringed. "Um..."

"When was the last time you made out with one of your guys?" he tried next.

All I could do was hang my head. "With you?"

"Yeah, doesn't count." He reached over to catch my chin and make me look at him. "Baby girl, we just talked about this the other night. I mean, unless that was a really good dream, I'm pretty sure you asked me to be your boyfriend because of it, right?"

"Yeah..."

"And I was serious," he told me. "Jeri, I do love you, but that's the thing. I love you enough I don't want to see you lose yourself in a mess that we might not be able to fix. I definitely don't want to see you destroy yourself in the process. I want you, my girlfriend, to be happy every so often. I want you to have a reason to live, and maybe even to live offline a little."

"But with everything that's happened..." I tried.

He just shook his head again. "I know you want to fix it all. I do. I also know we're stuck. I don't want to see you get depressed, fall into some darkness, and not be able to talk to me about it. I want you to realize these little shits might get away with this."

"No!" I snapped, sitting up.

He lifted a hand, begging me to listen. "Jeri, we have videos. We have stories. We know what they've done, and we've done something about it. They all lost their scholarships to college, right?"

"Yeah."

"And you said they're not as popular at school, so isn't that something?"

"But it's not enough!" I insisted. "Hottie, they don't get to fuck women over and be praised for it! This is wrong! It's all so fucking wrong, and it feels like no one is doing a damned thing about it except us!"

"Because that's the shitty nature of the world," he shot back. "It's how things are, Jeri, and yeah, it sucks. It's also not a good enough reason for me to watch you tear yourself apart. I love you, in case you missed that. I also can't bear losing you. Fuck everyone else. And you know what? If I have to choose between you and Zoe? Yeah, I'm choosing you. Don't get me wrong, I like that girl, but you? You are what I care about. You're why I'm doing this, so I'm all-in, but I'm worried you're too far in."

"I can't help it," I admitted.

He just nodded, showing he heard me. "I know. This is who you are. Believe it or not, I'm ok with that, but I'm going to keep trying to convince you to slow down, step back, and let the rest of us help a little."

"But we're stuck," I reminded him. "What can you help with if we have no leads? I mean, all we have left is getting someone to actually report those guys so we can use those videos!"

"It's not that easy," he countered. "Evan went to jail because Zoe was a minor. These girls?"

"Marissa turned eighteen in June," I mumbled, knowing where he was going.

Hottie leaned closer so he could push my dreads from my face. "So maybe we need to see why we can't find another way into the website. Maybe we need to change direction. I'm not telling you to stop, baby girl. I'm just asking you to remember that there's more to life than fixing other people's problems, ok?"

"I'm trying," I mumbled.

He smiled at me softly. "You're failing."

"And the bucket list was a bust, so now I'm stuck too."

Hottie just stood and offered me his hand. "To me, that sounds like an excuse to watch a movie. Time to get our minds off this and onto something else, right? Take a break, Jeri. Regroup. Step away from the computer for a little bit."

So I took his hand. "I think you talked me into it. But maybe tomorrow we can head over to Knock's to ask about hacking KoG?"

"Sold," he agreed.

CHAPTER 23

HOTSHOT

The next morning, I reminded Jericho to ask her friends about a Ruin meeting before I headed to work. She promised she would, and said she'd text me to let me know. When my phone buzzed less than an hour later, I wasn't surprised. The meeting was a go.

But since Jeri was heading over straight after school, I decided to drive myself. It just made sense. The problem was that I got there a little early. I tried to park out of the way, picking a spot that should have been at the end of the line of cars once everybody else got here.

The farm was quiet, but Quake was bouncing around the yard, proving that wasn't the same as abandoned. Climbing out of my car, I was headed towards the backyard when I saw Riley lead a horse out of the barn. She looked over and waved, but kept heading down towards the arena.

"You know your way around," she called to me. "Everyone else should be here soon."

So I let myself into her house and made myself comfortable. Not surprisingly, Quake followed. Thankfully, I didn't have to wait long before the guys showed up. Knock and Cade were first. Jeri came only a few minutes later, with Ripper right after. Zoe was the one who took the longest, but that was okay. The rest of us had gotten distracted by playing with the dog.

"I'm here," Zoe called out as she descended the stairs.

"Okay," I said. "That means we can finally start."

Knock laughed once at that. "Just because you get off work a couple of hours before we get out of school doesn't mean we're late."

I grunted and rolled my eyes. "Yeah, but what you don't realize is that this has been waiting since last night."

"Wait," Zoe said as she claimed her chair. "What's going on?"

"I want to hack KoG," I announced.

"Okay, hang on," Zoe begged as she pulled her phone and dialed. "I promised Jinxy I'd bring him in on this."

"Hey, baby," Jinxy said as he answered, unaware he was already on speaker.

"Well, hello to you too," Jeri teased.

Jinxy just groaned. "You, Jericho, are 'baby girl.' Zoe is 'baby.' Learn the difference. I'm also getting the impression I'm on speaker. Does this mean we're having the meeting?"

"Evidently so," Zoe said.

"Hottie wants to hack the KoG website," Knock said.

"I'm with Hot," Jinxy said.

Which made me nod in approval. Okay, so we'd already talked about this, but it was nice to know he had my back. Mostly because I had a funny feeling Knock wasn't going to like this idea.

"Why?" Cade asked. "I thought we already took the KoG forums off the table."

"We'll never get in," Knock explained. "The guy who runs the site knows what he's doing. If we try to hack in, it's more likely he'll send the entire power of KoG after us. All of you should know by now that it's not hard to back-hack. I mean, that's how *we* usually get in somewhere. We follow something, like we did with Dylan's homework. If you try to hack into KoG, then you won't even notice Soul Reaper diving into your system."

"So we do it as a team," Jeri said. "Hottie can handle the hack while Jinxy and I deal with anyone who might try to retaliate. Problem solved."

Knock ducked his head, shoving both hands into his blue hair. "It's also probably one of the most secure websites on the Internet. Hacking it isn't going to be easy. Without a username and password, you won't get very far. Even if you do get in, you still won't have the authorization for the higher levels."

Out of the corner of my eye, I caught movement on the stairs. Looking over, I found Riley paused about halfway down. Like the rest of us, she was listening. She also looked like she had a few opinions of her own, but this wasn't her gig.

"All that means is we have to get a username and password, Knock," I explained. "Like I told Jeri, brute-force cracking isn't the only way to get in. There's no reason we can't socially hack into these forums."

"Which is a whole problem in itself," Knock pointed out.

"No, it's actually pretty easy," Jeri said. "All we have to do is get into someone's email, use the 'forgot username' option, and reset everything. After that, we can even change it over so the account is using an email we set up."

"If," Ripper said, speaking up, "we actually can find the right email address that they're using. I mean, how many email addresses do you have, Jeri?"

"Like four or five," she admitted. "Probably five more I've forgotten about and don't remember the passwords for."

"Exactly," Ripper said. "Because while it's easy to get into someone's bank account that way – or so y'all say – I have a feeling the account information for a hate group isn't going to be their normal email address."

"I sure wouldn't use mine," Zoe said. "I mean, I would make a Gmail account specifically for that. And if that's the case, we have no clue what emails the Alpha Team are using."

"And while all of that is true, the bigger problem is the FBI case," Knock insisted. "The feds are watching those forums. If we try to break in, we're just asking to get arrested. Never mind that we might fuck up the case for Deviant Games."

"And there it is," Jinxy said. "I have a feeling that's the real reason we need to stay out of it."

"Tell them," Riley said, interrupting the discussion.

Knock's head jerked up as he looked at her. "I thought that was a house secret."

"And I think your friends have earned the right to know," Riley countered. "Besides, the secret's out. I think the more people we have on our side, the better chance we have to fuck these assholes up."

"What secret?" Zoe asked, looking completely confused.

Riley slowly began to descend the stairs. "We're helping the FBI. I happen to think Ruin should be helping the FBI too."

"Whoa," Jinxy said over the phone. "Yeah, I don't want any part of that."

"Sure you do," Riley said. "Because whether you know it or not, the FBI has already helped you. Zoe, how do you think Evan got busted?"

"I thought you had a connection with some guy that was here at the shooting," Zoe said.

Riley just flicked her brows up as if daring us to think about that a little harder. "Pretty much. We call him Cyn –"

"The hacker?" Jeri asked, looking at Knock in confusion.

"Yeah, look..." Knock tried.

"What the fuck?" Jinxy snapped. "You told a fed what we're doing? Are you trying to get all of us busted?"

And then the entire room went crazy. Naturally, I was right in the middle of it. What the hell was Knock thinking, telling law enforcement about our illegal activities? What happened to the rule about not talking about this? Was he trying to get all of us busted?

And yet I still caught Zoe look over at Cade. "Did you know?"

Because this whole time, he hadn't said much. He also didn't seem either upset or offended like the rest of us. Hell, even Ripper looked a little shocked. Granted, he was also the one who said Knock probably had a point, but I wasn't listening to that part.

"I recently found out," Cade admitted.

Which made me turn my focus on Knock. "Oh, so you tell your boyfriend what he needs to know to not get arrested, but not us? So you know, that's not how this group is supposed to work. I thought we were supposed to be taking care of each other? Shit, if nothing else, I figured you'd give a damn whether or not Jeri got arrested. Do you not realize she's eighteen now? If she gets busted for hacking, she goes to jail for a long time."

"Yeah, so do you," Ripper pointed out. "So do all of us, which is why I don't think Knock would –"

Which was when a piercing whistle ripped through the room, silencing all of us. "Shut the fuck up!" Cade bellowed. "Yes, Cyn is an FBI agent. He's also on our side. He's already helped us."

"Riley just said he's the reason Evan got arrested," Zoe insisted.

"Yeah," Knock said. "He's the one who had the idea about child pornography. He told me we needed to go that route because it was more likely to stick."

"Which is why we need to listen to him," Riley said. "Yes, Cyn works for the FBI. He's the only person who's out there trying to help the women who are being abused online. He's the one pushing the KoG case."

"You should also know he's not a very good FBI agent," Knock added. "I mean, he's a good guy for us, but I'm pretty sure the FBI wouldn't think he's the kind of person to make employee of the month."

"So we're basically throwing away the best chance we have to bust Alpha Team because this guy is your friend?" I asked.

But it was Riley who answered. "No, we are staying the fuck out of his way because this guy has already done the work for the rest of us. Grayson, who the hell do you think reviewed Nina's case? Who do you think ignored the mysterious appearance of all that proof in her email account? Yeah, it was this guy."

"Wait, he was involved in Nina's case?" Jeri asked.

"He's involved in *every* case that KoG is in," Riley said. "He's been there from the start. The problem is the rest of the Bureau doesn't want to give him a hand, so we're the only assistance he's getting."

My brain couldn't handle that. This random guy, who Knock and Riley said was an FBI agent, was the same guy who had gotten Nina's bullies arrested? This sounded like some kind of sick joke. There was no way it could be true. Jeri had gotten the information and tucked it carefully into Nina's email account. Never mind that the assholes hadn't gotten the kind of punishment I'd wanted.

"How do you know about him working on Nina's case?" I asked, because right now that was the first thing I needed to know.

Riley pushed out a heavy breath and lowered herself down onto the couch. "Because I spend a lot of time talking to the guy. His name is Jason Raige, and he saved my life. He saved Logan's life. Shit, he even saved Quake's life."

"When you had the shooting here," I realized.

Slowly, Riley nodded her head. "Yeah. The thing is, he was helping me before that. I actually met the guy because he thought Logan was a bad guy. He was watching over me to make sure I didn't get hurt. Grayson, he's been on this case far longer than any of us. He's been on this case since Dez was abused. The whole time, he's been doing everything in his power to try to keep the women on the internet as safe as he can, and now he's the one who's getting hurt for it."

"Wait, what?" Jinxy asked. "How is he hurt?"

"Did you hear about the shooting in New York?" Knock asked. "The one at that college? Yeah, he was there."

"I have questions..." Jeri said.

Cade just waved both of his hands in front of him. "Let me give you the simple version. Cyn works with the cyber division, but he also shoots people. It's kinda like he's undercover to help us get the assholes with KoG. Unlike us, he's not going after a group of high school guys. He's going after the fuckers running the show. The ones who are recruiting thousands of desperate men to torture and harass women online. He's trying to shut the whole thing down so no one else ever ends up like Nina."

"Shit," I breathed, because what else could I say? "Okay, so maybe hacking the KoG website is a bad idea."

"A real bad one," Knock insisted. "The guy who runs that thing isn't dumb. If he has any proof at all – and we all know it's easy to leave little traces when hacking – then he can get off scot-free because it's easy to say we planted evidence."

"Yeah," Jinxy said, "but all the evidence is on the KoG forums. We can't find where they're storing their videos. We know Amber got everything off the KOG site. So why isn't the FBI getting this stuff to make the case for us?"

"Because he's not high enough level," Knock explained. "He literally cannot abuse women to earn points to see what he needs to see. He's an FBI agent. It's not just that it disgusts him. It's that it would destroy the entire case just as much as hacking the site would."

"Well, shit," Jinxy grumbled.

"I know," I told him, because he just put my feelings into words.

"So we need to come up with a new plan. I mean, if this guy is actually making progress – and the assholes who bullied Nina to death did go to jail, so I'd call that progress –"

"And Evan got arrested," Zoe broke in. "Y'all, think about it. This guy told us how to break the law. He told us to do what we needed to do so that my rapist would go away."

"And he made sure Evan got arrested where everyone would see," Knock added. "He told Logan how to get the burner phone without leaving a trace. He walked us through it step-by-step, which included helping me hack into Alpha Team's phones. He's the one who's been teaching me everything I know. When I say he's helping, I mean this guy is actually fucking helping."

"So how do we help him shut down KoG?" Jeri asked.

It was Riley who answered. "Right now, the best way you can help is by making sure his name is not on the internet. Special Agent Jason Raige just stopped a mass murder at UNY-N. He was shot twice in the process. He's currently in the hospital, without access to his tech, and the media is going crazy with the story. They aren't supposed to print his name, but that isn't necessarily stopping them."

"Or his pictures," Cade said.

I just nodded, understanding what Riley was trying to say. "Which means this guy needs Ruin's help. We need to take him off the internet so he can keep on helping us, right?"

"It'd be nice," Riley said.

So I turned my chair towards the computer. "And while we do that, maybe we can come up with some ideas for our own problems, because we're stuck."

"One thing at a time," Riley said.

Jinxy just scoffed over the phone. "Fuck that," he said. "We're a hacktivist group. Multitasking is our specialty. Knock? This is a great opportunity to teach people how to use those toys in that toybox. Hot? We need a new plan. What do we have, and what can we do?"

"We have the information Amber gave us," Jeri offered. "The USB drive had some of her homework on it, which probably won't help, but we should look at it anyway."

Then Zoe spoke up. "What about the stuff on her phone? I know we looked at the videos she left you, Jeri. What about the rest of it? She had to have pictures, memes, and old text messages. Maybe John texted her something months ago?"

"Yeah, and then there's the big thing," Ripper said. "We have those videos. Videos have metadata."

"But that's for tomorrow," I decided. "Those videos are going to take our complete attention, and it sounds like we might owe Special Agent Jason Raige a favor first. Or if I'm honest, a few favors. One for Nina, one for not busting Jeri, and at least one for helping Zoe."

"Yeah, but he doesn't keep track like that," Riley assured me.

"It's still a damned good reason to make him disappear," Jeri said. "If nothing else, it'll convince him we're on his side. Hopefully, that'll be enough to get him to look the other way if and when we do fuck up."

CHAPTER 24

ZOE

We spent quite a few hours searching the internet for any reference to Knock's FBI friend. We found a lot. Thankfully, there were only two photos. Those got replaced by other images of the campus after the incident. Everything else was a line tucked into some article written by some unaffiliated journalist.

Blogs, some of the most obscure "independent journalistic websites" I'd ever seen, and comments on articles written by the big news sites were the biggest culprits. Sure, the comments part made sense. Those were normal people who hadn't gotten the memo they weren't supposed to name this guy. From the looks of it, some of them knew him from school.

But we got it done, and we would keep checking for as long as we needed to. Shit, just thinking about how this guy had done so much to help me was a little bit overwhelming. He didn't know me. He had no reason to care about me. I couldn't even begin to wrap my mind around why he would break so many rules and laws in order to help us set Evan up, but he had.

So now I would do this. I might not know how to hack very well, but I was learning. Plus, finding and replacing all those mentions of Cyn's name had helped me learn a lot. Scripts were starting to make a lot more sense. I knew what a spider was. Even better, I was pretty sure I could code my own. Not good ones like we had available in the toybox, but one that would *work*.

But the next day, we all headed back to finish what we'd started. This time, Hottie didn't drive himself. Jeri went home to pick him up, which meant Ripper and I beat them there. It gave me the chance to test my knowledge as I searched the internet again, making sure no new references to our secret friend had popped up.

Sadly, the handful I found weren't enough to stop what I knew came next. It was Friday, which meant the start of the weekend, so we had all night to focus on these videos. I had a funny feeling that was why Hottie had really wanted to wait. He knew this part would be hard.

"So here's the problem," Ripper said once everyone was there. "We know these videos trigger Zoe. I'm not going to make her watch them."

"But I came to help," I insisted.

Jeri just waved me down. "I'm actually with Ripper on this. The last time we had to look at these, you said you'd be okay – and you weren't. I'm not saying that to make you feel bad. I'm just saying this is clearly a trigger for you. We all get it. We're also okay with it, Zoe."

Yeah, but I wasn't. I hated that I couldn't help as much as everyone else. I felt like the token broken girl everyone was mollycoddling to make feel better. I wanted to be a hero too, so there had to be a way to work around this.

"I don't like listening to them," I admitted. "Do we really need the sound?"

"I actually have a set of headphones, and I can work on the sound," Knock offered.

Hottie just murmured like he wasn't so sure of my idea. "Zoe, what are you going to be able to help with?"

Ripper turned to look at him. "There are two girls we need to identify. Zoe pretty much knows all of the girls at school. If there's anyone in this room who will recognize them, it's her."

"Still don't like it," Cade grumbled.

"Can I at least try?" I begged. "I promise I will speak up before it gets as bad as last time. Okay?"

"Let her try," Jeri told them.

Oddly enough, that worked. It was clear the guys still didn't like it. They also grumbled about how I deserved the chance and they couldn't stop me. Still, I was willing to call this a win. If nothing else, just because it gave me the chance to stop feeling quite so weak. Or maybe to define the extent of my limits. I wasn't sure, but the truth was I needed to do both.

Yet identifying girls wasn't the only thing we needed to do. With Ripper handling the videos, Hottie told Cade to help Knock go through the sounds. Somewhere in the background noise could be a hint that would give us what we needed - whatever that might be. Then Jeri and Hottie pushed their chairs over towards the computer Ripper was working on.

"Okay," Jeri said, "we're all gonna look for artifacts, reflections, or anything that might give us a lead."

"Uh..." Ripper glanced nervously at me. "I was going to look at the metadata mostly. I figured I could take screenshots of the video and crop out the girl's head to see if Zoe recognizes her. That way, she wouldn't have to actually watch the videos."

Okay, I actually liked this idea. The truth was that while I wanted to help so badly, I wasn't sure I would be okay with seeing the horrible things that were done to these girls. The last time, it had made me feel like I was about ready to pass out. Worse, it made me relive what Evan had done to me.

This? I could do this. It would be easy to look at a cropped image of someone's head. After all, I already knew what had happened to these girls. It wasn't like that part was a secret. My trigger seemed to be the similarities with what had happened to me.

"I can just turn my chair around," I offered.

"You sure you're okay with that?" Hottie asked.

Yeah, that earned the guy a few bonus points. The fact that he was thinking about my ego as well as the likelihood of me getting triggered? It kinda made me feel less weak or useless. It was almost like being traumatized by all of this was normal. Okay, so it made sense, sure. That was not the same thing as being normal.

I still nodded. "I'm okay with not watching the videos," I assured them. "I just want to help in some way."

"Well, let's start with the metadata first," Ripper said. "Zoe, you can watch for this part. It's just looking at the coding of the videos. No photo representation involved."

Unfortunately, it didn't take long to figure out it was a bust. Sure, Ripper was able to see the videos had been on a website, but that website was the KoG forums. We already knew about that part. Video after video, each time he looked, it appeared anything that could trace back to the guys who'd taken it had been scrubbed.

"Those fuckers know too much," Hottie grumbled. "Why couldn't the Alpha Team be a bunch of technological idiots?"

"Because KoG appeals to nerds," Jeri said.

"But these guys aren't nerds," Ripper countered. "They were the most popular guys at school."

"Because of football," I pointed out. "Okay, and they're all kinda cute. Combine the two and that basically makes them cool."

"And cool guys usually don't bother learning how to hack." Hottie sighed in frustration. "Okay, maybe not hack, but at least cover their footprints. Removing your metadata from a video the way they did?"

"KoG probably taught them," Ripper said. "I mean, these guys aren't that good. Sure, they play Flawed. Yes, they do decently in PvP. I'm pretty sure they all started on consoles, and there's no coding when it comes to that."

"But a lot of those first-person shooters on consoles have a pretty sexist community," Jeri pointed out. "It would be a perfect recruiting ground."

"Do you think KoG is actively recruiting?" I asked. "I always assumed these guys just kind of found out about it and trickled in."

Jeri lifted one shoulder in a halfhearted shrug. "Even if they aren't intentionally and actively recruiting, they're still recruiting. Some loser is going to tell some other asshole about the place because they share the same bigoted views. For all intents and purposes, that's recruiting."

"Do we even know how long the Alpha Team have been members?" I asked. "I mean, wouldn't that give us a timeline?"

"Not necessarily," Hottie said. "Things like this could go either way, Zoe. They did something horrible to a woman, liked the way the power made them feel, and so sought out supportive misogynistic groups, or being a part of that misogynistic group encouraged them to do the acts which made them feel the power they liked. It's impossible to know for sure."

"But could it be a lead?" I said, because that was what we needed – a lead.

Hottie just shrugged. "Maybe? But if so, then it's so vague I don't know where it would even take us. I think we have a better chance of figuring out who these girls are and seeing if one of them will talk."

"And say what?" I asked.

It was Jeri who had the answer. "That Dylan, John, Parker, Landon, or Wade raped her. Zoe, that's an accusation. If she makes an accusation, we have the video proof, and all of that can be given to the cops."

"Who are going to do nothing," I grumbled. "I had a video, and they did nothing. I was willing to report a rape, and they did nothing. Why would these girls be any different?"

"A pattern," Ripper said. "You already tried to report your rape, Amber has a video on her phone that says she was raped, and if another girl says the same thing, then that's a pattern. If it's one of *these* girls, then we have video evidence for all of you – and the cops can't ignore that."

"Are you sure?" I asked.

Ripper simply sighed. "No. It's just the best we have."

"Which is better than nothing," Jeri reminded me. "It might also help us figure out how they're picking their targets. You and Amber were dating one of them. Marissa wasn't. So how do they decide who they're going to abuse?"

"And that," Hottie said, "would give us a real lead."

I just nodded and turned my chair away from all of them. "Okay, let's do this."

I heard the mouse click a few times. That was it. Well, if I didn't count the little sounds made by Hottie's chair creaking or Jeri shifting uncomfortably. Behind my back, my friends didn't talk. In front of me, I could see Knock and Cade looking at graphs scrolling across the screen. It looked just like when they played some audio clip on the news.

Every so often, Cade would point at the screen and Knock would highlight a section. That bit of audio would be enlarged, which made me think enhanced, and then played over and over again, but I couldn't hear any of it. Both of the guys had on headphones, which kept the sounds between them.

I wasn't sure how long I watched them, but it felt like a while. This was interesting, though. The little graphic that represented the sounds was much more detailed than I would've thought. When they enlarged it, even more of those lines showed up. In the middle of a quiet section, there might be a large line. Other times, a relatively loud section might have a gap where there was almost no noise. Over and over, those seemed to be the places Cade and Knock were most interested in.

But while I was invested in that, it seemed Riley had come downstairs. I didn't even hear her until she cleared her throat pointedly. Confused, I turned to look at her, and it seemed I wasn't the only one.

"Yeah?" Jeri asked.

"Please tell me you're not making Zoe sit through that," Riley said.

"I'm looking over there," I told her.

"She wanted to help," Hottie said. "We're letting her set her limits."

It seemed that wasn't a good enough answer for Riley. "And did any of you consider this might be triggering for her?"

"They all did," I assured her. "I also promised I'd say something if I started to feel triggered."

"She did," Ripper insisted.

"And she's not that weak," Jeri said. "Zoe knows her limits. She also knows none of us will judge her for being traumatized by a traumatic thing. She wants to help, and I'm not going to take that power away from her – and neither should you. So you know, my best friend is one of the toughest people I know, and the shit she's already been through and stood up to is the sort of thing that would break most people."

"Okay," Riley said before turning to head for her room.

I had no clue what that was about, but it felt good. Jeri thought I was tough? One of the strongest girls I'd ever met in my entire life thought *I* was strong? That may have been the best compliment I'd ever been given in my entire life.

But as I turned around to thank her for it, Riley came back out of her room. Without a word, she walked over, pushing between all of us, and dropped a very large bottle of tequila on the desk.

"We don't have shot glasses in this house. Knock knows where the alcohol glasses are, though," Riley said. "So, if you're all going to do this, then I think you might need some liquid courage – or whatever you're going to call it. Personally, I think of it as my superpower elixir."

I nodded because I liked that. "You know, we can drink straight out of the bottle too," I told her.

Which made Riley grin. "That's my preferred method. It also doesn't mean you can't stop. This shit is hard. It's not supposed to be easy, but someone has to do it." She was looking right at me as she said that. "But we gamer girls are the kind who can handle it. Somehow, we always find a way to make it work."

I nodded, because I wasn't sure what else I should do, but that seemed to be enough. Riley turned and jogged up the stairs, leaving us to our mess. While I watched her go, Jeri had grabbed the bottle and was trying to open it. When she failed, she pushed it at Hottie in a silent request.

"Zoe might need a sip of that," she said.

"Because of the pictures?" I asked.

Jeri just nodded. "Ripper's got them all cut out and ready to go."

"And the actual videos are closed so you can't see a thing," he promised.

I just waited until Hottie got the bottle open and then reached out a hand. He passed me the tequila, but I hesitated before taking a sip. The last time I'd had anything alcoholic had been that night. *Now* I knew that Evan – or one of his friends – had probably put drugs in my drink to go along with the alcohol. I hadn't just been drunk or gotten raped, I'd also been drugged.

But I had to look at the next victims. The previous ones? Not that it mattered. We had all been through the same thing, and it sucked, so was taking a sip of this really the best idea?

I was still trying to decide when Ripper swiveled his chair around so he could see me. "If you have too much of that, I'll make sure you get home safe."

"Fuck that," Cade said from the other side of the room where he was clearly listening in. "If she has too much of that, she can have our bed for the night. Knock and I can sleep on the couches."

"We also have living quarters in the horse trailer," Knock offered, "and Riley has at least two blow-up mattresses. In other words, all of you can drink some of that, but if you drink you are not driving. One drink means you agree to let us take care of you."

And those words were enough to convince me to tilt the bottle up to my lips. It was tequila, so it burned like a motherfucker as it went down, but I didn't take a little sip. I gulped. I also felt safe enough to do it. I had to look at the victims and see if I knew them, so right about now, I seriously needed a hit of something to make me feel like I had "superpowers."

Then I passed the bottle back to Hottie. "You have the pictures ready?" I asked.

"My screen is safe for you to look at," Ripper promised.

So I turned my chair enough to see his screen. Sure enough, it was. Lined up, side by side, were four head shots of four different women. I recognized the first one as Amber, but it didn't really look like what I'd seen on the video the last time I watched.

Ripper had taken screenshots, rotated the pictures, then cropped out the girls' heads so they looked more like candid photos. They weren't lying down anymore. Now, like this, it was as if they were standing in front of a curtain that I just happened to know was actually a bedspread.

The problem was how many of them I knew. "The first one is Amber," I said, even though we all knew that. "The second one is a girl named Scarlett. She's one of the cheerleaders. Junior varsity, I think, but she might have made the varsity team this year. I didn't really keep track of that. I don't know who the third girl is, but the fourth one is definitely Marissa."

"Scarlett," Jeri said. "That means we have the name of another victim."

"But who's the third girl?" Hottie asked. "Could she be a freshman or something?"

"I don't think she goes to our school," I admitted. "Maybe she was at one of the parties with some friends? I mean, a lot of us know people from Denton, Krum, Gainesville, and the other little towns around here."

"So she could be anyone," Jeri said.

"Well, you could try posting her on Dylan's Facebook to see if it tries to get you to tag someone before you actually post it," I suggested. "I don't know if Instagram has a feature like that, but maybe facial recognition can help?"

"Put it on the Squirrel," Hottie told Ripper. "Put all of those on the Squirrel, and we'll have Jinxy work on that."

"And I'll see if I can talk to Scarlett," Jeri told us. "Even if she won't report it, maybe she can help us figure out how they're picking their victims. I mean, she didn't date any of them, did she?"

I just shook my head. "No. She's never dated anyone in Alpha Team. Jeri, you also don't have a way to get in touch with her until we're back at school on Monday."

"Which means," Hottie said, "it's one more reason for you to take a break from this."

"We all need a break from this," I agreed.

Hottie just gave Jeri a pointed look. "See?"

And from across the room, Knock piped up, "I think we all

need to do something fun tomorrow. Something relaxing. Nothing with Ruin. So whatever you're trying to chase with these videos, you better get it done tonight."

"We identified another girl," Jeri told him. "A cheerleader named Scarlett. She's girl number two."

"And right now, she's the only lead we have," Knock said. "So pass me that tequila, because I really don't want to listen to any more of this. I'm about done."

"Yeah," I agreed. "I think we all are. This shit isn't easy."

Knock just canted his head and lifted his shoulder. "Nope, but it's not supposed to be. This shit is evil."

CHAPTER 25

RIPPER

Saturday morning started nice and late. Surprisingly, while we'd all tried Riley's tequila, none of us had gotten drunk on it. Zoe had more than anyone else, but at most, she'd gotten tipsy. I'd still convinced her to let me take her home - after not having a drink for two hours. Now, I had to wait for her to get in touch with me for a ride back to get her car.

That gave me a few hours to get lost in my book. Once, I would've spent the day lost in Flawed instead. Now, it wasn't as much fun without my guildmates. Yeah, I knew the other guys in Death over Dishonor would be online, but they didn't hold the same kind of appeal. I had to keep secrets from them. Ruin secrets.

So, I read, I relaxed, and I tried my hardest to not think about the Kings of Gaming at all. It only worked so much, because the villains in my books reminded me of them. It was almost like all of these incel gamer guys were trying their hardest to twirl their mustaches or something.

But right around sundown, Zoe finally sent me a text. Her excuse to her parents had been that she'd been too tired to drive, so I'd brought her home. Yeah, I got that. My parents would freak if they knew Knock's house had an open bar policy, and Zoe's would likely be worse. Still, I got my shit together and headed over to pick up my best friend.

"Hey," I greeted her when she climbed into my passenger seat. She'd clearly been watching for me, since I hadn't even sent a text yet to let her know I was here.

"Hey," she beamed. "Jinxy said you're a good guy and I should appreciate you more, so thank you."

I just chuckled, because she'd all but explained away her day. "Oh, so you spent all day on the phone with him, huh?" I asked as I backed out of her drive.

"Discord," she admitted. "Easier, because my headset is wireless. He made us a private room."

"Which I can't see." I murmured, doing my best to give her a hard time. "Trying to cut me out of your life already, huh? Found a cooler boy and no longer need me?"

She grunted, then made a production of rolling her eyes. "Yeah, says the guy who's all into Jeri."

"Not the same," I pointed out. "I have to share her attention. That's why I almost made it through my book."

"Same one?" she asked.

I nodded. "Yeah. It's a bit dry."

"And you like talking to Jeri more." She twisted in her seat to face me. "You know, you should hang out with her more."

"She's always busy," I countered.

"Exactly!" Zoe said. "She also sucks at hinting that she wants attention, which means you should push more." The girl was almost bouncing in her seat, clearly liking this idea even as she came up with it. "Look, if you're scared of Hottie being there, I get it, but Jeri's not. And, well, you kinda need to remind her you're still around."

"I promise she knows," I mumbled.

Zoe just reached over to rub my shoulder. "So I'm right, huh? You're feeling a little pushed out?"

"No," I countered. "It's just that things have been a bit crazy lately. What with Cade, Amber, and now these videos? Never mind that Hot's the best one to deal with how Jeri's freaking about Amber dying."

"You should tell her how you feel."

Wait, what? That was *not* what I'd expected her to say next. It confused me enough that I almost missed the entrance to Knock's place. I didn't, but once I was on the drive, I dared to glance over.

"Where did that come from?" I asked. "Are you and Jinxy at the whispered words of love stage or something?"

She didn't answer until I'd parked beside her car. "Um..." She looked over. "We may have talked about feelings today." She grimaced. "Bad idea, right?"

"So you told him you're in love?" I asked.

Zoe quickly shook her head. "No! Oh no, nothing like that. It was more that I actually like him, and talking to him makes me giddy. That sort of stuff. And he started it." A tiny little smile took over her mouth. "He says he waits for me to call and turns stupid when he sees my number."

"You two are cute," I assured her. "I'm happy for you."

She looked at me for a little too long, then wrinkled up her nose. "So I'm not stupid for actually liking some guy I've never met before?"

"Sounds to me as if you like him for his personality," I told her. "Not his looks. Not his popularity or money or stupid shit like that. I think you actually *like* this guy, Zoe, and it sounds like he's ok with moving at your pace. Why would there be anything wrong with that?"

"But what if I'm not the kind of girl he wants?" she asked. "I mean, when he gets here."

"Then it's a sign it wasn't meant to be," I told her, hoping it was a good enough line to ease her fears. "If nothing else, you look happier than you have in months, so I think he's worth it."

"So there's nothing wrong with me going back home and waiting for his study group to finish?" she asked.

I flapped both hands towards the door. "Get out of my truck, girl. Go. Get home so you're ready when he is. You know that's what you want to do!" Then I laughed. "And keep being cute with him, Zoe. It looks good on you."

"Ok!" she giggled, grabbing her stuff as she slid towards the door a bit more. "Call me if you're bored?"

"Not gonna happen," I promised even as she got out. "Bye, Zoe!" But while I waited for her to get in her car and start it up, I also pulled out my phone.

> **Ripper:**
> Hey, you want company?

I didn't expect an answer right away. I should've known better.

> **Jeri:**
> Would love some! I've spent all day cleaning.

> **Ripper:**
> Your mom home or something?

> **Jeri:**
> Saturdays are usually clean days. We missed last week, so the house is a mess. Come save me!

> **Ripper:**
> OMW!

Next I sent a text to Cade, letting him know we'd stopped by for Zoe's car. He replied, letting me know Zoe had told Knock the same, they were still in bed, and no, he wasn't planning on getting out of it today. Yep, that meant they were being cute too.

So heading to Jeri's was a no brainer. When we pulled onto the main road, Zoe went left, but I turned right. That was the fastest way to circle back around town to Jeri's place. When I reached her house, I sent my dad a text saying I was going to be out for a while.

Dad:
What's a while?

Elliot:
Dunno. Hanging with my gamer friends.

Dad:
Just let me know if you're spending the night so I don't worry.

Elliot:
Can do!

Evidently, staying out late at Knock's place so much had earned me a few benefits. Dad hadn't asked where I was, so I decided I didn't need to clarify. He and Mom thought it was perfectly normal to have mixed-gender hangout nights now. The last thing I wanted to do was ruin that.

I was just finishing my conversation with him when I rapped on the front door. Of course, when it opened, it wasn't Jeri standing there. Nope, it was Hot.

"Hey, man," he greeted me, stepping back to let me in. "She's up in her room."

"She said she was cleaning?" Because I was now confused.

Hot just nodded. "I picked rock. She went with paper. Means I had to clean downstairs and she basically has to worry about her room, vacuuming the hall, and the bathroom up there."

"So, the easy stuff," I joked. "Yep, sounds like her."

Hot just grinned. "I also throw rock every time, just so I can spoil her a little. Don't you dare tell on me."

I couldn't help but laugh. "Promise. Just tell me she's handling everything ok?"

He made a face. "She's spiraling again. Starting to hyperfocus on results instead of living, and things like that." He tilted his head at the stairs. "So go up there and distract her, hm? Just make her think about anything except those girls?"

My brow creased. "That bad?"

"It's what she does," he explained. "Also, right after she heard about Amber, she said something about how she should've been working harder to help. Ripper, she's blaming herself for not saving them, trying not to, and doomed to fail unless she figures out how to relax and step away."

"Well, yeah, but I dunno what I - "

He clasped my shoulder, cutting off my protest. "She relaxes with you. Just make her relax?"

"I'll try," I promised.

So Hot let me go and gestured to the stairs one more time. Ok, I was starting to feel like this was predestined or something. No, wait. That was the plot of my cheesy sci-fi novel. This? It was just Jeri being Jeri. It was kinda what made her so amazing. The girl didn't know how to be either meek or mild.

When I reached her room, I tapped at the half-open door. "You decent?" I asked.

She laughed. "Nope!" Then she pulled the door the rest of the way open to let me in. "Hey, you! What's going on?"

Thinking about what Hot had just told me, I headed over to her bed and dropped down on it. "My book sucks. Zoe had me run her to Knock's for her car, so I figured since I was out anyway..."

She closed her door, then came over to lie down beside me. "Sounds like you need a better book."

"No kidding," I said. "It's just that I've been trying to get through this one for months now, so I'm committed. I also want to see how it ends." I turned my head to look at her. "And Zoe's blowing me off for some guy."

Jeri giggled. "Um, one in Colorado?"

"Yep." Using one foot, I began to push off the shoe on the other, planning to get comfortable. "I guess they're up to the feelings stage now, which is really good for Zoe."

"Feelings?" she asked, just like I had earlier.

I nodded even as I switched to get my other shoe off. "Yeah, you know. That whole 'I feel something but don't know what' stage. She's still worried he's not going to like her once he meets her, though."

"I think we all have that fear," she admitted.

Now shoeless, I shifted higher up on the bed, then opened my arm for Jeri to come closer. "Do you really?" I asked. "Not trying to make that sound bad, but I just figured you were the kind of girl who didn't care if someone liked you. You'd just move on."

She scoffed but did snuggle up against my side. "I care. Not about everyone. I mean, fuck Dylan and guys like him, you know?"

"Nope, we're not talking about them today," I said. "Today is a happy day. It's our time to relax, refresh, and regroup mentally."

Her eyes narrowed. "Have you been talking to Hottie?"

"He said something," I admitted. "Then again, so did Knock last night."

Jeri just groaned and rolled onto her back - yet still kept her head on my arm. "I just feel like I'm slacking if I don't figure this out. I mean, we know what those guys are doing. We know they're not going to stop. Worse, we know the system is all but designed to make it easy for them, since they're the cool boys. They have excuse after excuse handed to them, whether they need it or not."

"We're not talking about them," I reminded her.

She just looked over. "I'm talking about me," she insisted.

"No, you're talking about them." I smiled softly to take the sting out of that. "Believe it or not, Jeri, you're a lot more than some hacktivist."

"I'm kinda not."

"You are to me."

Her eyes jumped up to meet mine just as my heart stalled out. Shit, that hadn't been what I'd intended to say. It had just kinda fallen out. Fuck. What if I'd gone too far?

"What am I?" she asked softly.

Ok, this was safer. This gave me a lot of wiggle room, and I was going to use every single inch of it. Fuck, no wonder Hot had asked me to talk to her. I had a feeling she'd put him in this same position at least once. Probably more. It was like being dropped into a minefield and waiting for her to blow.

"Um..." I had to think fast. "Well, we all know you're a kick-ass mech pilot. I know you're intense in PvP, a damned good tactical advisor for the big guild missions, and a hardcore gamer. I also know you're smart. Maybe you don't think school is important, so you don't really try, but you easily understand all the stuff. You could make straight As if you wanted to."

"Too much work," she agreed.

Which made me smile, because I wasn't crashing and burning yet. "And you're not shy at all. You like clothes and makeup. Not the same way Zoe does, but you still like it. It's like you've got this hint of girliness about you that's pretty sexy."

"Yeah?"

I nodded. "I think so. I love the dreads and how you manage to always look beautiful, even if it's just an old t-shirt and jeans. I think my favorite thing, though, is how you don't give one single shit about the opinions of others. You don't make friends to be cool. You don't chase guys because they're popular. You also don't need us, which is kinda like some sort of drug that makes us need you."

"Only you," she teased.

"And Knock, Cade, or even Hot," I countered. "Hell, Dingo!" Because her guildmate wasn't subtle.

"Dingo would fuck a rock if it consented," she assured me. "Too many months of being snowed in up there in Canada."

"It's not really that bad up there," I pointed out.

"*He* says it is!" she laughed. "Oh, to hear his stories, he's been living in an igloo for the last decade, they haven't discovered electricity yet, and more. He loves telling us shit like that." But she also turned to snuggle up beside me again. "But that's the thing, Ripper. I've spent almost my entire life online. I don't really know how to do people without a computer between us."

I reached over to brush away the fine hairs by her face that weren't in her dreads. "Yeah, but you're a hell of a lot better at people than me."

"Bullshit."

Which made me smile. "I'm serious," I insisted. "In case you missed it, I'm a dork."

"We're all dorks," she countered. "So, try again."

But she'd moved a little closer, looking up at me in a way that made me want to kiss her. I couldn't help but turn just a bit so I was partially on my side but not crushing her. It made it even easier to mess with her hair again.

"Do you remember when we rode horses at Knock's place?" I asked, knowing she would. "Seeing you up on that horse, laughing like that? It's how I always think about you."

"Laughing?"

I nodded. "Yeah, happy. I couldn't stop thinking about how stupid I must look, but you? You were just having fun, admitting you had no clue how to deal with the horse, and somehow looking cooler because of it. And beautiful. Definitely beautiful. I think that was my favorite day, though, because we all forgot to worry about KoG and their bullshit."

"I'm not beautiful," she grumbled, rolling her eyes.

I pushed my fingers into the hair at the back of her neck and tilted her head up. "No? So you're saying I have bad taste in girls, huh?"

"No!" she tried next.

"Because I think you're beautiful," I promised. "I think you're amazing, Jericho. I'm also falling in love with you and I can't seem to stop."

Her gaze jumped from one of my eyes to the other as she looked for the lie in that. Too bad for her, there wasn't one. But when she began to smile softly, my heart took that moment to take off, racing hard for some finish line I didn't know about.

"I don't want you to stop," she breathed - and then leaned in to kiss me.

CHAPTER 26

JERICHO

As I kissed Ripper, all I could think was that this guy had a way with words. He always managed to twist things to the point he wanted, and this time that point was me. He thought I was beautiful? He was falling for me?

This should be the scariest thing he could say, and yet all I felt was thrilled. I wanted to tell him that when I said "like," I meant more, but I couldn't. Even thinking about how to phrase that made the panic start to rise. Admitting the "more" was a *hell of a lot* more? I wasn't sure I could do that without fucking up so much it ripped us apart.

So I kissed him instead. I touched him, letting my hands slide across the side of his face, down his neck, and over his baggy t-shirt. When he didn't try to stop me, I even hooked a leg over his thigh, pulling the lower halves of our bodies together so I could kiss him a little harder.

Because this I could do. I might not know how to say what I felt, but I could show it. Every touch was me desperately trying to make him understand how much he meant to me. Ripper had been there for me every time I needed him. He was the one who'd first made me feel like I wasn't abnormal. He'd been my friend without hesitation, and now that friendship had grown to something else.

Something big.

Something I could no longer ignore.

Something I wanted more of.

Pushing my hands under the bottom of his shirt, I slid one palm around to his back while the other moved up his chest. His lips flickered as he smiled into our kiss, and then his hand moved lower to grab my ass. I gasped playfully, pulling back so I could see his face.

"Fair's fair," he teased.

"Yeah, well, if you keep that up, I might end up ripping your shirt off and having my way with you," I warned.

"And what's the downside again?" he asked.

Damn, this guy was cute. I loved it when he was sassy, even if his little smile was more shy than arrogant. There was just something so completely honest about him. I always knew where I stood, and with Ripper, he made me feel like it was at the top of a pedestal - or maybe an ivory tower.

This guy made me feel like the girl everyone wanted to be: beautiful, perfect, and irresistible. More than that, he talked to me like I was worth listening to, as if I was a hell of a lot more than something to conquer and forget.

As if I was important.

"Hey," I breathed as I began tugging at his shirt. "You make me feel things, you know."

He caught my wrist, stopping my best attempt to strip him. "Yeah?" And those pretty green eyes of his found mine.

My teeth clamped down on my lower lip, but I jiggled my head in a nervous little nod. "Yeah."

"Jeri," he said, releasing my arm so he could cup the side of my face, "you don't have to say something just because someone says it to you. You know that, right? Not me, not Cade, not Knock, and not even Hot."

"I know."

"Not ever," he insisted. "You also aren't responsible for my feelings. You don't have to work around them or try to be careful with them. Just because I feel something doesn't mean you owe me a damned thing, ok?"

"Ripper, I know," I promised.

But his response wasn't what I expected. The guy simply smiled softly. The sweet kind as his eyes held mine. It was as if he was trying to memorize my face or something. Then, he swallowed.

"I..." His thumb swept across my cheek. "I already fell. I try not to put pressure on you, but I want you to know that. Jeri, I am in love with you. I have been for a while, and I don't ever want to stop."

My breath rushed out, but my heart wasn't racing. My palms weren't getting clammy. My ears weren't ringing. Instead, my lips wanted to curl, and the feeling in my chest was nothing like fear. It was happiness.

"I don't do good with words," I explained.

"I said you don't have to feel anything," he reminded me.

I just nodded, because I'd heard him when he said that. "I know, but..."

"Shh," he begged. "I just wanted to be able to say it once. I want you to know. I love you, and I kinda love how that feels. I love being your friend. I love being your partner. Most of all, I just love how being around you makes me feel like I'm not some stupid, dorky loser. You make me feel like I really am the knight in shining armor."

"On a big black horse," I agreed, catching my lower lip again, but only for a second. "Maybe kinda like my hero?"

"One of them," he promised before leaning in slowly.

I watched as his gaze dropped to my lips before jumping back to my eyes. That was enough to let my lids slip closed, and then our mouths met again. Soft, sensual, and gentle, he kissed me. It was timid. No, this was loving.

That was the best way to describe it. Ripper kissed me like I was his, and he wanted to learn every inch of me. He kissed me in a way that made me never want him to stop. His tongue explored my mouth, his hands held my body so close against his, and the soft murmurs he made proved he liked this as much as I did.

But I wanted to show him. Maybe I wasn't any good with words, but I didn't need to be. I was good at doing. I excelled when I put things into action. My pulse dropped lower in my belly as he kissed me over and over again, and I certainly did not want him to pull away or try to cool this down.

So I tugged at his shirt again. Lying on our sides, face to face, it wasn't exactly easy, but he wasn't fighting me. As soon as I got the fabric a few inches over his jeans, he let go of me to pull it off. That allowed me to lean in and kiss his chest. When his hands found the back of my head and neck, I loved it.

He liked this. I liked this. Yeah, maybe Hot was right and I did spend too much time online, because it had been far too long since I'd had my way with this guy. Yet when I reached down to unbutton his jeans, he grabbed my wrists again.

"Hot says we're supposed to use condoms," he reminded me.

"Those, off," I ordered even as I crawled off the bed.

Then I headed towards my makeup dresser. Pulling open the drawer with my nail polish, I found the little plastic case, opened it up, and ripped off one of the condoms from a string I'd hidden there. Hot said he'd gladly keep them in his room, but that idea sucked. Mine kept us from needing to ask - and getting embarrassed.

"I have four in here," I told him.

Which was enough for Ripper to push his jeans down, stripping his underwear with them. What he didn't do was get off the bed. Not even as he quickly yanked off his socks last, tossing them off the bed without looking away from me.

"Your turn," he taunted.

"Glasses," I reminded him while pulling my shirt off.

"Nope," he said. "Need those to see you."

I flashed him a smile before pushing my pants down. Socks came next, leaving me in a pair of red panties with a white bra, but who cared if they matched. Clearly, from the state of Ripper's erection, he sure didn't, and I liked that a little too much, so I peeled off those last two articles of clothing as fast as I could.

"Mm, now that is beautiful," he breathed before pulling off his glasses and lazily setting them on the bedside table. "Now give me that condom."

Oh, but I had a better idea. Crawling my way onto the bed, I tossed the little foil packet his way, then grabbed him right at the base of his dick. Ripper sucked in a breath, but that turned into a long, deep, and very low moan as my mouth slipped over the head.

"Jeri..." he begged.

I simply murmured before pushing a little more in. Slowly, taking my time about it, I swallowed his length, getting him all nice and slick before I slid mostly off. Then, the next time I pushed my way downward, my lips glided easily over his skin.

"Oh fuck," he gasped.

Yeah, that was the response I wanted. I might not be able to tell him how the definition of "like" had changed for me recently. Maybe I was horrible at admitting how much I cared, but this? I could show it. I could make him feel the way he made me. I could prove my feelings, because actions were much stronger than words.

So I sucked, adding gentle pressure as I bobbed across his length. When his hand fisted in the covers, I slid my own hand up before pumping back down. Bit by bit, I drove him higher, wanting to take my time about this while loving every second.

Some guys were quiet while getting blown. Some tried to act like it was no big deal until they nutted in my mouth. Plenty had tried hard to take over, fucking my face instead of letting me toy with them the way I wanted. Ripper was like none of them.

His hand found the back of my head, but not to push. His fingers tangled in the mass of dreads as he held on. When I pressed with my tongue or toyed with the head, he didn't try to hide his moans and groans of pleasure. He simply gave in.

I gave and he took. This was me proving my feelings, and it felt like he understood. Faster, slower, and as deep as I could take him, I sucked him off to the best of my ability, but when I glanced up, his eyes were on me. He was watching - no, staring - in awe. His lips were parted slightly and he was breathing heavily, but when our eyes met, something changed.

"Jeri..." he whispered.

So I pushed down his length again, sliding my fist and hand together. This time, his hips twitched, pushing him deeper into my mouth, but I could also feel his dick change. Thicker, maybe? Harder? I wasn't sure, but something. He had to be so close. From the strangled little sounds, I was sure of it.

And then his fingers tightened in my hair and he lost control. With a deep grunt of satisfaction, he came, giving me just enough time to shove him to the back of my mouth, and I swallowed. Then I swallowed again before giving him up just to flop down on the bed beside him.

"Need a minute?" I teased.

He laughed softly. "That? Yeah. Wow."

Then he rolled, grabbed me by the waist, and heaved me higher in the bed. I bounced as he let go, giggling once at the show of manliness, but it seemed he wasn't close to done. Ripper leaned in to kiss me, but I still heard the tearing of the condom packet.

"My turn," he said before sitting up to roll on that ring of latex.

I watched. I couldn't help it. I wasn't sure if I was supposed to look away or stare as blatantly as I was, but I wanted to see all of him. This guy - who was so sure he wasn't good enough - was gorgeous to me. I liked the shape of his belly. I loved the softness of his chest. More than all of that, I just...

I felt something very, very strongly for him. Something that made my pulse kick up as he moved between my legs. It was a thing that had me reaching for him and kissing him desperately as he gently pushed into my body. And when my fingers dimpled his skin, holding on much too tight, it wasn't just because he felt so damned good.

It was also because I never wanted to let him get away.

My sweet Ripper. My beautiful Elliot. My partner in this insanity we were calling life, and he loved me. He could say it, even if I couldn't, and that felt good. It felt like affirmation or something. It also felt amazing as he pumped himself into me, riding my body higher with every single movement.

So I bucked in time, rolling my hips to take him a little deeper. Beneath me, my bed creaked, the sound too soft to carry, but it matched the heavy panting of our breath. One of my legs hooked behind his ass, guiding him the way I wanted, and he didn't try to resist.

Instead, he leaned back enough to see my face. Shifting his hips, he found another angle, and then a different one after that. On his third try, he pressed against something inside me that made me want to come undone.

My eyes closed, my mouth fell open, and I forgot I was

supposed to be helping. Yeah, I moved, but that was simply this primal dance we were doing. My body understood, even if my brain was doing its best to short circuit. And when a moan of pleasure slipped out, I didn't try to bite it back.

"That's my girl," he whispered before reaching down.

His thumb found my clit, pressing between our bodies, even though his rhythm never slowed. Holy hell, how was I supposed to show him my feelings if he was taking over like this? How was I going to make him understand? Then again, I definitely did not want him to stop, because that was absolutely amazing!

"Ripper..." I begged.

"This is me loving you," he promised. "Let me, Jeri."

I nodded, feeling that pressure growing in my body. The one that came right before I came hard. "I do," I panted. "I definitely do."

Because that was the best I had, but it made him hesitate for a split second. That was all the proof I got that he heard me before he redoubled his efforts. Circling his thumb around my clit, thrusting into my body at that angle I liked so much, and watching me like he couldn't get enough, this guy made love to me.

Hot, fast, intense love that was like nothing I'd ever imagined. He played my body, worshiping it with every touch, every kiss against my shoulder, neck, or even my mouth. He watched me like I was a work of art, and he never once stopped.

Until I could take no more. Grabbing at his back, I clung to him as I came, forgetting about everything else. I didn't scream, but I did groan, the sound loud in the silence of my room. He kept going, kept thrusting, prolonging my pleasure until he finally gave in and gasped, collapsing down onto his forearm with our faces so very close.

And we were both breathing hard. I still felt his eyes on me, so I pried mine open, just to smile at the look on his face. Adoration, maybe? I wasn't sure, but it made something inside me feel like it grew a bit.

"You do?" he finally asked, leaning back so he could slide out of my body and claim the spot beside me.

I flopped an arm at the corner of the room. "Trash can for condom."

"Mm, thanks." He pulled that off, then tied a knot in the top and headed for the trash. "Jeri, are you ignoring my question?"

"Yeah," I decided. "Because answering it makes me anxious."

"Which is an answer," he pointed out even as he crawled back up on the bed beside me. "It's also a good thing."

"Yeah?"

He nodded. "Yeah. Because I think I might even understand." Then he reached over to push my hair behind my shoulder. "I'm also pretty sure Hot knows what we just did."

I blew that off and waved it away, my movements languid because this guy had blown my mind. "I guess this means you should spend the night, huh? Maybe so we can do that again?"

"Uh..." Chuckling, he leaned over the edge of the bed, rummaging out of sight. "What if I just want to talk and cuddle?"

"That's allowed too," I promised. "But so is the sex."

"Lovemaking?" he suggested even as he rolled onto his back, holding his phone. "And I'm going to need to get some backup on this."

"This?"

"Spending the night," he explained. "Some of our parents have issues with their son spending the night with his girl."

His phone dinged and his thumbs started again. On his face, a few expressions flickered, but the smile won out before he began swiping again and typing a little more. Eventually, he was done and tossed his phone onto the table beside his glasses.

"Cade says I'm hanging with him, and Dad's cool with that." So

Ripper rolled onto his side to face me. "Which means you have me all night long."

"Mm, but what if I want more than that?" I teased.

He leaned in to kiss my brow. "Then you can have more than that."

And I still wasn't freaking out. Nope, those words made me so very happy.

CHAPTER 27

RIPPER

I woke up in the middle of the night with my right arm tingling from Jeri lying on it, and my mouth was amazingly dry. Carefully, I managed to get out from under the still-sleeping girl beside me, and then I slipped off the bed. My underwear was right there, so I pulled them on.

The clock on my phone said it was just after four in the morning. The house was silent. First, I headed into the bathroom for a little necessary relief. Unfortunately, there wasn't a glass in there, so I decided to go down to the kitchen. My throat felt like the Sahara Desert. I'd probably been snoring like a freight train, and that wasn't exactly how I wanted to impress my girl with our first whole night together.

I wasn't really awake. In truth, I was operating mostly on auto-pilot. I'd been to Jericho's place enough I knew my way around, so my feet led me while my eyes kept trying to blink for just a little too long. But when I opened the cabinet to get a glass, a soft chuckle made me freeze.

And now, I was completely awake.

"There are bottles of cold water in the fridge."

Hot's soft voice allowed me to relax, but I realized the blue light spilling across the walls was from the TV. Worse, I didn't have a damned shirt on. Fuck, I didn't even have pants on! Just underwear.

"Uh, yeah," I mumbled. "Thanks."

"Second shelf, right side," he added.

Pulling open the fridge, I found it. Of course, this was some of his super-healthy shit. Still, cold water sounded good, so I claimed a bottle and then wondered how I was going to get out of here without this getting extremely awkward.

Hot somehow knew how to fix that problem too. "She still sleeping?"

"Uh, yeah," I said again. Clearly my early morning vocabulary was limited.

"Good." Then he sat up, proving he was sprawled on the longest sofa in the living room. "I'm assuming the fuck-fest went well?"

And there it was. My face immediately began to burn, but the darkness should help hide it. Trying to buy myself a little time, I opened the water and took a long gulp. Next, I cleared my throat, trying to get that crackling feeling to go away, and then I took another gulp.

"Why are you up?" I asked, because it was the only recourse I had right now.

Hot just waved to one of the chairs beside him. "Well, the truth is I didn't really want to listen to the moaning and groaning. Was doing an anime marathon." Then he paused to lick his lips. "She's ok, right?"

"She's asleep," I said, moving that way but too aware of my fat belly hanging over the waistband of my undies. "I was just thirsty."

Hot just nodded. "I have this fear she's going to die if I can't hear her moving." He breathed a wry laugh. "Which is fucked up, because it goes away when you're with her. Well, any of you."

He meant the guys, and I got that. I could also hear the honesty in his words. Maybe vulnerability was more accurate? Either way, this guy was offering me something - trust, friendship, or maybe even weakness - and I'd be a fool to ignore it, so I claimed the chair beside him.

"I shoulda grabbed a shirt," I mumbled, finding one of those decorative pillows to drop on my lap in a weak attempt to hide my body.

Hot just scoffed before lying back down. "I have this sneaking suspicion your girl is fine with how you look. I mean, it could be from the hours upon hours I've listened to her talk about how cute you are, the dimples, the glasses, or even how nice it is to cuddle with you. She says I'm pointy."

"Uh huh." I nodded, but couldn't really take this. "Hot, what are you doing?"

Tossing the throw off his body, the man stood and headed into the kitchen instead of answering. Like me, he was only in his underwear, which made me even more self-conscious. Seeing that, I almost took the chance to retreat. Sure, I liked this guy, but he was intimidating as fuck. He was Jeri's best friend. He lived with her. He was also "so hot" and "the sexiest man" Zoe had ever seen.

In other words, he was the guy Jeri would end up with. He was the one letting all of this happen. He was the man who could send me packing, and I had a bad feeling Jeri might actually listen to him. So long as I was good for her, I was allowed to "play my part," but if I ever screwed up, I knew HotShot would be the one making sure I paid over and over.

"So," he said as he made his way back to sit on the couch, "I'm trying to get used to this idea."

"Which idea?" I asked, since I was not keeping up at all.

Hot just gestured from himself to me and back a few times. "Us. Her. This. My other best friend says it's not normal for me to be ok with my girl fucking other guys. You, Knock, and Cade all seem perfectly ok with the idea. Knock and Cade are fucking each other, so that kinda makes sense to me, but us?"

"I'm not into guys," I explained.

He laughed. "Me either. I'm just saying I've been thinking about our situation." He paused to crack open his water but didn't drink. "And I kinda feel like you get me."

"Me?" Fuck, that came out like a squeak.

"Relax," he told me. "Ripper, I'm not trying to chase you off. I'm kinda working my way up to asking for advice."

"From me?" Because that still didn't make sense.

"Yeah, you. The guy who makes that crazy woman feel a little bit sane." Finally, he took a drink. "I mean, she's ok, right?"

"Because we had sex?"

"No!" He waved that off. "Because she's Jericho. Because she's got the tiger by the tail and doesn't know how to let go. Because that girl is a bulldozer who can't stop herself once she gets an idea in her head."

"You mean Alpha Team," I realized.

Slowly, he nodded. "The Kings of Gaming. Man, they killed Nina. It was a little group of shit-fuckers like these guys too. Just a handful of nobodies who decided she'd make a good target, and I couldn't stop them. I watched as this woman I loved tried to fight back, lost, didn't tell me, and began to pull into herself. Then, one day, she was just gone."

"Jeri's not like that," I promised.

"But what if she is?"

I shook my head to make the point. "She's not. She gets louder. She gets crazier. She does really stupid shit that will get her hurt, but she doesn't withdraw. Hot, I don't think she knows how."

He lifted his head and gave me a weak little smile. "I'm scared that one night she's going to do something. If I'm not there, if she's alone, you know? I have to sleep beside her so I can feel her still breathing. I need to hear her move. I just..."

"You're scared."

"Yeah." He huffed a weak laugh. "Scared shitless, man. I love that girl." Then he blew out his breath. "I also know how fucked up that is. I really didn't mean to. It's just that she was my family, right? She was the only person I had. The one who couldn't be taken from me."

"What about Jinxy?"

"Not the same," he admitted. "Shawn was in a juvenile facility. His internet time was restricted as fuck. I never knew if he'd get out and vanish, or if he'd stick around. Well, online, I mean. Back then, he didn't talk about why he was there. I had no clue he was as much of a geek as I was. I just knew about Jeri. And after Russel died..."

"Her dad?" I guessed.

He nodded. "Yeah. Losing Drake - her brother - broke her. Shit, it broke me too. Losing her dad, though?" He took another drink, this one longer. "She found him, you know."

"That's what she told me."

"But it was also the day her mom broke. Jeri called 9-1-1. She stood in the hall while they took his body out. Melissa couldn't cope, so that put it all on Jeri. Once her dad's body was gone, she spent all night scrubbing the floor and walls to remove the last of him. Fifteen fucking years old, and she would not stop until there was no trace left to upset her mom."

"Fuck," I breathed.

"And that was the first time I met her in person," he explained. "I called, and she talked to me while she scrubbed. She wouldn't stop, so I knew I had to help. I got a flight, made it to her place, and together we figured out how to manage a funeral. Ripper, the house was spotless."

"Ok?" Once again, I wasn't keeping up.

"I'm saying she does what she thinks she has to," he clarified. "She doesn't quit. She doesn't know how to slow down. She will never give herself the chance to rest, because the world hasn't given her that option. Now this? All I hear from her is how she's going to catch these guys, and..." He pulled in a shaky breath. "I'm scared she's going to decide it's too much."

So I leaned over my pillow and looked right in his eyes. "So give her something to lean on."

"I'm fucking trying!" He gestured at me. "Isn't that what you are?"

"I meant you, dumbass."

Which made him laugh. "Ok. Yeah. Point made. I just don't know how to shift our relationship that way."

"You don't have to," I told him. "She already thinks of you as her partner in crime. Her backup, in a sense."

"Well, yeah, but - "

"Shut up, Hot," I told him. "Listen to me. That girl?" And I pointed up in the general area of her room. "She's not weak. She's not going to back down. She sure as shit isn't going to be scared off by some high school boys - no matter how horrifying they are. She's going to seek and destroy. She's going to make them pay. I mean, isn't that what we're all so drawn to about her?"

"What do you mean?"

"Jericho is a bulldozer," I said, agreeing with his earlier statement. "You? Me? Knock and Cade? We're the ones meant to clear the area. We're the bumpers. All she wants is to be turned loose and know that when she's done being a little crazy we'll still want to wrap our arms around her and give her a nice place to relax. From everything I've heard, Jeri has spent her entire life doing it on her own and then being reassured it's going to be ok. That there's still a reason to care. That there are people out there who see all of her destruction and damage and still want to be near her."

"That she's not too much," he said as if my words had given him an epiphany. "Fuck, that makes sense."

"So let her go all out," I told him. "Follow behind her and pick up the pieces."

"No," he said softly. "Ripper, I think that's your job. Mine is to point her in the right direction. To guide her without forcing her."

"Mm..." Yeah, he had a point with that. "Just don't try to stop her," I warned.

Which made him duck his head and shove a hand into his messy hair. "I want to."

"You'll lose her."

"But what if staying with her fucks her up?"

I swore I heard a record scratch in my brain. "What?"

"Ripper, I've been her mentor. I'm the man she looks to for advice. What if I'm fucking her up by trying to make her what I want? What if I don't even realize it? What if I'm being some creepy-ass stalker who is manipulating her because she's young and impressionable?" He sighed. "What if I'm the thing that fucks her up?"

"You," I told him, "are her best friend. Never mind that if you start that shit, I'll grab Knock and Cade to put you in your place."

"Yeah?"

"You might kick my ass," I admitted, "or maybe even theirs, but you won't kick hers."

And the guy did the last thing I expected. He smiled.

"I think you're my favorite."

Again, I was thrown into confusion. "Huh?"

Hot just laughed. "I like Knock and Cade. They're good for her, but I think you're my favorite of her guys."

"You're kinda one of her guys too."

"Yeah, but I'm talking about you three," he clarified. "And you're good for her. You make her soft, Ripper. It's something she's never had the chance to be before."

"It's also not exactly sexy, ends up being called boring, and makes me the first one to get voted off this island," I pointed out.

Hot just shook his head. "Not with her. I have a feeling she's not looking to pick and choose. She's not going to be comparing us to find the right guy in the end. No, this is Jericho we're talking about. She wants it, so she takes it. This time, that means all of us."

"And you're good with that?" I asked.

It took a little too long for him to answer, and when he did, it wasn't at all what I'd expected. "I'm scared she's going to stop breathing one day. I want to hover over her, shielding her from anything that might hurt her, but I can't. I think *we* can, though. I think all four of us might have a chance to keep her breathing, Ripper. So, yeah. I'm fucking good with that."

"Even if it means I fucked her tonight?" I asked, braced for the worst.

Hot just shrugged. "Do you care that I fucked her a few nights ago?"

"Kinda."

"Same," he agreed. "Kinda. A little jealousy, but no hate. A little worry that she'll like you more than me."

"Me?" I laughed, shaking my head. "Not gonna happen, man."

"And yet I'm still worried about it," he told me. "Pretty sure you feel the same thing? That fear she might like me more, right?"

"Because you're *Hottie*," I reminded him. "You're the guy she's always wanted. You're..." And my shoulders slumped, because I was going all-in with this. "Handsome, fit, older, smart, and shit."

"And you think you aren't," he realized. "You know that's bullshit, right?"

So I lifted the pillow. "See the fat?"

"Not as much as you do."

Those words made me pause. "What?"

"You're not fat," Hottie told me. "You're probably healthier than me, because I work out to distract myself. It's an evasion, and not really a good one. No more than a girl starving herself to be tiny is a good thing."

"But it's what girls like," I mumbled.

"And it seems Jericho likes you," Hot said. "And me. And those other two fuckers." He smiled to show he didn't have a problem with them. "Ripper, not all guys have hard abs. Not all girls want a gym rat. I'm not safe because I have abs or whatever. I mean, shit. I don't have dimples!"

"Not the same."

He shrugged. "She thinks it is. All I'm saying is you should be proud of who you are. That girl is completely into you. She's struggling to deal with having feelings - yes, for you."

"She kinda said something about that tonight," I admitted.

"And my point is proven," Hot said. "Just help me make sure she keeps breathing?"

"Help me figure out how to be as confident as you?" I shot back.

He looked up, scanned my face, and then smiled. "Yeah, I think I can help with that. But you help keep me from panicking when I can't see her?"

"Like a team effort, right?" I asked.

Hot just nodded. "Yeah. Because when you're with her - any of you boys - I know she's going to be ok. It's crazy. It doesn't make sense, but it's still there."

"Trauma isn't supposed to make sense," I told him.

"Maybe not, but I'm kinda glad you came downstairs tonight." He put his water on the end table, then fluffed the pillow he'd been lying on. "Now go fuck your girl again, or something. At least curl up with her. For some strange reason, I kinda feel like my mind can shut up now."

"Yeah," I said as I stood. "Night, Hot."

"Night, Ripper." I made it almost all the way to the stairs before he added, "And stop thinking my opinion matters. It's all about hers. Next time I start being a paranoid ass, just tell me to shut up and fuck off, ok?"

"Not what partners do," I reminded him.

"And that," he said, "is why you're a better man than me."

I wasn't sure about better, but the compliment still felt good. Good enough that when I crawled back into bed beside Jeri, I had a smile on my lips. Hot had made his point. I wasn't trying to be him. I was the complement to him. I was the guy this amazing girl could lean on, and that meant I was the best at my own thing.

And I was going to make sure she never wanted to let me go. Any of us.

CHAPTER 28

JERICHO

I woke up the next morning with my face pressed into Ripper's chest. Somewhere in the night, he'd put on his underwear, but I was still completely naked. Yet as I began to stir, so did he. The sweet kisses on my cheeks, wordless touches, and soft smiles were the perfect way to begin the day.

But he couldn't stay too long. His excuse had been that he'd crashed with Cade. His parents expected him back at a decent hour, which seemed to be around noon. So, after a breakfast made by Hottie, Ripper kissed me one last time and slipped away, leaving me smiling wistfully.

"So," Hottie said as he gathered the plates to wash them, "looks like last night went well."

"Is that weird?" I asked - because it was still a little weird for me.

He just made a face and shook his head. "Nah."

"Give me more?" I begged.

I heard the dishes clatter in the other room, and then Hottie was back, pulling out the chair across from me. "You have an open relationship. Your partners are good with it. Where's the weird part?"

"But you're my boyfriend."

He just shrugged. "And? I've also known you longer than those boys. I've had the chance to weasel my way into your good graces. Or to convince you I can be trusted. You know, depending on your perspective and all."

I chuckled, because he had a point. "And it doesn't bother you if I sleep with Ripper? Like, right across the hall!"

He rocked his head from side to side as if he was thinking about that. "So, I may have slept on the couch."

"Hottie!" I protested.

He just lifted a hand. "That's a me problem, Jericho. Not a you problem. It's not even that I mind hearing your little sex noises."

"Ok?"

He groaned. "I feel a little weird about hearing his."

"Jealous?" I guessed.

"No, just weird," he admitted. "Not invited type of weird. It's one of those things we'll all have to figure out, and it will take time to do it. Jeri, I'm fine with you fucking the guy - or the other guys. I'm fine with you caring about them." He paused. "No, that's a lie. I love that you care about them. I like seeing you putting yourself out there. I feel, um... Relaxed? I dunno. It's just that knowing they'll take care of you makes me less worried about what might happen when I can't."

Ok, that all made sense. Sadly, it didn't do a damned thing to deal with the slightly awkward feeling I had going on this morning. Not that I regretted spending the night with Ripper. Nope, not at all. I'd even do it again, just on principle, if nothing else. That didn't necessarily mean it made this one of those things that felt natural.

It felt like I was cheating. Worse, it felt like I was cheating on all of them. Knock and Cade because we hadn't talked about it, Hottie because I'd ignored him last night, and Ripper because I was sitting here trying to smooth things over with Hottie.

"This is weird," I explained.

Hottie just nodded his head slowly. "Yep, kinda how polyamorous relationships work. But here's the thing, Jeri. It *is* working. I'm good with the guys. The guys are good with each other and me. And you know what my favorite part is?"

"What?" I asked.

He smiled. "You've started looking at those guys as if they aren't disposable. You smile like a girl with a crush. You even giggle at times - and not just when Zoe is around. You, baby girl, like them."

"Yeah..."

"And you deserve to like them," he went on. "You also deserve to do whatever you want with them. If that means screwing Ripper's brains out all night, then good for you."

I tossed myself back in my chair. "It wasn't like that!"

"Then what was it like?"

"Like the last time I was with you," I mumbled, almost hoping he wouldn't hear.

"Mm, so like making love, not fucking, huh?"

"Maybe?"

Hottie just pushed himself to his feet and grabbed a few more things off the table. "Jeri, that's a good thing. Stop trying to make your decisions based on what some guy would want. I taught you better than that. You do you. Do it loudly and proudly. Figure out what *you* want, and forget anyone who isn't ok with that."

"Yeah, but..."

"I will always be ok with it," he swore. "Now go have a damned shower. You smell like sex."

I didn't. Well, I hoped I didn't, but I still had that shower. I also thought about what he'd said. I thought about what Ripper had said to me last night, and the words I'd been so close to saying back. I thought about Knock and Cade, and how they were figuring their own relationship out, but always making sure I knew they hadn't forgotten me.

In other words, I thought about us. From Zoe and Jinxy's new-found "feelings" to my own. I thought about what I'd always assumed I wanted and how it had changed over time. Mostly, I kept thinking about my friends, Ruin, and how I couldn't imagine losing any of them.

It didn't matter if they were lovers, pals, or anything else. I'd gotten close. In the months I'd been living here, I'd given a little bit of my heart to all of them. Zoe was like my happiness, always reminding me there was nothing wrong with being a girl. Ripper was my safe space. Knock was my partner in crime, and Cade was the brute force who stumbled into the right thing most days. Then there was Hottie.

He was complicated. Once, he'd been my brother, and when Mom came home, he fell into that role again. Now, he was my boyfriend. He was my mentor, and not just with gaming. His words of wisdom were meant to show me how to live. He tried to make me think my way around things rather than just going off or reacting. He also was no longer the most important thing in my life.

They were.

All of them, as a whole and individually. Each of those guys was different. Every one of them had quirks and flaws, but that was the thing. We were all flawed, but we were not alone. Together, we made something amazing. Sure, that thing might be confusing and complicated. It was definitely a little messy, relationship-wise. It was still exactly what I wanted.

So why was I still trying to hold them at arm's length?

That evening, I decided to do something about it. Hottie and I were in Flawed. I knew Ripper and Zoe would log in soon enough, but Knock and Cade had been playing their other game a lot. It had to do with some convention coming up and how Knock needed to make sure he could place high enough. So, to get them all together, I grabbed my phone and started sending out texts.

They were all the same. They were all personal, not part of some group chat. They also went to my guys, and only my guys. While Zoe and Jinxy might be my partners, this time, I didn't need their input. Shit, it was going to be hard enough with just the guys.

Sitting in the room called Damage Control, I watched as everyone logged in and jumped into the room. The notifications dinged. The icons for each person lit up as they checked their mics. There were a few greetings and then it was all on me.

"Ok," I said, deciding to just hit this head on. That usually worked for me. "So, Ripper spent the night last night, and - "

"Which is why you needed cover," Cade broke in.

"How you holding up, Hottie?" Knock asked.

"Didn't know I needed to hold up," Hottie replied. "Besides, Ripper and I are cool."

"Yeah..." Ripper said.

"Nope, what does that mean?" Cade asked.

"That I'm blushing like a motherfucker!" Ripper shot back with a laugh. "Fuck off, all of ya."

"Sounds to me like you were the one fucking," Knock joked.

I just dropped my head into my hands as they went off, completely stealing my thunder. The strange thing was it also helped. The anxiety hammering at my chest was giving way to the stupid smile on my face at their antics.

"Yeah, and I'm pretty sure you did some fucking too," Ripper told Knock. "Don't go trying to embarrass me."

"He did," Cade said. "A little him, a little me, a little more him."

"Is the condom drawer a little less full?" I teased.

"Wait," Hottie said. "You two are using condoms with each other?"

"Riley," Cade said. "Trust me, when that woman decides to talk about sexually transmitted infections, she's damned good at all the gross details. I will never fuck without a condom again. I mean, she brought pictures!"

"She likes pictures," Knock explained.

"Big, gross ones!" Cade went on. "Genital warts and herpes. Like, that shit ain't right. Syphilis!"

Hottie was laughing. "Thankfully, modern medicine can cure most of those, but it's still a good idea. I'm a little more worried about pregnancy."

"Can't get pregnant," Cade reminded him.

"And I'm not fucking *you*," Hottie pointed out. "Or Knock. Shit, no offense, Ripper, but not you either."

"Good with that," Ripper said. "I mean, I definitely want all the giggles from Cade about his fuck-fest of a weekend. But I also do not want to be anywhere near another guy's dick."

"Not even for a threesome?" Cade asked.

"Nope," Ripper said. "Y'all can do all the kinky shit. I'll deal with letting Jeri sleep with her head on my shoulder. If that means less sex, then I'm good with it. I kinda like the kissing just as much."

"I like seeing her on a mission," Hottie said.

Knock laughed once. "I like threesomes. Jeri, Cade and I got you covered there. If Hottie ever gets brave, he can join in, because I'd love to see him naked. Won't even touch."

"Much," Cade joked.

Which made Hottie laugh. "You were supposed to mention what you like about her, not upstage the rest of us who are trying to make her orgasm on our own."

"Oh, right," Knock said. "You mean like her brilliant mind?

How she's as much of a geek as I am, and makes me feel like it's ok to be this big of a nerd? That sort of shit?"

"Yep," Hottie said. "Cade?"

Cade breathed out a weak laugh. "I just like that she's stronger than me."

Those words hung there for a little bit. I got the feeling no one knew how to respond to that, and I certainly didn't. I still liked hearing it, but I also had questions.

"I'm kinda not," I reminded him.

"Not physically," he clarified. "I mean the mental kind. The emotional kind. You, Jericho, have the kind of inner strength that is sexy as fuck. Ok, and I really like your ass too. Tits. Lips. Those blue eyes. I mean, I can keep going if you'd like."

"No!" I groaned. "Guys, I didn't ask all of you to pop into Discord because I wanted a compliment fest or anything."

"I started that," Hottie told me.

"So why did you ask us to log in?" Ripper asked.

"Yeah, um...." Well, shit. "I mean, you remember what we talked about last night?"

"I think so..." he said.

Yep, I was completely fucking this up.

But Cade inadvertently helped me out. "The rest of us don't know. Fill us in?"

I pushed out a heavy breath and decided there was no good way to ease into this. Sometimes, saying things was terrifying. Every instinct in my body told me to make a joke, say something about the game, or wiggle out of this. It also wasn't what I really wanted.

Nope, when things were hard to say, there was only one way to deal with that. I pulled in a deep breath, focused my mind, and just let all the words fall out as I exhaled.

"I keep saying I like you guys," I rambled. "I do, but you see, it's different now. I didn't want anything serious because serious is dangerous, so Knock made the polycule. That works. Oh my god, that works so well, you know? And I like it, and I like all of you, but that's the thing."

"What's the thing?" Ripper asked gently, clearly encouraging me.

"Like!" I huffed. "That's the thing. I mean, what does that word even mean? And I didn't want to get close because when I care about people, bad things happen - but bad things are still happening. And last night, I was talking to you, Ripper, and I realized that just because I don't say the words doesn't make a thing not true, you know? Redefining words to make them safe is just stupid and childish. It's not fixing anything. If any of you left me, were hurt, killed, or died..."

"What are you saying, baby girl?" Hottie asked, using the same tone Ripper had.

"Boyfriends!" I blurted out. "I want all of you to be my boyfriends, ok? I mean, it's stupid, and it's just a word, but it's a word that means something, and it's more true than friends. I still like partners, and I don't want to lose Zoe and Jinxy as my partners, but why can Knock and Cade be boyfriends and partners? They make it work, so why can't I? Why can't we?"

"Jeri..." Knock breathed. "You're really asking us to be your boyfriends?"

"Mhm," I mumbled.

"Are you sure about that?" he asked.

Hottie spoke up right after. "Is this you thinking you have to use that word, or do you really want to?"

"Jeri," Ripper said next, "we're all happy with whatever you want. We like this. Words aren't as important as actions."

"Yeah?" I asked him, thinking back to last night.

"Sometimes," Ripper said, "we all need a little armor. For you, that's avoiding words that make you nervous. We all get it."

"Yeah, but..." Shit. How to explain this? "I mean, like isn't like anymore. And friends isn't keeping any of you at a distance. I care, ok? I care about all of you, and it's that kind of care, and I like that it's that kind of care, so I kinda was hoping that maybe I can try boyfriends?"

"I'm in," Cade said. "I like boyfriend, but I'm not dumping Knock."

"No!" I huffed, sure I'd completely screwed this up. "That's not what I meant."

"I know," Cade assured me. "Jeri, I was teasing. I can have a boyfriend and a girlfriend. That's all I'm saying. I'm cool with it, and for me, it doesn't really change anything. I've kinda been feeling that way for a bit."

"Same," Knock added. "I mean, I get it. Hooking up feels like it should be safer, and boyfriend or girlfriend feels more like a promise, right?"

"Yes!" I said, because he'd just put my confusion into words.

"I'm good with boyfriend," Hottie said. "Might make it easier to tell the old ladies at work I'm taken if I can call Jeri my girlfriend."

That made me pause, because he was already my boyfriend. We'd agreed to that a week ago. Why wasn't he bragging that he'd been my first boyfriend? And yet, it felt like a sweet thing. Like he was making this easier for all of us, even if I didn't understand why it would work like that.

"Ripper?" Cade asked. "You good with this?"

Ripper just chuckled. "Yeah, I am. I also don't care if she can ever say love. Like is enough for me."

"I'm trying!" I insisted.

"And I'm being serious," Ripper assured me. "I'm pretty sure all of these guys will agree with me. Words aren't as important as actions, Jericho. You're not a word person. You're the kind who just does."

"You," Knock said, "are my partner. This is a polycule. We all have bonds, and those bonds are all that matter. That's why we work, Jeri, because we don't need to define shit or play by someone else's rules. We figure this mess out for ourselves. So if you need to avoid words, then do. You're still my girlfriend. You will always be my partner."

"Yeah," Cade agreed. "That. And one day I'm going to get to be the guy with the good lines. Promise."

"But today is not that day," I teased.

"Nope," Cade said, "but I still got a girlfriend out of it, so I'm calling this a win."

"Yeah," I breathed. "Me too, and I'm not even freaking out."

CHAPTER 29

JERICHO

When everyone logged out of Discord about an hour later, I was damn near bouncing in my seat. That had gone so much better than I'd expected. Never mind that the guys seemed to actually like my idea. Granted, boyfriend was a much better title than friend. It was the kind of word that meant something. The best part of all was that I *did* mean it – whatever "it" was.

I didn't want to think about that, though. Nope, I wanted to giggle a little about how well they'd taken my impromptu meeting. I wanted to brag that I now had four actual boyfriends. I wanted to stop worrying about the things that made me nervous and allow myself to just be *happy* about this for a little bit. So, to make that happen, I texted Zoe.

Jericho:
Hey, you busy?

Jericho:
Because if you aren't, I will buy you a coffee if you'll listen to me giggle about boys. I'm in serious need of girl time!

I waited, watching my screen for her reply. I really needed her to be around. Shit, what would I do if she wasn't? Or maybe she was busy talking to Jinxy and didn't want to go out right now? Yeah, I should've thought about that first. Crap!

And then her response appeared.

Zoe:
I'm all yours! Meet you at Starbucks in ten?

Jericho:
OMW!

After grabbing my shoes, I headed over to Hottie's room to let him know I was going out. He smiled at me, demanded a kiss first, and then reminded me I had school in the morning. Yeah, as if I could forget. Still, the way he looked at me was perfect. His smile proved he didn't have any problems with this polycule thing we were doing.

Yep, that was one more thing I wanted to brag about. Needless to say, I managed to beat Zoe to Starbucks, so I ordered for both of us. Even better, I knew exactly what she'd want. There was this strange comfort to being friends with someone long enough to know their coffee order, and I liked it just a bit too much.

Maybe I was just riding the high of things going well? I didn't know, but I wasn't about to question it either. Knock had been right to make us all take the weekend off from chasing the Alpha Team. And in turn, that meant Hottie was right. I needed to pause sometimes and enjoy my own shit, otherwise I wouldn't have things like this to celebrate.

But the moment Zoe walked in, she gave me a suspicious look.

Crossing the room, she slid into the chair across from me, accepted her drink, and then leaned in.

"Why are you grinning like the Cheshire cat?" she asked.

I rolled my eyes. "Because I'm having a good day!"

"Uh huh." And she lifted a brow. "Spill."

"I just asked the guys to be my boyfriends and they all said yes."

It took a second for my words to make sense to her. When they did, her entire expression changed. Zoe's mouth dropped open, her eyes went wide, and slowly, the corners of her lips curled higher.

"Boyfriends? All of them? Even Hottie?"

"Well, yeah, but I kinda asked Hottie to be my boyfriend a while back," I admitted. "I mean, he didn't tell the other guys that, and he knew I was kinda doing a trial run, you know?"

"Nope," she said, dropping her arms on the table to give me her complete attention.

"Well, it was the same weekend Cade got kicked out, and everything was crazy," I explained. "So, he said he wanted me to relax, and I said I wanted to test out boyfriend with someone who couldn't leave me - "

"Him," Zoe said, proving she was keeping up.

"Yeah. So that's been going well," I continued. "And then Ripper came over last night, and he kinda said he loved me, so I kinda showed him how I feel."

"Naked," Zoe broke in, grinning at me. "Uh-huh."

"Yeah, but then we talked about feelings, and he understood what I meant and I dunno, it just made me realize that maybe I'm being stupid, you know? Because no matter what, losing any of you would kill me, so why not go all-in, right?"

Zoe just nodded, and quickly, like she was trying to make sure I didn't change my mind. "Yep. I agree. All-in with the romance for you. And that dork didn't tell me he spent the night with you!"

"Ha!" I stuck my tongue out. "For once, I know something you didn't know!"

"But he'd tell me tomorrow," she countered. "So, like, it was an all-night thing?"

"Mhm," I agreed. "Sleeping curled up next to him and everything."

"And the loving you part?" she pressed. "Jeri, are you actually ok with that?"

Yeah, that made me pause to take a sip of my coffee. "Um, yes and no. I mean, yes, I'm ok with it. I love the idea. It also makes me nervous, but that's just habit, you know? This is Ripper. He's not going to do anything, and I'm hoping that with Ruin being all of us, and this whole thing working like it does, that maybe nothing too bad will happen to him."

"Jinxy and I have your back too," she promised. "But now for the hard question. Do you love him back?"

"I..." My throat clenched. "He..." Nope, that wasn't any easier. "It's like..." And I sighed, because this was fucking hard. "Maybe?" I tried.

Zoe reached across the table to rub my arm. "Yeah, that's a pretty good answer. So, you like the guy a lot, you're freaking out over the idea of maybe being in love with someone - "

"But I say it to Hottie all the time," I countered.

"And he's been in your life forever," she pointed out. "Jeri, we all know this is a thing for you. It's ok. I'm just trying to figure out what you're doing and what you're really wanting."

"To be able to say it," I muttered.

"That," she told me, "is a good thing. So, maybe you do feel something for these guys?"

"Definitely something," I agreed. "The problem is that I don't know how to know if I'm in love with them. I mean, is it just really strong like? Is there some banner that drops from the sky and tells me when I'm there? How can I be sure I'm not guessing it's love and then fuck everything up and then I'm the one chasing them away?"

"You don't get a banner." She shrugged. "That's the shitty thing about relationships, you know? All you can do is go off what you know about a person. You decide if you like them enough to want to keep seeing them. And eventually, you reach a point where you feel so strongly for them that like just isn't cutting it."

"It's kinda not."

Which made her smile. "So you love Hottie, right?"

I nodded.

"And you've said you love me," she went on.

Again, I nodded.

"Do you like me more than Ripper?"

My mouth dropped open. "Zoe! No! I mean, he's amazing. Well, and he's really good in bed, but that's beside the point. He's just this wonderful guy who is always so sweet and kind and caring with me. It's like there's this trust between us I know isn't going anywhere."

"No, no, no, no..." she said, waving a hand to slow my roll. "Just a yes or no answer, Jeri. Do you like me more than Ripper?"

"No."

"Do you like Hottie more than Ripper?" she asked next.

This time, I just shook my head. "They're different, but not better or worse, you know?"

"And yet you just said you love me and you love Hottie," Zoe reminded me.

All the little puzzle pieces fell together as her questions suddenly made sense. Ok, it was more true to say they slapped me upside the head like a sledgehammer, but this was why I loved Zoe. This was why she was one of my best friends. No. Wait.

"But you and Hottie are my best friends," I told her. "Does that make a difference?"

"Does it?" she asked, grabbing her drink just to lean back proudly.

Which made me chuckle, because we both knew the answer. "No," I said. "It's just easier to say that word with you two because it doesn't feel as heavy."

"Like it's going to break things, right?" she asked. "Like admitting you love someone might chase them off? Trust me, I get it. Jinxy and I have kinda been talking about our feelings, and I keep thinking about that."

"That you love him?" I asked.

She shook her head. "No, not yet. I mean, it's more that I could, you know? I talk to this guy all the time now. I tell him about pretty much everything - even the shit I'd normally never admit out loud - and he just keeps coming back for more. He's amazing. Fuck, Jeri, he's perfect, but he's also kinda not real."

"Oh, he's very real," I promised.

She scoffed. "You know what I mean. Right now, he's just a disconnected voice that matches with some amazing pictures. What if all I'm seeing are the good things? What if he has tantrums that are dangerous, or he can't stop picking his nose, or maybe he farts all the time?"

I had to laugh at that. "Ok, I mean, he is a guy..."

"See!" she said, thrusting both hands out towards me. "That's my point! But at the same time, he's kinda amazing. I really like him, and I like talking to him."

"How's Gran doing?" I asked.

Zoe just shook her head. "Bad. Even worse, she doesn't want her kids coming down yet. She said she doesn't want them all sitting around while she's sick, but I think she's more worried about being in their way. From the sounds of it, she has a lot of kids she's taken in, and yeah. Jinxy says they're hoping for the best, but the nurses say it's not going to end well."

"Fuck," I grumbled. "Well, just make sure he knows my place is always open to him, ok?"

"I will," she agreed. "I'm also not going to bring this moment down with his bad news. I mean, you have boyfriends now, right? Plural? How'd that go?"

So I told her all about our little Discord chat, and how I'd basically just blurted it all out. The whole time, she was grinning at me. From the look on her face, I was clearly missing something.

"Ok, what?" I demanded.

"They love you," she teased.

I groaned. "Zoe..."

"No, seriously," she insisted. "And you love them back. I'm pretty sure you love all of them, just for being them. You love Knock and Cade, which is why you're so happy for them to get together with each other. You love Ripper because he's kinda lovable. You love Hottie for being your best friend and kinda sexy. But think about it. That means you love them all."

"Well, yeah, but - "

She just pointed at me. "And there it is."

Because I'd agreed. That one little word had been all she needed to get out of me, and the best part was I didn't really want to take it back. I had exactly zero urge to explain how her points didn't mean I should use the L-word, but Zoe had just worked right around that.

"Can we keep that to ourselves?" I asked instead.

She nodded. "Yep. But now *you* know it. That's all that matters, Jeri. You know you feel something, and maybe it's not love yet. Maybe it is. Maybe it's just a complete obsession, or trust, or anything else, but you feel something and you aren't trying to push them away because of it. That's a good thing, right?"

"Yeah," I breathed. "I really hope it is, at least. I mean, with all the shit that's going on..."

"Then you need some guys you can trust at your side," she

finished for me. "Jeri, you've gone from friends, through trusted friends, and now you're working on this new thing. Go all-in, girl. Stop trying to play it safe."

"That's kinda my problem," I admitted. "I keep thinking my curse is going to fuck with someone."

"And we've all been fucked with," she countered. "Hottie lost Nina. I got raped. Ripper was bullied so bad. Trust me, this year is good for him. Cade got kicked out of his house, and how many times has he been beat up? Then there's Knock."

"Who hasn't had much shit," I reminded her.

"Who's had more than you know," she told me. "His family kicked him out. He lost everything and then found something better. Shit, he's told this story enough. Jeri, someone shot up his house! I mean, how much worse can it get?"

"Yeah..." I breathed, thinking about it.

Because maybe that was what made all of us ok? Maybe our flaws really were our superpowers? Could it be that the shit we'd already waded through gave us some kind of life armor? And if not, would believing it was true help my stupid, fucked-up mind stop worrying about it?

"So this is ok?" I asked her.

"This," Zoe told me, "is amazing. I have a boyfriend. You have four. Maybe we're breaking our own rules about no boyfriends in high school, but I think we can be forgiven this time."

"Definitely," I laughed. "I mean, how can I say no to all of them?"

"*You* asked *them!*" she reminded me. "And good for you for doing it, but that isn't the same as 'saying no.'"

"Well, yeah," I agreed. "But still. I have these four guys, and they're all ok with me having the others?"

"And me!" she insisted.

"And you, and Jinxy," I added.

Which made her grin. "See, it's like one big happy family.

Maybe our polycule is kinda fucked up. Maybe this isn't how we're supposed to do it, but who the fuck cares? We're also not supposed to do half the shit we've been doing, you know?"

"Yeah," I said, thinking about the girls on those videos. "Zoe, how am I supposed to talk to Scarlett?"

She blew out a heavy breath. "Gently, I think. Like you're on her side. Do not accuse her of anything - not even failing to report it, because if you'd done that to me, I would've lied my ass off."

"Won't she do that anyways?" I asked.

"Maybe," Zoe said, "but if we don't ask, we're stuck again. I also think saying Amber sent you the tapes after she died might help."

I nodded. "Ok, because we have to fix this. I mean, I feel like I'm fucking around with my guys, having fun while everyone else is watching their lives burn to the ground."

"Yeah, but that doesn't mean you should burn yours just to fit in," she countered. "Jeri, I'm with Hottie on this. You can't save everyone. Some of us weren't ready to be saved yet. I mean, I wasn't. Not until I had no other choice."

"But won't Dylan and his friends just target someone else?"

She shrugged. "Maybe? I mean, their parties are done. Hopefully that's enough to kill their plans, right?"

"And if it's not?" I asked.

She grabbed my hand. "Then you still need to take care of your guys, Jericho. Not just strangers who get shit on by assholes, but also the guys you care about. Make sure they know they aren't throwing themselves into your project for nothing."

"Ok." Because what else could I say to that?

Which made her smile sadly. "And be happy sometimes. What good is fixing the rest of the world if you're miserable because of it? Can't we figure out how to get revenge and be happy?"

Which made me nod. "Ok, yeah. I like that. We're going to get revenge and be happy, because being happy will just piss Alpha Team off more!"

"To happiness - and boyfriends," Zoe said, lifting up her drink.

So I tapped my disposable cup against it. "To boyfriends, because they make the rest of this shit worthwhile."

CHAPTER 30

JERICHO

I made it back home early. This time, Hottie didn't even try to pretend he was sleeping in his room. Nope, when I went to bed, he joined me, called me his girlfriend a few too many times, and kissed me in the softest, most amazing way possible.

But while all of this should've been proof slowing down made things better, the only thing I could think about was how something could happen to them now. These guys were my boyfriends. Zoe was my best friend. Jinxy was Jinxy, and his own horror was already descending on him as his gran's health failed.

In other words, it made me want to fight, but fight what? Alpha Team, sure. That was a no-brainer. The real question was how. Punching them in the face sounded damned good, but it wouldn't exactly accomplish anything.

No, I needed a plan. I had to figure out some way to protect my crew. The people of Ruin were more to me than just friends, and I'd actually admitted that out loud now. It was out there, in the universe, which made me nervous in a way I didn't like at all - and yet I liked too much. Sadly, emotions sucked at making sense.

I was thinking about my options as I got to school the next morning. Knock's FBI friend, Cyn, had to have some ideas, right? Granted, he'd been shot, so I needed to be patient. The guy was in the fucking hospital. Still, he might be able to give us a path, and until then, we had Amber's videos to worry about. They had to be useful for more than just seeing too much sick shit. I was so lost in my thoughts I wandered up to our normal table on auto-pilot.

Then, "Hello, girlfriend," Knock said, cupping my face with both of his hands so I had to look at him.

A smile immediately claimed my lips. Boyfriend. Progress. The most amazing guys I'd ever met, and all four of them were willing to put up with my shit? Yeah, there was nothing at all bad about that!

My eyes met his, his gaze dropped to my lips, and then Knock leaned in to steal a long, slow, deep kiss. I felt a hand on the small of my back and relaxed into it only to have another mouth caress the side of my neck. A different mouth. One that was not the same as the one currently stealing my lips.

"Hello, girlfriend," Cade breathed against my skin a second before his body pressed up against mine.

Knock shifted closer, pinning me between them without giving up my mouth. Yep, I moaned. Fuck, there was no other way to make it clear how ok with this I was. Maybe we were at school, and I was pretty damned sure a lot of people would see, but that only made it better. That made this feel like bragging, and these guys were definitely the kind worth bragging about. Each and every one of them. Reaching back, I hooked Cade's waist, holding him there. My other hand slid up Knock's chest, and I gave in, letting this happen.

"Enough!" Zoe groaned. "Jesus, guys! Get a room or

something. You're giving the female population of Sanger High too many ideas."

"Good," Cade said before stealing one last kiss against my neck. Then he stepped back.

Knock stole a little peck and did the same, but he didn't let go of my arm. Yeah, that was a good thing, because I may have swayed a little. Hopefully, no one noticed.

"So, that happened," I said, trying - and failing - to regain my cool.

"It's the girlfriend thing," Ripper told me from where he was sitting beside Zoe. "We're down for it."

"And you do realize someone's going to try to make this a bad thing?" I asked, looking at each of them to make it clear that was an open question.

"So?" Cade asked.

I thrust out an arm towards Ripper. "He's been bullied enough!"

"Jeri," Ripper said, "I'm good with it. I mean, what can they say? That I'm gay? Well, if so, then I wouldn't be fucking you. That I'm desperate, taking sloppy seconds, or whatever crap people think will hurt? News flash, there's nothing wrong with not being a girl's first. That you're using me? C'mon, I know better than that."

"Yeah, but I don't want you to get shit," I mumbled.

"Her thing," Zoe explained. "She made you her boyfriend, and now her curse is supposed to kick in, remember? You getting bullied might be the curse."

"Ah..." He thrust out his lower lip and nodded. "I'm good with people thinking I'm getting boned by two cool guys. I'm not, but doesn't hurt my ego any. I'm down with people thinking some hot girl is jumping on my dick. This isn't the sort of thing that will hurt, Jeri, so it's ok."

"And no one fucks with my best friend," Cade added. "I got his back."

"Me too!" Zoe said.

"Chopped fucking liver," Knock grumbled, clearly joking. "But seriously. It's cool, Jeri. We also talked. So you know, the three of us actually like the idea of being able to admit this is a real thing. You know, not having to hide our relationship and all."

"One," Cade said, holding up a finger. "Singular. One relationship. Us. All of us - including Zoe - are together. No one needs to know how that together part works."

"So Zoe's my girlfriend now?" I asked, trying to make a joke of it.

"Well, I'm sure not a boy!" she huffed. "Yes, Jericho. I am your girl-friend. If people want to hear that as a lover, then let them. Who fucking cares? We are a polycule. We do us. The doing and the us parts can be left to the imagination. See? I can play on words too."

"Ok, ok, ok," I relented. "I mean, I'm good with being able to kiss on three guys at school. Doesn't bother me at all. I just didn't want to make things hard on anyone else."

"Definitely hard," Knock mumbled as he tugged at his jeans.

I just pointed at Cade. "Blame him!"

Which made everyone laugh, but it was nice. This was us. This was our new balance. This was what it meant to have boyfriends, and the guys were clearly taking this seriously. The title was a step up for them, and it wasn't as if the whole school hadn't already known we were kinda doing a thing before, so why was I worried?

Because worrying was what I did. It usually came right before some bone-headed move that either got me in shit or someone else hurt, and that was my big fear. I really didn't want my guys to suffer because they were with me. Ok, and logic said that was my own trauma speaking, so I did my best to ignore it.

Claiming a spot on the table beside Zoe and Ripper, I leaned over my knees. "Ok, so while I hate to admit it, I think taking the weekend off was a good thing."

"Uh, because boyfriends?" Ripper asked, bumping me with his shoulder.

I bumped him back. "Maybe..."

"And," Zoe told the guys, "Jinxy says that Hottie said that Jeri's working on an ulcer with her obsession over Alpha Team." She flashed me a smile. "Jinxy also said Hottie's a worry-wart, take his paranoia with a grain of salt, and to remind you that hacking isn't magic. It's just researching in places we shouldn't be looking."

"That's what makes Jinxy a bro," I told her. "Yep, he's clearly on my side."

"He's also trying to use facial recognition to find girl number three," Zoe said, leaning in a little closer so she could point off towards the football field. "But the blonde in the pink shirt? Yeah, that's Scarlett."

I followed her finger to see a group of girls heading towards the school with gym bags hanging off their shoulders. All of them looked freshly made up and beautiful, but they were coming from the direction of the football field. Considering football season was over, I was definitely confused.

"Uh..." I glanced to Zoe. "They're still doing cheer practice?"

"Basketball," Knock said. "Pretty sure that girl's not a senior either."

"She's not," Zoe agreed as she slid off the table. "So, are we doing this, Jeri? I mean, not like there's going to be a better time."

"We?"

She just jerked her head in a gesture for me to get moving. "Jeri, motivate! Let's go!"

"Ok," I muttered as I grabbed my bag. "Kiss me later, Ripper?" And then I was off, trailing after Zoe like I had some clue what was going on. I didn't. "What are you doing?" I whispered when we were a few steps away.

Zoe just shrugged. "You have the tact of a bull in a china shop. I know what this girl went through. So, I'm helping."

"Zoe..." Because that hadn't gone over well with the videos.

She glanced at me quickly, then forward again. "Jeri, this is something I really can help with, ok?"

"Ok," I relented. "I'm following your lead here."

And just like that, my best friend's shoulders settled a little better, her spine straightened, and her head came up. It wasn't much, but she looked prouder, maybe? I just had no idea if it was real or her faking it, but I had a funny feeling I was about to find out.

"Scarlett?" Zoe called as we reached the edge of the building.

The pretty blonde looked over with a smile on her face that began to wilt when she saw us. A moment later, her brow creased. "Yeah?" she asked.

"Hey, I have a question for you," Zoe told her. "Can we get a second alone before class?"

That crease on the girl's forehead got deeper. "Uh, sure? I mean, is this about the cheer tryouts? I thought you were a senior?"

"Not for me," Zoe explained as she waved to the side. "And I kinda... it's a little embarrassing, ok?"

"Yeah, um, ok," Scarlett said, giving her friends a look. "I'll meet you in a minute?"

"We'll be right over there," her friend promised, pointing to the edge of the student body.

"Perfect, thanks," Scarlett said before wandering back the way she'd come with Zoe and me. "Uh, you're Jericho, right?"

"Yeah," I said. "Evidently everyone knows my name."

The girl laughed. "It's the hair. Well, and the rumors."

"Rumors?" I asked, latching onto that.

261

Zoe gave me a dirty look, but Scarlett missed it. "Yeah, that you're dating more than one guy. I mean, you know, some people have opinions."

"Oh!" I nodded. "Yeah, I'm with three guys here at school. Boyfriends. It's a polycule."

"Consensual non-monogamy," Zoe said. "Open thing, you know? And speaking of that, um, the reason I kinda wanted you alone is to ask about a guy you may have hooked up with."

"Why?"

"Because..." Zoe looked at me as she faltered.

"Did you know Amber Callihan?" I asked instead.

Scarlett's eyes widened just a bit. "Yeah. We were on yearbook together."

I just nodded. "The day her death was announced at school, I got a package from her. Scarlett, it had videos."

"Like mine," Zoe said. "That's why Amber sent them to us. She wanted us to do something about it."

Scarlett had gone pale, but her chin was just a little higher, almost like she was trying her hardest to pretend nothing was weird about this talk at all.

"It?" she asked.

"The videos of girls who'd been drugged with ketamine and raped," Zoe said. "Four of them, plus there's the video of me. The FBI have that now, and Evan's in jail, but the rest? They aren't. Scarlett, we need to know what happened if we want to make those bastards pay."

"I don't know what you're talking about," she breathed, the words coming out weakly.

Zoe gently rubbed the girl's arm. "You do. We know you do and you know you do. We also get that you might not be ready to talk about it, but you're not alone, ok? Those nightmares that don't make sense? The memories that seem impossible? That's because of the drug they used. It makes you go limp, so you couldn't have fought back, or run, or even screamed."

"They drugged me with it too," I told her, "but my guys were there. They got me home."

The sound of her swallowing was loud. The rush of her breath that came next felt even louder. For much too long, Scarlett stood before us, her eyes jumping from Zoe to me and then back. Then, it seemed she made her decision.

"I haven't told anyone," she said, her voice soft enough it was hard to hear.

"I didn't either, for months," Zoe assured her. "Trust me, I get it. It's just that they can't be allowed to get away with this. Is there any way you'd be willing to report it to the police? I mean, we have a video that's proof."

"No!" Scarlett hissed, taking a half-step back.

I lifted both of my hands. "And that's a valid answer. Will you at least answer some questions?"

"Like what?"

"Like how you ran into them?" I asked.

"It was one of their parties," she explained. "Wade was flirting with me, and the girl he was with at the time was being a bitch. John and Amber were there, and um, a few other friends from the team and the squad, you know? We'd won that game."

I nodded to show I was keeping up. "But you weren't dating any of them? Or maybe things with you and Wade heated up?"

"No," she insisted. "Not like that. I was picking on him about his girlfriend. I think I called him a shitty boyfriend or something. Told him that if he pissed her off, he was supposed to make up for it. And, um, we were all laughing. Ok, and drinking."

"Where'd you get the drinks?" Zoe asked.

"From the team," Scarlett explained.

"Anyone in particular?" I pressed.

"Not really." She pulled in a breath. "John, Wade, Dylan, and the main crowd, you know?"

"Landon and Parker," I finished for her.

"And probably Evan," Zoe said.

Scarlett just nodded in agreement, but her movement was fast. Nervous. "And then things got weird, and I was drunk. John said I could crash on the sofa so my parents wouldn't be pissed. I figured that was ok, since Amber was there, but then she left, and before I knew it, we were all alone. That's about the time things got really weird."

"I saw an elephant," Zoe said.

Scarlett nodded. "Yeah, that kind of weird. I was flying through the rooms, like Icarus. Hell, I barely even remembered that myth before that night. And when I moved my hands, I saw colors radiating off them. I was laughing at first, until they threw me on the bed."

"And then it turned into a nightmare," I finished for her.

She nodded again. "I don't really remember more than bits and pieces after that."

"Where did you wake up?" Zoe asked.

Scarlett just licked her lips. "On the couch, just like I'd been when Amber left. Dressed and everything, but I hurt. I knew it hadn't been a dream because I could feel it, you know? Between my legs."

"Yeah," Zoe said softly, "I know."

"And I pretended like I didn't remember anything," Scarlett went on. "I complained about getting blackout drunk, that my parents would be pissed and shit. Wade gave me a ride home and I managed to sneak up to my room, but yeah. I never once let anyone know I suspected anything happened."

"Then we'll try our hardest to keep you out of it," I assured her. "Just know this might blow up."

"Wait." She looked at Zoe. "Because of your case?"

"Because we're pretty sure there are more than ten people they've done this to," Zoe told her. "A lot. It's a serial thing, and I have no fucking clue what happens when the cops bust something like that."

"Shit," Scarlett mumbled. "So it wasn't just us?"

"Not even close," I told her. "We just want to make sure you're kept in the loop, because no one deserves this."

"Yeah," the girl said, glancing over at her friends. "Thanks, I guess?" Then she took a step that way. "Um, if you can leave me out of it..."

"We'll try," Zoe promised, "but the guys have videos. If the cops find those, it's not because of us."

"I'm sorry," I told her.

She gave me a weak smile. "Yeah. Me too. I'm going to tell my friends you two know someone in middle school who wants to get into cheer, cool?"

"Works for me," I promised, but Scarlett was already walking away, stretching her legs as far as they would go.

"Another bust," Zoe said as we both watched her leave.

"But information," I pointed out. "Zoe, she was picking on Wade. She put him down in front of his friends. Do you think that's why she was picked?"

"I don't know," Zoe admitted. "I just know those assholes are some seriously sick fuckers. I know I hate them."

"And I want to watch them all burn," I agreed. "One way or another, I'll make sure they do."

CHAPTER 31

ZOE

The problem with talking about what had happened to me was that it made *me* remember what had happened. That rotten and disgusting feeling was like a film on my skin I just couldn't get off. And no, it didn't make me feel better to know Scarlett was probably feeling the exact same thing. In fact, it made me feel worse.

I'd brought it back up for her. Yeah, Jeri was right and we had to, but that didn't make it better. Still, there was no fucking way I was going to let these assholes get away with the shit they'd put us through. To Dylan and his friends, we were all just some commodity to use and abuse at their whim. They were also wrong.

We were women. We might not fight like men, but that didn't mean we gave up.

Between second and third period, I managed to slip a note to Tiffany in the halls that asked her to meet me in the library for lunch. Next, I sent a text to Ripper - and was a little proud of myself for starting to think of him by his game name now - asking him to babysit Jeri's boyfriends during lunch because we had girl business. And when all of that was done, I whipped off one more message to Jeri, telling her to meet me at my locker because we weren't doing normal lunch.

Then I waited. Naturally, with my plan partially enacted, third period dragged on slower than it ever had before. That was the nature of time, wasn't it? I was pretty sure there was some inverse relationship to excitement. I'd have to ask Ripper about it. He'd probably read some book with that as the plot.

Finally, it was time. The moment my class was over, I was out of my seat and heading for my locker. Jeri was there, and all alone. Snagging her, I turned for the library, propelling her along with our arms linked together. I figured it was easier to explain as we walked.

"Confused," Jeri muttered when we passed the cafeteria and the doors to the area out back.

"We're going to the library to meet Tiff," I said. "See, this crap is a mess, and I don't think we can deal with it alone. There are three kinds of hacking, right? Normal, viral, and social."

"Close enough," she agreed.

"It's time for social, and we can't do that on our own." I looked over with a smile. "We're not cool enough."

"And Tiff is," Jeri realized just as we reached the door for the library.

I pulled it open and all but propelled her in. She still paused just inside, but mostly to look around. Then again, this might be her first time here. For the rest of us, we'd had to do some research project or class thing in here at some point in our high school careers.

"Where are we going?" Jeri asked.

"Study area," I explained, leading the way.

And sure enough, Tiffany was sitting at a table, all alone, with a massive book open before her. Of course, with the library being as quiet as it was, she heard us coming. Looking up, she smiled at first, but it faded when she saw us.

"So, not good news," she said, keeping her voice down.

Jeri and I claimed the chairs across from her. "Anyone around?" I asked.

"Nope," Tiffany said. "Told Mrs. Limburg we have a group project, so we'll be ignored."

"Who?" Jeri asked.

"Librarian," I explained. "She's also mostly deaf, so it works out."

"So what's going on?" Tiffany asked.

Jeri immediately leaned over her arms to get closer and keep her voice from carrying. "Amber sent us four videos. One was her. Three weren't. We've identified two of those girls, but they won't report it."

"Shit," Tiffany hissed.

"But," Jeri went on, "they had some interesting information. It seems the incidents were always at those damned parties. Almost everyone was drugged."

"Almost?" Tiffany asked, picking up on that.

"Not the first one," I explained.

"Interesting." Tiff's eyes narrowed. "So, what do you think that means?"

"That they were learning," Jeri said. "Tiff, we watched the videos. They aren't nice."

"Duh," Tiff said. "But what does this have to do with my girls?"

Yep, I had this answer. "So we've been thinking they have storage, right? Well, Amber found them on that forum, but they had to start somewhere before that. We're trying to find the somewhere, but no one has a clue, yet all signs point to them using one place. Like one server."

"We're worried it might be a personal server," Jeri explained.

Tiffany just shook her head. "That means exactly nothing to me."

"Like an extra computer in the house," Jeri told her. "One set up to be accessed online by friends but not anyone else. Kinda like off-site storage, you know? But a little more home-made than Google Drive."

"Gotcha," Tiff said. "So let's see if I'm keeping up. Those assholes recorded themselves committing crimes, are keeping the videos - probably to jack off to - and they have the 'safe' for them hidden really fucking well, right?"

"Bingo," I told her. "Nailed it in one."

"So, this is just another dead-end update?"

Jeri started to nod, but I spoke up. "Not if you can help us."

"Huh?" Jeri asked.

"What?" Tiffany mumbled.

I breathed out a laugh, then glanced back to make sure the librarian wasn't in sight. "Ok, so here's the thing. We know they did this at their parties. All of the stories have that one thing in common. What we don't know is who they attacked. We can't seem to get anything that will make the cops do shit about it. That means we need to do something about it ourselves, right?" And I looked to Jeri to make sure she agreed.

"Like?" Jeri asked.

But Tiffany was starting to smile. "Well, you already started it, Jericho," she pointed out. "Those five all lost their college acceptances. They lost their football scholarships." Then her smile turned into a grin. "And it seems no one really thinks they're very cool anymore. Not after their last party."

"Where so many people got busted for underage drinking," I said. "Yep, that kind of something."

"Wait, wait, wait, wait..." Tiffany begged, her eyes losing focus as she thought. "Ok, so you know of how many girls?"

"Well, your four for sure," I said, "then me, Amber, and three others."

"Nine," Jeri said.

Tiffany just nodded slowly. "Girls at the parties. Fuck." She leaned her head back and groaned. "Guys, that freshman chick!"

"Who?" Jeri asked.

"The freshman Dylan was hitting on the night he drugged us." She paused to clench her jaw in annoyance. "Fuck, that makes so much sense. We got drugged. We bailed. The next morning, that one girl who overdosed? Yeah, the same one he was chatting up when you and your guys arrived."

"So you think she's number ten? Because I was kinda wondering that too." I said. "But do we know that for sure?"

"We don't," Tiffany admitted.

Yet Jeri had a different thought. "And that's how they're picking."

"Huh? How?" Tiffany asked.

Yeah, Jeri had my full attention, because I wasn't sure how she'd gotten from here to there. Then again, this was Jeri, and her mind worked in some wild ways.

"The first time I went to a party at John's place," Jeri explained, "was because Dylan invited me. It was supposed to be to take the heat off Cade because I'd pissed you off, Tiff. Dylan also promised that a gamer friend of mine, a guy named Qry, would be there. I had no idea Qry was Cade."

"Ok?" I asked, still not keeping up.

"So I showed up," Jeri went on, "and Dylan gave me a drink. He and his friends were all thrilled about it. I'm talking high fives and shit. Well, I know better than to drink something like that, but Dylan said I'd find Qry out back, so I went to hang, and then Tiff and Cade got into a loud fight, and Knock kinda appeared. He saw me sniffing my drink and said not to drink it, so I poured it out. Knock gave me his, got another, and yeah. I was fine."

"And?" I pressed.

Jeri just huffed. "Zoe, I pissed the guy off before that party. I was public enemy number one in Dylan's world. I was targeted! Don't you see? They were hyped because they'd drugged my drink. Knock wasn't a target, so they didn't drug his, and because he gave me his, I didn't get fucked-up. Now, think about that. The freshman girl? The cheerleader? Our gamer friend?"

"You can use their names," Tiffany said. "I'm not about to spread this shit around."

"I don't know the freshman," I told her, "but the others are Scarlett and Marissa."

"No..." Tiffany breathed. "Marissa? Is that why she and Carson..."

I just shoved my head into my hands as all these tiny little pieces of things began to paint a much bigger picture. "Marissa cheated on Carson, but she didn't. She was raped. Fuck!"

"Oh, I'm going to fuck those assholes up," Tiffany grumbled.

"How?" Jeri asked. "I keep hitting dead ends."

"And I don't do things your way," Tiffany said. "Jericho, I know how to be a bitch. Call me a bully if you want, but you know what? I'm damned good at revenge. This time, I think a few girls at school need to get some from the five guys we all happen to hate."

"How?" Jeri pressed.

Tiffany just smiled. "I think it's time I told my girls what's really going on. No names. No details. They just need to know their little fun was a lot less innocent than they hoped it was."

"And then?" I asked.

"Think of this as a class-action bitchfest against the guys who made the biggest mistake of their lives," Tiffany said. "Oh, and maybe a bit of a support group. I mean, I need to put a club on my college applications anyway, right? A few things to make me impossible to refuse?"

Ok, I could see her point, but she was missing the big thing here. "And when Dylan finds out?" I asked. "Tiff, he said he'll get you, one way or another."

"Which means I have nothing to lose," she insisted. "That asshole thinks he can take what he wants, but he's never met a woman like me."

"Uh..." I subtly pointed at Jericho.

"You know what I mean," Tiffany laughed, flashing Jeri a smile. "Besides, we fight differently."

"I still don't get how this will help," Jeri admitted. "Don't get me wrong, I'm all-in for making those dicks as uncomfortable as possible, but how does it get us closer to getting them arrested?"

"Because girls talk," I realized. "Shit, and Tiff's about to make a place for them to do it. For all of these girls to admit what happened, accept they aren't to blame, and to create a place for women to protect each other."

"Exactly," Tiffany said. "Hopefully, once I do that, some of them will say some things that might help you two find those videos and destroy them."

"Turn them over to the cops," Jeri said.

"Either way," Tiffany told me.

"No!" Jeri insisted. "Tiff, your friends were raped too, don't you get that? What Dylan and his friends did to them, manipulating them like that? It's not what they consented to. It was planned. That shit is hinky as fuck."

"Oh, so now you agree with me? Yeah, they were, and we all know that no judge in the world would ever convict those guys for it," Tiffany countered. "It's just like what happened with Zoe. They did consent. Maybe not to a setup, and I agree with you that should count as rape, but they *did* consent to *something*. That wiggle room is all it will take for us to become whores and those boys to have every man in town feeling bad for them. Just more 'false rape reports,' right?"

I groaned in frustration, because she wasn't wrong. "Look, we have me and Amber. The current thought is that if we can get one more victim to report what happened, then we can make a serial rape report to the cops. If it's serial, they have to listen, right?"

"Not really," Tiff told me. "Zoe, I know they should. I know we want to think they would. I also watch the news, and I know exactly what happens in rape cases. Women's lives are ruined and men get a slap on the wrist at worst. *That* is the problem. So fuck the system. Let's show these guys what it feels like to have no power."

"I'm in with that," Jeri said. "If I can help..."

Tiffany just smiled at her. "Not yet. You're too obvious. I mean, the fight you've already picked with Dylan might scare some of these girls off."

"Most of us don't fight like you do," I reminded her. "We prefer safer, more subtle methods."

"We prefer," Tiffany said, "to make it out alive. That means bullying is back on the table."

"And this time," Jeri told her, "I'm completely on board."

"Yeah, kinda thought you would be." Then Tiffany offered her hand. "Allies?"

"And maybe even friends," Jeri said as she accepted.

CHAPTER 32

JERICHO

All the new information was sitting like a bomb in the back of my mind. Since we couldn't really talk about this at school, we all agreed to meet up at Knock's place. At least those of us at school did. Hottie and Jinxy could get updated later, because I had a feeling we'd find more to work with as we talked it through.

I was the third car in line when I pulled up to park, and the place looked deserted. Even the arena was empty, which wasn't normal for this time of day. That meant everyone had to be inside, right? Yet before I turned my car off, Ripper's truck claimed the spot beside me. Zoe was right after him, so now we were all here. But when I climbed out, I found Ripper waiting at the front of my car.

"Hey, you," I greeted him.

"Aww, and now you're going to be cute," Zoe said as she made her way past. "Knock and Cade beat us, huh?"

"They always do," Ripper said. "I also think Cade drove today, so yeah. Definitely beat us."

I laughed at the implication that Cade drove too fast. In truth, I'd never ridden with him, so I didn't know. Granted, I also wouldn't put it past him. Yet as Zoe headed for the backyard, Ripper caught my hand, holding me in place until she was out of sight.

"You ok?" I asked, confused.

Those pretty green eyes of his found mine. His black-rimmed glasses really brought out his dark lashes, making him look amazingly seductive, but the lack of a smile on his lips had me just a little nervous.

"I have a question," he admitted. "You can blow me off, and that's ok, but I've kinda been thinking about it since our Discord chat."

"Ok?"

"Did you ask us to be your boyfriends because of me?"

Whoa, ok, that was kinda a heavy question. I also wasn't sure of the right answer. This was the sort of thing that felt leading, like screwing it up might make us implode, and yet he was giving me exactly zero hints.

"A little," I squeaked, wrinkling my nose at him. "I mean, yes and no?"

"Does not really give me much to work with," he said, and that smile finally began to show, easing my fears.

"I'd been thinking about it," I admitted. "I mean, partner is nice, but boyfriend? That's what you guys feel like, and when you said you love me, it just kinda, um..."

"Fell into place," he offered.

I wobbled my head from side to side. "It made me want to say it back, but it's hard. I mean, that's a big word."

"Just four letters," he countered.

I rolled my eyes and groaned. "You know what I mean!"

His fingers tightened on mine and he shifted a bit closer. "I do, Jeri. I also know you said you *do*. Words are hard for you, but your actions scream volumes. I just wanted to say that if this is too fast, or too much, or stressing you out, I'll handle the other guys, ok?"

"No, it's perfect," I assured him. "I mean, I wanted to kiss you this morning, but Zoe told me to hurry up, and - "

"It's ok," he broke in. "Jeri, you don't have to constantly keep track to keep things even. It's not a case of kiss him, the other him, and then me. Besides, I got to spend the night curled up against you. I think my pre-boyfriend celebration was much better than those two showing off at school where they can't do too much."

"Yeah?" I asked. "So I'm not ignoring you?"

"You," he told me, "are trying to tear yourself apart at the seams. You want to give so much of yourself to everyone else, and sometimes I wonder if you forget to keep a bit for yourself. To be a little greedy, Jeri. To enjoy that you have two boyfriends who like a threesome - just because you can. I swear to you that if the situation was reversed, I'd be enjoying it every chance I could."

"Yeah, but what about you?" I asked.

He reached up to cup the side of my face. "I am your boyfriend. That's it. When I feel lonely, I will speak up. See, Zoe taught me that. She says guys are needy all the time, and girls have shit to do, so guys need to learn how to communicate. This is me communicating."

"Ok," I said, pulling in a deep breath. "So this is me trying to do the same." I paused.

Yes, I wanted to do this. I fucking *needed* to do this. All I had to do was blurt it out, but words meant things, and those things had consequences. Still, I knew what happened when things were said too late. I knew how bitter regret tasted, and it wasn't something I wanted to deal with again. Pulling in a big, deep breath, I closed my eyes and let the words fall from my lips.

"I think I'm in love with you."

The sound he made was soft, like all the air rushing from his lungs without any pressure. When I dared to open my eyes, I found his waiting, jumping back and forth between mine. Immediately, my heart picked up, trying to panic because the expression on his face wasn't one I could read.

And then he kissed me. Ripper didn't bother to say a thing. He just pressed his mouth to mine, hard, and kissed me like he was drinking in my soul. His hand on my face was soft. The feel of him moving closer, pulling our bodies together was gentle. His mouth wasn't.

His tongue explored, his lips caressed, and he devoured me in the best way. This time, he was the one showing instead of saying. Every touch was fueled with both passion and something else. Something deeper, better, and too amazing for words to truly convey. Something that could only be called love.

Then he leaned back, his eyes immediately searching mine. "Yeah?"

I nodded. "But don't expect me to say it a lot."

"Once is more than enough," he promised. "Fuck, that's a hell of a lot better than just boyfriend, and I was going to tell you how much I liked that."

"Being my boyfriend?"

"Being yours, in any way you'll have me," he clarified. "Jericho, you are the most amazing girl I've ever met. Now, considering Zoe's my best friend, that kinda says a lot. Being loved by a woman like you? It's..." He paused to moisten his lips. "Guys like me don't get this. It doesn't mean we don't dream of it, and I kinda feel like I'm going to wake up."

I pressed my forehead into his chest and let a soft laugh slip out. "But girls like me want guys like you, Ripper. We want men who are real, who can be soft, and who actually fucking listen."

"Then that means this is perfect," he said, wrapping his arms around my back to hold me against him. "We also need to get in there before Zoe gets impatient and starts without us."

"Yeah," I breathed, pulling away only to grab his hand. "So this is ok?"

"This is our secret until you're less freaked out by the word," he assured me.

Hand in hand, we headed inside. Quake met us at the back door with his entire body wiggling. In unison, we both bent to pet the silly puppy, then Ripper found my hand again, holding it as we descended the stairs. It was nice. It was easy. It felt so fucking good.

Normal, even.

But as we reached the computer room, Cade spotted us. His eyes immediately fell on our laced fingers before he pouted. Yeah, he had to work at it, but then he hurried over to the couch, reaching out a hand towards me.

"My turn!" he proclaimed.

"Cade's turn," Ripper said with a laugh as he nudged me that way.

So I went. Flopping down on the couch I curled up next to my other boyfriend. Cade shifted so he was sitting sideways, I managed to wiggle up between his legs to use his chest as my backrest, and then his arms came around me.

Zoe was in her usual chair. Same with Knock. Ripper claimed the one he normally used, but they all swiveled around to face us. In that little pause while everyone got situated, I swore I heard a man's voice in the distance. Confused, I tried to locate it.

"Riley and Logan are in her room," Cade explained when he saw my head twitch.

I just nodded. "Cool." Because who knew what they were up to this time.

So Cade took the chance to steal a kiss against my neck. "So you just called us all here for a little special time with your polycule, huh?"

"Boyfriends," Zoe fake-whispered.

"I was trying not to overuse the word," Cade admitted.

Which made me laugh. "No, that's actually not it. I - "

"But I liked the idea of polycule time," Cade fake-whined. "More cuddle time, and I feel a little short on cuddle time." Then he sighed, making a production of it. "Ok, but seriously. What's going on?"

"So, today was interesting," I started.

"So interesting," Zoe said, taking over in her excitement. "We talked to Scarlett, and while she doesn't want to be involved, she admitted it happened."

"Fuck," Knock grumbled. "Poor girl."

"Yeah," Zoe said, but then kept going. "So, she said Alpha Team was giving her drinks all night long. She had the same symptoms of hallucinating that I did."

"Mine weren't as bad," I pointed out.

"And you didn't drink as much," Zoe explained. "I was trying to get drunk. When I first felt woozy, I assumed it was the alcohol. You and Tiff? You had a few sips and still got partial effects, right?"

"Which is how ketamine works," Knock agreed. "Low doses make it a sedative. Higher doses make it an anesthetic. I mean, for the horses it does."

"But what I found interesting," I said, taking over, "is that Scarlett was picking on Wade about his girlfriend. She called him a shitty boyfriend and things like that. I pissed off Dylan before my first party, but Knock swapped my drink. I didn't end up getting drugged even though I'd really pissed their crew off. Tiff also pissed off Dylan. This seems to be Alpha Team targeting girls to put them in their place, no?"

"Which would explain Marissa," Zoe added. "Dylan knew her from gaming. He'd made a few comments about her kicking his ass. Then she supposedly cheats on Carson with him? Yeah, no. That was set up to fuck up her life."

"Fuck..." Knock groaned. "Shit, that explains so much. Marissa has never had a problem holding her tongue. Kinda like Jeri. The difference is Jeri doesn't care about fitting in, and Marissa does. Hell, most of us do."

"So," Ripper said, holding up a finger, "does this mean Dylan expected the same thing to work on Jeri?"

"Probably," Cade answered. "He thinks all girls are idiots, they just want a guy for his money, and that sort of incel bullshit. He also said it was why he and his friends could get any girl they wanted. Their families had what these 'sluts' wanted, and shit like that."

"Ok," Knock said, leaning over his knees. "So Alpha Team isn't just raping girls to get off. They're doing it for power. Kinda what we expected, but this is pretty damned close to proof, right?"

"I think so," I agreed.

"And," Zoe told him, "Jeri and I talked to Tiff at lunch."

"About?" Cade asked, the sound of his ex's name making him sit up.

"All of it," Zoe said. "Mostly how the girls won't talk to us, so Tiff's going to see if they'll talk to her. She and her friends are going to make a support group of sorts."

"Yeah," I laughed. "The kind of support group that trashes the men who hurt them. She called it something."

"A class-action bitchfest," Zoe supplied. "I kinda like the idea."

"Which means," I told the guys, "that Tiffany is handling the social hacking. It was Zoe's idea, and a damned good one. She can take a little heat off us, and she knows we're trying to find their storage server. So if we get lucky, then maybe someone will have heard - "

The door to Riley's bedroom opened so hard it hit the wall. "Knock?" she demanded, storming into the middle of our meeting.

"Kinda busy," he said. "What's up?"

A second later, Logan walked out of the bedroom with his phone still in his hand. "Cyn's gone," he said.

Knock jerked straight. "What?"

"I just talked to Murder," Riley said. "Zara's with him. Cyn's gone. His house has been emptied."

"The FBI fucking pulled him," Logan finished.

"No..." Knock breathed.

But my heart had also stalled out. That was our FBI guy. He was the one who was supposed to make this work. Our connection to him was the only way we'd be able to do anything with this case!

"So what do we do now?" I asked, turning to look at Knock. "How the fuck do we bust these fuckers if your friend's no longer on the goddamn case?"

"It's worse than that," Riley said. "He's not just off the case. He's fucking gone. Missing. No contact."

"Which means everything he had is now useless," Cade realized. "Fuck!"

"For all of it," Riley agreed. "Yeah, I think 'fuck' is putting it mildly."

CHAPTER 33

KNOCK

"They can't pull him!" I snapped. "This had to be fucking Bradley!"

"Knock, it doesn't matter," Riley told me. "The problem is that he's gone, he may not be coming back, and now we're on our own with the Kings of Gaming."

"Fuck!" Jericho hissed. "We already know the cops won't listen to us!"

"So what can we do?" Zoe asked.

"This isn't about your little 'case,'" Riley said.

Which made everyone in the room turn to glare at her. "It's not?" I asked. "Really, Q? I have a group of KoG asshats in my fucking school, serial-raping girls, and our FBI guy is no longer able to help us. Does it suck that he's gone? Yeah. More than you can imagine. But if you think letting rapists get off scot-free..."

Riley just hung her head and sighed. "That wasn't what I meant."

"Then what did you mean?" Zoe demanded.

"Look," Riley said, "this guy matters for a lot more than *one* case. He's trying to tear the Kings of Gaming down, and without him, we're fucked. There will be a thousand more groups like these Alpha Team boys, Zoe. There will be dead girls, rapes, abuse, and more. That's what I meant. It's not about one case. It's about cutting these fuckers off at the base!"

"I know," I assured her, lifting a hand so everyone would let me talk. "But dealing with Alpha Team is what he asked *us* to do." Reaching up, I rubbed at the bridge of my nose, feeling like a stress headache was coming. "Has anyone tried getting in touch with Bradley?"

"Who's Bradley?" Ripper asked.

"Cyn's handler," Logan explained. "He's an uptight, self-righteous prick who has no idea we even know who the guy really is. So no, Knock, we're leaving that alone. The last thing Cyn needs is for his chain of command to know just how far in he is with us."

"Yeah, good point," I grumbled, not liking it. "So what about the Squirrel? Does he still have access to that? I mean, he was just telling me some of the shit we put together was helping him stay on the Deviant case."

"Our shit?" Jeri asked.

I nodded slowly. "It's all tied together, Jeri. Kings of Gaming. Alpha Team is still a part of that, and a step into their little incel hate group. It also proves that real crimes are being committed against women."

"Wait, wait, wait, wait," she begged. "So, if that's the case, then maybe we still have a chance?"

And now all eyes were on her. "What do you mean?" Cade asked, relaxing his arms a bit so he could lean around to see her face.

Her brow furrowed and her eyes dropped to the floor. "Ok," she said, clearly thinking hard as she tried to explain. "So, if we can prove there are real crimes, then maybe we can get the FBI to help in some other way? I don't know, like just call the helpline or something?"

"Not likely," Logan said. "As much as I wish that was true, this is a local crime. It doesn't fall under the FBI's jurisdiction unless they've been called in."

"Which means we're back to the cops," Cade grumbled.

Around the room, everyone nodded, but Jeri was not ready to give up yet. "Ok, so that means we have to make a case good enough the cops can't ignore it, right?"

"How?" Riley asked, but it sounded like she was encouraging, not trying to stop her.

Jeri's face went through a few expressions, but her eyes never left whatever she was staring at. "Amber's death," she mumbled. "Zoe's rape has already been picked up by the FBI. That's two. If we can show this is a serial thing, repeating over and over, and make it clear that even when some consent is given, these boys are still going too far? I mean, Amber killing herself proves that, right?"

"How does it prove it?" Riley pressed.

"I don't fucking know!" Jeri snapped.

I tossed a warning look at my big sister, then patted the air to calm things down. "Ok, so what we need is enough evidence to make it clear this isn't ok, right?"

"A crime," Logan said. "You have to show a crime, Knock."

Yeah, and that made it harder, because Alpha Team had been so consistent with getting the girls to nod in their videos. Well, fuck.

"What if we look at other crimes?" Ripper asked. "I mean, if they aren't going to take rape seriously, then why can't we just do what we did with Zoe and find something else that might stick?"

"Like what?" I asked.

"Drugs," Jeri said softly.

"The ketamine," Cade realized. "Ok, so let's play this out a few ways? I mean, if we show they're giving ketamine to people against their will - slipping it into drinks - that has to be illegal, right? And if we pair that with the sexual abuse - which includes Tiff's friends and the rapes - then it makes it worse?"

"We need to make it foolproof," I told them. "That's what Cyn told me. We can't jump to conclusions. We have to fucking *prove* each step. We need to get evidence of some kind that walks us from point A to point Z."

"Which means we need to organize this shit," Ripper said. "I dunno, make like a murder wall or something?"

"A what?" Cade asked.

But Riley laughed. "One of those big boards with strings linking things together, Cade. Like that meme, or like in the cop shows."

"Will the chat logs Dez gave us help prove anything?" Zoe asked.

"I have no idea," I admitted. "I'm just thinking we need to get too much proof for everything, just so if anything is written off, we'll still have a backup."

"And then?" Jeri pressed.

But it was Logan who answered. "And then we take it to the local cops. If they won't listen, we'll call the local FBI office. If *they* won't listen, we'll give it to the news."

"And if that doesn't work," Jeri said, a cruel smile curling her lips, "then we can give it to the internet."

"The internet is unreliable," Riley countered.

Jeri murmured like she didn't necessarily agree. "It might not be inherently on our side, but it is damned good at spreading shit."

"Ok, there's that," Riley agreed. "So where do we start?"

That made me pause. "I thought you were worrying about Cyn?"

She just tossed up her hands. "And how does that help?

Knock, he's gone. His number goes to nothing. The only valid email we have for him is one we don't dare use."

"Which?" Jeri asked, picking up on that.

"His official FBI email," I explained. "The problem is we're not supposed to know he's a fed. We do, he helps us, but if his bosses had any idea, then he'd get fired."

"Which would not help us with this, and might make things worse," Riley explained.

Jeri just sighed, and the room fell silent. I was pretty sure we were all thinking hard. Hell, I knew I was. Losing Cyn? This was going to hurt! I had a feeling there were a few people feeling the pain worse than we were, but that didn't negate the danger of Dylan and his friends.

These guys were a menace. They were skating on their family reputations and the local mentality that this was just what boys did. Still, Jeri was right. We couldn't give up. We couldn't let those assholes get away with what they'd done to so many girls!

"We need to finish this," I breathed. "With or without Cyn, we have to."

"No shit," Jeri said.

"Yeah, but listen," I begged her. "We've been going off the idea that all we had to do was find the storage location, right? We thought that if we could delete those videos, send a few others to the feds, then we'd all have things work out in the end, but that's not the case anymore."

"Was it ever?" she asked.

Which made me pause. "Huh?"

"The cops don't care about rape," Jeri explained. "Ok, maybe that's not fair, but that's sure how it feels. Juries sure as fuck don't care. I mean, guys barely get punished when they're convicted at all. We've been trying to find girls willing to make a report, but then what? She gets torn down? I mean, that's why Zoe didn't want to go through with it."

"But I did!" Zoe insisted.

"I mean with the local cops," Jeri clarified. "They'd tell your parents, and the lawyers would tear you down, and maybe Evan would still get off. It wasn't worth it, but child porn stuck, so it was. The whole risk and reward balance, right?"

"Yeah, ok," Zoe agreed. "And telling my parents was the scariest thing I'd ever done. I thought they'd be disappointed with me, or pissed, or something. I mean, I expected them to blame me."

"And all these girls are going to think the same," Jeri told us. "That's why Marissa all but told me to fuck off. It's why Scarlett wants to be left out of it. Rape is the one crime where women lose more for reporting it than they do for ignoring it. Sluts, right? What was she wearing and all that bullshit?"

"So what do we do?" I asked.

Closing her eyes, Jeri groaned in frustration. "I don't fucking know, but we have to do something!"

"We make the case so blatant no one can ignore it," Cade offered. "We put this shit in order, fill in all the gaps, and have all the answers - with proof! Then, we can give the cops here a chance to do the right thing."

"And they might," Riley said. "Some of those cops have been pretty cool with me."

"And you weren't raped," Logan reminded her. "Property damage and rape are very different crimes."

"Ok, yeah," she relented.

"But that's it," Ripper said. "We make this impossible to ignore. From drugs to rape to any other crimes we can find, we organize it. Lay that shit out. We do Cyn's job for him, since he's not here to do it himself, right?"

"And then we dare the world to ignore it," Jeri said. "So where do we start?"

Riley turned around and headed to the wall at the back of the room, the one that separated the computer room from the bathroom. "Logan, put this painting somewhere else?"

"And then?" he asked, accepting it when Riley pressed the framed image into his hands.

Riley's answer was simply to yell, "Kitty!" at the top of her lungs.

"What?" came from upstairs.

"I need the damned printer!"

"I'll grab that when I put this away," Logan said as he headed up the stairs.

"Jeri, call Hottie," I told her. "Zoe, get Jinxy updated."

And then I stared at the blank wall Riley had just given us. A murder board, right? Using strings to line up one thing with the next would be a mess, so how would we do this? Cyn had said we had to prove things. Jeri kept pointing out how these guys learned from their mistakes, but often repeated things that worked.

"We need a fucking timeline," I realized.

"You have the whole wall," Riley said as she headed back into her room.

"The videos aren't dated," Jeri pointed out. "How do we make a timeline, Knock?"

"We ask Tiff," Zoe offered. "She'll at least have a good idea when things happened with her friends."

"And she might be able to get it from the other girls," Cade said. "I mean, since she said she was going to try to talk to them."

"So I need to let her know we need that," Zoe muttered, her thumbs going crazy on her phone.

Jeri had her own phone in her hands. "Hottie's on his way over. He says we need to fucking find the storage so we have videos to fill in the gaps."

Which was when Riley came back out of her room holding a handful of Sharpie markers. "Color-code shit," she said, popping the cap off one to make a mark directly on the wall.

"You do know that doesn't wash off," I told her.

Riley just rolled her eyes. "And we can repaint the damned thing once we win."

Yeah, once we won. That was the problem. For all I knew, without Cyn's help, we might not win. The cops would laugh at a group of high school kids trying to put together an investigation. Never mind the questions about how we got our evidence.

"Someone's going to go to jail over this," I realized.

"That's kinda the point," Jeri grumbled.

"No," I said, the reality of how big this had just become weighing on me. "Jeri, one of us is going to go to jail. There's no other way to get the evidence. We're hacking someone, and that's not legal. If we want this shit to be accepted by the courts, someone's going to go to jail."

She just looked up, her pretty blue eyes meeting mine. "I'm good with that. Blame me."

Yeah, that was not happening. I also wouldn't tell her that. Instead, I just nodded, letting her think I accepted it, but I was already trying to figure out how to make this work. Someone was going to go to jail for this, and I had a very bad feeling it wasn't going to be the guys from Alpha Team.

But that didn't mean I'd give up.

CHAPTER 34

JERICHO

We stayed up late. Too late. Hottie arrived, got filled in, and then we went to town on our little murder board. I liked that name better than what it really was: a rape board. Still, using Ripper's cropped headshots and the open space of wall, we started to figure out the timeline.

Marissa was first. After that, the times were all a jumble. We knew when Zoe had been victimized, so that gave us a second point, but the rest was all guesswork. What we needed was more information to make this into something organized and easy to follow, and that meant talking to Tiffany.

Surprisingly, the next morning at school, she was sitting at our table, waiting. Well, talking to Ripper was a little more accurate. Zoe wasn't here yet, but when I claimed a spot, Tiffany turned to me with a half-asleep smile.

"Ok, fill me in?" she asked. "Your boyfriend here said he's not sure what I'm allowed to know."

I glanced at Ripper, smiled, then looked back to Tiffany. "Well, since you already know way too much, I guess it doesn't make sense to cut you out, huh?"

"I just want to fuck up those assholes," she promised.

"We need - "

I didn't get to finish, because that was when Cade and Knock arrived. "Tiffany?" Cade asked, calling from enough of a distance that I stopped and turned to locate him.

Tiffany waved. "Hey, guys. I'm getting the scoop."

"Is that a good idea?" Cade asked her. "I mean, you're just asking to be dragged deeper into this."

Tiffany grinned at him. "So are you a hacker too?"

"Fuck off," Cade grumbled.

"He's more of a hardware guy," Knock told her. "Brute force is his best strength, but he's damned good at using toys."

"Oh, is that what we're calling it now?" Tiff teased.

And Cade's face began to turn pink. "That's not... Fuck off."

Tiffany just laughed, turning to me with a shit-eating grin. "Ok, he's better with you than he ever was with me. But where's Zoe?"

"Coffee run," Ripper said.

"She's always getting the coffee," I pointed out. "We should probably toss some money her way. I mean, I know things are tight in her family."

"No, I have this prepaid credit card," Ripper explained. "She has the card, and I put money on it. Since the coffee shop is on her way here, she picks it up for us."

"So we should be paying you," Cade realized.

"Give me a link," Knock told him.

"Guys," Ripper said, "it's fine. It's coffee."

"It's fucking Starbucks," Knock countered. "That shit isn't cheap. C'mon, man. Let me at least contribute?"

"He's rich," Cade pointed out.

Which made Ripper laugh. "Ok, fine! We can do that tonight."

"And I won't forge-"

"Coffee!" Zoe yelled. "Someone grab this. I'm running out of hands!"

Cade was right there, jumping in to help without hesitation. He also grabbed the heavier of the two trays she was carrying. Zoe gave him a sweet smile, and then the pair managed to set the coffees out on the table.

"Ok, and I got a caramel macchiato for Tiffany," Zoe announced, passing one to the girl in question, which all but proved she'd asked Tiff to meet with us. "Mochas are here. Regulars are there."

We all claimed one, and there was a little chaos while everyone found a spot. In the end, Ripper gave up his regular spot on the table so that we girls could sit there. He took the end of the bench beside my legs. Knock claimed the other side next to Zoe. That left Cade standing before us, but he didn't seem to mind.

"Ok, story time," I said, looking over at Tiffany. "We need general dates from the girls."

"Dates?"

"Like when it happened," I clarified. "Your friends, anyone else you can get to talk, and so on. We're trying to put together a timeline."

"Which means this is no longer just a hunt for storage," Tiffany realized.

So I filled her in on everything we'd discussed last night. What I didn't tell her about was the FBI guy. Nope, that was none of her business, and it might be a bridge too far for Knock. The rest? Yeah, I made it very clear that even if we couldn't find the storage, we still wanted to make this something that would destroy the assholes who'd thought it was ok to abuse women.

"Well," Tiffany said, "I can tell you Scarlett talked to me. So did that freshman girl, Olive. Now, they didn't say much, but they did admit Dylan and his friends abused them." She licked her lips. "Olive had a rape kit run."

"Fuck," Zoe breathed. "When she overdosed?"

"Olive is the girl who overdosed?" Ripper asked.

We three girls all nodded. "Yeah," I said. "Tiffany put that together."

"And I had a thought," Zoe added. "Scarlett's story? She said Wade had a girlfriend, right?"

"Which was back in like late July, early August," Tiffany clarified. "He was with Toni, the soccer player."

That made Zoe pause. "Huh."

"What?" I asked.

"They didn't date very long," Zoe explained. "Tiff, when did the orgies start with your girls?"

"I'm not sure."

"Guess," Zoe insisted.

Tiffany blew out a breath. "Um, September? Late August?"

"After me," Zoe realized, nodding her head slowly. "Jeri, I think I have another piece."

"Ok?" Because I wasn't keeping up.

"Toni dumped Wade," she explained. "He hasn't had a girlfriend since, but the others have. They also made sure their girls couldn't leave, even when they treated them like shit, right?"

"Yeah..." I needed her to give me just a bit more.

"And it all started in August," she said. "Or thereabouts. Wade pulls the same dick moves the rest want to, he gets dumped, so they realized they needed a way to prevent that. To keep their girls on a leash. That was why they made the videos."

"And," Tiffany said, "it could even be that in doing those orgy videos, they got a taste for the group stuff."

"Nope," I told her. "That started with the first one. Then again..." I looked at Zoe.

"I don't know," she said softly, clearly guessing what I was thinking. "My video just had Evan, and I only remember him, but Jeri, *I don't know*."

"And you shouldn't have to think about it," Ripper told her.

"Yes," Zoe countered, "I should. I'm the only one in Ruin who experienced this. I'm the one who needs to be able to think of this shit."

"Zoe," I said, but Tiffany was faster.

She grabbed Zoe's leg gently. "That's not how it works. You were the victim. It's not your responsibility to do anything but work through it. You need to worry about you, and the rest of us will worry about filling in the gaps, ok? They drugged you, and trust me, I know exactly how many gaps that leaves. You aren't failing because you aren't sure. You're going above and beyond because you're even trying."

So I reached up to rub Tiffany's shoulder. "Yeah, that. Thanks."

Tiffany gave me a quick smile, but then turned to Cade. "Don't you dare let them pressure her about this. You hear me?"

"Not how it works with us," he promised. "Zoe's harder on herself than we'll ever be. She's also a badass who's helping more than she realizes."

Which made Tiffany nod. "Ok." Then she sighed. "So you need to figure out their progression, right? From drinking and being dumb boys to becoming rapists." Her eyes narrowed. "Do you think there were incidents before this?"

"We can't know for sure," I told her. "We think we have the first because she wasn't drugged."

"Marissa," Zoe explained.

"Who fucked with her? Dylan?" Tiffany asked.

"All of them," I admitted.

Tiffany just pressed her lips tightly together. "Then there had to be more before. The kind with only one of them, you know? Since I'm sure it wasn't always a group thing. I'll see if I can talk to their exes." She laughed once. "I mean, since I was making a list for Zoe anyway."

"Because they had to warm up," I realized. "One rapist gets the rest involved, and after they're all criminals, there's no way they can back out without implicating themselves."

"And KoG does nothing but encourage them to get worse and worse," Knock said. "But the biggest thing we need now are dates. A way to set this up, find the gaps, track the parties, and figure out who all was abused."

"Raped," Tiffany corrected.

"Abused," Cade said, "because we're including your friends in this."

Which made her nod. "Ok, fair enough. I'll see if I can get Marissa in my little group next. I have a feeling she'll have the information y'all need most."

"If she'll talk to you," I grumbled.

"She'll talk," Tiffany promised. "Yvette has been sharing her stories, and it makes the others open up. We're also doing some girl time after school, and the idea of fucking over these assholes has an appeal you can't match, Jericho. No offense."

"None taken," I assured her. "And more power to you for being able to make it happen."

"And that," Cade told us, "is fucking weird."

"What is?" I asked.

He just pointed at me, Tiffany, then me again. "You two being friends. In case you forgot, the first time you talked to each other, you made my life hell."

"Because we didn't know there was a bigger enemy," Tiffany told him. "I also didn't have a clue she made pretty good backup."

Then she smiled at me. It was a conspiratorial look, but I understood completely. Somewhere this year, I'd gone from hating the girl to actually thinking of her as a friend. Watching her stand up for her friends proved there wasn't a damned thing weak or pathetic about being girly.

It made me want to be more like her, if I was honest. Tiffany was beautiful, powerful, and determined. She was cruel when she had to be, kind when she could be, and she never felt bad for either one. Nope, she based her actions on what she thought was best, and even when she fucked up - which we all had a tendency to do - she somehow still found a way to make it work.

"See if you can get an idea of where the guys go online too," Ripper said, ruining our moment.

"Huh?" Tiffany asked.

"A logo of a website," Ripper explained. "I dunno, or any hints. These girls have been to their houses. Someone had to see something, right? If we can just get a hint of where they kept their crap, we might be able to get it back."

"It's called social hacking," Zoe told her. "It's getting information from the real world that can get us into the data that exists in the virtual one."

"Pet names, mothers' maiden names, and shit like that," Cade added. "All of that information is often easier to get in a face-to-face conversation. The problem is we can't exactly talk to Alpha Team anymore."

"Who?" Tiffany asked.

"They call themselves 'Alpha Team' online," Cade said. "That's the five of them. Used to be six before Evan was arrested, but it's their group name. It's what they call themselves when they terrorize women or try to pathetically hack someone."

"Because they suck at hacking," Knock said. "Mostly, they just use the name when they're ranting online, trying to make some kind of viral outrage, which typically goes nowhere."

"Gotcha," Tiffany said. "It's also an easier way to talk about them, because I keep wanting to say the football team, but it's not the whole team, you know? And while Dylan seems to be the leader of their little butt-buddy group, Wade's just as bad. Landon, Parker, and John are followers, but Dylan and Wade? Yeah, they're the real problems."

"So maybe we need to convince Wade it's time to knock Dylan off his throne?" I suggested.

"Shit," Tiffany grumbled. "Fuck that. It's time to knock all of them off their thrones. No, Jericho, I'm making their biggest nightmare. I mean, just imagine how these fucknuggets are going to feel when confronted with all the women they've taken advantage of, fucked over, and pissed off."

"Talk about the perfect revenge," Zoe said.

Tiffany just nodded. "Yep. Funny how that works, huh? When we women stop fighting against each other and start fighting for each other, we're formidable."

"And you're the best one to make that happen," Cade told her. "Just make sure none of these girls get hurt in the process?"

"Promise," Tiffany swore. "Because I'm sick and fucking tired of us always being the victims. It's the Alpha Team's turn now."

CHAPTER 35

ZOE

I thought the rest of the day was going to be pretty normal, and it was - at first. Right up until the break between fourth and fifth period. I was wandering to my locker, my mind on how we could possibly find the storage these guys were using, when Marissa stepped right in front of me.

Not walking the same way. Not accidentally crossing the flow of traffic. No, she planted herself before me, forcing me to stop.

"We need to talk," she said. "Now."

"Uh..." I glanced around. "Bathroom?"

"Alone," she hissed.

"So we'll find one that's empty, or wait until it is." Tilting my head, I encouraged her to follow me to the closest girl's room.

It wasn't far, just up a short hall and around the corner. When we walked in, a girl was headed out, leaving the space empty for the two of us. Not surprisingly, Marissa pushed open the doors on each stall, making sure. Once she was done, she turned to me, her short, dark hair unusually frazzled, and just sighed.

"Who all knows?" she demanded.

"Knows what?" I asked, not wanting to say the wrong thing.

Her eyes narrowed. "Jericho said she saw a video. Who all knows about it?"

"The people who need to," I said gently. "The ones trying to put those assholes in jail." Then I dropped my bag on the ground and stepped close enough to clasp her upper arm. "I also figured out what happened between you and Carson."

"Who told you that?" she snapped.

"I literally figured it out," I said again. "I put the pieces together. The same people who raped me did it to you first. You didn't cheat on Carson. You were hurt, didn't want to say what had happened, and he assumed you'd gone for the more popular guy because 'that's what girls do,' right?"

And just like that, all the fight went out of her. Marissa reached up to shove her hair back, proving why it was in such disarray, then slowly began to nod.

"Yeah. I didn't want to talk about it. I didn't want him to blame me. All he knew was Dylan said he'd fucked me, and yeah. Um, he kicked me out of BAD for it."

"And he was wrong," I told her. "I also know that sometimes it's easier to ignore it, because this shit isn't easy to think about - let alone *talk* about."

"But now Tiffany is asking me about it," Marissa said. "She stopped me in the halls to ask if I wanted to join her support group. I mean, what the fuck is that about?"

"Dylan said he fucked you," I reminded her. "He and his friends fucked over her friends. No, not in the same way. They just know there's some serious shit going on, and Tiffany's Tiffany, you know?"

"Fucking popular bitch sticking her nose in everyone's business," Marissa grumbled.

"Who's trying to help girls deal with abuse," I clarified. "A girl who has nothing at all to gain by this, didn't ask to be born pretty, and is doing everything she can to protect women who've been hurt."

Pushing out a heavy breath, Marissa tossed her bag at the far wall, turned, and then leaned her ass against the sink. Using both of her hands, she scrubbed at her face, almost like she was trying to wash away her memories. Sadly, I knew that feeling. I could also see this girl unraveling before me, and I didn't have a fucking clue how to help her.

"We know you weren't drugged," I said softly. "I was. I can't remember if it was just Evan or all of them. I know they all raped Amber, though. She was pregnant when she died, and she didn't even remember it. Not one second, so I guess I should feel thankful I have the bits and pieces I do."

"Shit," Marissa drawled. "Trust me, it's not better."

"But at least you know," I said. "You can tell when the nightmares are real or just fear taking over. For me, I feel like my body was stolen. The drugs kicked me out, and all that's left are these little bits and pieces that prove it was horrible, but it's not enough to *know*. Just enough to make me worry about it. Like flashes in the darkness, tormenting me with how powerless I was."

"They held me down," she snapped. "You want to talk about powerless? Well how's that for ya? You at least had drugs to explain that away. I fucking tried to fight back. I kicked. I screamed. I bit and punched and still couldn't get away. I was fucking *helpless*, because they decided torturing me was fun, and then you know what they did? They plugged every single hole they could, talking about how I had to like it like that and shit. They fucking *laughed*!"

"That's what I remember too," I mumbled. "The laughter. All of them, like I was a joke. Like my pain was the funniest thing they could imagine."

Marissa just turned her eyes to the ceiling. "Yeah. Fuck, but I want to make them pay."

"Then help us," I begged. "Shit, don't you get it? That's the only reason Jeri even tried asking you about it, because we don't know enough to put it all together."

"All what?"

"We know of nine victims," I said. "No, ten now. The number keeps getting bigger. Marissa, ten girls our age have been abused by those fuckers in one way or another. Rape, blackmail, sexual assault, physical abuse, and more. And then!" I groaned. "Yeah, then they go and post it on their little incel forums."

"Kings of Gaming," she said, proving she was enough of a gamer to know about them.

"Yeah. That's where Amber got your video. John had posted it."

Her throat bobbed as she swallowed, but she didn't bother turning to look at me. "I'm not shocked, you know? I mean, they had a tablet there to record the whole thing. Like, in the middle, the guys would look over at it and crack some joke. Sick jokes, like mushroom stamp shit, you know? Like they were putting on a show to enjoy later."

"For the ones who'd see us," I said. "I'm probably on there too."

"I think it was for each other," she admitted. "Landon said something about how they'd each need a turn with the damned thing."

"Which thing?" I asked.

"The tablet," she said. "Like, he was talking as if he wanted it for porn. I can't remember what exactly he said - it's been too long - but that's the impression I got. They thought they were making their own amateur porn or something. And when I cried, they loved it."

"Shit," I breathed. "Marissa, I'm so sorry."

She waved that off. "Yeah. Sorry doesn't change anything

though." Then she inhaled hard. "But I tried to, you know? When Jericho asked me about it, she said they changed. She wanted to know why they started making girls nod."

"Do you know?" I asked, unsure where she was going with this.

"Not for sure, but I might have a guess." Again, she shoved a hand through her hair. "Fuck!"

"It's ok," I told her. "Look, neither of us are trying to blame you. We know this shit sucks, and however you handled it, that's fine. That's more than fair. Hell, just surviving this shit is hard as fuck, and trust me, I know that!"

It was as if my words slowly sank in. Before me, Marissa began to relax. She blinked a few times too many, pressed her black lips together, and then her entire body slumped like she'd just given in. Eventually, she nodded. The gesture seemed to be mostly for herself, but I still saw it.

"Afterwards," she said, her voice much too calm. "And I mean after Carson dumped me. After my life was complete shit, you know? Like, a few weeks. Maybe a month?"

"Afterwards," I agreed, understanding completely.

"Well..." Finally, she turned to look at me. "I decided to do something about it. Dylan had raped me. He and his friends, and someone had to do something about it. I had no proof, and I hadn't gone to the hospital, so it was too late to go to the cops, so I decided to talk to his dad."

"Dylan's dad?" I asked, making sure I was keeping up.

She nodded. "Yeah, he's a vet, you know? He has a clinic. So, um, I kinda went there and said I wanted to talk about his son. Um, he took me into his office, and I told him what happened. I told him how all six of them had grabbed me, pinned me down, and then what they did. I told him they recorded it, so he didn't even have to believe me!"

"Shit, was he pissed?" I asked.

Her entire face scrunched up. "Kinda? But not like I would've expected, you know? He was more frustrated, and he wanted to know what I wanted. I tried to explain that I wanted him to make sure it stopped, that Dylan didn't come after me. I didn't want to talk to him, hear from him, or have him say shit about me again. I told him how Dylan had been bragging about it and my boyfriend had dumped me, and how fucked-up my life was and shit, right?"

"Right," I agreed.

"So he..." Her tongue darted out to wet her lips. "He grabbed his checkbook, Zoe. Ten thousand dollars. He asked me if that would be enough to make up for it. I tried to tell him no, that I wasn't trying to get a payout. I wanted to be sure Dylan and his friends wouldn't hurt me again, but Dr. Marshall said he'd make sure of it. He said I could have the money, and Dylan wouldn't even look at me until he'd paid it back."

"So you took it," I realized.

She nodded. "Yeah. I took it. I mean, I was thinking it'd be at least a year to earn that much, right? A year of peace. And that's the thing! Ever since I got that check, Dylan hasn't talked to me, he hasn't said my name, he and his friends don't mess with me or anything. It kinda worked out in the end."

"Good for you," I said. "Marissa, I honestly mean that. Fucking good for you."

"But that's what changed," she told me. "Zoe, that's why they made the girls nod on the videos. I didn't, and I could've gone to the cops. I mean, I know that now, but I didn't then. I could've gotten them in a lot of shit. Instead, I took the money."

"And there isn't a damned thing wrong with that," I insisted. "I mean, the cops basically told me I'd get torn apart by the attorneys, they'd have to tell my parents, and all that shit. You fixed your problem and got something back. More back than I would've otherwise."

"If Evan hadn't been arrested for sharing..." She paused, her eyes narrowing. "How did you know he was sharing it?"

I just smiled. "We're going to make them pay, Marissa. That's what we've been trying to tell you."

"Who's we?" she asked.

I just shook my head. "I can't tell you that."

"Ruin," she breathed. "The gamers have been talking about them. A hacktivist group that pissed off Dylan and his friends. You're a part of that?"

"I know someone who knows someone," I explained. "Remember, Knock has a *lot* of connections."

"Dez," Marissa said. "Has to be, because Carson said it was in Flawed's game chat."

I just mimed zipping my lips and locking them. "Can't say. Please don't ask."

Which made the girl laugh, even if it was weak and still fretful sounding. "Then I won't ask, but tell Jericho she can ask me. I don't want everyone to know. I don't want to be seen as the victim, but fuck those guys. Fuck them, their families, and everyone who's helping them get away with it."

"And maybe Ripper can talk to Carson?" I asked. "Just say that he may have heard the whole breakup was for all the wrong reasons?"

"He won't forgive me," she said.

"But what if he would?" I asked. "I mean, if Ripper happens to mention Dylan trashed you because he's part of KoG, wants to hurt women, and knew the idea of you cheating would fuck you over?"

"No rape?" she asked.

"That's for you to tell him," I promised. "But Marissa, maybe you should? Maybe, if you honestly like this guy as much as you think you do, then you need to give him a chance? You need to trust him - otherwise, why be with him?"

"But what if he..." The words trailed off when she couldn't finish the sentence.

"What if he doesn't?" I countered blindly. "What if this guy is still single because he's still not over you? What if learning that you didn't want to replace him is all he needs to hear? What if he wants to help, to be there for you? What if he's not a piece of shit, Marissa? And how will you know if you never give him the chance to prove it?"

"But what if he *is* a piece of shit?" she asked. "Zoe, what if I tell him and he says I'm trash now? What if he thinks I was asking for it?"

"Then you dump his ass and wait for the guy who won't say that," I said. "But I don't think he will. Just say this is ok? That Ripper can say something?"

She finally nodded. "Yeah. He can say something. And um, if you need anything else, ask. But like, maybe quietly?"

"Promise," I assured her. "Because this is no one else's business, but we all have to help to make sure these fuckers fry."

"One way or another," she agreed, turning for her bag. "And ten grand isn't enough, just so you know. It doesn't stop the nightmares."

CHAPTER 36

JINXY

I was sitting at the tiny little work desk in my dorm-apartment with a text book open before me, but my mind wasn't on it. Every time I tried to read a line, my thoughts jumped. Sometimes it was to Gran and her failing health. I couldn't imagine what I'd do without her, and yet I'd been on my own long enough to know I'd figure it out.

Other times, it jumped to Zoe. I'd been pissed as hell when I found out we had a fed working with our group. Knock's fucking friend, of course. Shit, it made sense, but the memories of being arrested as a kid were still a bit too raw for me to have any love for law enforcement. And yet, losing the guy sucked in a way I couldn't quite put into words.

A connection with the FBI who was cool with us? One who'd been helping? A man who could push this shit to the right people and get someone to actually pay a little fucking attention to it? Just the chance of being able to get revenge for what had been done to Zoe was worth taking every risk imaginable, and now one of our options was simply gone.

Fuck!

Giving up, I closed the book and leaned back in my chair just as my phone rang. Confused, I looked at the clock, realizing Zoe should be out of school - so I lunged for my phone. Sure enough, there on the screen was her name and that very first picture Ripper had sent of her.

"Hey!" I answered on the third ring. "Please tell me there's good news today?"

She laughed gently in that way of hers. It was such an easy sound, and one I wanted to hear as often as I could. I also knew it didn't necessarily mean things were going well. No, this was just Zoe being Zoe.

"Well, we got a few leads," she told me. "Not good ones, so don't get too excited."

"I'll take anything," I admitted. "I'm over here trying to study, and my brain isn't on quantum computing. So, hit me with your best news."

"Alpha Team seems to be targeting girls who pissed them off," she said. "That could be for something as minor as picking on them or as serious as kicking their ass in gaming - which still isn't serious. But we know Marissa, Jeri, and Tiffany all pushed their buttons. Scarlett seems to have done the same with Wade. That's four, right? And I pissed off Evan because I wouldn't fuck him, so five for five?"

I groaned. "Yeah, that sounds more like misogyny, Zoe."

"Huh?"

"These guys are trying to put women 'in their place,'" I explained. "They pick the girls who are too uppity, make waves, or try to be empowered. You, as an example. By choosing when and how to have sex with someone, you were being empowered. Jeri made waves. Sounds to me like this Tiffany girl might be what they consider to be uppity. It's misogyny. These boys are trying to force strong women to act like weak ones."

"Oh."

And then she was silent. Fuck, had I just screwed up? Did I make things harder for her recovery? Was she now blaming herself for doing the right thing?

"Zoe?" I begged.

"Sorry, I was just thinking about that," she admitted. "And I might be changing clothes too. I mean, we're all headed over to Knock's again to work on the murder board."

"There's a murder now?"

"No!" This time, her laugh was the bright kind. My favorite kind. "We're doing like they do in police shows. You know, the board with the victims on it, and all the corroborating evidence. Somehow we started calling it a murder board, and it just kinda stuck."

"Ok, good." Because while that made sense, I also wouldn't have been surprised if these assholes killed someone. They were that kind of wrong. "So how do I help?"

She made a little noise. "Um, I was kinda thinking there might be something in the chat logs from Flawed. See, Ripper's working on a timeline. Well, we all are, but he took charge of it last night. So if we can find them chatting about why they changed their methods, or things like that?"

"Which means I get to read all those chat logs again," I realized. "Ok, I can do that. Probably about as much fun as studying."

"Yeah, but you have to graduate," she reminded me. "Otherwise, you won't get to hang out with us next year at college."

Ok, now that was a thought I really liked. "Maybe some study groups?" I asked, only partially teasing. "I mean, if you need a tutor in undergraduate computer science stuff, I offer myself as tribute."

Once again, she laughed. "Only if you graduate." Then she sighed. "I also talked to Marissa today. Shawn, she told Dylan's dad what happened. The man paid her off."

"For his son raping her?"

"Yeah," she breathed. "I mean, I get it. She wasn't asking for a payout, but she took the money when offered. I get it. I really do. It's just that something about her story bothers me, and I can't quite put my finger on it."

"Maybe because it means Dylan's father knows what his son is doing?"

Which made her suck in a little breath. "Shit! Fuck. Oh my god, Jinxy, that's it! After Marissa, they started consenting!"

"Ok?" Because she'd just left me behind.

"So did his dad give him the idea?" she went on in a rush. "That's what I couldn't figure out. Dr. Marshall hears his son raped a girl, and now they have ketamine and make the girls nod? I mean, I could be wrong, but that sure sounds like dad's in on it, right?"

"Or dad chewed them out, said something about not fucking a girl unless she specifically consents, nods, or says yes," I offered.

"But that it changed at the same time they started using the drugs?" she pressed.

Yeah, I grumbled at that. "Ok, I admit, it's suspicious as fuck. It could still be that Dylan decided he'd rather take the risk of stealing from his dad - since his dad covered for him once, he'll probably do it again. So taking the drugs is better than a girl reporting them? I'm just trying to play the devil's advocate here, Zoe."

"Which we need," she admitted. "It's so easy to think we know what we're doing, but Knock says we have to prove each and every step. We can't guess. We can't make assumptions. We have to find proof."

"And hence the chat logs," I realized. "Ok, but that'll be easier if I have updates on the timeline," I told her. "Those chats are all time and date stamped."

"I can work on that," she promised.

"And updates on how you're holding up," I added. "Seriously, beautiful. How are you handling all of this? I mean, it can't be easy."

"No, I'm fine," she promised.

I knew that was a lie. "Bullshit."

That earned me a weak little huff. "I'm trying to be fine?"

"Better," I told her. "Baby, it's ok for this to be hard."

"Well, yeah," she said, "but I don't want to be the weak link."

"You're not!" I insisted. "Zoe, what you went through? There's nothing weak about it."

"There is if everyone else is diving in to save the next girl, and then the one after that. My friends are trying to be superheroes, Shawn! They're doing something to help people, and I can't keep up. I mean, I couldn't even watch the damned videos!"

"I couldn't watch the videos," I countered. "You calling me weak and useless now?"

"No..." she mumbled.

"Zoe, it's not weak to be hurting. It's not weak to be scared. It's not weak to be triggered or traumatized. Baby, that's called life. It's the fucking smart thing to do. We avoid the bits that will hurt us so we don't get hurt! So don't you dare think there's anything wrong with taking care of your own mental health first, ok?"

"I still want to help," she muttered.

"And you are," I promised. "Zoe, you're right there in the middle of shit that would destroy most people. Looking your own monsters in the eye and daring them to try something? I mean, isn't that basically what you're doing?"

"I never really thought about it like that," she admitted.

I just murmured in response. "So how are you really doing, baby? I'm over here, all alone, and kinda worried about you. I know Jericho well enough to bet she's diving in, full steam ahead, and all that shit. Hot's so blinded by his devotion to her he's probably following her lead like a needy puppy. And from the sounds of it, her boy toys aren't much better."

"Boyfriends now," she informed me. "But yeah, they all kinda do what she says. Kinda, though. I mean, they also do their best to keep her from getting in over her head."

"Which is why that mess works," I agreed. "But I want to know about you, Miss Thing."

That earned me a little giggle. "I'm holding in there."

"Weak," I groaned. "You can give me a better answer than that."

She blew out a breath. "Ok..." Then she paused, probably to think of an answer. "I think it makes me stronger. Every day, I have to face what they did to me. I find holes in what I know, and I can make guesses, but not be sure. I have memories I've been picking apart, but I fucking hate thinking about them, you know? And yet, the more I do it, the easier it gets to do it the next time."

"So is that a good thing, a bad one, or a neutral one?" I asked.

She made a little noise. "Good, maybe? Not super good, but neutral leaning towards good." Then she sighed. "But I do feel stronger. I feel less like a victim, Shawn."

"And more like?" I asked.

"I don't know that part. More like I'm reclaiming the part of me they stole?"

"And that is called courage," I told her. "Zoe, I'm not saying you have to do this. I'm definitely not trying to push you into crossing your own limits, but I want you to think about this. For most people, when shit goes bad, what do they do? They run, they hide, and they try to not deal with it. To let it pass them by, right?"

"Ok?"

"But not you," I went on. "You're the one running at the threat. You, Zoe, are using your own worst day to make a weapon. You're figuring out - even if it's sometimes hard as fuck - how to fight back in your own way. And I mean thinking about it, baby. Just fucking thinking about what they did to you takes more courage than you can imagine, and I get that. Maybe you don't, but I sure as hell do."

"Yeah?" she asked.

"Oh yeah," I promised. "Know what else takes courage?"

"What?"

"Telling them when you can't. Setting boundaries. Enforcing those boundaries. All of those things are hard, and most people can't do it. So I'm hoping you'll put as much effort into finding your limits as you are in pushing at the hard stuff, ok?"

She hummed thoughtfully. "I think this is why I like talking to you, Shawn. You always make me feel like I'm not fucked up."

"Because you aren't."

"But I am," she insisted. "Hell, I think every teenager is, aren't we? You still find ways to make me proud of the mess I'm dealing with, simply because I'm trying to actually deal with it. So, I dunno, thank you?"

"It's something my Gran taught me," I admitted. "She always talked about that phrase, you know the one about mountains and molehills?"

"Making a mountain out of a molehill," she offered.

"Yep," I agreed. "Gran said it was funny how everyone talks about that, but no one ever mentioned the people who try to make molehills out of mountains. She said that for most of us, we had a mountain in our way, and the rest of the world was doing its best to convince us it was just a molehill - but we still had to climb it. I figure this is your mountain, right?"

"Getting raped?" she asked.

"Well, dealing with all of it," I explained. "The rape, the fallout, telling your parents, hearing about other victims, and on and on. To other people, it might seem like this is a tiny little molehill that can easily be handled. It all happened to someone else, after all. To you, though..."

"It's a mountain," she breathed.

"A fucking Everest," I said, "and you're scaling it all on your own. This is just me trying to offer any help I can."

"And it does help," she assured me. "Jesus, Shawn, you have no idea how much it helps, but it also makes me want to help you back."

"Yeah, but I'm kinda good right now," I pointed out.

"Are you really?" she asked.

Pushing out of my chair, I moved over to my bed and sank down on the edge of it. "Right now, yes," I finally said. "Tomorrow, that might be a different story. Gran's dying, Zoe."

"I know," she said softly. "I'm sorry."

"And it means I'm coming back to Texas for a bit," I warned her.

"I know," she said again. "Shawn, I want to help. I mean, even if that's doing nothing but hugging you when you need to cry, I get it. She's like your mom. You don't have to pretend it's not happening, ok? Not with me."

Which was enough to make me crack a bit. "She doesn't want me to come down yet," I breathed.

"Maybe you should ignore her and do it anyway?" she asked.

I laughed once, because I'd thought about that. "Next week," I told her. "I've already talked to my professors, and they all say they'll work with me. So long as I can pass the final exams, they'll make sure I pass, even if I miss a lot of coursework in between. So, yeah. I think I'm going to come down next week, just so I can make sure Gran knows how much she means to me."

"And if you need a break..." she offered. "I can even drive out there, you know. I mean, sounds like it's the middle of nowhere, but I'm pretty sure I can find my way."

"I'll probably come to Sanger," I assured her. "Hot and Jeri already offered me a room."

"So we might meet?" she asked.

"Under the worst circumstances ever," I said, "but yeah. Just don't think poorly of me for having red eyes, ok?"

"Cross my heart," she told me. "I was actually thinking that maybe it might be nice to have someone willing to listen when you want to talk about her and don't know what to say. So you know, this is me volunteering."

I chuckled once. "Yeah, you. The bravest woman I know. Zoe, those are the things that make you so amazing, just so you know."

"Because I'm willing to listen?" she asked.

"Because you're willing to wade into someone else's shit to help," I clarified. "You don't care if it might be hard, or messy, or even awkward. You still help, and that makes you a damned good person. The kind of person that doesn't come around very often, which is why I can't get enough of talking to you. So yeah, I'm going to take you up on that. Promise. And while I'm there, I'll even listen to you back."

"Which makes you a pretty good person too, Jinxy," she said. "Don't ever forget that part. It's kinda why I keep calling."

Which was enough to put a little smile on my face. Even when things were turning to complete shit, this girl somehow could make that happen. Fuck. If she kept this up, I was going to end up falling hard.

CHAPTER 37

JERICHO

God, I hated school. It got in my way. If Mom hadn't made her rules, I could be at home right now, working on something actually useful. Instead, I was walking to my next class, shuffling along behind the mob of students trundling in front of me, and pretty much bored to tears.

That was why I was looking around. I didn't need to pay attention to where I was going. The traffic in the halls was almost automated. But there, at the side, leaning up against one of the lockers, something beautiful and blue caught my eye.

It was Knock's shirt, the one with the triangle logo that he liked so much. I was pretty sure it was for his outfit in that other game. His hair was a few shades lighter than the shirt, faded once again, but the overall look was definitely working for him. The way his muscles played under the loose fabric, proving he had one hell of a nice chest hidden away? It was entirely possible I was drooling.

Which was when he looked up. His nearly-black eyes found

mine, a smile curled half his mouth, and then he pushed away from the walls. The guy he'd been talking to - Carson - just watched with his mouth hanging open in astonishment. A moment later, Carson laughed, shook his head, and reached up to close his locker. Knock, however, was headed straight for me.

"Hey, good lookin'," he said, falling in beside me. "What's a girl like you doing in a place like this?"

"Supposedly, getting an education," I joked, flashing him a smile.

"And giving me some very sexy looks," he pointed out as he draped his arm over my shoulders.

Then he hooked my neck with his elbow so he could pull my head closer. The kiss on my temple was warm and sweet. The way he held me so casually was even better. My eyes found his, and for a second, I managed to get lost in those dark depths.

Knock was casual. He was determined and driven. He was nothing like most boys in high school, and I'd always liked that about him. And yet somehow, I'd gotten used to the way he could easily make me feel like the most amazing girl in the world. Kinda like he was doing right now.

"Going to be one of those old-school boyfriends and walk me to class?" I asked.

He just shrugged. "Sure, if that means I get to spend more time with you." Then his little smirk faltered. "Fuck, that came out wrong. Jeri, you know I haven't been avoiding you, right?"

"Yeah, we've been a little busy," I agreed.

"I kinda meant with Cade," he muttered.

I leaned in so I could wrap my arm around his waist. "Yeah, our boyfriend who got kicked out, outed himself by accident, and has been having one crisis after another? I think he needed you more."

"I wouldn't mind if you needed me too," he said softly.

I glanced back up. "Knock, I prefer not to need anyone."

"Mm," he muttered. "Yeah, I can see that. I'm the same. Doesn't mean it won't happen, though. And just so you know, if it ever does, I'm here. Kinda like I'm hoping you'll be there when it's reversed."

A giggle slipped out and I pressed my head against his shoulder. "I'm that transparent, huh?"

"I live with a lot of strong women," he reminded me. "I know how much it hurts your pride to think of being in that position. I also know everyone ends up there at one time or another. Me, Logan, and even Riley have. I can only assume you'll eventually have a moment where you ask for help."

"And you'll be there for me," I repeated, nodding to show I heard, but I wasn't sure how I felt about it.

"Probably with this herd of guys you're into," he teased. "And I'm kinda fucking up my best attempt to impress you. Shit. I'm sorry, Jeri."

That made me slow. "Huh?"

Knock simply dragged me forward with him. "I liked our date. I still think about that time in my bed, the kiss at the party, and pretty much every second I've had a chance to be alone with you. Like in your room when you were going to go rogue to save Zoe?" He moaned like I'd done something sexy. "Yeah. So I was going to be real subtle and try to convince you to spend some alone time with me."

"Just you?"

"Or us," he conceded, "but I was kinda thinking just me."

Grabbing his hand, I pulled him to a stop. "Now that," I said, stretching for his mouth, "is the sort of thing I really like to hear."

He sighed just before our mouths met, but he didn't hesitate to kiss me. Nope, this was my boyfriend. Maybe one of four, and of the group, he was one of the most likely to end up as my partner in crime, but I liked it. A lot. I couldn't get enough of how easy it was to be with this guy - in all ways.

The bodies in the hall bumped us as we kissed, but neither of us cared. This one moment was ours, and I actually liked that people could see. I wanted everyone to know he was mine. Cade's too, but still mine. I'd caught this hunk. I was dating this amazing guy. Somehow, I had ended up as the lucky girl with the guy they all *should* want, even if they were too blind to see it.

Slowly, I broke the kiss, lowering myself down from my tippy-toes. "I want to ride horses again."

He groaned playfully. "Jericho, you are killing me. Can you be any more perfect?"

I just shrugged and tilted my head back up the hall. "Well, I can probably make you late for your next class, because I don't think you go this way."

"I kinda do," he admitted as we started walking again. "Different hall, but not too far out of my way. That's why you always see me about now."

"And I don't even know your whole schedule," I admitted. "Isn't that something I should obsess over as your girlfriend?"

He grinned. "Well, I can give it to you, but I kinda like that you're not that kind of girlfriend. You sorta march to your own - " His words trailed off as his eyes jumped up.

Confused, I turned to see what he was looking at. It felt like we both understood what we were seeing at the same time. There, just around the corner in one of the side halls, was Dylan. That was normal. The asshole did still go to school here. The problem was the person he'd backed up against the wall. The girl he was clearly threatening? Marissa.

"Oh, I don't fucking think so," I growled, storming forward.

Knock was right there with me. Side by side, we reached the asshole. I hit his right shoulder. Knock slammed into the left, and together we pushed him at least two paces back. The dick hadn't even seen us coming.

"Marissa?" I asked, not daring to look back to see if she was ok.

"He wanted to know who I was talking to," she explained.

"Because you've been talking!" Dylan snapped at her, thrusting his arm out to point like he was threatening her somehow. "Did you think I wouldn't notice you spending time with Tiffany? Did you expect me not to put that together with her buddying up with Scarlett?"

"You dated Scarlett or something?" I asked, seeing my opening.

"Fuck," he grumbled. "Hooked up. But Tiff's trying to break the truce."

Hooked up? *Hooked-fucking-up?* No. That was not what he'd done. He'd raped the girl! Dylan and his friends had drugged her, had their way with her, and recorded it! Nothing about that was a goddamned *hookup!*

But Knock turned back for Marissa before I could go off. "Go. We got this."

"Knock..." she breathed.

"It's ok. Go," he told her.

I heard feet, but I was keeping my body planted firmly between Dylan and where Marissa had been. If he wanted to rush after her, he'd have to get through me first, and I was ready to kill the fucker. The best part was how Knock let me. He didn't try to plant himself in my way. He didn't act like I was something weak or breakable. Nope, he was right at my side, like the perfect partner in crime.

"Talking to people wasn't part of the truce," I reminded Dylan. "Leaving those girls alone was."

"Oh, fuck you," he snapped, taking a step forward.

Beside me, Knock let his bag slip to the ground, clearly ready for things to get out of hand. I did the same, feeling my lips curl into a smile, because I had this.

"And if you want to talk about truces," I went on, "then let's talk. Cade? Look at how you fucked him over. Oh, but I shouldn't get free rein because of that? Why not? Tell me, Dylan, exactly *why* you think you get to have all the privileges and none of the responsibilities."

"And if you want to talk about videos," Knock added, "then we can do that too. I mean, drugging girls wasn't the extent of it, hm? Bet the cops would love to see what we have. I mean, if this is *really* what you want to do."

"Fuck off," Dylan grumbled.

"Or," Knock said, "we can keep deleting them. Does KoG remove points if your video is no longer available?"

And that was one push too far. Dylan lunged forward, reaching for Knock's neck with both hands. I tried to grab him, intending to yank him off, but Knock was faster. Ducking, he grabbed his right fist with his left hand, and then used both arms to jab his right elbow into Dylan's sternum.

The guy staggered back, coughing as the wind refused to enter his lungs, but we'd been noticed. People were moving in, and quite a few of them.

"Don't fuck with us," I told Dylan. "That includes Marissa, you hear me?"

"You can't add on people anytime you feel like it!" he snapped.

"Or what?" some guy in the crowd asked. "You gonna go after her like the pussy you are?"

"See," a girl said. "Told you these guys were last year's news. Fucking losers now."

Unable to help myself, I stormed forward and leaned right into Dylan's face. Knock caught my arm, tugging to hold me back, but I ignored him. This had to be done. It needed to be said.

So, with my free hand, I caught the asshole's chin and lifted his face so he had to look at me. "Unlike you, I'm not fucking around. Try me, Dylan. I dare you. When I say leave someone alone, you leave them the fuck alone - no questions asked. Got it?"

"Fuck you," he snarled.

Which was when the guy in the crowd lost his cool. Knock

pulled as a group of people pushed in. I felt myself bump against them as I was forcibly extracted from that mess, but it was worth it. This was so worth it. And once we were free, Knock passed my bag to me, the pair of us walking quickly for the end of the hall.

"Don't give him too much," he warned.

"Nope," I agreed. "I'm just clarifying the rules. You're the one that was letting him know what we have."

"Hopefully, to get him to turn on that fucking tablet," Knock said. "If Marissa thinks the videos are on there, then that's what we need to get, and we can't. Jeri, that could be their Squirrel."

My feet stalled out at the next hallway, the one where my class was located. "You really think it's that simple?"

"It hasn't turned on," he said. "It has plenty of storage. Yeah, I looked up the model. It could be where everything is hidden, and we can't see it because it's always turned off. I mean, it makes the most sense, right?"

"So we *need* to get into it," I realized.

Knock just nodded even as he cupped the side of my face. "Yeah. So you check with Hottie and Jinxy tonight to see if they have any ideas on how to force-power it on. I'll do what I can with my contacts, deal?"

"Deal," I agreed. "But pretty sure there's no magic power option."

He kissed me, but it was just a soft peck. "Probably not. And so you know, I think you're the most beautiful when you're pissed like that." He paused to smile. "Damn, you get me going."

"Keep sweet-talking me, Knock," I breathed. "I like the way you do it a little too much."

"Yeah," he said. "I'm working on that four-letter kind of like. The other four-letter word."

And I felt warmth rushing to my cheeks. It wasn't a normal thing for me, so it stood out. I was also too proud to duck my head in some feeble attempt to try to hide it.

"Close," I told him. "I just don't do so good with words."

"Nope, but our partner says you do just fine with action. Pretty sure you just proved it." Then he let me go and stepped back. "Class, Jericho. Get out of my sight before I vow to follow you anywhere."

Smiling, I took a step towards my class, but I couldn't pull my eyes off him. "Knock? You should do this more, you know."

"This?"

"Spoil me," I told him. "I like the flirty version of you. It's sexy."

And the smile that earned me? Yep. I had a funny feeling I was going to get a whole lot more of this. I also didn't mind. Nope, not at all.

CHAPTER 38

CADE

On the drive home, Knock told me all about how he and Jeri had caught Dylan trying to scare Marissa. I didn't really know the girl, but I knew of her. I was pretty sure most of us who hung out in the gamer circles did, and the idea of Marissa being scared? It didn't sit right with me.

Worse, Dylan had tried to push back against Jeri. The asshole had been willing to go after my boyfriend and my girlfriend. Right now, he was probably sitting with his little Alpha Team friends, trying to find some way to fuck us over without getting their videos released.

None of it sat right with me. Sure, I was starting to get used to the idea that my significant others could take care of themselves, but that didn't mean I had to like it. I wanted to beat the shit out of Dylan just on principle, and this was one more reason to add to my very long list.

And yet, none of that helped with our chores. So, once we made it home, Knock and I hurried inside to put our shit away, changed, kissed a few times, and then headed to the barn. Kitty was paying me to be a full-time stall cleaner for Andrews Shires, so I had to keep up my end of this sweet bargain. Cleaning the stalls was also relaxing. It was the sort of thing that let me work out my anger and frustration without making things worse.

"So," Knock said out of the blue, "I was thinking about maybe taking Jeri on a date again."

"Too much guy time, huh?" I asked, glancing over.

He looked up, smiled, and then headed for another pile of shit. "Too little girl time, if I'm honest," he said. "I want all the guy time and all the girl time."

"I'm good with that," I assured him. "I kinda feel like we've been ignoring her. From the sounds of it, Ripper and Hot are just sliding in to steal the show."

Which made Knock laugh. "Yeah. Ripper. Fucker deserves her, though."

"Yeah, he does," I agreed. "Zoe says he's in love with her."

Knock just nodded. "I can see that."

I grunted, knowing when someone was avoiding something when I heard it. I also was the kind of guy to push. "What about you?"

"With Jeri?" he asked as he made his way to the waiting wheel barrow.

"With anyone," I said, trying hard - and failing - to be subtle.

Knock paused at the open stall door to lean his shoulder against it. "I'm living with my boyfriend, chasing down a group of serial sexual abusers, and pretty much fucking it up with the girl. I think that's called fucked up."

"Not what I was asking and you know it," I pointed out.

So he jerked his chin at me. "What about you?"

"I'm getting a bad case of feelings," I said, scanning the floor all of a sudden in the hopes of more horse shit. "I like this polycule thing."

"Yeah, that about sums up how I'm feeling too," Knock said, pointing at the floor. "Grab that and we'll move to the next stall?"

I saw the poop he was talking about, scooped it up with my stall fork, and dumped it in the wheelbarrow. Together, we moved that to the next stall, opened the door, and began again, but the conversation was still hanging between us.

"I don't like Dylan threatening you, you know," I said as I got to work.

"I don't like him threatening the girls," Knock tossed back.

"Me either," I agreed, "but in this case I'm talking about you. Just hearing about it makes me want to punch him in the face."

"But not for Jeri?" he asked.

"Oh, for her too," I promised. "Maybe more for her, because I have a feeling you could punch just fine on your own. I mean, I know Jeri can too. Fuck, I saw her do it! Doesn't make me stop wanting to protect her, though. Well, or you."

"Feelings," Knock said. "Yeah, I'm with ya. I just keep thinking that if we can get into that damned tablet, we can fix this shit and have enough time to sort the rest out."

"Rest?"

"Us," he clarified. "All seven of us."

I chuckled once at that. "Ok, yeah. I mean, I barely know Jinxy, but Zoe's super into him. Hot's still a bit out of the loop. Well, with us."

"More you than me," Knock admitted. "But he mostly talks to me about geek shit, not Jeri shit."

"Ripper and Zoe are easy," I offered. "I mean, it's almost like they're trying the most."

Knock murmured at that. "I don't know about trying. I think Hottie's trying his damnedest to protect Jeri, and that's what matters most to him. Not being with her, but just keeping her safe."

Which made me pause, leaning my rake against the wall

before I thumped my back beside it. "Knock, have you thought about that?"

"Yeah," he breathed. "Someone's getting arrested for this shit. Without Cyn, the only way to admit we got these videos is for one of us to admit to hacking. I mean, I figure Logan will get me probation or something."

"I want to do it," I said. "You've got a good job. Ripper and Zoe have a future ahead of them. We need to keep Jeri moving forward, right? So I'll say I hacked it."

"How?" Knock asked. "Cade, that's the problem. Anyone worth his salt would tear you up in an interrogation. How did you get in, how did you get the videos, how did you crack the passwords, and so on."

"Scripts?" I offered.

Knock grunted, unimpressed. "It needs to be me. I'm the only one that makes sense. I also have a job that won't fire me for doing the right-ish thing. I'm pretty sure Logan can make it work, so - "

"What's Logan doing?" Riley asked as she walked her horse into the barn.

"Getting me out of shit," Knock told her. "In theory."

Riley moved the gelding to the cross ties and began to secure him in the middle of the aisle. "What theory?"

"Without Cyn," I explained, "the only way to admit we got the videos is for someone to say they hacked them."

"Mm..." Riley pulled off the horse's bridle, traded it for a halter, then slapped its neck. "Well, that's a shitty plan."

"It's the only one we've got," I reminded her. "Because so far as I care, letting these guys get away with it is worse."

"No, I agree with you," she said as she moved to slide the saddle from the horse's back. "But I have news..." And then the crazy-ass bitch headed into the tack room to put away the horse's stuff, leaving us hanging.

Still, her words were enough to make Knock move to my side,

the pair of us leaning out of the stall while we waited for her to get back. Luckily, it didn't take very long, and when Riley returned, she picked up right where she'd left off.

"So, Dez called this morning about the next CGI shoot with the horses," she said, pausing to pick up a brush. "While we were chatting about it, I filled her in on Ruin."

"And Cyn?" Knock asked.

"She knows Cyn's gone," Riley promised. "She's also pissed about it. Sounds like Bradley and his boss got an earful from Chance." Riley looked at me. "Dez's partner." Then back to Knock. "But that's where things got interesting."

"Ok?" Knock asked.

"Well, I told her about how the one thing you can't get inside is that tablet, because it never turns on. Dez said there has to be a cloud version of this shit somewhere. If there's anything on that tablet you need, it'll be saved on the cloud - in the same place as all the other shit you're trying to find. Likely, the tablet is inconsequential. Regardless, she said you'll never find it the way you're trying."

"Ok?" This time I was the one saying that.

Which made Riley smile. "You two are a cute little matched set, aren't ya?" Then she flicked her brows up. "But our little chat resulted in Dez giving me a keylogger. I put it on a USB drive. Supposedly, this will work even better than remoting in - and you're working above my pay grade now."

"She gave you a keylogger?" Knock asked.

"Uh..." I looked at him. "Fill me in?"

"A program to record and send us every button or click someone makes on their machine," Knock explained. "Usernames, passwords, special key presses, macros, and anything else will be recorded. It basically gives us a step-by-step trail of what someone does on their computer, phone, tablet, or whatever we put it on."

"Oh?" I asked.

That made Riley smile. "Yeah. She even tweaked it to record everything on the Squirrel. Shit name, she said, but it made her almost laugh." Then Riley paused in her brushing. "There's one downside."

"We have to put it on the computer," Knock said.

"And?" I asked.

"No," Knock told me. "Cade, I don't mean we hack it on. I mean someone has to plug the USB drive into his actual computer - or the tablet!"

"Or both," I realized, nodding. "Ok."

Which made both of them turn to look at me. "Ok?" Riley demanded. "What the fuck does that mean?"

"It means we know the tablet is at Dylan's house," I told her. "It means I know where that is." Then I glanced at Knock. "I've been to his place dozens of times. I can do this. Just make sure I know how to activate that program and I can fucking do this."

"Which is breaking and entering!" Knock countered.

"Or going to have a talk with Dylan," I countered.

Knock's eyes narrowed. "What are you thinking?"

"That fucker told my dad," I reminded him. "He tried to start shit with my girlfriend today. He would love to beat the crap out of my boyfriend. I'm thinking that maybe it's time for me to get up in his face and remind him I'm not scared of him."

"Which would make a good distraction for putting the keylogger on," Riley agreed.

"He'll beat the shit out of you again," Knock pointed out.

I just shrugged. "Took a few friends to help him last time. I think I can take him."

"I have drugs," Riley reminded us.

"Stop fucking helping!" Knock snapped. "Q, don't you get it? He's talking about going alone to this fucker's house!"

"And you've been willing to do some pretty stupid shit too," she countered. "I mean, should we talk about your fake ID? Do I need to mention the hacking? Screwing around instead of getting your kills-to-deaths at a decent rate? You want to talk about stupid shit? Well, I think this is a house filled with people who are damned good at making stupid work. You just have to learn to trust when someone says they can do it, even if it makes you nervous."

"It does," Knock said, his eyes on me.

I nodded to show I heard. "But if I don't, then what? You couldn't get in there. Tiffany wouldn't be safe. Ripper and Zoe? I'm not even going to ask. Knock, it has to be me."

"And when he tries to beat the shit out of you?" Knock asked.

"I'm pissed, babe," I explained. "I've been pissed. I have all this rage just building up, and there's nowhere to let it out. Never mind what you said about the girls!"

"What did you say?" Riley asked.

Knock groaned. "I told Cade about how men yelling makes girls nervous, and how we have to bottle up our anger so we're not emotionally abusing them."

"In fewer words," I agreed. "But with Zoe? There's no fucking way I'm going to make her feel worse, even if I do want to punch a damned wall. I won't scream about the shit done to her, because she doesn't. I've been sitting in the computer room, looking at all the crap done to girls I fucking know, by guys who were supposed to be my friends, and having to just deal?"

"And you need an outlet," Riley realized.

I nodded. "Yeah, and I kinda think Dylan's face is a good one. Not saying it'll be easy, but I do think I can do this. I also think screaming at him about outing me will be enough to let me get that drive into his machine. Just promise me it will auto-update?"

"Maybe," Riley said. "Depends on his antivirus."

"Which means this won't be easy," Knock said.

I just shrugged. "I'm still doing it. I think that tomorrow, we're both driving, because I'm going to do this, and you're going to trust that I can make it happen."

"And worry the whole time," Knock admitted.

"Because he likes you that much," Riley said as she began brushing her horse again. "The shitty thing is I kinda do too, so make sure you don't get too fucked-up, Cade. That would piss me off."

"Yeah," I said, knowing she didn't mean it quite like that. "I'll try to be safe, Riley. And I will make it home to you, Knock. Promise."

CHAPTER 39

CADE

Knock spent the rest of the evening teaching me how to make this keylogger work. In theory, it was simple: plug in the USB. In reality, I had to worry about how to disable the antivirus options, how to make sure it wasn't noticed, and more. In other words, doing this without Dylan noticing? Yeah, not fucking likely.

But I didn't say that. I simply learned all the options, tried to make sure I wouldn't forget anything, and desperately wanted to take notes. I did write down a few things on my phone, but I had to keep it vague so it wouldn't come back and bite me later. Things like that counted as "proof" in a court of law.

But Friday morning dawned much too early - just like all school days. Knock took his car. I took my Impala. Normally, we rode together, but this afternoon was my chance. Throughout the day, I ran over the steps again and again, my thoughts only broken by the memory of my father's face when he'd come in my room that last time.

"Is it true?"

"Dylan says you're a damned little faggot..."

Yeah, this fucker had tried to get me killed. He'd known exactly what my father would do if he had any idea I liked guys, and Dylan had weaponized that. He'd hurt so many girls. He'd gone after my girlfriend! Seeing her drugged and losing control? Then there was what had happened to Zoe!

Little by little, all of the suppressed rage I'd been carrying around for months was leaking to the surface. Every time I thought about talking to Dylan, it grew a little more - and I let it. For once, I didn't try to tamp it down or push it away. I embraced it.

So when my last class of the day was done, I was more than ready for this. That little USB drive was tucked into the front pocket of my jeans. It was basically all I needed. Well, except for stealing a kiss from Knock before heading for my car.

I knew the way to Dylan's house like the back of my hand. I'd been driving this way for years. Before that, my dad had driven me. And even before that, I'd cut through the pastures behind our houses, because my dad lived just a street over, in a country sense of the word. So a few hundred acres away.

When I pulled up in the drive, the place was empty. Turning my car so it was pointed out, I killed the engine and climbed out, leaning against the front bumper to wait. Sadly, no matter how I tried to hold onto that anger, it only helped so much. What if his friends showed up with him? I already had first-hand experience with how that would go down. What if it was his dad? Not likely, but not completely impossible.

But I waited. I was doing this.

Eventually, Dylan's big black truck pulled into the drive - and paused. Yeah, I knew my car stood out. That was part of why I loved it. I had a feeling it also meant Dylan knew exactly who was waiting here for him. Soon enough, the truck started moving again, making its way forward to stop only a few yards in front of my car.

"What the fuck are you doing here?" Dylan asked as he climbed out - alone.

I felt a sly little smile curling my lips. "I came to talk."

"Your little bitch already got in my face. And I mean the blue-haired one," he shot back.

My smile didn't slip at all. "What about the pink-haired one? Heard she had more of an impact."

Dylan grunted and made his way closer. "So you're here to talk about our truce, huh? Guess they sent the expendable one?"

"Makes the most sense, doesn't it?" I asked, refusing to let him bait me. "Leave the girls alone, Dylan."

He just scoffed. "Yeah. You got your phone recording me or something?"

My eyes narrowed, because I hadn't thought of that. "Saying there's something to record?"

"Jericho's been all up in my shit," he said. "Dumb cunt thinks she's so tough, but we both know what happened to her at my party. Funny how you ended up carrying the *other* girl, though, isn't it?"

"Not my fault girls are into me," I said, shrugging that off. "But I actually came for a different reason." And I pushed my ass off my car and stood up.

Dylan jerked his chin at me. "Fuck off, Cade."

"You outed me," I said, slowly closing the distance between us. "We had a damned truce, and you still told my dad."

"I got fucking suspended!" he roared into my face. "Do you think Dad's ok with that? And the principal told him I was fighting a damned *girl*!"

"And?" I taunted. "Not my problem. No one made you hit her - or get hit by her."

"Oh, fuck off," Dylan grumbled, pushing at my shoulder as he made to storm past me.

But that was all I needed. I shoved back, once again putting myself in his way. "Fuck off. That's all you can say?" I demanded. "Do you have any fucking idea what Dad did to me?" My voice was getting louder. "Did you laugh when you told him? When you knew he was on his way home? When I showed up at school with the bruises?"

"Yeah, I did," he snarled.

So I leaned right into his face. "And I know all about the girls. Each and every one of them."

"Can't help it if the bitches love me," Dylan quipped.

"It's called rape," I growled, shoving him with both hands. "I've seen the damned videos. We know what you've done, but you forgot one fucking thing."

"Yeah, what's that?" he asked.

And that sly little smile returned to my lips much too easily. "I'm nothing like you."

Then I swung.

My fist caught the left side of his face before Dylan even knew what was happening. He staggered, and I took the chance to hit him again. Fuck fair. How fair had it been when his entire gang jumped me? How fair had it been when they drugged those girls? This asshole needed a real good lesson on being the one to get fucked-up, and I was here to give it.

I managed to hit the edge of his eye next, then his jaw. Over and over, I pounded the fucker as fast as I could, but Dylan wasn't a weakling. Sadly, this guy had learned how to take a few hits in football. About the time my fourth hit landed, he'd caught his bearings again, and was on me.

I felt his fist slam into my ribs, but it let me hike my knee into his chest. Both of my hands came down on the back of his head. Now, it was truly on. There in his front yard, the pair of us fought like rabid dogs. There was nothing pretty about this. It wasn't MMA or boxing. Nope, this was a full-out brawl.

The dry rocks of the driveway made dust as our feet scuffled on it. The warmth of the afternoon had us both sweating quickly. I could feel my shirt trying to stick to my damp skin, but ignored it as I swung yet again.

For every hit Dylan got, I landed two. All that rage, fear, and desperation was flowing through my fists. I felt the skin on my knuckles split. I knew I was going to have at least a few bruises from this, and I didn't give one single fuck. All I could think of was Zoe.

Seeing her eyes get so big before she'd jumped up from the lunch table and bolted to the restroom. Hearing her sob like that. The way she'd shrunk when she admitted she'd been raped - and knowing Dylan had been there?

I didn't even care if he'd touched her. It didn't matter to me if he'd done nothing more than encourage Evan. Dylan had still supplied the drugs, and that meant it was his fault. It was all of their fucking fault, and now my friend had to deal with it. My friend, the girl who'd gone so far out of her way to help me pull my head out of my ass with Jeri, the girl who made me feel like I finally belonged somewhere, needed someone to stand up for her.

To protect her.

To protect them all.

To fucking make these assholes pay.

So I hit, and I hit. Pain, exhaustion, and consequences no longer mattered. As Dylan and I danced around each other, slamming our bodies together in an attempt to hurt the other more, I stopped caring completely. This, right here, was my own vengeance. This was what I could do for Ruin. This was where I belonged. I took the fucking hits - and gave them back tenfold.

Just when I was sure this was never going to end, Dylan made the mistake of looking up. My fist was already in motion, so I leaned into it. With all my weight behind the punch, I slammed my hand into the soft spot of his temple and watched as the bastard's eyes rolled up in his head.

He staggered. He stumbled. Dylan didn't even make it a whole step before his body was flat out on the ground, completely unconscious. And my damned hand was burning with pain.

Ignoring that, I knew this was my chance. I patted his pockets until I found his keys. Sliding those out, I jogged for the door, gasping for breath. My fucking hands were shaking. My body just wanted me to stop, but not yet. Not until I got this done.

A twist of the key unlocked the front door. Inside, the house was quiet. Neither of his parents should be home. I had at least two hours - or until Dylan woke up. I needed to work fast.

In his room, Dylan's computer was still on. That made this easier. Popping the drive into the forward-facing USB slot, I moved to the mouse, jiggling that to wake up the monitor. Naturally, his screen was covered with some mostly-naked girl. Some cheesy porn-style wallpaper. Typical.

Within seconds, his antivirus software popped up a warning. This was what Knock had spent all night teaching me to work around. I clicked for exceptions. I found the place to turn off malware scans. I made sure that unless he specifically checked, nothing on his computer would warn him that I'd fucked with it.

Then I executed the script on my little drive. While it did its thing, I turned to scan the rest of the room. Somewhere, these guys were storing their videos. Half of us thought they had to be on the tablet, so where was the damned thing?

There. Lying flat on the bookshelf, it was easy to overlook. Two steps carried me to it. A press powered it on. While the tablet booted up, I pulled out my phone and decided Knock could have his first update.

Cade:
Working well. Dylan's taking a nap. Have the mystery device too.

Knock:
Clone it!

Cade:
That was not in my damned lessons!

Knock:
Texting you a script file.

Cade:
and then? Fucker! I don't have a cable.

Knock:
Plug it into the PC. I'm waiting.

Ok, now that was a whole hell of a lot easier. Beside the computer was a slew of charging cables. We all had them for our phones, our externals, and pretty much everything that was rechargeable in the world. A glance showed me the port type. A little rummaging found a cable to go with it.

Once the USB drive said it was good, I pulled it out, plugged in the cable, and went to connect the tablet. There was just one *big* problem. The lock screen was asking for a face to open it.

Dylan's face.

Well, now if that wasn't fucking convenient! Spinning on my heel, I raced back through the empty house and outside, carrying the tablet in my hands. Thankfully, Dylan was right where I'd left him in the driveway. A push at his shoulder rolled him flat on his back, and I held the screen to his face.

Eyes must be open.

Fuck! Wait. I had this. Dozens of times I'd unlocked a screen with my face. I'd always thought it was funny that blinking was an issue when covering my eyes wasn't, which meant there was an easy workaround.

Rushing to my car, I grabbed my sunglasses from where I'd hung them on the visor. Bending, I didn't even bother putting them on Dylan. I just held them in front of his face and tried again. And the screen changed, showing the Kings of Gaming wallpaper. I was in!

As I hurried back to the house and Dylan's computer, I pulled out my phone. Fuck texting. I didn't have time for that shit because I had no clue how long Dylan was going to be out. It only rang twice before Knock answered.

"I can't see the tablet yet."

"Because it's in my hands," I told him. "Had to get Dylan's face to unlock it."

"You got it unlocked?" he breathed.

I murmured an agreement while my hands fumbled with the cable. The computer made a sound, recognizing something new had been plugged in.

"And now you should be able to - "

"Got it," he said, cutting me off. "I'm cloning that shit. Fuck, Cade. That you got into it means we can..." His words trailed off. "Yeah, this thing's packed. Where's Dylan?"

The quick change of topic confused me for a moment. "Uh, outside."

"How did you get inside?" he asked.

"I'll explain when I'm home," I promised. "Knock, just hurry, because I'm not sure how much time I have. I figure I can take this with us, and then we'll have some real proof, right?"

"No," he said, cutting me off. "Turn it off when I'm done and put it back. Like nothing was there. No signs of us, Cade. No proof."

"Yeah, but..."

"No," Knock said. "I'm almost done. We'll have everything on it and won't need it. This will buy us more time."

"Gotcha," I agreed, even though I didn't like it.

And for a moment, silence fell between us. I could hear Knock's fingers flying on his keyboard, but nothing else. He was busy, focused on getting what we needed, and the last thing I wanted to do was distract him.

Then, "Done, power it down and get out," he ordered. "Safely!"

"See you at home, babe," I told him before hanging up.

The tablet turned off easily. The cable went back with the others. My USB drive was in my pocket. The only thing that might give me away was the fact that his monitor was on, but I knew how to deal with that. Clicking start, I told his system to reboot, which would pull up a lock screen and look like a standard reboot for an update. Happened all the time and no one usually noticed.

And then I got the fuck out of there. When I pulled around his truck and out of the driveway, Dylan was still lying faceup, but his keys were back in his pocket, his front door was locked again, and there was no way to prove I'd ever been there.

This time, he got to be the one fucking off.

CHAPTER 40

JERICHO

I was tearing down some enemies in-game - random ones - when the text came in. Finishing up my latest kill, I quickly retreated to a safe area before reaching for my phone. I didn't even manage to get my hands on it before Jinxy's voice spoke up in our main Discord channel.

"Go," he said. "All of you."

"Dude," Dingo grumbled. "This super-secret shit's starting to suck. I wanna get spy missions too!"

I laughed as I hit the recall button to send my character back to home base. "You want to go back to high school, Dingo?"

"If it meant time alone with you, sure?" he joked. "I'm also seriously curious to know what the fuck is going on at your high school, kid."

"Reapers," I told him just as my screen went black to move me. "We're trying to fuck them up in real life."

"Sweet!" he cheered. "Here's me doing my part. Jinxy, I'm reloading into a mech. I'll hold off the planes while Jericho's gone."

"Deal," Jinxy told him. "Rooster, you got any big guns?"

"On it," Rooster promised. "You cool kids think of this as us doing our part. Maybe one day we'll get to know what we're covering for?"

"One day," I promised before logging my character out, giving my goodbyes, and then *finally* finding my phone.

And in the time it took me to do that, most of my friends had already responded, the conversation well in progress.

Knock:
Cade did it. Need all Ruin at my place
ASAP. This could be it.

Ripper:
Zoe, pick me up?

Zoe:
On the way! ETA to you, Rip, is 3 minutes.

Hottie:
I'll get our gamer girl. She's on a kill streak.

But Cade hadn't said a thing. I was about to scroll up to see what was going on when my bedroom door opened. Hottie was standing there with his brows up like he expected something. Confused, I turned my chair - and saw the keys in his hand.

"ASAP means now," he told me. "Shoes?"

"Shit, I just read the message!" I told him as I rushed to find something for my feet. "What did they get?"

"No idea, and I really don't want any of them putting it into a text," he said. "Jeri, let's just get over there, then we'll know."

"Yeah, but what about all the texts Zoe's sending to Jinxy?" I asked while slipping my feet into a pair of Chucks.

"She uses code and calls him a lot," he assured me. "Sounds like those two have already started making their own love language. Toys, tricks, assholes, and such all have specific meanings. Jinxy's able to keep up, and nothing is there to be used against us."

"We hope," I grumbled before standing. "Ok, let's go."

Together, we hurried to his car, and then across town. Hottie was driving just a bit fast. Not enough to get us pulled over or anything, but there was an excitement to it. Knock had caused that with one little phrase: *This could be it.*

What was "this," though? Which "it" could it be? I had no clue and really didn't want to get my hopes up, but as we pulled into the farm, I realized the parking area was already full. Not completely, but enough to prove Zoe and Ripper had beaten us here. Considering they'd had further to come, that proved just how slow I'd been moving.

"Please be a good thing," I begged as I got out of the car.

Hottie chuckled, exiting on his side, but our doors were barely closed before Cade's Impala limped into the driveway. That big engine had a sound to it, like it was lazy and waiting for a reason to wake up. It was also impossible to miss. Hottie and I, in tandem, turned to watch as the thing found a spot and fell silent.

Cade pulled himself out a moment later. "Everyone's here?" he asked, sounding completely wiped.

"Fuck," Hottie breathed, seeing him. "Who beat your ass?"

I wasn't sure what he was talking about until Cade moved from behind the car. Then I saw it. His clothes were rumpled. He was covered in pale dust. A bruise was growing at the corner of his mouth, there was a red mark on his arm that looked painful, and the guy was a complete mess.

Limping towards the backyard, Cade simply said, "Dylan."

"No, no, no, no," I muttered as I hurried to catch up. "Are you ok?" And I wrapped my arm around his waist, giving him something to lean on.

The best part was that he actually did. Cade grunted as he draped his arm over my shoulder, making it clear he hurt, but he also allowed me to hold part of his weight. A split second later, Hottie moved to his other side.

"I'm not that bad, guys," he promised.

"You will be," Hottie told him. "Just fucking take the help, man. Set a good example for the rest."

And that was all it took. Cade let us all but carry him through the backyard, up the steps to the porch, and then inside. There, Riley was pacing the length of the rarely-used living room. The moment she saw us, she paused. Her eyes raked over Cade, and then the woman smiled in a way that was almost cruel.

"Did you win?" she asked.

"Fuck yeah," Cade promised. "Knocked Dylan's ass out."

So Riley grabbed a glass of water and a bottle on one of the end tables. "No more than two of these every eight hours. Use as needed."

Cade took the pills first, opened the bottle to pull out a pair, then put the lid back on. Next, he accepted the water, tossed the pills back, and swallowed. When he kept drinking, Riley smiled again, waiting until he was done before taking the glass back and waving to the stairs.

"The rest are waiting. I'll brew coffee," she promised.

"Thanks, big sis," Cade told her.

"And," Riley added, looking at me and Hottie, "don't let him fall down those stairs!"

This woman was the strangest mix of enabling and protecting that I'd ever seen. The crazy thing was that I loved it. It was almost as if she'd figured out how to give everyone their own power while still making sure they knew how much they meant to her. A skill, I decided, I wanted to master for myself.

But down in the basement was the rest of the crew. From the sounds of it, Jinxy was already on speaker too. Cade limped with each step, proving down was much harder than walking on flat ground. Hottie took most of his weight, the stairs being too narrow for all three of us side by side, but I hovered behind them, wishing there was something else I could do to help.

I heard Knock gasp first. "Babe?" he breathed, standing up in shock.

"I'm fine," Cade promised. "Riley already drugged me. It was also worth it, if you got the clone."

"Clone?" Hottie asked.

"Put him on the couch," Knock ordered. "I'll get a pillow. Jeri, get his shoes off."

"What the fuck?" Jinxy asked. "Blind here."

"Cade got beat up again," Zoe said. "Said something about a clone, and we're all trying to figure out what's going on, so you're not out of the loop."

But Cade couldn't stop smiling. "Clone," he said proudly. "As in the tablet. I knocked Dylan's ass out, unlocked the thing, and Knock said he got it."

"I did," Knock promised as he returned with the promised pillow. "Currently uploading a copy to the Squirrel."

"Stop!" I demanded before pulling off one of Cade's shoes. "Let's go back to the beginning and put this in order?"

So they did. Knock explained about Riley's well-timed chat with Dez. A business meeting about the horses, but those two women couldn't leave well enough alone - thankfully. Riley mentioned something, Dez had a solution, and the next thing the guys knew, they had one more toy for the toybox: a keylogger. They just had to get it on Dylan's computer.

Which was where Cade picked up his part. He admitted he'd been pissed to hear about Dylan yelling at his boyfriend and girlfriend - me! He said he went to Dylan's house knowing his parents wouldn't be home for a couple of hours. It was the best chance to catch the guy alone. Then, he picked a fight.

And from there, Knock took over again. "So now we have a computer constantly recording every keystroke or mouse click

Dylan makes. We will be able to get all of his passwords, including the one to KoG. We'll be able to see the websites he goes to. If they have usernames and passwords, we'll get those too. I'm going to set up alerts for the KoG site and the tablet."

"You skipped the tablet part," Jinxy said.

"Cade saw it, turned it on, and used an unconscious guy's face to unlock it," Knock explained. "Then he plugged it into the computer. Open, I could get right in, clone the whole thing, and leave sorting through the data for later."

"Lost," Zoe said.

"He means," Jinxy explained, "that we won't be trying to avoid Dylan while we devour everything on the tablet. If we have a clone of it - unlocked - then we have full access. No need to wait for them to turn it on."

"And this can lead us to the storage site?" Ripper asked.

Hottie murmured in a way that was not encouraging. "Maybe," he said. "Maybe not. If nothing else, it'll give us a list of internet history to narrow down the options. If that doesn't work, though..."

"Then there's the KoG site," Jinxy finished for him. "We can potentially follow that back."

But I saw one glaring problem already. "What if it just leads to the tablet?"

"Then," Knock answered, "that means all the shit is on the tablet and we already have them. But guys? It's a lot of shit. This is going to be an all-hands-on deck thing to just organize it, let alone look at each file to see what it is."

Ripper sighed. "I'll handle the videos."

We all turned to look at him. "You sure?" I asked. "Because that isn't going to be easy."

"And I'd rather do it than have Zoe see the wrong thing," he explained. "I'm also the only one in Ruin who can spot a splice, an edit, or that kind of stuff. Jeri, videos are my thing. Digital editing is what I plan to study next year. If *I* do this, we're less likely to miss something."

"And I'll keep the alcohol stocked," Riley said as she made her way down the stairs to join us with hands full of coffee mugs.

"Getting drunk won't help," Hottie countered.

"But it does blur the edges," she countered. "I'm not saying anyone has to drink. I'm certainly not pushing it on you underage fuckers. All I'm offering is a way to cope in an environment that's a lot less likely to make it become a crutch."

"She's got a point," Jinxy said. "A shot to numb things is a lot different from a bottle, alone, to drown it."

"Maybe just coffee?" Ripper asked.

With a smile, Riley passed him a bright purple mug. "I think this is your color. Cade, you get orange, Hottie, you're stuck with this yellow thing now."

"Gold," Hottie countered.

"Oh, is that your preferred color?" she asked, but her eyes jumped to Knock, giving her away.

"I said," Knock groaned, clearly trying to defend himself, "that his in-game team was gold. I don't know if he loves it."

"Well, I hate that cup, that marigold color, and everything about it," Riley said as she passed Hottie a coffee. "So I've decided it's his. Pink for Jericho, red for Zoe, dark blue for you, Knock, and rainbow for me."

On the couch, Cade chuckled. "And that," he informed the rest of us, "is her way of letting you know you now have permanent coffee cups in her house, which means you're part of the family."

"Also means," Zoe said, "that we can brew the coffee now so she doesn't always have to."

"Ok," I said, waving my hands before me to get everyone's attention. "Back to the subject at hand. Cade just got his ass kicked - again - and for what? We got a clone of the tablet and a keylogger. Guys, now what?"

"Now," Knock said, "we find out what they've been hiding, where they're going, and see all the shit that prick never wanted us to know about."

"Which means more waiting," Hottie told me.

"And organizing," Ripper added. "Filling in the timeline."

"Sorting the data," Zoe added. "If we want this to be a good, clean case, then we need to have it all in labeled folders, easy to follow."

"And as tedious as that is," Jinxy said, "I think they're all right. Sorry, Jeri. No nukes today, but this? This is a big fucking win."

And yet I wasn't ready to believe it. A step, sure - but this was not enough of a break to make a win. Over and over, we'd been let down, and I was not about to get my hopes up just to have them dashed all over again.

Still, I was willing to hope that somewhere in all the data we'd just stolen there might be a gem waiting to be found. Something good. Something more than the pain we'd been limited to so far.

Something that might break this case wide open, if we were patient enough to find it.

CHAPTER 41

CADE

It didn't take long before Riley's leftover prescription painkillers started to take effect. When my head started bobbing, Knock and Hot all but carried me to bed. There I lay, listening to the soft but jumbled voices of my friends. They were fixing things. I knew it. I also had no clue how I was supposed to help like this.

At some point, my eyes closed. They didn't open again until a swath of light leaked through the door as it opened. Murmuring, I tried to sit up, only to hear a deep and soothing voice.

"It's just me." Even backlit, Logan was easy to identify.

"Is everyone gone?" I asked.

"Mhm," he agreed as he moved to drop a bottle on the table beside me. "Ruin divvied up sections to sort and headed home so you could rest. Knock and Riley are in the barn, cleaning it for you. Kitty's at a pregnancy or family class. I can't keep track, and she won't let me go with her."

"Because you're not the baby daddy," I teased.

He tipped his head to the side, accepting that. "True, but I hate that she's doing it on her own." Then he gestured for me to shift over. "How are you doing, Cade? Your face looks like shit."

I huffed out a laugh. "Yeah, probably. Still, we got the keylogger on Dylan's computer and finally got into that damned tablet."

"And the whole time," Logan told me, "Knock was pacing the basement in a panic."

"What?"

He just nodded slowly. "According to Riley, your boyfriend was *very* worried about you. He doesn't want to make you feel bad about it, and he'd probably be embarrassed to admit it, but that doesn't stop him from being scared you'd get hurt bad this time."

"Yeah, but I could do this," I insisted.

Which made Logan give me a sad smile. "Cade, you can do a lot of things. Shit, at the rate you've been learning about tech? Hardware, software, internet security, and more? You're a smart guy. That's why Knock's into you, so just don't take it for granted, ok?"

Grunting, I pushed myself up a little higher. "Logan, I'm the muscle for this group. If someone needs to take the hits, it needs to be me. I mean, Knock's talking about how someone's going to go to jail for this - and I think he's right - but it needs to be me."

"Why?" Logan asked.

Which threw me off because it wasn't the response I'd expected. "What?"

"Why does it need to be you?" he pressed. "Why not Jericho, or Hot, or any of the others?"

"Um, Jinxy has a record," I said, trying to think through the fuzz these pills made of my brain. "If he got arrested, it'd be worse, right?"

"It would."

"And Jericho would do too well in jail," I said, laughing to show

I didn't really mean that. "No, in all honesty, I think going to jail would derail her entire life. She'd give up. We all agree it can't be her."

"Makes sense," Logan said. "But why you?"

"Well, Ripper and Zoe have these perfect little lives," I tried to explain. "And Knock! I mean, he's a professional gamer!"

"Sponsored," he corrected, "but what does his job have to do with this?"

"He has a fucking future!" I finally snapped. "They all do. Me?" I scoffed. "I'm the screwup who's lucky enough to have friends who'll help. Shouldn't I help them back? Isn't this how I make sure they know how much I appreciate it?"

Logan gently reached up to clasp my shoulder. It was an almost paternal gesture, not the sort of thing I was used to. Especially not with him sitting on the edge of my bed.

"I'm going to guess your father didn't have a high opinion of you?" he asked.

I huff-grunted, because that should've been obvious.

Which made Logan almost smile. "Yeah, kinda what I thought. But here's the thing." He rubbed gently. "He was wrong, Cade. Your father put his fears and failures on your shoulders and expected you to carry them. That's not your job, and it's not fucking fair, ok?"

"Ok..."

"And," he went on, "you're a smart guy. Trust me, I've been sharing a space with you long enough to be positive of that. You have a future too, and a damned good one - so long as you don't throw it away. That means you need to stop thinking you're useless, the weak link, or anything else."

"No, I..." I wasn't sure what to say, because I did kinda think those things.

"Trust me, I've been there," he promised. "When I was your age, I was so fucked up about everything. I wanted to make my father proud. I wanted to make the girls like me. I wanted to be this perfect guy, and I had no fucking clue how."

"Yeah, but you're... you!" I countered.

"I am now," he agreed. "Back then I was just a zit-faced dork who loved video games. I was an attorney's kid, raised with a silver spoon in my mouth. I had the entire world laid out ahead of me on a silver fucking platter - and I still thought I was a fuckup. Why? Because no one told me I wasn't." Then he smiled. "So this is me telling you. You, Cade, are not a fuckup. You are not the extra. You are not a burden or a pity case. You're a young man who somehow managed to make the meanest bitch in the world respect him, and that should say a hell of a lot."

"Jericho?" I asked, trying to figure out who was the mean bitch.

He laughed. "No, Riley. Trust me, Jericho's got potential, but Riley's mastered the skill. Never mind that young man you have wrapped around your finger."

"Knock," I realized.

He nodded. "That kid has become like a brother to me. I adore him, and I will tear the world apart at its seams to keep him safe. Here's the thing. I see him look at you with the same expression. I'm not sure what's going on with your relationship, and I'm sure as shit not about to try to figure it out. The polycule works for the group of you, and that's all that matters - but don't think it doesn't mean it can't be serious."

"Yeah," I breathed, not sure what else to say.

Logan simply leaned back. "Too much, huh?"

"No, it's just that I don't know what you want from me."

He murmured in response. "Ok, fair. I think I'm wanting to see you value yourself. I'm wanting you to accept that you now have an entire house filled with people who have your back. I want you to stop running into dangerous situations and showing up at home black and blue. Most of all, I want you to realize what it means when your boyfriend is worried."

"Was he that worried?" I asked. "Because, when I called, he got right to work."

"To keep from making you feel like he was emasculating you," Logan said. "After all, it has to be hard to date a man, right?"

That made my face scrunch up in confusion. "What do you mean?"

"Well, with a woman, it's usually easy," he explained. "Not Riley or Jericho, but most girls. You tell them they're beautiful and they giggle. Buy them a few presents and they feel spoiled. The rules are simple, and so long as we guys follow the steps, we can't fuck it up too bad."

"Kinda like me and Tiffany," I said, proving I was following along. "But I never really felt that close with her."

"You do with Jeri?" he asked.

This time, I was the one nodding. "Yeah. It's raw. She lays it all out, blunt-like. If I fuck up, she makes sure I know, and yet she keeps giving me the chance to fix it."

"What about with Knock?" he asked.

My mouth opened and hung there.

Logan grunted, seeing the expression. "Harder, huh?"

"Yeah," I relented. "I mean, we talk. Fuck, we talk all the time, but it's different."

"You talk about things, not internal stuff," he guessed. "Cleaning the barn instead of being frustrated about these boys. Being horny instead of how much you like him. That sort of stuff?"

"Yeah..."

"You know it's ok to tell him things you'd tell Jeri, right?"

"Huh?" My head twitched as I tried to make sense of that.

"That you need him," Logan offered. "That you want to protect him. That you *like* him. That he's beautiful, or handsome. Whichever word you like more. How he makes you feel warm inside when he smiles at you, or all the stupid gushy shit we drop on girls when we're into them."

I heard him. I really did, but there was one problem. "Yeah, but it's not the same."

"Could be," Logan told me. "If you've got the balls to put it out there, I mean. And here's the part no man is going to tell you." He paused, waiting until he had my full attention. "There's nothing wrong with wanting to be loved. It doesn't make you less of a man."

"I know," I promised.

"Do you?" he countered. "Because it took me a long time to figure that out. As a man, I was supposed to take it or leave it. There was always another piece of ass out there. I was successful, powerful, and rich. Women should want *me*. And yet, I spent too many years feeling lonely because I didn't realize that one simple truth."

"Oh."

"It's ok to want to be loved," he said again. "Not fucked. Not worshiped. It's completely normal for a man to long for someone to care about him - with all his flaws - and to take care of him. Someone he can take care of in return. Cade, it's the most natural thing in the world, and it doesn't make you weak to long for your man's arms around you, his head on your shoulder - or yours on his. You're not simply allowed to feel giddy around him, have a crush on him, or fall in love with him. You *need* to. Stop trying to hold back. Stop being scared of saying too much too soon, sounding like a pussy, or anything else that will run through your mind, and simply lean into it."

"With Knock?" I asked.

"With all of them," he assured me. "Love them, Cade, because I think that group is starting to love you, and none of them want you throwing your future away for them. They want to protect you just as much as you want to protect them, but you have this wall up. A big, strong emotional barrier that keeps the pain at a distance, right?"

"I've been trying to stop that," I admitted.

He smiled at me proudly. "Good. It's hard as fuck, huh?"

"Yeah." I breathed a single laugh. "I just don't want to be like Dylan and those guys, so I've been trying to, I dunno, not be."

"Then accept that you're a good man," he said. "Stop thinking that what men are *supposed* to do is right. Most of all, when your partner makes you feel like you're so full of excitement and warmth and stupid-happiness, tell them. Let them in, because it takes a damned strong man to take that risk first, and Knock doesn't know how either."

Oddly, that last line made me feel a lot better. It made me feel less like I was failing at something and more like this was just the type of wisdom a father - or big brother - would impart to a guy. Never mind that I'd never had anyone in my life willing to talk to me like this before.

Nope, my dad had yelled and ranted about what it took to be a "real man." He'd laughed at me for crying as a child. He'd done his best to "toughen me up," and shit. Not once had he ever sat with me like this and talked. Certainly not about things like *this*.

"Logan?" I finally asked. "Why are you telling me this?"

"Because once upon a time, my father sat me down and told me the same thing, or close enough. It was when I was ready to throw away my entire career for some wild woman who was barely giving me any hints of what she wanted. I was torn between writing her off - because I thought I should - and following her to the ends of the earth."

"Riley?" I guessed.

He nodded. "This whole family. I fell in love with the wind, and I had no clue how to handle it. My dad..." His eyes jumped to the wall and Logan smiled. "He told me that when 'the one' comes around, a man knows. The only way to catch them, though, is to surrender completely. Let love happen. Don't fight it. Don't try to be strong in the face of it. He said that even getting my heart broken would be worth it if I loved hard enough, because loving is a win on its own. It's not about what we get back, Cade. It's about what we can give. That, little brother, is love, and I think you're standing right at the edge of the cliff, looking at the drop and scared to fall, even though you're willing to throw everything else away for them."

"Yeah," I said softly. "That's kinda how it feels."

"Then don't fall, Cade. Jump." He palmed the back of my neck and smiled. "Be a man and go all-in. I've got your back on this, ok?"

"And when I make a fool out of myself?" I asked.

He bit back a laugh. "Like today? Going to that guy's house on your own, getting beaten up? Risking yourself without thinking about how that would crush every single person in this house? Not just Knock or Jericho, but me, Riley, and Kitty?"

"Yeah, but..."

"Jump," he told me again. "Love someone so hard that throwing your life away is no longer an option, and I will always have your back. Legally, physically, or anything else. It's what family does, ok?"

"Ok," I agreed.

Then he nudged the bottle he'd put on the table. "This is horse liniment. It'll help with the aches. Do *not* use it on your dick. Just trust me on that. Do have Knock help rub it on everywhere else." And he moved to stand.

"Logan?" I asked before he could leave.

"Mm?"

"How do I..." I paused, at a loss for words. "With Knock, I mean? Like, how do I tell him that I kinda, um..."

"Like him?" he offered.

I just nodded.

"Do you?"

Again, I nodded.

"Then tell him you care about him," he said. "It's that easy. Just lay it out there like a gift. He can either take it or not."

My next words came out almost too soft to hear. "What if he doesn't?"

"Then you still have a home," Logan assured me. "You are still family. Besides, it takes guts to take a risk, right? Well, so you know, risks don't always have to be putting your face in the way of someone's fist. That's the easy shit. This? Growing a relationship? That's what makes a 'real man.'" Then he reached for the door. "And if you have more questions, I'm always here to talk it out. Brother to brother. No shame." And then he was gone, but those last words hung in the air.

No shame. For some reason, that was exactly what I'd needed to hear.

CHAPTER 42

KNOCK

I spoiled Cade with a long soak in the bath that night. Later, I rubbed him down with Riley's horse liniment. The best part, though, was how he snuggled up into the crook of my arm before falling asleep. That was why, the next morning, I woke with a smile on my face.

Cade was still out cold. Not surprising, considering he'd taken a second dose of Riley's pain pills. I also really didn't want to wake him. So, carefully sliding my arm out from under his neck, I extracted myself from the bed and decided to get started on sorting the data he'd gotten his ass kicked for.

When I stumbled out of the room, the sound of key clicks made me look over to see Riley already lost in a game. Her headset was on, keeping the sounds of it to herself, and her brow was creased in concentration. On her screen, the kill list was flying, yet she still managed to jerk her chin in something near my direction as a greeting.

I just shook my head and kept going towards the bathroom. It wasn't what most people would call "early," but in this house it was. I was pretty sure the clock showed it was a quarter till noon when I'd left my room, so why was Riley awake?

Once I was done with my morning routine, I went back to ask - but she was gone. Giving in, I dropped down into my own chair and fired up my computer. Before the thing had even finished booting up, a dark-blue coffee mug was placed just above my mousepad.

"Why are you awake?" I asked, turning to see Riley making her way back to her own chair with her latest favorite coffee mug.

"That damned dog," she said, leaning back just to kick her feet up on the desk.

Which meant she wasn't diving back into the game. So, turning my chair, I shifted so I could face her. Then I claimed my coffee, took a sip, and leaned back to match her.

"So did you leave Quake outside?" I tried next.

She paused to take a long drink of her own coffee. "He abandoned me for Kitty. Where's Cade?"

"Sleeping," I said, feeling my lips curl again. "Pretty sure you knocked his ass out with those pills."

"He needs it," she pointed out. "But if he's sleeping, then that means you might tell me how you're doing with all of this?"

"Of what?"

She pointed towards my bedroom door and then waggled her entire arm. "That. The boyfriend living with you. The boyfriend getting beat up *again*. The bullshit with KoG and this tablet, and the girls at your school getting fucked over." Then she rocked her head from side to side. "And how that girl is fitting into your life, if you're in too deep, and those sorts of little things."

"Damn," I joked, "hit me with the easy shit before coffee, huh?"

"Means you'll say more than you want," she countered with a sly grin.

Which made me laugh, because she was probably right. "I

want to say I'm good, but the truth is that I don't think I know anymore."

"How so?"

I just flopped an arm at my computer. "This shit! Riley, these guys are serially raping women, and we don't know how to stop them."

"And the cops aren't an option?" she asked, but her tone made it clear she had ulterior motives to her question.

I grunted, then took another drink of coffee. "They should be, but they really aren't. I don't think it's their fault either. Cyn says there's only so much we can do with videos and no victims."

"But you could still give it to them and wipe your hands of this mess," she countered. "Knock, that's their job, not yours."

"And nothing would get done!" I snapped.

She lifted a hand to calm me down. "Zoe's handled," she said. "These other girls are in a big mess. I'm not disagreeing with you at all. I'm just trying to give you the flip side of things. If this is too much, then turn it over to the police and get out."

"Which means nothing would happen," I said. "Riley, that's what's weighing on me. Not the doing it part. Not even looking at the shit these boys do - and trust me, that's fucking horrific. No, it's knowing they're 'just girls.' They were 'asking for it.' They were drinking, so clearly, it's 'their fault.' It's no fucking different than listening to the fuckers go off on you at the PLG!"

And she smiled slowly. "Yeah, that's pretty much what I expected you to say. I think we broke you."

"Fixed," I corrected. "You opened my eyes, gave me the tools to become a superhero, and accepted it when that was the path I decided to follow." I shrugged. "I dunno. It's not supposed to be easy, right?"

"Nope," she agreed. "It's supposed to be a fire that burns in your gut, making you want to do the dumbest shit ever just because someone has to do something. It should make you long to stand up when no one else does, not care if they like you, and refuse to sit your ass back down until shit's right again."

I just tilted my head at her. "And I learned from the best."

Which made Riley murmur thoughtfully. "I don't know if I'd go that far. I think it's more of a team effort. For you. For me. For all of us." Then she flicked a finger at my room again. "So how's that team working out?"

"Good, I think."

"You think?" But before I could reply to that, she added, "Logan talked to him last night."

"About?"

"You."

Yep, I was going to need one more sip of my coffee, because that didn't necessarily sound good. It also made me think they were ganging up on us. Granted, that wasn't out of the realm of possibilities for these two. Plus, I knew that if they were, Kitty would likely join in shortly.

"Are we a problem?" I asked. "Is there something I need to know?"

"You're not a problem," she promised. "But I saw you pacing this room yesterday when he wasn't here. When I gave him the drive, I thought you were ok with thi- " She paused as one of the doors opened.

We both turned to check my room, then twisted to look at hers. Barely awake, Logan staggered out in a loose pair of emoji pajama bottoms. His bare feet peeked from the bottom and he didn't have on a shirt. The cutest part, however, was his disheveled hair and the way his eyes were barely open.

"Sit," Riley told him even as she hopped up. "I'll get you a coffee."

"That is why I love you," he breathed before pulling her against his chest to steal a kiss. "How's Cade?"

"Sleeping," Riley answered.

Logan nodded, letting her go even as he continued towards the bathroom. Taking the chance, I snuck in a few more gulps of coffee, but I wasn't quite ready to start in on the Squirrel yet. I debated a few rounds of Eternal Combat, but knew that would suck me in. What I needed to do was wake the rest of the way up and then actually make some progress.

After all, Cade had gone through so much to get this for us. When he'd said he was going to Dylan's place, I'd gotten the impression he was going to *talk* to the guy. I assumed he'd sneak the drive into one of the ports, distracting Dylan with a verbal fight at worst. I'd hoped he would be safe, but this?

Never in a million years would I have imagined knocking someone out cold, taking their keys, and sneaking into their home. Yeah, it had worked out, but shit. Cade had planned that fight. He'd known he'd get hurt in the process. He'd also considered it worthwhile because there was a damned *chance* we might find something useful.

Just for a fucking chance.

I was smiling at my boyfriend's stupidity - and courage - when Logan made his way out of the bathroom. His hair was in better shape. His chest was still bare. He also looked like he didn't give a shit at all as he claimed his seat beside me.

"Cade's not hurt too bad, is he?" he asked.

I shrugged. "It's hard to tell with him. I mean, he's got a pretty good bruise on his face, and I bet he's going to be moving slow today, but if asked he'll just say he's fine."

"The joy of loving the protectors," Logan murmured as he turned his chair around. "We get to sit our asses at home, know they're throwing themselves in shit, and not have a damned way to help without removing all their power."

"That's how you feel with Riley?" I asked.

"What about me?" she asked on her way down the stairs.

"Loving the protectors," Logan repeated. "I knew what I was

getting into with you. Pretty sure Knock's getting a few hard lessons, though."

"I'm not that bad," Riley grumbled as she passed Logan his own coffee mug - a stainless steel one.

He accepted the cup, but scoffed at her. "Yeah, Q, you are. You're probably worse than that. Shit, you were willing to chew my ass out for just trying to help."

"Because I didn't want to need it," she admitted.

Logan just looked at me and lifted a brow. "And this is what you chose for yourself."

"Twice," Riley said. "Cade and Jericho."

"But I know how to deal with you," I told Riley.

"It's different," Logan said. "When it's someone you love - or just care about - it hits harder. Besides, you've made yourself Riley's sidekick. That puts her in the position of power. However, I'm willing to bet that's not how it works with your partners, hm?"

"Not really," I admitted. "I'm not sure if we have a hierarchy like that, though."

"Sure you do," Riley said. "Everyone does. Maybe it changes, but sometimes you'll be lead for a thing you know. Other times, someone else will be."

"But that's the thing," I pointed out. "We're all lead on our own things. Ripper's the video guy. He and Zoe are damned good at organizing. I mean, she does the file moving, and he tracks all the details. Hottie and Jinxy know hacking pretty well. Jericho's the one who drags us into shit."

"And you?" Riley asked. "Because I can already guess Cade's the one who gets in fights to keep anyone else from being hit."

"I keep us within the lines," I said. "I can't say I'm a better hacker than Jeri, Jinxy, or Hottie. I can say I know more about what limits we have to work around. Cyn taught me that."

"Which means you organize the whole," Logan offered.

"Probably makes it even harder when your cute little boyfriend runs off to do something stupid, hm?"

"Makes me feel more helpless," I admitted.

"And that's ok," Logan said. "The hard part is making sure you don't try to stop them."

"Sometimes I want to," I admitted.

He nodded slowly. "Trust me, I get it. Sometimes I want to stop her. I also know I can't. Not just because I don't think it would work, but also because she has to. If Riley doesn't do this, then who will?"

"And Cade can take a hit better than you," Riley added.

Logan groaned. "You're not helping."

"I am!" she insisted. "Listen to me. Knock, you're a tough guy. Could you survive a fight like that? Fuck yeah! That doesn't mean you'd be good at it, though. Doesn't mean you'd accomplish what you wanted, right?"

"Probably not," I admitted. "I mean, I wouldn't know how to knock someone out."

"But Cade does," she said. "He proved it. The why is the hard part. Did he learn from avoiding his dad, fighting with those guys, or somewhere else? Doesn't matter, but he did learn. That means this is what he's good at."

"He's good at a hell of a lot more than just fighting," Logan snapped.

"Didn't say he wasn't," Riley assured him. "But he *is* good at fighting. He's good at knowing what data they needed. The guy also picks up shit fast. That means he's the best for the job."

"And maybe Knock has a problem with wondering if Cade's getting his ass handed to him?" Logan countered. "Or maybe how broken he'll be when he gets home? Maybe, Riley, it's fucking hard to be the one who protects the protectors." Then he looked at me. "But someone has to, Knock. They won't fucking protect themselves, you know. I think it's part of what draws us to them."

"That little bit of wild," I realized.

Logan began to smile even as he nodded. "Yeah. Like loving the wind. But the one thing these wild ones won't tell you? They need a soft spot to crash. They need a safety net. They hate that they need it, but it doesn't stop them from doing so. They aren't trying to make us worry. In truth, they think they're saving us."

My eyes dropped down to my coffee and I nodded slowly. "Yeah, I can see that. Cade keeps trying to protect everyone. Me, Jeri, Ripper, and definitely Zoe. Even his ex, when he can."

"And you like it, right?" Logan asked.

"Yeah..." I breathed.

"Because it means he cares about people," he went on. "It's the only way he knows to show how he feels. He thinks he has to take the pain because no one has ever taught him otherwise. To people like Cade and Riley, life hurts. It's one hit after another. Sometimes physical, sometimes mental, always emotional. They also feel safer knowing the pain is coming at them, because they can handle it. And here's the thing: they really can. We might hate it, but they *can* handle it."

"Which is why I keep trusting you to do stupid shit," Riley said softly.

And she had a point. How many times had she pointed out that she had drugs if things went bad? How often had our plan been to get in shit, and she'd just gone along with it? Some might call that being a bad influence, but it really wasn't. It was nothing more than my big sister accepting we knew our own limits, and trusting us to ask for help when we might need it.

"But what if Cade doesn't realize he has other options?" I asked. "What if he doesn't know we can help, or it might be too much for him, or I dunno. Those things?"

"Tell him," Logan said. "Knock, that guy is your boyfriend. Tell him he doesn't have to always win. Lay it out there so he isn't trying to guess what you expect from him. Make it clear you care about him enough that you worry about him."

"And that you'll always have his back, stand at his side, or jump in front of him when he needs it," Riley added. "Let him know you're his partner, not his responsibility."

"Yeah..." I said, thinking about what they were trying to tell me.

Because they had a point. Cade and I were circling around each other, trying to figure ourselves out. We shouldn't be living together yet. It was too soon, too fast, and too unexpected. It was also the best option, considering the circumstances.

But wasn't the same thing true with Jeri? Not the part about too fast, but about being her partner. Throughout her life, she'd only had Hottie to lean on. Now she had all of us, and while we tried to make sure she knew that, I was pretty sure none of us had ever said it quite so bluntly. We'd never given her the option to be weak. We'd never reassured her that we'd still care about her if she was.

I needed to do all of that - with both of them. Fuck, in truth, I needed to say the same thing to all of my partners. Zoe, Ripper, and even Hottie probably needed to hear it just as much. Jinxy too, but I didn't really know him as well. Then again, would I ever if I didn't take a bit of a risk?

But mostly Cade. Jeri had Hottie to lean on. Ripper had Zoe. Even Jinxy had Hottie and Zoe. Who did Cade have besides me? Jeri would never think to say anything. That wasn't her nature. Cade still needed to hear it, which meant this was up to me. And that was when I realized something else.

"You two are meddling in my relationship mess for a reason, aren't you?" I asked, looking between them both.

Riley just smiled and kicked her feet back up. "Maybe..."

Logan grunted at her, unimpressed. "Yes, Knock. This thing you have? Seven people, all in some mess of a relationship, all doing their own thing? It's not going to be easy under the best circumstances."

"No relationship is," Riley pointed out.

"But," Logan went on, "it's a lot easier when someone is willing to start the communication. When someone can teach the others to talk about the emotional stuff."

I just nodded slowly. "Which kinda puts a whole new spin on mentoring me, just so you two know."

"Family," Riley corrected. "Call this being a good influence."

"Or some kind of influence," Logan joked. "It's also our way of saying we have your back. Kitty too."

"Because some of this was her idea," Riley said. "Well, the whole emotional baggage bit, at least. Your partners are fucked, Knock."

"So am I," I reminded her.

She shrugged that off. "And the best part is it doesn't have to be a bad thing. Cade probably learned to fight because his dad beat the crap out of him. He took something bad and made it amazing. You, little brother, know exactly how that works. So help the rest of your polycule figure it out."

CHAPTER 43

RIPPER

Friday night, we did nothing but move files around, separating video, audio, text, and more. Everyone but Cade and Knock was on Discord, working together to make this happen. Knock needed to take care of his boyfriend, and from what I'd seen, Cade was hurting pretty good. Even better, since it was the weekend, we could all stay up until it was finally done. That would be one less thing for those two to worry about.

The next morning, I had nothing stopping me from diving in. I'd volunteered to take the videos. I was going to go through all of these and hopefully find what we needed. Pulling out my headphones, I locked the door to my room so my parents wouldn't accidentally walk in and think the wrong thing, then got to work.

On the Squirrel was now a folder titled "Videos." Simple and easy to find. I just didn't expect it to be filled when I opened it. So many fucking videos! All of them were titled with numbers, but a moment of looking made me realize those weren't just dates. It also had the damned time in the file name! And they'd been sorted from oldest to newest.

Bracing myself, I played the first one. Two seconds in, I wanted to stop, but I couldn't. I'd known this would be hard. I could do this. Someone fucking had to, and if I didn't, then who would? Besides, I had to find a point where I could get a headshot of the girl.

Once I got that, I clipped it out, named it to match the video it had come from, and dropped it in a subfolder I made. This way, I could have Zoe look through the girls. She used to know everyone, so hopefully she'd be able to assign names to these victims.

Then I moved to the next.

Watching these in chronological order made it even worse. Like this, I could see the progression these fuckers made. Worse, Marissa was not the first. Nope, she was number three. For the first few videos in the folder, they alternated between the entire group and simply one of the guys raping their victim.

Then I came across Zoe's.

Smacking at the space bar paused the video, but my stomach turned. I wrenched off my headphones, hopped up, and rushed to unlock my door. Saliva began to fill my mouth, forcing me to swallow it back, and I raced for the bathroom at the end of the hall. I barely made it. Closing the door behind me, my guts began to heave.

I breathed, forcing the horror back. I also knelt before the toilet, not sure if I would win this battle. That had been my best friend on the screen. To see her glazed eyes and limp body? To know she'd been alone, helpless, and I should've fucking been there? Worse, to violate her yet again by watching that?

No, I couldn't do this. I wasn't sure how long I spent in the bathroom, but when my insides finally accepted there was nothing to purge, I made my way back to my room. On my screen, the frozen image of my best friend was still waiting. Needless to say, I closed the tab quickly.

Propping my elbows up on my desk, I scrubbed at my face. That didn't help, even if it all but forced me to breathe. Slowly, I filled my lungs, pushing the air out when done with it. I had to do this. I needed to push through this. Zoe needed me to watch that because I'd already seen most of it, and this appeared to be the unedited version - but I didn't want to.

I hated this idea so much that my eyes were tearing up. My fingers were trembling. Crap like this was supposed to be in a horror movie, and we were supposed to know it wasn't real. This was! All of this shit was much too real, and while I felt disconnected from most of the victims, it was different for Zoe.

For much too long, I sat there, paralyzed between wanting to help and not wanting to watch that. Every time I was sure I'd talked myself into it, I found another reason to hesitate. Cade could've done this. Knock could've. Fuck, Hot definitely would be able to push through it.

Me? I needed help.

Desperate to see who was around, I opened Discord. The server was mostly empty, since it was still early, but sitting in the main room was the one man who might be able to help me right now. So, picking up my headphones again, I joined the channel and decided to accept I was too much of a pussy to do this.

"Jinxy?" I said as soon as my mic was active.

"Morning, man," he responded. "Wanna come help me with this quest?"

"Um..."

"Damage Control then," he said, vanishing from the channel.

I clicked to follow, once again waiting while the system logged me all the way in. The pair of us were alone in this chat space, but I wasn't sure that made me feel better. Shit, in truth I didn't even know how to bring any of this up.

"What's going on?" he asked, making it easy.

"I found Zoe's video," I breathed.

"Fuck."

He didn't yell the word. He just said it calmly. Too calmly. Somehow, that seemed even more appropriate, though. It made me feel like the weight crushing my mind was valid.

"Did you watch it?" he finally asked.

"I can't," I admitted. "I've been staring at my monitor for... Shit, half an hour? I almost puked, Jinxy."

"But you've seen it before," he said.

"The fucking edited version!" I snapped.

"Wait." He seemed surprised. "You have the unedited videos?"

"Yeah," I breathed. "From the thumbnails, I think I might have the edited ones too. There are so many fucking videos in here, and a lot of them look like the same girls, but I'm not that far in."

"Ok," he said. "Take a break, man. Don't try to push through this. And if you want, I'll ask Jeri to watch Zoe's videos."

"Not you?"

"Not me," he replied. "The last thing I want is to see that shit. Fuck no. There's a reason I didn't fight to get in on that, Ripper. I couldn't do it."

My next words were barely a whisper. "I can't either."

"But you are," he reminded me.

"No!" I snapped. "Fuck, don't you get it? I can't do this shit!" And I flung myself back in my chair. "Jinxy, it's too much. This? It's like... I'm watching these assholes learn, you know? And Marissa wasn't the first!"

"She was just the one that caused the change," he realized.

I grunted, not caring so much about that right now. "All these girls, and not a single one said it's ok for me to see this shit. I feel like I'm raping them all over again!"

"You're helping them," he promised.

"Doesn't change the lack of consent."

That made him pause, the silence in our chat feeling much too loud. I pushed out a heavy breath, because that wasn't all of my problem. A big part, sure. I didn't want to be anything like Alpha Team, but I also knew someone would see these. Someone had to review them. Someone had to make sure these girls got the justice they deserved, and I had the skills to help.

But something else made it even worse. "We hear about it," I said, not sure how to put this into words. "Rape. It's on the news. It's in our movies, social media, and all of that. We cheered on the MeToo Movement, right? But this?" I shook my head, even though he couldn't see. "Jinxy, it's different."

"It's real," he explained. "All that other shit is just a theory. It's someone else, somewhere else. Ripper, it's no different than how every time there's a mass shooting, someone always says, 'I never thought it could happen here.' We disconnect from it to protect ourselves. Our minds."

"But it's still real!" I whined. "All these girls, Jinxy. Worse, none of them are talking about it. I mean, no. That sounds wrong. It's like, I hate that they can't talk about it. That if they do, it gets worse. Women complain about men being assholes. They talk about domestic violence and sexual assault. They scream it all over the internet, but it's distant. It's someone else. I believe them. I fucking do! I just don't think I really get it."

"What do you mean?" he asked.

"The pain," I tried to explain. "The helplessness. It's not the pushing the guy off. It's the asking for help and getting nothing but blame. It's that the entire world is telling them to shut up and like it. That rape is their fault. Things like that. It's so..." I sighed. "Evil. That's the only word I have for this. It's fucking evil, man."

"And this is us trying to fight back," he soothed. "Ripper, if no one will listen to those women when they say a man hurt them, then it's up to us to scream about it."

"Ruin?" I asked.

"No, men," he clarified. "We have to stand up and scream that this is not ok. That women are not here to amuse us. They are not objects! These girls..." He grunted. "Fuck, Zoe, you know? They're not a thing to amuse us. They have thoughts and feelings. They have futures. They have value outside of being a fuck-receptacle!"

"They should," I agreed.

"And to get that, they're going to need our help," he went on. "Seriously, do you think guys like the Alpha Team are going to listen to a woman?"

"But they aren't going to listen to a loser like me either," I shot back.

"No, but their friends might," he countered. "Someone has to do this, Ripper. Someone has to pick the fight. The girls can't do it, because they're already the victims. If we want to be their heroes? That means it's up to us. Fuck saying *we* didn't hurt them. Fuck pointing out how we're the good guys. Nope, if we want to be heroes, we need to put in the work, and this is the work."

"And it fucking sucks, ok?"

"Yeah, it does," he agreed. "It should."

I huffed in frustration. "But you're not willing to do it."

Jinxy pulled in a breath that sounded like it was through his teeth. "Yeah. Guess that means you're a better hero than me?"

"Not really helping," I told him.

"Fuck, man," he groaned. "I'm trying here. I mean, this shit shouldn't be easy. Some things should leave marks on our souls, and I think this is a damned good example. Wanna know something else?" He didn't want for me to respond. "I also think you're the right guy for this. I think you're one of the few people who can see this shit and not change your opinion about a girl."

"Why would I?"

"Because it's what people do," he said. "I know I would. Seeing

Zoe like that? I'd feel bad for her. I'd try to baby her, be gentle with her, and shit like that. I'd feel like she'd been hurt or broken, and like she needed me - the big man - to step up and take care of her. Spoiler: she doesn't."

"No, she doesn't," I agreed. "She likes the help, but she doesn't want it done for her. She doesn't want to lose any more power."

"That." He paused, the word hanging between us. "None of those girls want to lose any more power. They also don't need to know *you* watched those videos. That *you* are the hero who found some hint somewhere in that shit that put their abusers in jail, you know? Downside, however, is that you won't get the credit for being a hero."

"I don't want it," I promised.

"I know," he assured me. "I think that's why I like you, Ripper. You're one of the few guys who has his shit together. You truly see women as your equal, while the rest of us are still working on it. Maybe that's why it hurts so much?"

"Maybe," I relented. "I dunno. I just don't think I can keep doing this."

"Take it in pieces," he said. "A few at a time. Don't try to do it all in a day." Then he sighed, the sound much too heavy. "And when you break, I'm here to listen, ok? I might suck at it, and I'm probably not saying what you need to hear, but I'm fucking trying."

"It's actually helping," I told him. "I guess I just needed a reminder that I'm helping?"

"You," he swore, "are tackling the hardest part. You're also picking up little bits of their trauma and carrying them on your shoulders. It's going to add up, Ripper. Maybe it didn't happen to you, but it's still trauma. It's a crack in your perception of fairness, the world, or whatever the fuck you want to call it. *It fucking hurts.* Takes a real man to intentionally take on that kind of wound."

"Yeah..." I breathed. "Not sure that phrase is a good one

anymore, Jinxy. I'm starting to think I'd rather be a fake man. I dunno, a pussy?"

"One of the girls?" he offered, half joking.

Which made me huff something near a laugh. "Yeah, I'm cool with that too. I just think we need a better word for the people who refuse to fall in line."

"What line?"

"This one!" I said, waving at my screen even though he couldn't see. "The one that says real men are strong. Real men can fuck any girl he wants. Proper women obey their man."

"Ah, gender roles," he realized. "Yeah, that shit's bullshit. Fuck it. But I might have a word to solve your problem."

"Ok?"

"You're a gentleman, Ripper. A very gentle man. Kind, compassionate, and honest. Fuck ranking ourselves by alphas or betas. Fuck toxic masculinity, real masculinity, and all the other labels people keep trying to come up with. How about we simply strive to be kind, gentle men? The kind of men women can run to, not from. The kind of men we decide we're going to be."

"Gentlemen," I repeated. "Yeah, I think it's time to take that word back. I don't care if I'm real. I do care if I'm gentle, because my partners deserve nothing else."

CHAPTER 44

KNOCK

None of this was easy. For most of Saturday, we focused on trying to make sense of the information on Dylan's tablet. Jinxy, Hottie, Jeri, and I were trying to look through the history of the device. Jinxy was hunting for evidence of deleted files. Hottie was trying to track the wifi locations where this thing had connected. Jeri and I were doing our best to identify any websites that might be another storage location.

At the same time, Zoe was identifying girls. From the sounds of it, we had all of Tiffany's friends' videos now, even if these might not be the only copies. Ripper was in the process of matching his cropped headshots to both the unedited and edited versions of the videos. With the dates on those, that left Cade to fill in our "murder board," updating it with as much data as we could get.

And there was still so much more - yet not enough! At some point, I'd started dozing off in my chair. Cade, even as busted-up as he was, had done his best to get me to bed. It had only taken a little pouting to convince him to stay there with me, but on Sunday morning, we were both right back at it.

The data had to be here. I knew it did. Technology always left some little trace, but Dylan wasn't a dumbass. Well, not enough of one. He'd been wiping his history, clearing his cache, and removing his temp files. The fucker even had a "Clean Up" app so all he had to do was activate it.

The one thing we really needed was their online storage. Hottie was starting to think there might not be one. He even suggested what was on the tablet might be the extent of their crimes - and I had too, initially - but there was one big problem with that idea. Amber wasn't on it. So far, everyone else we knew about was, but Amber was missing, which meant they had videos somewhere else.

The question was how many?

Was it just Amber? Could there be more? One? A hundred? There was no way to know unless we found it, and I almost felt like everyone was trying to grasp at the easy answers just to call this done. But it wasn't done! This wasn't going to get fixed like this, and I didn't know enough to get the information I needed!

Slamming back my keyboard, I pushed to my feet and turned for the stairs. Behind me, I heard Cade turn towards me, shocked at my reaction. I didn't really blame him, but I was right at the breaking point. I needed space. I needed to move. I fucking needed *something*!

"I'm going for a walk," I told him.

I wasn't even halfway up the stairs before he was out of his chair and following me. "Sounds like a good idea," he agreed.

I just kept going. I didn't want to yell. I certainly wasn't about to blow up, but I really wanted to. I wanted to open my mouth and scream, or punch a wall, or do something fucking stupid to get this feeling out of the back of my head. Sadly, the only way I knew how to do that was to walk, because I wasn't one of those tough guys. I'd never been given the chance to rage like Cade could. Nope, I'd always had to push it down, and this was not something I wanted to keep bottled up.

Leaving through the backyard, I made for the gate. Once I was through that, I turned my feet towards the side of the property, passing by the carriage house. I didn't make it, though. Cade caught up and grabbed my arm, pulling me around to face him.

"Knock?" he asked, clearly concerned.

I just waved an arm back towards the house. "It's not there! I've been over that tablet a dozen times, and it's just not there. Dylan fucking wiped that shit clean. It's like he knows what he's doing or something."

"We'll find it," Cade promised me.

I grunted in frustration. "Not there, we won't. And without their storage, we're fucked. All those girls they've raped? We can't fucking help them if we can't prove all of this. That's the thing, Cade. We can't make guesses. We can't assume we know what they did or why they did it. We have to have proof. Fucking real, hard evidence. Something good enough the cops can't fucking ignore this anymore!"

"And we'll get there," he assured me, rubbing my arm gently. "Knock, this is a step. A good one, right? I mean, we got a timeline now, at least?"

"And?" I asked. "Yay, we fucking know when they raped people." Leaning my head back, I shoved both hands into my blue hair. "We know it was rape. They know it was rape. Yet we don't have shit to *prove* it was rape, Cade. The girls nod! That's what fucked up Zoe when she tried to report it. It's what the cops will say if we dump this on them. They nod, so there's nothing we can do, but we have to fucking do something! All those girls are depending on us!"

"You'll find it," he soothed. "If anyone can, you will. I believe in you."

"Then you're a damned fool," I grumbled.

"Maybe," he said. "But I'd rather be a fool who believes in the guy who's actually trying to do something."

Turning, I flopped against the back of the carriage house, letting it hold me up. "I was so sure I could get something off that damn tablet. I'd convinced myself that all we needed was the data and we could fix this, but we can't, can we? You risked everything so we could clone the damned thing, and it's all but useless."

"I didn't risk shit," he assured me. "Knock, cloning the tablet was just good luck. So what if it's a bust? We're still going to fix this. We're not giving up yet."

So I reached up to trace the bruise on the side of his face. "Yeah, but this had to hurt."

Tilting his head slightly, he pressed his cheek into my hand. "It was worth it. The rest of you strain your brains all day long to figure this shit out. I got a bruise."

"One or two," I pointed out.

Which made him smile. "Yeah. Something like that. But we were stuck. Now we have ideas again. Besides, I know you'll figure something out. You always do."

"You have too much faith in me. I'm not that good."

He just shrugged. "Yeah, Knock, you are. I kinda think you're the most amazing guy ever."

And my damned heart forgot to beat. My eyes jumped up, finding his, and for a moment we just looked at each other. Fuck, he was gorgeous. The lock of hair that always fell across his face was there, daring me to push it back, so I did.

"You're not supposed to think I'm amazing when I'm failing," I breathed.

He moved a little closer, planting his body in front of mine. "But I do. Look, I'm probably fucking this up."

"Fucking what up?"

He ducked his head and let out a little chuckle. "Um, Logan

kinda said I should talk to you the way I talk to Jeri. To just lay it out there, so I'm trying, ok?"

"Ok," I agreed, waiting to see what he meant.

"And I like you," he said. "Fuck. That doesn't do it justice. I have a crush. You make me feel stupid and awkward and like I don't know how to play it cool. You're so fucking smart, and so damned chill about everything. It's like you've got your shit together, and I feel like a complete train wreck, but then you look at me like that, and I don't even care." He gestured at his chest. "I just feel this thing. And I don't know the words for it, or how to tell you, or what I should do about it, but it's fucking there, and it says you're perfect. It says you can do anything, so I fucking believe you can do anything."

I felt like I couldn't breathe. All I could do was nod my head, letting him know I'd heard, but all the words in the English language had just abandoned my brain. He thought I was smart? Not right now I wasn't.

"I wish I was more like you," I finally managed to mumble.

He just shook his head. "No, you really don't."

"But you're brave and charming," I told him. "You're so fucking sexy that it's unbelievable. And you're so good to the girls. Fuck, to all of us! You're kind and amazing, and I'm a dumb fuck who keeps waiting for you to get tired of him."

Those warm brown eyes of his sparkled a bit even as his lips curled higher. "So you maybe like me back?"

"Uh, yeah!" Which had us both laughing.

Then Cade clasped the side of my neck and moved even closer, only stopping when our chests were touching. "I like you, Knock. I like how you've got shit figured out - "

"I don't," I assured him.

"You do," he countered. "Trust me, compared to the rest of us? You got your shit together, and it makes me not just like you, but also respect you. Even when things aren't going the way we want, your first thought is about others. You want to save the damned world, and you know what? I honestly think you can."

"But the data isn't there," I reminded him.

So he leaned in and kissed me, halting my protest. "Listen," he whispered against my lips. "I think you'll figure this out. I also think you need a break. Fuck, we all probably do, but you never give yourself that luxury, do you? When you aren't trying to direct Ruin, you're working on your stats for Eternal Combat, working with the horses, or something else."

"Well, yeah, but - "

Again, he kissed me. "Shh," he breathed. "For once in your life, just stop, Jeff. Just stop trying to be all things for all people. Just stop for one minute."

There was something about hearing my real name in his voice, spoken so softly. It made me grab his shirt and pull him closer, intending to kiss him again, deeper.

But Cade smiled. "You wanted something to take your mind off the frustration, right?"

"I think you're a good distraction," I assured him, pulling at his shirt again.

This time, Cade followed and our mouths met. He didn't kiss me softly, though. Oh no, he kissed me hard, like he was daring me to worry about anything else but him. I caught the side of his head, holding his mouth to mine, and swept my tongue between his teeth.

Then I jerked my hand away. "Fuck, your bruises!"

"Which don't hurt that much," he assured me even as his hand slid down my chest. "Promise." His finger tripped over the waistband of my jeans. "It's private out here on the farm, right?"

"Uh huh," I breathed, feeling my dick getting hard fast.

The devious little smirk Cade gave me made it clear he noticed the ridge in my pants. "Good, because I want to try something." And then he dropped down to his knees.

Oh damn. Holy shit. Fucking wow.

My brain completely forgot about all my suddenly-unimportant problems with this guy looking up at me like that. When he reached for the button on my jeans, popping it open? Yeah, I was pretty sure my entire nervous system shorted out. I was also smiling stupidly. Very, very stupidly, and yet not dumb enough to tell him to stop.

"Hold your shirt up," he told me as he forced my zipper down.

I obeyed, grabbing the hem and hiking it up above my belly button. Cade pushed my jeans down, then slowly teased my underwear lower, taking his time about it. My dick was now throbbing with excitement, so once the fabric was low enough, the damned thing sprang free, flopping right towards his face.

"Nice," he said, wrapping his fingers around the base.

And then he pushed his mouth over it. Heat. That was the first thing I was aware of. Wet came next. Then it was nothing but pleasure. Trying not to move, I looked down, wanting to watch every second of this. His lips stretched as he slid down my shaft. His fist pushed lower.

"Oh, god," I breathed. "I'm not gonna last long."

His response was to murmur, which sent all those vibrations right over that highly sensitive skin. My knees damned near buckled, but I forced them to stay straight. There was no way I'd ruin my boyfriend's first blowjob. Hell, or my first time to have this done by a guy.

He slid off, playing with me, and my eyes wanted to roll up in my head. This was different from when Jeri had done it, but neither better nor worse. Cade played with me like he wanted to make me break. He licked at the sensitive spot under the head of my dick. His hand set a rhythm, nice and slow. Then his mouth followed.

All I could do was breathe. A few of those were rough as the air rushed from my lungs. Others were sharp as I struggled not to gasp. My eyes were locked on his face, entranced with how good he looked like that. This guy - *my* guy - was sucking me off, and it felt so good I forgot about anything else but the next time he swallowed me.

His mouth moved faster. His fist gripped me just a bit tighter. His tongue began to play with me, and I struggled to hold in my moans of pleasure. My hips wanted to twitch, but I fought to keep them still. I let my other hand, the one not holding my shirt, rest on the back of his head, and I gave in.

If this was him not knowing what he was doing, then damn. It felt so good. Maybe part of it was the excitement of being outside. Some of it was the stress and pressure all needing an outlet, and his mouth was a damned good one. Nothing else mattered but the next pass of his mouth, the feel of him bobbing across my length, and those words he'd said only a few minutes ago.

He liked me. This guy felt something for me. Whatever we were doing was about a whole hell of a lot more than sex, but the sex was fucking amazing too. This was mind-blowing. It was so good that I barely had the sense to gasp his name in warning because I was about to come.

"Cade," I begged.

He didn't slow at all, but I heard the back door of the house. I also couldn't stop my orgasm if I'd wanted to, and I didn't. Closing my eyes, I gave in, feeling the rush of pleasure hit, taking over my entire body as I spilled down my boyfriend's throat.

"Hey, there's..." Logan broke off to yelp. "Sorry!"

I gasped as my head jerked over. Cade quickly backed off my dick, doing the same. There, in the backyard, Logan stood with his back towards us and both hands over his face.

"What the fuck?" I asked.

"Sorry," he said again. "I didn't see shit. I mean, not too much shit." Then he groaned and dropped his head forward like he was giving up. "Can I fucking turn around yet?"

I scrambled for my underwear, pulling those into place so I could close my jeans. "Yeah. What do you want, Logan?"

He turned back around, making me realize Quake was by his side. "So, that alarm on your laptop? It's going off. I didn't want to disable it because I wasn't sure what it's for."

"On my laptop?" I asked, still working to button and zip my jeans.

"Yep."

I looked down at Cade, who was still on his knees. "Shit, that's the keylogger. It's set to go off if he tries to log into the KoG forums!"

"Fuck!" Cade said as he pushed to his feet. "We need to tell Ruin!"

Logan just tossed his hands in the air. "At least fucking kiss the guy, Knock! He just blew you!"

"Later," Cade said as he grabbed my arm and hauled me towards the gate. "We have work to do."

CHAPTER 45

CADE

The moment we made it downstairs, I grabbed my coffee cup and took a long swig to wash the taste of cum from my mouth. Then I sat down and texted Ruin. We had a group chat for things like this. The message was short, sweet, and right to the point.

Cade:
Discord. Now! We got something!

Beside me, Knock was pulling on his headset and tapping at his keyboard. I made sure I was active in the right channel on Discord, then reached for my own headset, but before I could put it on, a hand clasped my shoulder. Looking back, I saw Logan.

"Sorry to interrupt that."

"It was for a good reason," I said, feeling my face getting warmer. "Thanks for letting us know about the alarm. He was a little stressed."

"Don't be embarrassed," he said, his voice lowering a bit so it was between us. "Things like that happen around here. We still ok?"

"We're good," I promised. "I mean, I think we are."

Which made him smile. "Good. Get to work. Yell if you need us."

I nodded, pulled my headphones on, and was immediately assaulted with voices.

"You're recording that, right?" Hot was asking.

"Keeping a record of all of it," Knock promised.

"Does anyone know if KoG allows double logins?" Jeri asked.

"Don't try it," Jinxy warned her. "Too risky."

"I don't know what the excitement is about!" Zoe snapped. "Y'all need to slow down and break it down for me."

"It's the keylogger," Ripper told her.

"And?" she pressed.

This was something I actually knew how to handle. "Zoe, that keylogger is recording every button and click on Dylan's computer. In this case, that means it's recording his keyboard keys as he's logging into the Kings of Gaming forums. You know, giving us his username and password."

"So we can get in?" she asked.

"Careful..." Jinxy warned.

"Why?" Ripper demanded. "We've been waiting how long for this, and we just fucking got it!"

"Because it might require two-factor authentication," Jinxy said. "Or maybe it has a device tracker. Possibly it'll kick Dylan off the site, telling him another user is logged in with those credentials. We don't know how that fucking site works, and Knock says the guy who made it knows his shit."

"He does," Knock agreed. "Cyn couldn't get in, so I think Jinxy's right. We need to be patient with this."

"I'm so fucking tired of being patient!" Jeri grumbled.

"Yeah, but would you rather fuck everything up because you can't wait?" Jinxy asked.

"No..."

"I have a question," I said. "Why are we so excited about getting into the forums if we have the tablet?"

"Because it's KoG," Hot growled. "Because no one can get in if they aren't a sick motherfucker who's done horrible shit to earn rank."

"Because we have no clue how they work," Knock explained. "We have some ideas, but we're basically playing blind while they have an entire forum designed to keep them safe. They can coordinate, make plans, and brag about their crimes."

"And Amber found all those videos on there," Jeri added.

"Which means," Zoe said, "that Alpha Team has probably made posts that talk about what they did. Posts where they call it rape, making it clear they knew what they did was wrong."

"More proof to add to the pile," Ripper said.

Ok, those were all good points. Never mind that we needed to discuss what we'd all found anyway. So, instead of letting everyone freak out about something we couldn't exactly use right now, I decided to nudge them that way while hoping I wouldn't set Knock off again.

"Did anyone get anything useful from the tablet data?" I asked.

Ripper groaned. "Depends on what you call useful. I can prove the videos were usually taken in John's bedroom."

"And you know it's John's because..." Jeri asked.

"Me," Zoe said. "That's John's room, and it's in enough of the videos that it means they're raping these girls on his bed, filming it, and then he's sleeping there afterwards. I mean, talk about skeezy!"

"He probably gets off on that," Jinxy told her.

"I don't care!" Zoe said. "That's just gross!"

"It's all gross," I agreed. "But did we get anything else? I mean, we've all been at this all weekend."

"I've been trying to see what wifi connections the thing has had," Hot told us. "My hope is we can trace where it's been, giving us proof it was located at the scenes of the crimes."

"Which I kinda already had," Jinxy told him.

"But I didn't fucking know they were all at John's!" Hot shot back.

"Not all," Ripper said. "We've got a video with Yvette that's not at John's."

"I'll do my best to match that up," Hot said. "Is it her place or Dylan's? Somewhere else?"

"Looks like Dylan's," Zoe said. "I'd need Cade to make sure of that, though, since he's been there."

"Send me a screen grab," I told Ripper. "I know his room pretty well, and that's where we found the tablet."

"I've been trying to find deleted files," Jinxy told us. "I was hoping for some hint of videos that had been scrubbed. Sadly, the cloned copy doesn't give me much. It's not the actual hard drive in the tablet, so I'm doing my best to find shrapnel from old files. It's basically a bust."

"Any luck with a website, Jeri?" Knock asked.

Hot immediately groaned. "Don't ask her that!"

"No!" Jeri snapped. "I don't know how this fucker learned to clean up after himself. Self-righteous asshats like him are usually the kind to leave evidence all over the internet behind them, but there's jack and shit. I even tried to break into his password manager, and got nothing. Who doesn't have a password manager on their device? Google's, a master password program, or something! Nope, not this motherfucker."

"Same," Knock told her. "I did find an app called - "

"Clean Up," Jeri finished for him. "Yep. I saw that too. Know what else I found? The damned thing was created by someone called Soul Reaper. Pretty sure I've heard that name before."

"Fuck!" Knock snapped.

"What?" Ripper asked.

"Soul Reaper's the fucker who made the KoG site," he explained. "If these guys have an app for cleaning up their devices, made by the leader of the Kings of Gaming, that can't be good."

"Makes me think this buttmunch is minding his flock," Jinxy joked. Then he paused. "Shit, is that a bad phrase now? I mean, since you two are..."

I shoved my face in my hands, but I was laughing. "No, Jinxy, it's fine. I'm also starting to think the entire world is trying to cockblock me, but that's beside the point."

"Oh?" Ripper asked. "How so?"

"Logan interrupted my first attempt to give a blow job," I told him.

"Dude, you ok there, Knock?" Hot asked. "Suffering a little now?"

"He finished," Knock mumbled.

Which made the entire group laugh. The girls most of all. "So how bad was it?" Jeri asked.

"Who's that supposed to be to?" Ripper asked.

"Cade!" Zoe answered for her. "I mean, he's the one who had to deal with the finish!"

Fuck. My face was getting hot again, and they couldn't even see me! I used to think I was good about not blushing, but I'd been failing at that all day today. The strangest part of this, however, was that I also found myself smiling.

"Um, it's not as bad as I'd feared," I assured them. "I just haven't gotten my report card yet, since Logan broke up our fun time due to a certain alarm going off."

"For the keylogger," Knock explained.

"So?" Jeri asked. "How was it, Knock?"

"Shit," he grumbled. "Um... Good? I mean, how the fuck am I supposed to answer that?"

"He got off," Jinxy said. "Means it was pretty good."

"Knock, you're supposed to say it was the best blowjob ever. You can't imagine anything better," Ripper teased.

"Nope," Zoe said. "Jeri's in the channel. That would get him in shit."

"And now I'm finally seeing a downside to this whole polycule thing," Jinxy said. "Knock, have fun with the mess you made."

"Oh, I am," Knock assured him. "And I can honestly say it was the best I've ever had. Means Jeri has to work to keep up."

"Oh!" she laughed. "Ok, I can do that."

"Do not want to know," Hot groaned.

"Lies!" Zoe told him.

"Ok, ok, ok..." I begged. "Guys, I'm fucking blushing. Weren't we talking about the tablet? Like, progress or something?"

"And we just made fucking progress," Knock assured me. "Cade, this login? It's going to let us see into the blind spots. I mean, if they think their forums are impenetrable, then how much shit is out there?"

"And your FBI guy is still gone," Hot reminded him. "Think we can get the cops to give a shit about this?"

"I think we'll get enough to solidify our timeline," Ripper said. "That's the worst-case scenario. The best case, we get them confessing. And if they were dumb enough to use their game names - which we all think they would - then the chat logs will tie those things together, and that should be more than enough to make the cops do shit, right?"

"That's the plan," Knock agreed.

"But!" Hot said. "If you're right about this website's security, I think we need to wait until tomorrow before trying the username and password."

"Why?" Jeri asked. "I mean, if we just wait until Dylan's out of there - or even asleep?"

"And if it texts his phone?" Hot asked. "We don't know if he's using two-factor verification for his login, baby girl. If Dylan sees that, he might change his password, freak out, and start deleting shit."

"The deleting is the problem," Knock told her. "The password we'd get again, thanks to Cade putting that keylogger on his computer."

"Well, fuck," Jeri grumbled.

"I'll cut class and help tomorrow," Jinxy offered.

"Yeah," Hot said. "I'm already texting the evening manager to see if he wants some extra hours. While the kids are at school, they tend to keep their phones silenced."

"Not even vibrate," Zoe said. "Most of our teachers will hear that and get pissed. Airplane mode or totally silent."

"Which is perfect," Jinxy said.

"Mhm," Hot agreed. "If anything goes wrong, we'll have enough time to cover our tracks before Dylan realizes anything has happened. We'll hit them in the middle of a class. I'll be on the computer, because you're better with phones."

"Works for me," Jinxy said. "Time?"

"Fourth period," Jeri offered. "Hit him then. He'll have just checked his phone at lunch, and you might get away with him not looking again until school's out."

"Sounds good," Hot said. "And once we're in?"

It was Ripper who answered. "Then we'll divide out the work again, break it up, and take turns. I don't know about anyone else, but I'm having a hard time with this."

"Me too," Knock said.

"I feel like I'm not doing enough," I admitted.

"Shit," Jeri said. "Cade, you got your ass kicked to get us this far!"

"And you're doing the murder board stuff," Zoe reminded him.

"Which is all the easy shit," I pointed out.

Knock twisted in his seat to look at me. "So help me? Pretty sure you can surf a web forum."

"I can."

"And none of you are wrong," Hot said. "Guys, this is heavy shit we're dealing with. It's a lot of pressure, not to mention the trauma. And some of us - I mean you, Zoe - are a little closer to it. So we need to check up on each other, ok?"

"Which is why we're partners," Jinxy said.

"I still want my cowboy hat, Cade!" Zoe called out.

Which made me laugh. "I'll get you one. I just need the chance to go shopping for it. And no, I'm not buying you one of those million dollar felt things."

"I just want a red one," she told me.

Jeri laughed. "Think they make them in orange? That's Cade's favorite color, isn't it?"

"Assigned by Riley, so it's permanent," Knock said. "It also works for him."

I looked up and he was smiling at me. For the third time today, my stupid-ass face decided it wanted to warm up, but this time I liked it. There was something soft in his eyes. Something tender. Something that looked like more than just friends.

Yeah, that look was worth making a fool out of myself to get. It felt like a happy ending - in more ways than one!

CHAPTER 46

HOTSHOT

It took fifty bucks, but the afternoon manager agreed to come in at noon so I could head home early. Worth it, in my opinion, if we could get into the Kings of Gaming website. Still, that was cutting it a little close, so I rushed home to fire up both my desktop and my laptop.

The desktop loaded first. After opening Discord, I somehow wasn't shocked at all to see Jinxy's name in Damage Control. He'd said he'd be here to help, and he was. I also had a feeling he'd been here a while.

"Did you skip all your classes today?" I asked the moment I was logged in.

Jinxy's response was to laugh. "Yeah, pretty much. I also have a damned good excuse."

And that, right there, made me feel like shit. "Gran?" I asked. "She's not doing any better?"

"No, and she's not going to," he said, yet somehow his voice was calm. Too calm. "Grayson, she's dying. She's in hospice care."

"Fuck," I muttered. "Shawn, you should be worrying about her, not this."

"She doesn't want to be gawked at, she says." He huffed, clearly not agreeing. "I convinced her to let me come visit during Spring Break, but she said she's fine. She told me to focus on my future and all that old lady bullshit she does."

"Are you ok?" I asked.

It took much too long before he answered. My hands were busy on my laptop, activating my VPN, the secondary encryption, and even this cool little program from the toybox that would hide my MAC address. Easy stuff, but it made me overly aware of the silence hanging in the channel.

Then, "No, not really. My Gran is dying, man. She's got fucking cancer, they can't fix her, and I fucking hate it. I'm fucking pissed about it, because I can't really be anything else. So how about we let me use this anger against someone who deserves it?"

"We can do that," I assured him. "I'm getting everything ready right now. Just waiting on a text from Jeri to know when she's on her way to fourth period. I'm also willing to listen, you know."

"I do," Jinxy promised. "Fuck, man. I promise I do. It's just that I kinda want to think of some lighter shit, if you're cool with that?"

"Like Zoe?" I offered.

He groaned. "I dunno if that's lighter. I mean, I'm *going* to be coming down there. If I'm that close, I'm not going to head back without stopping to see you and Jeri, right?"

"And we have a room for you," I assured him. "Mine, but I'm ok with sleeping in Jeri's bed."

He laughed. "I bet you are. Hitting that barely-old-enough ass like you are."

"It's not like that," I hurried to tell him.

"I know," he promised. "Shit, man, I do know. Zoe's even younger."

"Yeah, but so are you."

He murmured, almost as if realizing that for the first time. "Fair point. Still, I know the thing with you being her 'big brother' is screwing with you. I know she doesn't give a shit. I'm kinda hoping that giving you a hard time about it will pull your head out of your ass."

"I just don't want to become one of those creepy guys," I admitted.

"And I think Ruin will make sure you don't," he promised. "So give in, bro. Admit you're completely whipped, you like it like that, and let me give you some shit? I mean, you know, since you feel all bad for me or something?"

"Or something," I grumbled, but I was only teasing him. "Ok, fine. You can give me shit about my official girlfriend all you want. I'm man enough to take it."

"Keep telling yourself that," he joked. "But seriously, meeting Zoe? I'm nervous as shit about it."

"Why?" Because the pair had been talking for months now.

"Because what if she expects me to look like you!" he snapped. "Seriously, Grayson. I'm like six-four, skinny as fuck, and wear glasses!"

"And she thinks you're hot," I assured him. "She also isn't looking for a sex object, Shawn. She wants a nice guy. The real kind of nice. Yeah, and here's the shitty part for you. Her best friend? Well, he kinda sets the bar for kick-ass nice guys. Fucker's barely eighteen years old and putting both of us to shame - and that's what Zoe's used to!"

"Yeah, no," he agreed. "Ripper's cool as fuck." Then he breathed out a laugh. "You know he got in touch with me this weekend? Found Zoe's video on that tablet and couldn't take it. Like, the guy was beside himself about it."

"Damn," I breathed. "Yeah, that would be hard."

"Mhm," Jinxy said. "But he was doing it. The first time I met the guy, I thought he'd be one of those pushover types, you know? But there he was, diving right in to the kind of shit that makes my skin crawl, and he was worried because he couldn't handle seeing his best friend in that mess. Like, is this guy even real?"

"Very real," I promised just as my phone went off. Picking it up, I kept talking. "He also has low self-esteem, thinks he's the pity fuck of the group, can't see how good he is for either of his girls, and is making the rest of us look like shit the whole time because he's honestly that cool of a dude." My eyes scanned the text I'd just gotten. "And Jeri says we're a go in five."

"Let's make it ten," he decided. "Get them into class before we start poking around."

"I'm good with that," I told him. "As for you and Zoe? I think you'll be fine. She's mostly gotten over the touching problem. Granted, if you surprise her by grabbing her, she might kick you in the balls, but otherwise she's doing pretty good. A lot better than I would've expected, if I'm honest."

"Yeah, I dunno how girls do it," he said. "If the situation was reversed, I'd be curled in a ball for a few more years, but they just push through it and keep going. Shit, Jeri's the same!"

"No kidding," I agreed. "And she's rabid about this Alpha Team bullshit."

"Do you blame her?"

"Wrong kind of rabid," I explained. "We all want to make them pay. Jericho wants to make it hurt while she's at it. She wants to destroy them, Shawn. Not just justice, but vengeance."

"That's our baby girl," he joked.

"My baby girl. Your bro. Keep your hands to your own chick."

He laughed, but in the background, there was a second sound. One I knew a little too well: his alarm. "It's time," he told me. "Give me a sec to open up some shit and get into that fucker's phone, ok?"

"We've got all afternoon," I reminded him. "I'd like to avoid the times they're in the halls, but otherwise? Fifth period? Sixth? Doesn't much matter to me."

"Cool," he said, but I could hear the clicking of his keyboard. "Ok, so Knock says this website should be a death trap. How bad do you think it's really going to be?"

"No fucking idea," I admitted. "I'm more worried about Dylan catching us and going after Jeri, truth be told. I mean, if we have the guy's username and password, what's the worst that can happen?"

"That he has a key fob for random code generation to authenticate his login," Jinxy said. "You know, if you want the absolute worst option."

"Keep that shit to yourself," I grumbled, because I hadn't even thought of that. "What are the chances they'd set it up like that?"

"Slim," Jinxy promised. "Those things might be cheap, but the system isn't, and that would require their blind followers to pay to keep it all going - or for *someone* to be paying. It's more likely to email a code, or text one, if even that."

"Ok, so we'll have to sneak in every time?" I asked.

"Won't know until we try," he pointed out. "Hot, for all we know, having the password means we'll get right in. This'll be fine. Stop fucking around and let's do this shit?"

"Doing," I promised even as I began typing. "Ok, I have my laptop about as stealthed as it can possibly be. Hopefully, Dez's script actually works, even if I don't know how it could."

"Because it's Destiny Pierce," he pointed out. "Swear to god that woman has coolant fluid in her veins or something."

"Be less of a dork," I taunted while the Kings of Gaming website loaded onto my screen. "Ok. Here we go. Slime420..." I typed in the entire username we'd caught, then the password and took a deep breath. "And go!" Then I hit enter.

Immediately, the portal opened, giving me access to the site.

Up at the top, I could see a spot for user activity. Clicking that, I set "Dylan" to invisible, then paused to take in what was before me. This was an old-school forum. Sections were broken out like on video game websites. Beneath those were more options. The titles were all the worst shit I could think of.

"Fuck..." I breathed.

"And we have a problem," Jinxy said. "Shit! Ok, I'm on it."

"What?" I snapped, seeing nothing at all on my side that would cause a concern.

"It fucking sent out an email!" Jinxy hissed. "You've logged in with a new device, please confirm this is you."

"Fuck!" I said, growling the word this time. "I'm cracking his computer to make sure it won't show up there."

"Deleting from the account," Jinxy told me. "Checking his texts. Jesus! Yeah, there's one there too. Looks like this Soul Reaper guy borrowed the Google account method."

"Where else would they have sent it?" I asked as I dove into Dylan's home computer on my own desktop. "Alternate accounts? What if we miss one?"

"Checking!"

Shit, this could be bad. If Dylan realized someone else was using his shit, he'd figure out it was us. There weren't really any other options. It wasn't like some spammers from Nigeria would hack into the Kings of Gaming! Nope, they'd want a bank or payment site like PayPal. Social media, maybe. Wait, could we use that to our advantage?

"Find the code, Jinxy," I ordered. "See if it's sent to everything he has, or just what he listed."

"I'm fucking trying," he grumbled. "Man, this is a damned email. I have to work backwards! Ok. I found the list server. Yeah, um..." There was a long pause. Eventually, a sigh. "Fuck me, we should be good."

"Really?" Because Dylan's computer didn't have a hint of that email on it, which meant Jinxy had already cleared it. I checked the account's trash just to be sure. "What if we missed something? I mean, it can't be this easy, can it?"

"Could," Jinxy said, but he was still typing in the background. "It works for Google, man. It's all about recognizing the device, and people get new phones or use a friend's all the time. I clicked that we're good, so we should be good from now on."

"On this laptop," I added.

But Jinxy laughed. "I dunno. Maybe just that MAC address?"

Which made me smile, because it was spoofed. Dez's program had given me a fictitious one, but would it give me the option to use the same one again?

"Wanna test it?" I asked.

"Activating the program now," he told me. "I'm in the options and..." He began to chuckle. "This woman? She's a fucking genius. I want to have her brain children or something. Wow. Ok, hit me with the MAC address you're using?"

"How does this thing work?" I asked before reading off the falsified MAC address. "That number's supposed to be an identifier for a computer."

"Just trust Dez," he told me. "I'm starting to realize that's the only way some of this shit makes sense. I mean, a MAC address is just an identifier, right? That means software is involved to read it. And where there's software, Dez has the ability to make some pretty strange things happen."

"So we do not let this script out of our sight," I decided. "But Jinxy? I'm in."

"Yeah..." he breathed. "Funny thing that. I am too. His phone is quiet. No more notices about a new device. We're both logged in and neither of us is being kicked off. Do you fucking know what this means?"

Those words made my entire body still. "Holy shit," I said. "It means KoG is ours."

"And we can see everything these pricks have ever done in private," Jinxy agreed. "So let's rape them back - digitally speaking."

"Show them just how it feels," I agreed.

CHAPTER 47

JERICHO

I'd sent Hottie a text on my way into fourth period. When that class got out, however, I still hadn't heard a damned thing. There were no waiting notifications on my phone. Did that mean there was a problem?

I made it into the hall and immediately called. Thankfully, Hottie answered on the second ring. "Is everything ok?" I demanded. "What the fuck, Hottie? Are you still working on it?"

His answer was a soft laugh. "It's good, baby girl. All done and handled."

"And?!" I demanded.

"And it seems KoG has a moderately decent ability to recognize the devices someone uses."

Right. Yeah. As if that really told me anything. "And?" I asked again.

He just sighed. "And Jinxy was watching Dylan's phone. Jeri, I used the login info we have. It worked. Popped me right in. It also sent an email and a text to Dylan's account. One email. One text. Both of them said a new device was used and asked if it was allowed. Jinxy approved it and then deleted all the evidence."

"On Dylan's phone?" I breathed, glancing around to make sure no one around me could hear.

"On his phone," Hottie agreed. "Don't panic. I checked his desktop at home and it was all removed from the server. Nothing there. We checked and double-checked anything we can get into, ok?"

Those were the words that finally let me relax. "Ok," I told him. "So we have access? Will this happen every time? Doesn't this make that login all but useless?"

"Nope," he bragged. "You see, it recognized the MAC address. The spoofed one, thanks to that toybox Knock got for us. Jinxy and I even made sure we can replicate it. He and I were logged in at the same time with no problem and no new emails."

My feet stalled out. "What?"

So Hottie repeated all of that, saying it in even simpler terms. Not that it mattered. I wasn't asking him to break it down for me. I was just stunned at the implications of this. If Hottie and Jinxy had both been on KoG's website, with Dylan's level of access...

"We can pull everything off there!" I gasped, completely interrupting.

"Yeah..." And for the first time, my best friend made it sound like there might be a problem.

"Fuck, what?" I demanded.

"Jeri, there's a lot."

"Yeah, but we knew that."

"No," he said. "I mean a *lot*. Dylan has over five thousand posts. The others aren't as bad, but they're heavy users."

"Videos?" I asked, feeling my heart stall out.

"Mostly discussions," he assured me. "Don't get me wrong, there are a shit-ton of videos too. Pictures as well. Fuck, and some of these posts? Jeri, these guys were giving each other ideas. I mean, it reads like they're just joking around, but from what we already know they did? And they've been members a long ass time. Um..." He paused. "Looks like about three years."

"Most of high school," I realized.

"Which is right about the age guys start to give a shit about this incel bullshit," he agreed. "Look, I think we're going to find a lot of stuff to build this case, and there's a good chance we'll find evidence of more victims. It's just that it's a *fucking lot*. It's going to take time."

"And we're not going to give up," I promised. "I think this means we need to meet at Knock's place after school and get a plan together, huh?"

"Definitely," he agreed. "Jinxy and I are already working out some ideas. Right now, we're just snooping around, trying to see what all might be in here. But there's something else to consider."

"Hm?"

"Alpha Team aren't the only sick fuckers in the world, and I'm pretty sure all of them are members of this horror-site."

"Fuck." I forced my feet to move again, but changed my direction from my next class to Knock's locker. "How many?"

"The site doesn't have a list of members."

"How fucking many, Hottie?"

"Probably a few million," he guessed. "Jeri, the boards are active, too. This place is jumping, and I don't want Zoe in here."

"Let her decide that," I told him.

"No, you don't - "

"So fill her in," I interrupted, "and then let her set her own boundaries, ok? Same for the rest of us."

"No, you're right," he relented. "My bigger problem is Dylan."

"What do you mean?"

"Did he notice," Hottie clarified. "Keep an eye on him today. See if that fucker's acting weird, because we can't be sure he wouldn't have seen the email. We don't know which way his eyes were pointed. The chances of him having a clue are slim, but that's not the same as zero."

"Ok, and I'll tell the rest," I said as I turned the corner. "Hey, I'm almost to Knock's locker. I'm going to fill the crew in and we'll finish up at Knock's place?"

"I'll meet you there," he told me. "Stay safe, baby girl. Love you."

Which made all the bad feelings that had been building stop in their tracks. A smile touched my lips and I ducked my head, loving how easily he added that last bit in.

"Love you too. Bye."

I disconnected the call, put my phone away, and didn't stop until I reached Knock's locker. He and Cade were there, heads together, talking much too seriously about something.

"So!" I said as a greeting.

Both guys flinched, spinning to look at me. "What the fuck?" Cade snapped.

I grinned. "It's done."

"It?" Knock asked.

I leaned in and lowered my voice. "Hottie and Jinxy are on KoG's site. Yes, both. Yes, at the same time. I told Hottie we need to have a meeting at your place after school. Cool?"

"Cool," Knock agreed.

So I looked over at Cade. "What is making you both look guilty as fuck?"

"We were talking about how I got the keylogger on and whether there was any evidence left behind," Cade explained.

"Yeah. Well, Hottie wants us all to keep an eye on Dylan to see if he's acting funny." I looked from one guy to the other. "Is he?"

"Not that I can tell," Knock said.

Cade just shook his head. "No. Heard them all talking about their big plans for Spring Break earlier today, but just being their normal selves."

"Good." Turning, I flopped my back against the line of lockers. "Supposedly, there's a literal shit-ton of stuff that we're going to have to go through. Hottie says he doesn't want Zoe in there."

Knock canted his head like he thought Hottie had a point, but Cade was shaking his slowly. "Zoe's tough," Cade reminded us. "She also hates being left out."

"Kinda what I said," I admitted. "I told him to warn her and let her decide."

"Same for Ripper," Knock said. "Last night, Jinxy mentioned the videos are harder than he thought."

"I can do videos," Cade offered. "Let Ripper handle data correlation?"

"But Ripper's the - " I jerked in place as a flash of red bounced into place beside me.

"What about Ripper?" Zoe asked.

Laughing at how I'd flinched the exact same way the guys had when I'd walked up, I filled her in. I didn't even skip the part about how she might not want to get on the site, but Hottie would have more information about how bad it was. Then I picked up where I'd left off.

"Ripper's our video guy," I said. "He's the one who knows about splices and edits and how to spot that shit."

"But if we're just downloading and organizing," Cade countered, "then why can't I say, 'this is a video, save it to the video file'?"

"He's got a point," Zoe said. "I can focus on sorting the screens of the posts into topics, right? Like these are about rape, these are about torture, and those are about abuse. I figure they won't have many more topics than that."

"Which means reading that shit," I reminded her.

The look she gave me could've burned lesser people. "Jeri..."

"I'm just saying!"

"But," Knock said, speaking up before the pair of us could derail the conversation, "someone needs to tell Ripper."

"Whoever sees him first," Cade decided. "I'd rather he heard it too much than not enough." He chuckled once. "I can't believe we're in."

"Full access to KoG," Zoe said, keeping her voice down.

"Not full," Knock countered. "More than anyone has had before, though. Well, the good guys, at any rate."

"Wish Cyn could have it," I mumbled.

"Same," Knock agreed. "Shit, if I had a fucking clue how to get in touch with him, this shit would be closed by now!"

"But we're in," Zoe said. "What else do we need?"

"To make the case," Knock told her. "Zoe, we have to put it together, prove the connections, and organize this in a way that leaves zero room for doubts. We know the cops don't want to deal with it. We know the justice system doesn't really think crimes against women are a big deal. That means we need to make this more. We need to make it a serial thing, prove it's not just a little fun, and hammer home - with no room for doubt - that this is the kind of problem that can't simply be ignored or explained away."

"Or a different crime," she breathed, nodding to show she understood. "Is there another crime we could call it? I mean, if rapists get like six months in jail, then is there something worse?"

"The drugging will add on," Cade said. "I have a feeling stealing that shit is probably more jail time than the rapes."

"Hate crimes too," Knock pointed out. "I'm sure once we're in the site, we'll find evidence for more. Let's just make it all run in line. Leave nothing out, and make sure we do this right, ok?"

"Ok," I said. "And I have to get to class."

"Same," Zoe said, lifting a hand to wave bye to the guys. "And I'm going to use makeup on you if you get bruised again, Cade."

"Dunno why I like you, Zoe," he called back, lifting his hand the same way.

Zoe and I headed up the hall. Knock and Cade headed down. I had a feeling our little pause was going to make me late for class, but I was getting used to that. Although my teachers had probably stopped caring, which I was willing to think of as a bonus.

Then Zoe leaned in a bit. "We need to tell Tiff."

"About KoG?" I asked.

"About all of it," she insisted. "Jeri, her little band of pissed-off girls? They're starting to make a difference."

Which had my complete attention. "How?"

"I just saw a few talking earlier today," she explained. "Natalie with Marissa? I mean that's a pair that never would've been near each other a week ago. Makes me think her plan's working."

"The support group?"

Zoe nodded. "And if all those girls, across all those friend groups, are now talking? What do you think it's doing to Dylan's reputation? To the chances of Landon, Parker, Wade, or even John getting another girlfriend?"

"John should be mourning Amber," I grumbled.

Zoe just rolled her eyes. "Yeah. I'm sure he would - while fucking someone else. They're all pigs, but that's the point. If we're all calling them pigs, and everyone is warning everyone else that they're pretty but not worth it?"

"I'd rather fuck a nerd boy," I told her.

Which made her bump my shoulder. "Same. Well, eventually, but in theory and all that. All I'm saying is Tiff and her friends? Yeah, so if they're handling ruining these dicks at school, then it means we can focus more on the busting, right?"

"I like how you think," I told her. "We just have to figure out when we can snag Tiffany."

"After this class," Zoe decided. "Meet me in the girls' room on the science wing?"

"By the library?" I asked.

She nodded. "That's the one. I always see Tiff, and I'll drag her that way." Then she smiled. "And it's good news, you know. This? It means we're winning, Jeri."

"Not winning yet," I told her.

So she grabbed my hand. "Stop. We're *winning*. Over and over, we keep winning, because we're the ones doing the right thing. Stop overthinking this and let yourself get excited! This is a good thing!"

"A good thing," I repeated, putting a little excitement into my voice.

She nodded like she accepted that, then turned down the hall to her next class. I kept going, heading for mine, but I was thinking too hard.

We were making progress, sure, so why did I feel like there was still a hammer hanging over my head? Because I really didn't know anything else. I was cursed. I was supposed to always be braced for the worst, but that was the strange thing about Ruin.

Together, the seven of us somehow made things work. No, it wasn't always easy, but we did not quit. We never gave up. We'd all known what it was like to suffer, so we were willing to take the hard knocks to reach our goals.

And we just had. We'd fucking hacked into the Kings of Gaming forums. They'd said it couldn't be done, but we'd fucking *done* it. And now, we had complete access to use their deepest, darkest secrets against these assholes.

Yeah, that did kinda sound like winning.

CHAPTER 48

JERICHO

The bathroom by the library was a bit of a hike from my fourth-period class. I stretched my legs, but I could only go as fast as the bottleneck of human bodies in the school halls. Eventually, I made it - yet the moment I walked into the bathroom, a pissed-off voice was waiting.

"Find another!" Tiffany snapped. "This one is out of commission."

I rounded the corner, smirking at how damned predictable she was. "But I like this one."

"You made it," Zoe greeted me. "Ok. I told Tiff we had news, but this shit is above my pay grade."

I nodded at her, then turned to Tiff. "Dylan has a tablet. Cade has bruises on his face today because none of the other methods were working. He managed to get us access to both Dylan's computer and that tablet, which means we've found some of the videos."

"Which videos?" she asked.

"All of your friends'," I assured her. "Now, I can't promise these are the only ones, and we haven't deleted them, but we have them."

"And what good does that do?" she asked.

I licked my lips, trying to figure out how to break all this technical shit down to her comprehension level without coming off like a bitch. "Um..." Yeah, this was going to get complicated. "Tiff, we're trying to make a case the cops can't ignore. That means we can't let Dylan know what we're doing. We have reason to worry that deleting those videos might show our hand."

She nodded slowly. "Ok. But what does this mean for us?"

"Well, Knock kinda made it clear to Dylan that we have some bad shit," I admitted. "So, the truce is still holding."

"Kinda," Zoe told her. "Dylan's pissed about you making friends with all those other girls."

"Fuck him," Tiff said.

I laughed once. "Kinda what I think too. What I can say is that we'll be able to delete them before he could share them."

"We have people watching this shit all the time," Zoe promised. "They put alerts on things turning on and all that."

Tiffany just shook her head, but a smile was on her face. "So this is really like some bad-ass hacker thing? Do you have a secret lair too?"

"Knock's place," I admitted. "You know, where you spent the night that time. In other words, you've been there."

"Makes me almost feel like I belong," she joked. "Ok, so this is good news, right?"

"One step closer to making sure these fuckers pay for what they did," I explained. "I can't promise the cops will do anything, but I can promise we're going to make it hard for them not to. We're also ready to go to the media if it's pushed under the rug - without leaking who any of you are. Just that there are multiple videos, a serial problem, and all that. High school jocks terrorizing girls in small-town Texas? I have a feeling that will hit hard."

"I'll make sure they're all braced for it," Tiffany promised. "I mean, just in case. You do know that's not the best-case scenario though, right?"

"I do," I assured her. "Ideally, we'd like to see these guys rot in jail with no big splash. No repercussions for any of us. It might also be a pipe dream."

"No, I'm with ya," she agreed.

"But," Zoe added, "if all of you are already leaning on each other, then it will be easier, won't it?"

"That's the hope," Tiffany agreed. "And I've got quite a few girls. Twelve now."

"What?!" I gasped, because I only knew of ten so far.

"She already gave me names," Zoe promised.

"Yeah," Tiff sighed, pushing the word out. "So, apparently when I started talking to people, they talked to others, and the next thing I knew, new faces were showing up at our little girl time. Jeri, I also know Marissa wasn't the first."

"We got that off the tablet," Zoe confirmed. "We just hadn't identified everyone yet."

"And we're about to get more," I told Tiffany. "Today, we cracked into their little online hate group. That means we can see all the shit they've posted as a brag. Videos, pictures, and everything else. We'll also get them talking and planning in a place they think is safe. So, keep an eye on Dylan and make sure he isn't acting weird?"

"Oh, he's acting weird," Tiffany assured me. "See, the bitch squad has made it our mission to fuck those guys over. All five of them have been trying to plan a big party for Spring Break next week, right? Well, they want to have another one of their ragers that first weekend. We're making sure no one will go."

"Someone will go," I grumbled. "They're football stars."

"Not with the rest of the team on our side," Tiffany countered. "Jericho, you forget the most important rule in the world. We have the pussy. All guys want it, and plenty of them will do anything they can to get it. Most of them will bend over backwards if it's also the right thing."

"Ok?" I asked.

Which made her smile deviously. "And when their girlfriends, crushes, and pals are all saying Dylan's a creep, lame, and that we shouldn't go? When they mention how those boys hurt girls? Yeah, let's just say that having the football, basketball, baseball, and soccer teams all cancel them? It kinda has an effect."

"Oh damn!" Zoe breathed. "Nice!"

Tiffany nodded proudly. "Yep, although that was mostly Scarlett. She has connections with the jocks. The point is we're going to make them regret what they've done. See, those boys? They fucked with the wrong girls. They assumed we were all alone, but now we're not."

"You found your fellow Flawed," Zoe told her.

"My what?"

"Your fellow Flawed," Zoe repeated. "See, that's the line from our game. 'We are all flawed, but we're not alone.' And the whole thing is that it's true. We're all fucked up in some way, but we think we can't talk about it. We think we have to do this shit on our own, yet when we find our fellow Flawed, it somehow gets easier."

"It really does," Tiffany agreed. "Just seeing my friends feel like they can finally talk about it? And sure, we've had a few hangouts that turned into crying sessions. God, and it sucks to hear what was done to them, but they need it, you know? They need to talk to someone else who can actually understand." Then she looked over at Zoe. "And you can come any time you want. You know that, right?"

Zoe made a face, but I couldn't quite read it. "Yeah, but I think I'm doing better my way. No offense."

"None taken," Tiffany promised her. "Just making sure you knew the invitation's there."

"What about you?" I asked. "How are you fitting into their support group?"

"I got away," Tiffany explained. "And we all know it's true. Doesn't matter if we're talking about him drugging us that night or the promises he made. Does anyone doubt that Dylan would've raped me if he had the chance?"

"Or Jeri," Zoe said softly.

I just shook my head. "I think he wanted to hurt me, not rape me."

"And you're a damned fool," Tiffany snapped. "None of those guys care about the sex part of it. They're doing this because of the *power*. Every story I hear is the same thing. One of those girls spoke up, spoke back, or made a fool of those guys. They made her pay. Well, you know what? You've made the biggest fool of all of them, and they *will* rape you, Jericho. They will do it just to destroy you, because they aren't that fucking dumb. They know exactly how bad this fucks us up, and they *like* that it does!"

"Yeah, but - "

"No!" Zoe said, cutting me off. "She's right. You know she's right. And maybe you like to think you're untouchable, or not worth it, or whatever stupid fucking thing is in your head, but you're wrong."

"You're so wrong," Tiffany agreed. "And you are worth it, Jeri. You're the unstoppable one. You're like Dylan's damned white whale!"

"Moby Dick," I realized, pushing out a breath. "Ok. Hopefully, I can be the monster that destroys him too, because that's what we're trying to do."

"Fingers crossed," Tiffany said.

"But," I added, "while we're focused on making this mess of data into a case that can be used, do you think you and your bitch army - "

"Bitch squad," she corrected. "They like that name."

"Bitch squad," I agreed. "Maybe all of you can keep the guys distracted enough they won't pay attention to us?"

"Become a bigger problem?" she asked. "Sure. I mean, how far can we go?"

"As far as you want to," I assured her. "Just know that if you get arrested, I can't help. So, make fools of them, harass them, toilet paper their houses, throw eggs at their trucks, or whatever people in the country do for fun. Go fucking wild, Tiffany, and make sure the entire damned school is laughing at them by the time the year is over."

"I can do that," she agreed.

"Because if we don't have to fight with stupid boys, that gives us more time to fight with data and internet security."

"And I don't understand any of that," she admitted. "Well, not enough. Just *try* to keep Cade from getting his face broken again? It's too pretty of a thing to waste."

"No shit, right?" I asked. "Although he gets a little credit for this one. He knocked Dylan out, said it was for outing him, then put spyware all over the asshole's computer. Tiffany, Cade took a few hits so we could get this shit. He intentionally picked a fight because he's trying to do the right thing."

"To take care of you," Zoe told her.

"Shit," Tiffany mumbled. "Jeri, I just want to make it clear I'm not - "

I waved her off before she could finish that. "No, I didn't think that," I promised. "I know you and Cade aren't involved. Hell, the guy doesn't have the time to be cheating on us."

"Us," she repeated with a little laugh. "You and Knock - and you say it so easily."

"Because it works for us," I admitted. "I also don't have a problem with you two being friends. It's a good thing."

"Should be a more common thing," Zoe said.

I nodded at that, but Tiffany was looking between us, almost like she was confused. "You know," she finally said, "I always thought I had to tear down other girls in order to get noticed by the right guys. When you first moved here and Cade went stupid over you, Jericho? I was so sure you'd steal him away. It never dawned on me to put the blame on him."

"It's always the other girls, right?" Zoe asked. "And do you know what Jeri told Cade the first time he asked her out?"

"No," Tiffany said.

Which made Zoe smile. "She told him dumping a girl for her isn't impressive. It just means he'll dump her for the next one, so to stop acting like he did her any favors. She also turned him down, Tiff."

"I don't poach from other girls," I mumbled.

Which made Tiffany clasp my arm. "I know that now. I also know Cade and I were all wrong. I was only dating him to keep Dylan at a distance. He was only dating me because Dylan was blackmailing him. Talk about a recipe for failure, right? But he's a great guy, and he deserves to be happy. We had almost nothing in common, but in the time we were together, I realized we could be friends, so I'm enjoying that he's still letting me - even after I was a pretty big bitch to him."

"You kinda were," I agreed, "but I think it's your signature move."

"Yeah, it is," she said. "One I plan to turn right on Dylan, Landon, Parker, John, and Wade. Fuck those asshats. I want to make sure they'll never forget that just because women can be nice, it doesn't mean we're weak."

"And I want to see them as miserable as they made the rest of us," Zoe said. "They thought they were on top of the world, but it's past time for the mighty to fall."

"Because they laughed at us," I agreed. "Video after video, those fuckers *laugh* at the women they abuse, and I think it's the thing that pisses me off the most. Destroy them, Tiff."

"Gladly," she agreed.

CHAPTER 49

JERICHO

Meeting at Knock's after school became the new thing. Monday, Hottie met me there to fill us all in. On Tuesday, he headed over right after work because Riley had invited him, beating us by a few hours. Together, we were all diving into the horror-world of KoG and tearing apart anything that might possibly relate to our case.

Knock explained to us what Cynister had told him about the evidence needed for a conviction. Hopefully, what was good enough for the FBI would be good enough for the Sanger Police Department too. Sadly, none of us knew shit about the law, but since this was what we had to go on, this was how we were going to build our case.

Yet once Kitty announced dinner was ready, we were done. Those were the rules we all agreed to. No deep-diving into hate speech after eating. Nope, that was our time to remember we were human. It was the space to keep us all from getting overwhelmed with this shit. And maybe the idea had come from Knock's family, but since none of us could really say they were wrong, we agreed to obey it.

Like we had the rest of the week, once school was out on Wednesday, Zoe and I headed out to our cars. Her parking space was closer than mine, so I waved at her and told her I'd meet her there. The boys were either already gone or right behind us. I wasn't sure, and in truth I didn't care. The sooner we got there, the more time we had to play with Quake!

I made it to my car, opened the driver's door to let the heat out, and was reaching for the back to throw my book bag in when a body slammed me into the door, shutting it again. The air rushed from my lungs at the surprise attack. Fear rushed in. Instinct took over and I pushed, managing to get the weight off me, but only enough to spin around.

Then he was on me again. This guy was stronger than me, but that didn't mean I wouldn't fight back. Everything was happening too fast. I didn't have the chance to take in who, what, or any of those details. I just struggled to get free!

I pushed, he blocked, and my car prevented me from escaping. For far too long - which was probably mere seconds - the pair of us struggled, until his arm pressed across my throat as a threat, forcing me to stop. His weight held me in place. My blood ran cold, knowing I'd lost even as my eyes found my attacker. With his face inches from mine, it was impossible not to recognize Dylan. Worse, all four of his friends were lined up behind him.

"Hello, Freak Show," Dylan snarled. "Thought we had a truce?"

Fuck. Fuck, fuck, fuck! There was no way this could be good, but maybe I could play it off? I wanted to scream for help, but the only thing that would accomplish was making these guys laugh. Instead, I nudged him back, encouraging Dylan to give me a little space. Hopefully, I could talk my way out of this.

"Yeah, I thought we had a truce too, and slamming me into my car isn't a good way to keep it," I pointed out.

But I was scared. Zoe had just left. The guys wouldn't come looking for me! These five assholes had already beaten the shit out of Cade in this parking lot, and I had no doubts they'd do a hell of a lot worse to me. My only consolation was the other cars around us. We weren't alone. It wasn't late in the day. More people would come - and that meant witnesses.

Struggling not to glance around us too much - because Dylan would notice - I tried to convince myself I wouldn't get murdered or raped today. Not out in the open, in broad daylight, surely? And yet Tiffany's warning from Monday ran through the back of my mind.

Dylan hated me. His friends hated me. I'd been fucking with them for months, which was why I did my best not to be alone around them - and now this? These guys didn't abuse women because they needed to get off. They were looking for power. What excited them was putting girls back in our places, and I'd risen far above what they thought should be mine. Yet if this was going to suck, then I was determined to make sure I went down fighting.

"You're fucking with my party plans," Dylan finally said, jerking his chin at me as if demanding an answer.

"What party?" I asked.

John grunted, clearly not buying my act. "Don't pull that shit, cunt. You keep coming to them."

"I thought they were canceled," I said. Ok, it wasn't completely a lie, but close enough. "The last I heard, after the cops busted all of you, the parties were off."

"Because of you!" Dylan roared. "We know you called that in."

"I was fucking drugged!" I screamed into his face, trying to match his intensity. "So look in the mirror, dumbass. Maybe try taking a little blame for yourself for once. Stop and think about how your actions are what get those reactions. *You* drugged me. I was *drugged*. My friends were busy trying to figure out if I needed to go to the fucking hospital. Your damned party wasn't exactly high on our list at that moment."

"Still think she did it," Wade said. "We should give her a reminder. On principle, if nothing else."

Fuck! How the hell was I supposed to get out of this? My best plan was to act pissed off and hope they saw me as competition and not a victim. Then again, that probably wouldn't save me from getting a beating. Damn it. Yeah, my options right about now sucked.

But while I was thinking, Dylan glanced back, shooting Wade a warning look. "And the truce?"

"The fucking videos," Landon snapped. "C'mon, we all know what we're talking about."

"She doesn't have any," Parker said. "Bitch is bluffing."

My damned heart was hammering so hard I could hear the blood in my ears. My hands were getting sweaty as I braced for the worst. I didn't like anything about this, but what could I do? I was quickly running out of options, so I decided to go with the truth.

"Amber sent them," I said calmly. It wasn't easy, but I was a little proud that I managed.

But my answer made John snarl. "Why the fuck would she do that? Hm? You weren't even her friend!"

"Nope, but I'm the one who keeps getting under your skin," I reminded them. "That's literally what she said. Oh, and I know about the baby too."

That was what made the guys look at each other. From the expression on John's face, the pregnancy was news to him. Sadly, I didn't get to enjoy my little victory, because Dylan slammed me into the car again.

"Shut the fuck up!" he snapped.

I just lifted my chin, refusing to let him see my fear, but I wasn't quite dumb enough to keep taunting them.

"We agreed to back off, Jericho," he said, a clear warning in his tone. "We broke up with our girlfriends. We haven't talked to them since. If you'd just left us alone, things would've been good, but you couldn't do that, could you? You had to fucking stick your nose in shit."

"Which shit this time?" I asked.

"You mean besides fucking up our scholarships? Besides making us all start over with applications? Well, no one's coming to the party," he told me. "This is supposed to be our big Spring Break bash. One of the last celebrations of high school, and now our friends suddenly want nothing to do with us. The girls?" He scoffed. "Oh, they say they've heard *stories*."

"I'm not used to getting turned down," Parker sneered. "Don't know what lies you're spreading - "

"Oh, please," I said, cutting him off. If I was going to get out of this, I needed to go big or go home. "We're not beating around the bush, right? So how about you guys just call it what it is. The word you want is *rape*. And so you know, I haven't said shit about it. I've been a little busy dealing with my own stuff. But it's funny how you've never considered who else might know what you did. Like, maybe *the fucking girls you raped?*"

"It wasn't rape," Wade shot back. "Fuck you, Jericho. They all agreed. They fucking consented."

"They were drugged!" I hissed.

"And?" he asked. "No one made them drink."

"Not our fault they wanted it," Landon added.

Parker just laughed, and beside him John crossed his arms over his chest, looking like he wanted to pop my head off my body. Ok, that was fucking intimidating. Damn, that fucker was big.

"What do you care about a few sluts getting laid anyway?" Dylan asked. "Thought you didn't give a shit about high school drama."

Ok, so they weren't hitting yet, which meant this was working.

Now all I had to do was make it clear I had shit they really didn't want to get out. A reason to leave me alone, right? To not piss me off.

"Nope, but I give a shit about my friends," I countered. "Maybe you remember Zoe? Is it possible you also remember the edited clip someone put on her phone? Yeah, well the unedited version captures the laughter. The very thing she remembers." I lifted my hand and made a little circle with my finger around us. "It was all of you laughing." Then I leaned closer to Dylan's face. "And that pissed me off."

"So you're breaking our truce?" he taunted.

Letting out a groan, I rolled my eyes, playing this up. "The truce is easy," I told him. "You don't release their videos and I don't release yours. I haven't released shit, Dylan. Truce is still on."

"And you're fucking up our lives!" Landon bellowed. "This isn't how it's supposed to work!"

"That's what she wants, dumbass," Parker told him.

"Doesn't matter," Landon said. "She's already gloating. Just look at her."

"I say we make her hurt," John grumbled. "Leave her on the ground and see if her dear friends actually notice."

"Mm, now wouldn't that be a great idea," Dylan said, evil taking over his voice. "That wouldn't break our truce either, according to your rules, hm?"

No, sadly, it wouldn't. Fuck. For a second there, I'd actually thought I was winning, but I'd fucked up. I didn't even have a good comeback, just the racing of my heart. I really hoped none of them could hear it, because I was convinced the damned thing had to be loud enough. My whole rib cage was starting to hurt.

Dylan just kept going, aware he finally had the upper hand. "Stay out of my business, Jericho. Stay away from me and my guys. Keep your *fucking nose* out of our fun or you will regret it, do you understand me?"

"No, not really," I replied, unable to keep my idiot mouth shut.

"If you don't, I will kill you," he said - and his voice was completely serious. "Not hurt. Not embarrass. If you keep trying to fuck with me, I will make sure you can't do it again. Is that fucking clear enough for - "

"Jericho!"

I didn't recognize the voice at first. I also didn't care! Female. From behind me. That was all that mattered. Whoever she was, she saw me, and that meant she was about to be my savior.

"Over here!" I called back, praying she could see me.

"I told you to wait for me!" This time, I realized it was Tiffany yelling, and she was getting a lot closer.

There weren't words for the feeling of relief that rushed through my body. It tingled. In front of me, the guys were starting to look concerned. Unsettled, maybe? I wasn't sure, but the anger and hatred that had been written on their faces a second ago had vanished. Now, they were all shuffling like they wanted to bolt.

Dylan just leaned a little closer, putting our faces close enough I could feel his body heat. "I will kill you," he swore, the words too soft for anyone else to hear. "So leave us alone, understand?"

"Yep," I agreed, because I was too scared to say anything else.

Then he pushed, using the motion to lift himself off me. "Hi Tiff," he called over my head even as he gestured for his guys to leave.

"Later, guys," Tiffany said, her voice no longer a yell because she was close enough she didn't need to. "Hope you're planning a real good Spring Break!"

John just lifted his hand and flipped her off, which made multiple women giggle. Wait, multiple? With Dylan no longer holding me down, I spun to see Tiffany and eight other girls spread out in a lazy line, all glaring at the guys.

It was a power move. They were standing in a way to be intentionally threatening. Half of them had their phones in their hands, which was probably their best weapon. In other words, this group of badass bitches had just intervened. They'd just *saved my fucking ass!*

The moment the Alpha Team was out of sight, Tiffany rushed around my car to hug me. "Shit, Jericho, I was so sure Dylan was about to prove me right! Are you ok?"

I nodded, hugging her back. "God, your timing couldn't have been better."

My hands were shaking. My knees were weak. I was sure Tiffany could feel it, but she didn't say a thing. The girl just leaned back to look me over, then hugged me again, all but holding me up - and I needed it.

"I called her over," Marissa said. "Saw the crowd around your car, thought it was your guys, but John is a lot bigger than Ripper."

"So we all came," Scarlett explained. "We had to make sure it wouldn't happen to you too."

"Wait," Yvette said. "She knows about what you..."

"She knows," Tiffany assured them. "She's been helping Zoe."

Which was an easy enough excuse for these women. Hearing that, the entire crew moved closer, all but making a circle around me. Some faces I knew. Others I didn't, and it didn't really matter. I'd seen the way those guys had reacted.

"They're scared of you," I realized.

"Who?" Tiffany asked, letting me go just to move to my side, still giving me support.

"All of you," I explained. "Dylan was threatening me to leave him alone - because he thinks I'm fucking up his party plans - but when he saw the group of you, it was like they all had their balls crawl up their asses."

"And they should," one of the girls I didn't know said. "Fuck them!"

"Fuck all of them," Marissa agreed. "Hope they like being afraid."

"And we'll give them something to fear," Tiffany promised before looking over at me again. "But are you really ok? They didn't..."

She meant rape. She was worried they'd somehow managed to rape me right here, with dozens of students walking by. I shook my head, but something about that made my blood run cold. I'd been so sure I was safe here at school.

So many people. No way to have the privacy for that sort of a crime, right? And yet Dylan had accidentally made it clear they wouldn't need privacy. They just needed no one else to care.

Leaning my head back, I let out a relieved sigh, because someone did. These girls. They cared, and they were taking back their power! They were standing up and doing something about the assholes who'd taken advantage of them.

"Thank you," I said softly, making their conversation stop. "Seriously," I told them all. "Thank you, because I don't know what they were going to do, but I was scared shitless."

"Oh, Jeri..." Marissa breathed.

Then others followed, all of them crowding closer to reassure me that they had my back, it would be ok, and I'd made it through. The strangest part was I took it. I fucking *needed* it.

And the whole time, all I could think was that I didn't deserve any of this. I wasn't the strong one here. I wasn't the one who'd been hurt. I'd been fucking scared for a few seconds, but it was over. All of my worries were done now that they'd left.

Which meant I owed these women the same sort of closure. One day, they would also be able to say it was over, that their abusers were gone - locked far away - and wouldn't be coming back. I'd make damned sure of it.

CHAPTER 50

ZOE

Jeri told me about how Dylan had caught her at her car. She hadn't wanted to tell the guys, but I didn't have that problem. Sure enough, Hottie had been pissed. Knock and Cade had been worried. Ripper, however, had just pulled her into his lap, wrapped his arms around her, and did his best to make her feel ok again.

It worked. In less than an hour, Jeri was back to her old self and the crew was back to sorting through all the bullshit on the KoG website. Over the course of the week, the Squirrel had been inundated with screenshots, videos, and photos they'd downloaded. My job was to sort it all. Letting the guys simply save everything into the main area sped them up a lot, and this kept me from feeling useless.

At some point, I'd learned the server we were using wasn't in the house. I'd never really thought about it, but that made sense. It also wasn't small. Evidently, Logan had access to a bank used for confidential information at his law office. He paid a fee - he called it a small one, but the guy was loaded - to use the space. He also had it set to expand if we needed more.

That was one layer of protection. The encryption was a second. According to Knock, there were about fifteen more layers to keep private everything they needed to protect, and that included their TeamSpeak program. We didn't use it, but the gamers in Eternal Combat did, and they were working on a case of their own, sorta.

But when we met up on Thursday, I couldn't get a hold of Jinxy. He wasn't on Discord. Just as I was about to panic, he sent me a text that something came up and he was busy. Ok, I was pretty sure he had a few tests to worry about, and since this was his last semester at college, I didn't think much of it. We had this.

It was almost ten that night when my phone rang. Seeing his icon, I swiped to answer, expecting to hear an apology for being busy. Instead, he was breathing too hard. Hard enough for it to be the first thing I heard.

"Shawn?" I asked, sitting up.

He murmured. "Yeah," he tried, but his voice broke in the middle. Quickly, he cleared his throat. "Um, yeah," he said, better this time, but still not good. "I, uh, thought I should let you know I'm headed to Texas tomorrow morning."

And my heart stalled out. "Is she..."

"No," he promised. "Gran's not dead yet, but the nurse said she's crashing." He sucked in a trembling breath. "Zoe, she has *days* left!" The words ended on a wail.

"Oh my god, Shawn, I'm so sorry!" I breathed. "What do you need?"

"No, I'm good," he promised. "I told my professors a few weeks ago. Grades are fine. I'm covered there. I have a plane ticket bought. I, uh, have my suit..."

For a funeral, I realized. He was coming to Texas because this was it. This was the nightmare he'd been trying to run away from by losing himself in Ruin's mess. Now, there was nowhere left to run. The woman who'd all but raised him was dying, nothing would stop it, and I felt completely powerless to make it hurt any less.

"Oh, Shawn," I breathed. "God. Do you want me to tell the others?"

"Mhm," he agreed. "I mean, I have to talk to Hot, but yeah. I dunno. I'm just so fucking tired of talking about it!"

"Oh."

Because he hadn't really wanted to talk about it before. He admitted she was sick, but this guy never spoke about his fears, how much it hurt, or any of the emotional stuff. Not with me, not on Discord, and from the sounds of it, not with anyone else in Ruin.

"My family," he explained, "is made of like a million people. Ok, not that many, but Gran..." He breathed a soft and sad laugh. "She made us, Zoe. That woman took in all these broken little kids, right? And then she gave us glue and allowed us to piece ourselves together how we wanted. I mean, Bea helped too, but she's been gone for a bit now, and Gran's all I have left."

"And the rest of your family," I reminded him.

"Mostly Violet," he breathed. "I just don't know if she'll come back. I don't know if my home is gone, you know? That place broke Vi, and I wouldn't blame her if she would rather stay away from it."

"But that doesn't mean she doesn't exist," I soothed. "She's still your sister, right?"

"Not exactly," he tried to explain. "I mean, she's the only one of us really related to Gran. The rest of us are just hangers-on, so if she wanted to..."

"But would she?" I pressed.

This time, his breathy laugh was a little less sad. "No, I don't think so. I just don't know what to do, and if this hurts me this bad, is it going to break her all over again?"

"Losing a parent hurts the entire family," I said. "That's one of those things I read when looking up grief." Then I groaned. "And you probably know that, so I sound dumb."

"You sound like you care," he assured me. "Zoe, you sound like a hug, and I fucking need that right now. I just... I don't know what I'm going to do without her. Gran was always the glue between the rest of us. I mean, what the fuck do I have in common with someone like Ashton Walker?"

"Who?" I asked.

"The guy who made that fancy-ass lingerie company," he explained. "Never mind. It doesn't matter. All I'm saying is that we all grew up different, you know? I went into computers. Others went into fashion, or medicine, or law. Gran made sure we all did well for ourselves, too. I'm like the baby of the family, though. She stopped taking in kids right around the time I got out, so there aren't too many of us. Well, younger ones. But, like, the older..." He stopped. "I'm not making any sense, huh?"

"Not really," I assured him, "but it also doesn't matter. There are a lot of kids who that place helped, you don't have an exact count, and yet they all feel like family, right?"

"Most," he agreed. "Some did their time and bailed. Shit, I can barely remember their names, but I'd say more than half of us joined Gran's little rainbow. She gave us colors, you see. I'm Teal. It's my favorite color, so that was what she named me, and she calls all of her kids 'her rainbow.'"

"That," I said, "is about the cutest thing I can imagine. You also seem like a Teal."

"I know, right?" His laugh was even easier this time. Then he sighed like he was letting go of all his stress - or maybe taking more on. It was hard to be sure. "Zoe, I just wanted to say it's ok if you don't want to see me. I mean, I know you might not be ready, and I'm not coming into town to pressure you or anything, but since I'll be that close, I really want to see Hot and Jeri. I'd kinda like to see you too."

"Yeah," I murmured, suddenly feeling like I was at a loss for words. "You have to at least let me buy you a coffee, ok?"

"So you're good with the idea of meeting up?"

"I..." That sentence failed me. "Yes?" I squeaked.

"Doesn't sound so ok," he told me. "Baby, I'm honestly ok with it if you're not ready yet."

"I want to be ready," I promised. "I just hate why you're coming here, and I'm scared to death you won't like me once you meet me."

"I'll like you," he swore. "I'm kinda scared you're going to get your vision of me destroyed."

"That you're cute?" I asked.

"I'm a fucking nerd," he reminded me. "Beanpole, baby. I'm like stupidly tall, ok? A fucking giant, right? But I weigh about half as much as Hot, and I swear to god none of it is muscle."

"So?" I asked. "I'm not really into gym rats."

He laughed. "Lies! I've heard what you say about him."

"To encourage Jeri," I admitted. "Ok, and he's cute too. I mean, he has a nice face and all, but I'm kinda more into the skater boy look than the barbarian."

"Yeah?" And now he sounded a little bit happy.

"Don't you dare tell Jericho!" I hissed. "She would never let me live it down!"

"Hell, Jeri would probably fuck a tree if she was in the mood," he joked. "That girl's standards for one-night stands are not something to mimic, ok? Granted, she also doesn't want to talk to them, so there's that."

"Are you calling her a slut?" I teased.

"No," he assured me. "I'm just saying my guildmate judges

people by what they give her, and sometimes that giving is nothing more than an orgasm, which makes them disposable."

"Yeah, she does kinda do that," I agreed, having heard enough stories. "What about you, Jinxy? What makes you decide someone's worth it?"

"Uh..." He paused for a long moment, then chuckled. "I honestly have no idea. It's a gut feeling for me, baby. You're worth it, though."

"Me?"

"Mhm," he agreed. "My gut feeling about you says yes."

"But what if - " I tried, only for him to cut me off again.

"Stop!" he begged. "Oh my god, Zoe, you're killing me here. I'm nervous to meet you too, but I'm thinking you're going to be the bright spot in my trip, ok? Can't you just let me have this one thing?"

"Ok," I relented. "I mean, it's kinda shitty why you have to come here, so yeah. I guess that's the least I can do - but I'll still be nervous!"

He just laughed. "No shit. Same. You can also cancel at any time, you know. I mean, I'm not coming to Sanger to see you. I'm coming there to see Hot and Jeri, so it's super low-pressure."

Which made me snort, since we'd just gone around all of this stuff a second ago. "We're a mess, huh?"

"Completely," he agreed. "And I happen to like my girlfriend. Gran wants to see a picture, so I'm going to show her the one from you at school, ok?"

"My hair's kinda crappy in that one."

"No," he told me, "it's not. It makes you look beautiful and sweet. Trust me, those are two things Gran will approve of."

"Yeah, but my fire-engine red hair?" I asked.

"Is considered calm in her world," he assured me. "Her granddaughter has this pastel, multicolored thing. She'll love it.

And I'm seriously hoping she'll still be coherent enough to say that..." he mumbled, his voice once again breaking near the end.

"She loves you," I reminded him. "That's why she put in the effort, right? You're not even her own flesh and blood, but she took you in, claimed you as her own, and helped you as much as she could. To me, that kinda sounds like she loved you because she *wanted* to. Not because she had to, Shawn. She *chose* you."

"Yeah," he breathed. "She kinda did, and the world is going to be a darker place without her in it."

"And I'll help you fix that," I promised. "I also meant it when I said I'd go and hold your hand if you need support. This isn't the kind of thing someone should do alone."

"No offense," he said, "but if it comes to a funeral assistant, I'm claiming Jeri. She's kinda a pro at these things by now." He huffed, trying to laugh. "Hot's not far behind."

"Or maybe you just need someone there for you," I reminded him. "That's ok too."

"No, I think I'll save that part for when I don't have a zillion eyes on me."

"The offer's still there," I promised.

"But what about Alpha Team?" he asked. "I mean, if I'm with Gran, I won't really be able to help, and you deserve to get revenge too, baby. I feel like I'm letting you down."

"We're fine," I promised. "Jinxy, we're all going to be fine. This is your time, and I get that. Just like I needed time and space to figure out what had happened to me, you're going to need to do that with your Gran. You deserve it." I almost stopped there, but couldn't help myself. "And I like you enough I want to make sure you get it."

"Yeah?"

"Yeah," I said.

"Because I like you too, Zoe. A lot." He pulled in a long breath. "Enough that I don't want to abandon you like this."

"It's not abandoning me," I promised. "This is you taking care of you, and it makes me respect you more."

"That," he said. "You asked what made someone worth it? Well, I think I just figured it out."

"What's that?"

He murmured thoughtfully. "The people who feel worth it to me are the ones who truly care about helping. They give a shit about how others feel. Most of all, they manage to make being around them into a good thing. You know, the way you do with everyone."

"Me?"

"You, Zoe," he said. "That's why I can't stop thinking about you. That's why I know that even if this sucks, I'm going to be ok - because I have a feeling you won't rest until I am."

"Promise," I assured him. "It's kinda the least I can do."

CHAPTER 51

JINXY

I talked to Zoe for much too long. By the time I got off the phone with her, it was almost midnight in their time zone, but I had a feeling Hot would still be awake. Since this was happening, and I was flying out in about eight hours, I needed to make sure I gave him a head's up.

"Yeah?" Hot answered his phone.

"Hey, man," I said, "it's Shawn. I'm flying to Texas in the morning."

"Fuck."

Yep. That pretty much summed up things, but it also meant I didn't have to repeat all of the same sad shit I'd told Zoe.

"Is she gone?" he asked next.

"No, but she's fading," I admitted. "The nurse called. Evidently, I was like ninth on the list, so I guess they're telling all of us. I'm working on an email to my brother to make sure everyone gets informed, but sounds like it's only a few more days."

"And you want to be there," he said, proving he understood. "Call if you need anything? Jeri and I aren't that far away. Food, clothes, or anything else? An extra hand? Seriously, Shawn. Any single thing. We're here for you."

Fuck it. My damned throat chose that exact moment to get all tight and stupid again. The murmur I managed made it clear I heard him, but I had to sniff to get this shit to relax. He heard it. I knew he must've. The strange thing was that I didn't care.

"So," I said, pausing to clear my throat, "I was thinking about taking you up on your offer, but I don't know when. I mean, I can stay at Southwind, I'm sure. I figure Bonham probably has a hotel or two."

"Maybe," Hot replied. "That's a tiny little town, man."

"Yeah, and Cats Peak is smaller."

"Which is why we'll make room if we have to," he assured me. "Open invitation. I'll send you the code for the back door, so even if I'm at work, you can get inside, ok?"

"Probably won't be for a few days," I assured him. "Some of us are going to crash at the hospital. Those pull-out beds and fold-down chairs suck, but being close is more important."

"Nope, I gotcha," he swore.

"But," I went on, "this Ruin stuff - "

"Is not your problem now," he assured me. "You deal with what you need to, Shawn. I'll let Jeri know, and we'll cover the rest. Besides, it's not like the Kings of Gaming are going anywhere, right?"

"No, that's a good point," I realized. "It's just that I'm worried about Zoe. I don't want to put too much on her, and I don't want to hold her back. I mean, if you can get what you need to finish this, then do it?"

"Promise," he said. "But, bro? How are you really doing?"

Pushing out a heavy breath, I flopped down onto my too-small bed. "Grayson, I'm a fucking mess."

"Kinda figured."

"I mean, I'm trying to keep it together, but I'm up here in Colorado, feeling like I'm out of touch with the rest of the world. Sure, Cyan's close, but - "

"So put in the effort to talk to your brother," he told me.

I groaned. "He's busy. Shit, they're all busy. That's the problem, you know? Without Gran to keep us all circling the same thing - Southwind - I'm scared to death we're going to just drift apart."

"And we'll always be here for you," he told me. "Death over Dishonor, brother. We made a pact when we named our guild that, and it's one I will never forget. I also meant every word."

"All three of them," I joked. "But no, that actually helps. I'm just..."

"Feeling like your mom's dying?" he supplied.

Which made me sigh again. "Yeah, pretty much. Fuck, this sucks."

"No shit."

"Just ask Jeri to keep an eye on Zoe for me?" I begged. "I know it's stupid, and I know she'll be ok, but I feel like I need to know someone's looking out for her so I can relax. Not that I'm really doing anything, but you know how it goes."

"Kinda do," Hot agreed. "I'll also make sure she's fine. You know Ripper will. Pretty sure Cade's gotten close to Zoe too, and Knock watches out for all of us."

"Yeah," I breathed. "Kinda why we work, right?"

"Mhm," he agreed. "Our own little mashup of a family. Also sounds like you really like this girl. Anything you want to tell me?"

"Such as?" I asked.

"Oh, about how you told her you love her. Or maybe how she gets this stupid smile on her face when you call her baby?"

"She does?"

"Mhm," he agreed. "Her eyes also light up when she calls you.

Probably on Discord too, but I don't get to see that. The girl's into you, Shawn. I mean, she's got some baggage, but she's seriously into you."

"I don't give a damn about her 'baggage,'" I assured him. "I do care about her hurting. I hate the idea of what they did to her, and I want to rip those fuckers apart, limb from limb."

"That's the grief talking," he told me.

"Probably," I admitted. "It just feels like I can't fucking change things, you know? How long have we been at this?"

"Months," he agreed.

"And we're barely any closer to busting them than we were at Christmas!" A groan slipped from my lips. "It's like I can't even help give her closure, and now I'm bailing on her when we finally get into KoG's site! What the fuck is she going to think of me?"

"That your Gran is dying," he said gently. "Shawn, you didn't plan this."

"But I'm bailing on her!"

"So do you want to come here instead of there? Do you want to tell Gran you'll catch up with her later? Do you think she'd understand how important this girl is to you and why you're willing to not even bother saying goodbye to her because of a fucking crush?"

"She's more than a damned crush!" I snapped - and immediately wished I could take it back. "Ah, fuck."

But Hot just murmured like he'd won that round. "I know that. You know that. I have a feeling everyone in Ruin except Zoe knows that. You're falling in love with a girl you've never seen, and you want to be her hero. It's normal. Shit, it's a sweet thing! You also can't rewind time, Shawn. Trust me on that."

"No, I know."

"Do you?" he pressed. "Because knowing she's dying is very, *very* different from the moment someone says she's gone. There's still hope right now. There's possibility and chances. Once Gran's gone, it's going to hit you so fucking hard and you won't be able to breathe. You'll be begging for more time, hating the time you wasted up there in school, and thinking about how another semester would've been worth it to see her a little more. That's what happens."

"Yeah..."

"And it's ok to feel all of that," Hot assured me. "It really is. It's ok to stop thinking about Zoe for a bit because you need to think about yourself. Shawn, I swear to you that Jericho will not let anything happen to her. I won't let anything happen to Jericho, which means I have to keep all of these kids safe. Now, it'll be a little more work without you around to help me herd up these cats - er, kids - but I'm willing to take one for the team."

Which finally got me to laugh. It wasn't a real one, but it felt like some of the tension in the back of my neck finally relaxed. I was willing to take it.

"But do you think we can really bust these guys?" I asked. "Give it to me straight, Grayson. Is this project of Jeri's a pipe dream, or do we have a chance of actually getting the fuckers who abused my girl thrown in jail?"

"We have a chance," he swore. "It might be messy, but it's a chance. Why?"

"Because I'm going to see my family," I reminded him.

"And?"

Yeah, that was a lot harder to explain. "Uh..." I thought of a vague way to put this. "So, some of my siblings have connections."

"To shady shit?" he guessed.

"Kinda, yeah," I admitted. "Let's just say they're the ones you want on your side, you know?"

"And you haven't asked them for help because?"

Which made me sigh again. "Um, because sometimes they ask

for a favor back," I tried to explain. "Look, Southwind made me who I am, but Gran did that by ignoring the court order that said I couldn't get online. Violet ignored that by giving me her laptop so it would look like it was her playing those games. Bea pointed out that she didn't know a damned thing about 'these internets,' so I had best learn enough for both of us, because it wasn't going away. They took risks on me, Hot."

"I know they did," he said soothingly.

"But those risks could've bit them in the ass. This? The shit with Alpha Team? If I asked for a favor, my siblings would take a risk, and it would bite them in the ass. They'd get tangled in it, just like we are, but they don't know shit about the internet."

"No, that's fair," he assured me. "And this is illegal. I can't imagine any of them would want to get busted again."

"Do we?" I countered. "I mean, I sure don't."

"We don't," he agreed, "but that doesn't mean it won't happen. Hacking is illegal. Ruin is good. Hell, those kids have learned a shit-ton doing this. I'm pretty convinced that if we turned them loose, they could perform miracles. I also really don't want them locked in a dark cell, never to see the spark of the internet again."

"Same," I assured him. "Trust me, it sucks!"

Which made Hot laugh. "Oh, I believe you. I mean, how would I order pizza without this miracle of technology? But don't worry about Alpha Team or the KoG site. There's so much crap on there to sort through that we'll be at it for at least another week. Maybe more."

"It shouldn't take so long," I grumbled.

"It's a lot of data," he countered.

"Yeah, yeah," I mumbled playfully, "and we have to put this case together so it'll stick. No, I gotcha."

"But speaking of the internet," Hot said, slightly changing the subject, "are you coming to the Dallas convention? Knock's competing, and Jericho wants to at least enter."

"That first-person shooter tournament?" I asked.

"Mhm," he agreed. "It's the Professional League of Gamers. It's in Dallas. It's at the end of the month. I was thinking that maybe we'd make a fun trip out of it, get everyone to stop thinking about this damned case for a minute, and just have some good, wholesome fun."

"Wholesome and shooting people in the heads doesn't usually go together," I joked. "But probably not. I mean, if I'm still in Texas at that point, then yeah! I'll gladly go. I just don't think I will be."

"And you have a degree to earn," he said, showing he was keeping up. "How hard is it going to be to recover from this time off?"

"I'm only missing a day," I assured him. "Well, tomorrow. After that is my Spring Break - "

"Same as Sanger High," he agreed.

"And the nurses don't think she'll make it that long. The funeral should happen pretty quick, since so many of us are from out of town." Groaning, I scrubbed at my face. "Fuck! I hate that I know that."

"Because you stood beside the rest of us when we stumbled through our losses," Hot reminded me. "Bro, it's now my turn to have your back. That's how this works, and it's ok."

"I know," I assured him.

"Shawn," he said, his voice sounding like a warm hug, "we've got you. We will always have you. I love you too much to let you worry about any of this, you hear me? Brothers take care of brothers, and we fucking have you."

Letting my eyes close, I could feel the sting of the first tears wanting to fall. "I love you too, man. I think I kinda needed to hear that."

"Then I'll say it more often," he swore. "Now go ahead and cry. I'm not going to tell a damned soul, but I will listen. All the blubbering, Jinxy. All the snot-sniffing and shit you need to get out there, you just do it. I'm not leaving you because you didn't leave me."

And that was what made me finally break.

CHAPTER 52

JERICHO

The next day, we continued on without Jinxy. It didn't feel like the start of Spring Break, though. When classes ended on Friday, the rest of Ruin headed to Knock's place to do what we always did: bust Alpha Team. There were no parties planned. The lack of school simply meant more time to work.

Zoe updated everyone on Jinxy's Gran's health, and we all agreed he needed to put his family first. The sad truth was his absence wouldn't change anything. Mostly because all we were doing was following posts, copying crap, and saving it.

On that wall above the charging area, however, the "murder board" was getting full. Initially, it had started with Riley making a few lines with her Sharpie markers. Now? Fuck, we had pictures of girls, dates marked in red, corroborating evidence from posts and photos listed below each girl, and almost no blank space left.

The timeline was the terrifying thing, though. No one had thought to keep track of every single party that had been held at

John's house, and I'd moved here long after they'd started. Still, it looked like there was good reason to believe that every single rape, assault, or sexual manipulation had happened at one. It was almost like those guys had organized the parties because they needed to get their fix.

The idea of them treating our female bodies as some cheap entertainment disgusted me.

But there it was. From the videos Ripper had seen, Evan had been involved in all of the horrible crap too. So many of them included six guys. Once Evan was arrested, the other five just continued on like it wasn't a big deal. Sure, they'd taken some precautions with their data, but their posts on KoG hadn't slowed down at all.

"Dylan has a pretty good rant about you, Jeri," Cade said at one point.

"Oh yeah?" I asked.

"Yeah, looks like it was about when Evan was arrested," he told us. "Just after."

"It's right around when he tried to say you were running Ruin," Hottie added. "Just found Wade chiming in like an obedient bitch."

"Not so sure he's obedient," Knock said. "I'm on a post where he and Landon are talking about how they need to 'ramp things up.' No idea what that's supposed to mean, but they're pissed they're being 'held back.'"

"When?" Ripper asked from his place by the wall.

"Um..." Knock's brow creased. "Looks like early February. The thread runs from the third to the fifth."

So Ripper added that to the wall. "I have a feeling we're going to be adding more girls to this."

"Yeah, Tiffany says she has twelve victims in her bitch squad," I told them. "We only named ten on our own."

"Well, nine," Zoe clarified. "Tiffany knew that freshman girl, who made ten. Evidently, she found the two Ripper was going to make me ID later."

"And we'll probably find more," Hottie warned us. "So let's make sure we save every single thing that might apply to our case, and then we'll start wading through it. I don't want to accidentally double up any more than we have to."

"Double up?" I asked, twisting to see him.

It was Cade who answered. "Like if two of us save the same video. If we're only saving things from the person we're tracking, it's less likely. If one person is trying to save everything?"

"They'll forget what they already saved," Knock finished for him. "That's why we have one of us for each of them, kinda."

Because Jinxy had been following John, but he was spending time with Gran before she passed. None of us knew how far he'd gotten, so we'd agreed that whoever finished first would take over for him. I had Parker. Knock had Landon. Hottie had Wade, and Cade had claimed Dylan. Naturally, all of these fuckers liked to not only post, but also comment on just about everything. That was turning our search into a full-time job.

Then, Saturday afternoon, Zoe's phone vibrated. We all turned in our chairs to check, but we knew what had happened before she even said a word. The tears welling up in her eyes said enough, but just to make sure we all knew, she lifted her head and looked around the room.

"Shawn's Gran is in Heaven."

"Fuck," I breathed, dropping my head into my hands. "When's the funeral?"

"Tuesday," she told us. "He said the last of his family is making their way there." Then she let out a soft little whimper. "Oh no, and they didn't all get to see her first!"

"Fuck," Cade mumbled.

Knock just nodded in agreement. Ripper looked sad, but none of them really understood how hard this would be for Jinxy. Sure, in theory we all knew how much losing someone might hurt, but none of them had had it happen yet. Knock and Cade might have shitty relationships with their parents, but they were still alive. The same was true for Zoe and Ripper.

And yet they still cared. They didn't get it, but they cared about Jinxy enough to feel bad for him. I, however, knew that pain. I'd been there. I'd learned how to keep the tears from my eyes and make polite conversation at the funerals. It sucked. God, did it suck, but I'd make sure he was eventually ok.

Then Zoe's phone buzzed again. Her brow creased for a single second before she looked at me. "Jeri, he says he's coming to your house Tuesday afternoon."

"Hottie should've given him the address already," I assured her. "Make sure he knows I'll be ready."

But when Tuesday came around, I wasn't. Trying to scrape as much data from the KoG website as possible, it felt like everything else had been put on hold. When I woke up on Tuesday morning, I realized our house was a mess!

Maybe we didn't use the first floor that much, but over time, things built up. There was a blanket sinking into the corner of the couch. Dust coated everything because no one had been dusting. Never mind the carpet! I couldn't remember the last time it had been vacuumed. If Mom decided to make another stop home, she'd be pissed at the way we'd let this go.

So I let the rest know I wasn't going to Knock's today and started cleaning. At least on the upside, I didn't have to go to school this week. We were officially on Spring Break. The rest of Ruin would continue harvesting data, and they promised it was ok for me to skip a day. The extra hours would make up for my absence. Besides, Jinxy deserved nothing less, they pointed out.

But turning on the vacuum alerted Hottie to what I was doing. Before I even finished cleaning that one room, he'd made his way downstairs and was standing in the space between the living room and kitchen. When I finished and turned it off, he gestured for me to pass the thing over.

"We're doing a full cleaning, huh?" he asked.

"Jinxy's coming in a bit," I reminded him. "I don't know what time, but he's going to spend all day at a funeral, and I don't want this place looking like a shit heap."

He nodded. "Ok. I'll vacuum the stairs, upstairs hall, and my room - since that's where he'll be staying. You good with me skipping your room?"

"Yep," I decided. "I'm supposed to be a messy teen, right?"

He just scoffed at that as he wound up the cord and rolled the vacuum towards the stairs. "And turn on the TV while you're at it? News, or talk, or something. I can't clean without voices in the room."

"On it," I assured him, reaching for the remote.

It ended up on the local Dallas-Fort Worth station. It was the last thing that had been on, so good enough for me. Mostly because *I* didn't need sound to focus on cleaning. That was Hottie's deal. Nope, I had no problem letting my mind wander on its own.

Of course, it wandered right to Dylan and his friends. It hadn't looked like there'd been a party at John's over the weekend. With that said, I also hadn't checked religiously or anything. We'd been a little more focused on saving shit to the Squirrel. But if there *had* been a party, it hadn't been very wild, the backyard hadn't been filled with people, and nothing had stood out that I could've seen from my window.

So I was going with no. Tiffany and her bitch squad must've killed that, which served the Alpha Team right. Fuck them. Fuck their rape-fests. Fuck their sleezy and skeevy habits that had worked for far too long.

I made it through picking up the clutter, trying to figure out how long they'd been at this. From what I could tell, they'd started last summer, but why? What had been the trigger for six guys to start having orgies? Even if they'd been consensual at first - because there could've been some kink before they started recording - what made them keep doing it?

And how the fuck did they justify that to themselves if they were so upset about homosexuality? God, bigots drove me insane. Their shit never made sense, but I supposed it didn't have to, to them. Nope, they just wanted to hate, and all five of those assholes hated women, it seemed.

They also had no plans to stop. That was the part that pissed me off the most. If Hottie hadn't called the cops, how many more girls from school would've been victimized? I should've seen that one thing as a win, yet it was hard to think that way when looking at the growing number of pictures on the murder board at Knock's place.

I was in the middle of dusting when the vacuum upstairs finally shut off. Immediately, the sound of the television beside me came across as much too loud. Worse, it was on the news.

"The body of a sophomore from Denton High School was found by hikers at the Isle du Bois park just outside Denton city limits this morning," the anchor was saying. "There have been three other incidents reported at that location over the weekend, and the police have requested that anyone with information call the tip line on your screen. Visitors are encouraged to be extra vigilant or to avoid the area if at all possible."

I just closed my eyes and groaned. Another woman hurt. There was *always* another hurt, wasn't there? It was like this shit was never-ending. Dylan and his friends weren't the only assholes out there in the world. They were just my current problem. They were one in a million, most likely, and not in a good way.

Nope, I wouldn't be surprised at all if there were at least a million rapists running around, thinking they had the right to our bodies. *That* was what made all of this shit so hard to fight against. And yet, in that moment, a strange calm came over me.

"Jeri?" Hottie asked, walking into the room to see me standing there, staring at the bookshelf. "You ok?"

"Our work is never going to be done, is it?" I asked as I turned around to face him. "Once we bust the Alpha Team, there will just be another, won't there?"

"Yeah," he breathed. "Baby girl, there's a lot of bad in the world. We both know that. It's also not our fault."

"But we can do something about it!" I told him. "Some girl got killed at a campsite in Denton over the weekend. Tomorrow, another will get raped in a mall parking lot. They won't stop, Hottie. Don't you get that? Men won't ever fucking stop abusing us, and no one is doing a damned thing about it!"

"We are," he said as he closed the distance between us. Clasping my arms, he dipped his head to look right in my face. "Jeri, we're someone. We're doing something. I mean, once we deal with the Alpha Team, then why can't we move on to the next group of assholes on those forums? We'll keep going until we've cleaned it up, even if we're like eighty years old by then."

"But you keep saying you want me to be safe," I reminded him.

He leaned in a little more to kiss my brow. "Safe, baby girl, is not the same as passive. This means something to you. This drives you, Jeri, and I can see that. Fuck, the last thing I want to do is put out your fire. So you lead and I'll follow, ok?"

"And Ruin?" I asked.

"You'll have to ask them, but I think they'll - "

The sound of the doorbell cut him off. We both paused in confusion for a second, and then had our epiphany in tandem.

"Jinxy!" I breathed.

But Hottie was already headed to the door. Pulling it open, he revealed an amazingly tall man with elegant and understated wire-frame glasses on the other side. He was wearing a suit with the most amazing turquoise accents. The tie and the handkerchief in his pocket matched each other, and they were only a few shades darker than his shirt, making him kinda look like some sort of mafia boss or something. I liked it.

"Wow," I said, heading that way. "Bro, you clean up nice!"

"Jericho!" he sighed, stepping inside but not stopping until he had me wrapped up in a bone-crushing hug. "Girl, you look good. I think Texas works for you."

"Thanks," Hottie said. "Not even here five minutes and you're hitting on my girl."

"Complimenting my little sister," he clarified. "I also think I might be stuck on 'polite mode' now. Fuck, small-town Texas is whack. I mean, did you know people wear cowboy hats and boots to a funeral?"

I immediately looked down to see his very nice - and shiny - shoes. "Clearly you didn't," I teased.

"Didn't get out much when I lived here," he admitted. "Now come give me a hug too, Grayson. I think I've earned one."

"And I can get your bags from your car," I offered.

Together, both men spun to face me and said, "No!"

So I stopped and lifted my hands in surrender. "Well, ok then."

"But I won't turn down a coffee," Jinxy told me. "Fuck, water, a chair. Some friends who are *not* going to ask me a million times how I'm doing or say anything at all about being sorry. Deal?"

"And I'll get your bags," Hottie offered, leaning in to give him a hard side-hug. "It's good to see you again, bro, even if the reason is shit."

"Complete shit," Jinxy agreed, "but this?" He laughed softly. "Crazy as this is going to sound, your house has that feeling that kinda screams home." And then he dropped down on my couch and leaned back. "I think it might have something to do with the people."

CHAPTER 53

ZOE

I was just getting into my car, about to leave Knock's place, when my phone rang. Confused, I pulled it out and saw Jinxy's real name on the screen. Of course, I was swiping as fast as I could.

"Shawn?" I gasped.

"Hey, baby," he purred, sounding better than he had in days. "Just wanted to let you know I'm in Sanger. Got to Jericho's place a bit ago, she had to feed me - and damn, can she cook - but now I have a free hand."

"Yeah, Kitty just stuffed all of us," I said. "It's getting to be a habit around here."

"Which here?"

"Knock's place," I explained. "We work on getting the data we need, Riley and Logan help out when they can. Um, Riley keeps offering alcohol in case anyone needs a break, and Kitty cooks. But once we have dinner, no more deep diving into that hellhole."

"Nice," he said. "So, I'm probably going to be in town for a few days. Just so you know."

"Have a car?" I asked.

"A rental."

So I started my car. "Well, if you'd like to head to Starbucks, I'll buy you a coffee. I mean, unless you're already all relaxed and sick of driving. We can do it tomorrow too, but I'm going right past there and don't really have to be home for a few more hours."

"Now?" he asked.

"It was just an option..."

"Now's good," he promised. Then the phone went scratchy and I heard him yell, "Hot! I need to know how to get to the right Starbucks."

"There's only one," I told him. "We're in a small town, Shawn."

"Busted," he said around a little laugh. "But you're sure about this?"

I looked down at what I was wearing and almost changed my mind. But my mouth said, "I'm sure. I'm more than ready to meet you."

"Ok," he breathed. "I'll be the one wearing teal."

"I'm the one with red hair," I said. "Now type Starbucks into Google maps, and I'll meet you there in five, ok?"

"On my way," he swore.

I hung up, but it was with a smile on my face. I wasn't all dressed up, and I didn't have super-fancy makeup on or anything, but did it matter? Eventually, he'd have to see me in my less-than-perfect phase, so why not start out that way? Lowered expectations, or something.

Trying to convince myself I wasn't making the biggest mistake ever because of my excitement, I sent a text off to my parents, letting them know I was meeting a friend at Starbucks, so I wouldn't be home until late. Then I finally left the farm and headed that way.

The drive was a short one, since Sanger really was a small town, but Knock lived on the exact opposite side from the coffee shop. I made it the whole way just fine, but the moment I pulled into the parking lot, my anxiety decided to make an appearance. Nothing too bad, yet I was damned near vibrating.

I wanted to meet Jinxy more than I could imagine. I hated why he was here. I was terrified I wouldn't be what he was expecting. There was also a tiny little worry that he'd be nothing at all like the guy he'd been on the phone. I didn't mean looks. No, that he'd be rude, or not funny, or something!

It was all stupid, but that was the problem with meeting someone I felt like I knew well but had never seen before. There was this disconnect, because we'd done things backwards. I wanted this to work. Fuck, but did I! I was also convinced I'd overhyped things and somehow screwed it all up.

So, steeling myself, I squared my shoulders and walked into the little store. The place was mostly empty, since it was early evening on Tuesday. That made the man at the counter stand out a little more. Clearly, he'd already ordered and was waiting for his drink.

And his shirt was teal.

"Shawn?" I asked, forcing my feet to head that way.

He turned, revealing a face I'd only seen in pictures, but the real thing was so much better. His jaw was one of those sharp ones. His nose was narrow and while not too small, it fit his face perfectly. His glasses were round, with the smallest little wire frames, making them almost disappear. I couldn't tell if the metal was gold or if that was just the reflection from the lights.

And he was tall. Not kinda tall, like the guys. Nope, this guy was definitely pushing six and a half feet. He had to be! His chest was lean but fit. His arms weren't bulging, but they weren't toothpicks either. The shirt he was wearing was caught perfectly between blue and green, with a tie that was just a few shades darker, and his black slacks and shiny shoes made it clear he hadn't changed yet.

The best part, though, was how his eyes found me, jumped up to my hair, and then he smiled. "Zoe?"

"Yeah," I said, closing the distance between us. "Hey!"

He spread his arms. "So, this is me."

On impulse, I kept going. Kept moving. I refused to stop until I was chest to chest with him and wrapping my arms around his neck in a hug. Jinxy froze for a moment, then bent to wrap his own arms around my back, making it so I didn't have to stretch so much.

He smelled amazing. There was a hint of some cologne or aftershave that had almost faded away. His shirt had a bit of lavender, like the detergent he'd used. His hair was citrusy, brown, and just long enough for my fingers to slip against it at the back of his neck.

We hugged. There was no swaying from side to side or roaming hands. We just hugged, our bodies pressed so close together as I held this dream of a man against me. So many times I'd spilled my guts to him. I couldn't count the number of hours we'd talked, nor the topics we'd gone over. All I knew was that in this moment, he was real. Finally, completely real.

And then the barista had to ruin it. "Shawn!" she called out.

With a soft chuckle, he let me go. "Um, Jeri said you like mocha?"

"Yeah?"

So he turned to claim two large paper cups and passed me one before thanking the barista. Smiling, and feeling only slightly awkward, I gestured to my favorite of the chairs in this place. Some were hard wooden things. Others were fancy-looking, but not meant for a conversation. But in the far corner was a little booth where Jeri and I always ended up talking.

"You know," I said as I slid into one side, "you were supposed to let me buy you a coffee."

"You can get the next round," he promised, joining me. "Also, I love the hair. No eyeliner today, though?"

"Uh, no," I grumbled. "I got up early to start organizing the Squirrel. Didn't want to mess with makeup."

His lips did a million maneuvers before he licked them, trying to calm the wild things down. I was pretty sure that was his best attempt to hide a smile. Giving up, he took a sip of his coffee.

"If this is you without trying, I'm kinda scared." His dark eyes jumped up to mine. "Zoe, you're beautiful."

"Yeah?" My stupid face was heating up, and fast.

Jinxy just nodded. "Yeah. I do have bad news, though. You do not qualify as fat."

"I'll take it," I assured him. "I also didn't believe you when you said you were a giant."

"Six foot, four inches," he told me. "You?"

"Five-four."

"Shorty."

Which made me laugh. "Hey, I wear heels that get me up to five-six!"

His lips curled deviously. "Shorty," he said again.

"And I can kick you under this table!"

But he shrugged. "I like short. It's cute - and I mean that in a good way, so do not start kicking." Setting his cup down, he turned it slowly. "I also didn't expect the hug."

"I kinda didn't either, but I wanted to," I admitted. "I mean, I've been getting better with the physical stuff."

"Just to put it out there, that's all the physical I'm looking for."

Which made me set my own cup down. "No," I said, leaning in so I could lower my voice. "Shawn, that's a bullshit line. It's not what guys think, or feel. It's what y'all say to convince a girl you're harmless, and I get it, but don't lie to me?"

"I'm not lying!" he insisted. "Shit, Zoe. I've been celibate for..." He groaned. "A *while*. Between classes, studying, and gaming? Yeah, let's just say that fucking everything that moves is low on my list of priorities, ok? I'm serious. The things I think of with you? Holding your hand. Maybe a hug. Definitely having you feel comfortable enough to lean up against me, or cuddle with me. That's it."

"But why?" I asked. "I mean, shit. You're hot. You could have a dozen girls in your bed."

He gave me a surprised look. "Me?"

"Yes!"

"I think you're going blind or something," he joked. "Zoe, I'm a dork. A nerd. I get turned down a hell of a lot more than I get to take a girl out. Oh, and I'm shit at asking. I get nervous, fuck it up, and yeah. Just not good."

"I'd say yes," I assured him.

That earned me a little smile. "So does that make this a date?"

Lifting my chin, I struggled not to smile. "Yes."

"Nice..."

There was a little pause as we both reached for our drinks. That little bit of awkwardness was there, and yet he was kinda easy to talk to. He also sounded just like he did over the phone. His voice was warm, deep enough to be sexy, and gentle. Nothing about Jinxy was threatening, and for me, that was a good thing. An *amazing* thing!

Eventually, he changed the subject. "So, how's everything going with Alpha Team? Weren't they supposed to have some big party over the weekend?"

I groaned. "Tiffany said they were trying, and Dylan yelled at Jeri for ruining it. Not that she did, but he hates her. So it kinda sounds like no. Hottie and Jeri didn't see shit at John's place, at least. There's nothing on social media about it. In fact, one of the football guys said those losers all went camping instead, since no one else would hang with them."

"Alpha Team went camping?" he asked.

I shrugged. "Away from parents, probably with alcohol, and somewhere they can meet girls who don't know them? Yeah, it's possible."

"And there are places to do that around here?"

I nodded. "Tons. The whole Greenbelt thing. It's a string of parks that connect to each other. Granted, that's just the ones I know about. They could've gone out in Dylan's back pasture for all I know. Plus, it's not like they've slowed down on their posting."

"Of course they haven't," he said. "Fucking assholes like that need someone to validate their existence, and KoG seems like the place for it."

"Yeah," I breathed. "But how about you, Shawn? I mean, how was her funeral, how are you doing? All of that stuff?"

He paused to take a long drink. "The funeral was about as perfect as it could be," he admitted. "We did this thing with carnations. Each of us had one in our color. Well, Violet had violets, but she's real family."

I just nodded, not knowing any of the people he was talking about. "But did it give you closure?"

A tiny, sad smile touched his mouth. "They buried her next to Bea, Zoe. In a small town where gay isn't something people talk about, we had a rainbow of flowers and she was buried next to her partner. Yeah, that's the kind of closure she deserved. Those women loved each other, and they should have been able to tell the world, but now it doesn't matter. They ended up side by side, and that is what they deserve."

"And you?" I pressed.

He reached forward to pick at the surface of the table, revealing a hint of ink on his arm. "I'm going to be ok. There are so many colors out there, and somehow we always find our way to each other. That's my family, and it's wild, it's intense, and it's impossible. It's also still there. I'm not alone, you know?"

"Yeah," I breathed, knowing that feeling.

"And it's hard, but this is life. I want her back. I wish I could turn back the clock and change everything, but life doesn't work that way. That means I have to be happy with the fact that she's buried beside Bea, the rainbow still exists, and I had her in my life. It wasn't long enough, and it didn't end how I wanted, but at least I had her."

"That's kinda how I feel," I admitted.

"About the Alpha Team?" he asked.

I nodded. "I wish I could turn back the clock. I long for the person I was before I woke up in that bathtub. I also know that shit is what led me here. It sucked, and I'm not saying I wanted it to happen, but I can't help but wonder if I would've been friends with Jeri before that."

"Ripper would've, and he would've dragged the pair of you together," he countered.

I made a little noise because I wasn't so sure of that. "Shawn, before that? I was one of *those* girls. I didn't stop and think shit through. I would've hated Jeri for stealing my best friend away, you know? I would've been trying to change myself to impress a guy. I dunno. I think that sometimes, we need a little pain to make us realize the good things."

"I don't," he said. "I think bad shit sucks. I think surviving it proves you were already strong. It didn't *make* you that way. It certainly didn't mold you. No, you had all of that before. It's just that you - not the rest of us, but you - can see it now."

"Yeah," I breathed. "I kinda like that."

"And I think you're an amazing woman who doesn't give herself enough credit," he continued. "You, Zoe, are sweet and soft and brilliant. You're a damned good hacker who hasn't yet realized you can keep up with the rest of us now. I think you're so used to hearing about all the things you can't do, or being told you're 'cute' when you try something new, that you haven't yet realized that somewhere along the way you became amazing. Powerful, even."

"I don't feel like it."

So he reached his hand across the table to trace the top of mine. "But I see it. That's why this is enough. Your time, Zoe, is more than enough. Knowing someone like you?" He smiled. "It made today bearable."

CHAPTER 54

HOTSHOT

Jinxy stayed out late with Zoe. Since it was Spring Break, the girl didn't have to get to bed early, but I still told Jeri to send her a reminder at midnight. The last thing we wanted was her first meeting with Jinxy getting her in trouble. Half an hour later, Jinxy dragged his ass through the front door with an adorable smile on his face.

Yeah, I knew that look. The guy was smitten. The girl he'd only known online, the one whose personality had enchanted him, had turned out to be as beautiful as he could've hoped for. Granted, I happened to prefer Jeri's look to Zoe's, but I wasn't about to bitch that my oldest friend didn't share my taste. One less guy chasing her sounded good to me!

I was happy for Jinxy, though. If Zoe could be a little light in his darkest time, then more power to him. If he could be a bit of light for her as well, then that made them a matched set, didn't it? Hopefully, they might even have a chance of working out.

But the day had taken its toll. The guy was still wearing half the suit he'd been in for the funeral. Sending him to enjoy a hot shower, I got my room ready to become his, and then moved what I needed across the hall. That night, I didn't need to hide the fact that I fell asleep curled up and hugging Jericho against my chest.

The next morning, I woke to the sound of laughter. It was coming from downstairs. The spot beside me was empty, and I hadn't even stirred. So pulling myself out of bed, I managed to get cleaned up and dressed, then went to join Jinxy and Jeri in the kitchen.

Jeri was cooking. She had an entire pan filled with eggs. There was another with pancakes slowly browning. Jinxy was sitting at the counter on one of the stools, sipping at a cup of coffee while they talked.

"She has the most amazing eyes," he was saying. "Like brown, but not. I don't even know what that color is called and I'm obsessed with it."

"Hazel," I supplied as I claimed the stool beside him. "Zoe's eyes are hazel."

"What the actual fuck is hazel?" he asked.

"Like two colors mixed together," I said. "Usually it's brown with some green or amber. Sometimes grey. I dunno. But when I Googled it - "

"You Googled Zoe's eye color?" Jeri asked.

Groaning, I pointed to the coffee pot in a silent request for help. "I Googled the color," I explained. "It was before I knew Zoe."

"Why?" she asked, a little smirk on her face.

"Some girl," Jinxy guessed.

I shot him a dirty look. "Stop helping me. It was an actress, ok? She said her eyes were hazel in an interview, and I thought they looked green, so I wanted to see what the difference was."

"Nerd," he teased.

He wasn't wrong, but that was beside the point. This was

supposed to be about picking on him. "So, how was that first kiss, hm?" I asked.

"No kissing," he said.

"Hottie," Jeri groaned, "she's not ready for that."

"Zoe?" I scoffed. "That girl will surprise you, Jeri."

"Well, she surprised me with a hug," Jinxy said. "Walked right in and wrapped her arms around my neck."

"Could she reach?" Jeri joked.

"I had to bend," he admitted, "but I kinda like that. There's something hot about a short girl, you know?"

"Makes sex easier if she's taller," I countered.

Which got me a dirty look. "And we're not even at kissing, so can we please leave sex out of this? Don't care if you and Jeri are boinking like bunnies, bro."

"Nice alliteration," I shot back.

"Impressive, huh?" he agreed. "Put a whole two seconds into that one. But my point is I do like her. Fuck, I like that girl a lot. Unlike you, I'm not weird about dating a high school girl, I'm totally cool with her taking time to figure out what she's comfortable with, and seeing her yesterday..." His words trailed off.

Jeri dropped a cup of coffee in front of me, made the way I liked it. "A little something to distract you, hm?" she asked him. "I just hope she didn't over-'sorry' you."

"She didn't," he promised.

But I jerked my chin at him. "So I'm going to. Shawn, are you actually doing ok? I mean, this is a lot. She was your Gran."

"Yeah," he agreed, "she was. It also wasn't a shock, I got to see her, and I had enough time to say goodbye. It matters, Grayson. Don't get me wrong. I still don't want to hear any more awkward attempts at sympathy. I'm full up with those. I also know you both get it. You've been there, you've had to smile kindly because someone else doesn't know how to make you feel better."

"Because they can't," I reminded him. "And that's ok."

"But it's also ok to enjoy the moments when it's not weighing on you," Jeri pointed out. "There's no law that says you can't remember the good things - even if it's just to distract yourself."

"That!" Jinxy said, pointing at her. "Yep, that's the path I'm on right now. A little crying myself to sleep last night, a bit of smiling about a cute girl, and you're going to burn those pancakes if you don't flip them."

"She won't burn them," I promised.

Jinxy just glanced over at me. "Bro, you're whipped. You know that, right?"

"I'm spoiled," I corrected. "I'm also going to have to do the dishes now, because that's our deal. I think it's worth it to get her to cook, though."

"I'm kinda good at it now," she bragged. "I mean, I've basically been raising myself since I was fourteen. I started buying the groceries when I could drive."

"And half the time, you only had a permit," I reminded her.

"Worked to get to the store when Mom forgot the year again," she admitted.

"How is Melissa doing anyway?" Jinxy asked.

Which made us both sigh. "Well," I told him, "she's great so long as she's not in the house. That's why we've encouraged her to make fewer visits home. It's really for the best."

"Even after moving?" he asked.

Jeri nodded. "Yeah. Even worse, she thinks Hottie's Drake half the time. It's as if her son actually grew up, so her fantasy came true."

"Which sucks when she's telling Jeri to listen to her brother," Hottie said.

"More when he snuck into my room the night before," Jeri admitted. "It's just cringe all the way around. But so long as she's not here, she's great. I mean, she calls once a week to check in on me, and she remembers Hottie is Hottie then!"

"She calls me too," I told him. "Thanks me for keeping an eye on Jeri and all that. I don't have the heart to tell her we're together."

"No kidding," Jinxy said. "Might make her crack a little more. She just seems like a good lady who was handed too much, you know? Losing her son and her husband like that?"

"It was hard," Jeri agreed.

"But you didn't break," he reminded her.

Which made Jeri roll her eyes. "Didn't I? Didn't we all? I mean, we've lost too many people and it just keeps happening, you know? It's like we barely get over one and the next is around the corner."

"We're stronger together, though," I said.

Jinxy just nodded. "We really are, Jeri. Shit, you definitely are. I mean, the difference in you this year?"

"Me?" she asked.

"You," he agreed. "Before you moved to Texas, you were hardcore into Flawed. You hated the world. Fuck, you were a scary bitch. Now, I think you're scared of nothing, and that's a good thing."

"Not so much," I grumbled.

"Why not?" Jeri asked.

I just gaped at her. "Did you forget Dylan shoving you against your car already?"

"I missed this," Jinxy said.

"The fucker tried to jump her in the parking lot," I explained. "Not alone. No, that limp-dicked fucker had his entire crew with him. Five guys against Jeri? As mean as she is, she couldn't have stood against them."

"Which is why running is a good option," Jinxy said before pointing to himself. "It's my favorite."

"If I could've gotten away from him, I would've," she admitted. "He had me pinned to my car door, but Tiffany and her girls showed up. Damn, those guys are scared of her."

"Of all of them," I guessed. "I mean, when their victims start working together, that can't be good."

"Well, I just want to meet the rest of the crew," Jinxy said. Then he smiled. "Or should I just call them your boyfriends, Jeri?"

"Either way," she said much too easily. "I was thinking we could head over after breakfast. Knock's place is pretty cool. They have all the tech, and I have a feeling there'll be a spare computer you can use."

"Got my laptop with me," he promised. "The one thing I do not leave home without is my tech."

The words were barely out of his mouth before all of our phones began to make sounds. Different sounds, depending on our notification choices, but it turned the kitchen into a cacophony. I managed to grab mine first. Jeri pulled the food off the heat, then reached for hers. Jinxy was fumbling, trying to get to his front pocket, yet we all managed to see the message right around the same time.

> **Unknown Number:**
> The status of the device [Tablet] has been updated to: ACTIVE

I knew all the words. I understood them. It still took a moment for the information to sink in. Jinxy, however, didn't have that problem. The guy sucked in a breath and jumped to his feet.

"The tablet's on!" he gasped.

"Dylan's?" Jeri asked, spinning to turn off the burners.

"Yeah," Jinxy said, pausing to grab one last gulp of coffee. "That's the script I wrote for the alert. If the tablet turns on and connects to Dylan's router, the computer we have watching it will send out texts to all of us."

"Discord!" I snapped.

"Breakfast!" Jeri said, waving me at it. "You handle that, Hottie."

"Let it get cold," I told her as we all raced for the stairs. "Fuck, if he's actually downloading something?"

I ran for my room, because that was where my desktop was. Jinxy followed, grabbing his laptop from where it was charging. Jeri went to her room, but somehow the brat beat me into Discord. I was willing to bet she was also halfway into Dylan's router before my computer booted all the way up too.

Then I connected to Damage Control, our private chat room. "What do we have?" I demanded.

"Nice script," Knock said in greeting. "The text woke me up."

"Everything here is secure," Cade said, clearly answering something that had been asked before I logged in.

"I'm looking for data transfer," Jeri announced.

"Slow your roll," Knock told her.

Then Jinxy joined us. "I've got a strong connection on Dylan's router by the tablet," he said. "We have multiple layers of encryption, and he's trying to ping pong around the world like a jack rabbit."

"It's spoofed," Knock told him. "Hook the data and follow it."

"I'm trying!" Jeri said. "Would be easier with something we'd given him."

"And that's not an option," Ripper said proving he'd also logged in.

Then, of all people, Zoe spoke up. "Guys? Is it just me, or is that a lot of data?"

"Enough," Jinxy decided. "I'm in the process of getting my claws in it, but the more of us who try, the better our chances are of catching a fish."

So we tried. For a long moment, the chat was filled with nothing but the sounds of keys clicking as we worked. Each of us had a slightly different method. Some were probably using scripts from the toybox or that they'd written themselves. It didn't matter. Nothing mattered but seeing if we could actually trace where that tablet's data was going.

Because with that much data, it had to be another video. Maybe one he'd had for a while, but my fear was they'd made new ones. It was Spring Break, after all. And new videos meant new crimes, but this could be our chance.

If they were uploading a video to that elusive storage site, with all of us working on this, someone would have to figure it out. We didn't suck. Maybe the limitations of technology tied our hands at times, but this crew?

Yeah, Jericho had found just the right people. We were hackers, all of us, and this was the most important hack we'd done yet.

CHAPTER 55

JERICHO

"Got it!"

The voice screaming into our ears wasn't the one I expected, but I understood the enthusiasm.

"Are you sure, Zoe?" Jinxy asked.

"Fuck," she breathed. "Yeah, um, hang on..." Then she started calling out numbers separated by periods. "I used that dark web browser," she explained.

"Someone check it!" Knock snapped.

"Already on it," Hottie promised. "I've got Tor on my desktop."

A long lull took over the chat, and I could feel my heart beating with excitement and anticipation while I continued to work. I didn't want to stop in case she'd grabbed the wrong thing, but what if she'd really got it? Could this really be it? After so long waiting, trying, and fucking failing, did we finally know where those assholes were hiding all of their dirty secrets?

Then, "I'm at a login for a server on the dark web," Hottie told us.

"Try his info from KoG," Cade suggested. "Username and password. He's not inventive, guys. Same shit is what he uses for all his games too."

Silence.

Anxiety.

"I'm in," Hottie breathed. "Fuck. I'm looking at his cloud."

"Do not touch anything yet!" Ripper snapped. "If he's uploading still, he might be actively looking."

"I just need someone else to check it," Hottie begged.

"I'm in," Zoe said.

"Same," Cade agreed.

"Don't have Tor," I admitted. "I'm locked out of the dark web."

"As it should be," Jinxy said, "but I'm in on a clean open. I've also saved that address in about a million different places."

"Including the Squirrel?" Zoe asked.

"That was the first, baby," he promised.

"Good," Knock said. "Which means we have two options. First, we can sit here and congratulate ourselves for a job well done without touching a damned thing until we know the tablet is off again..."

"Or?" I asked.

He chuckled. "Come over, Jeri. Bring your other brother - "

"Not her brother," Hottie grumbled.

"Party at our place," Cade said instead. "From the amount of icons I'm seeing on this drive, we're going to need a game plan anyway. The coffee will be brewed, and..." His words trailed off. "Hey, Jinxy? What color coffee cup do you want?"

"Got a teal or turquoise one?" he asked.

"Something close enough," Knock promised. "My big sister has a thing with collecting all the colors so everyone gets their own."

"I claim teal," Jinxy told us. "Now let me try this breakfast Jeri was making while someone else keeps an eye on that tablet?"

"I'm watching the tablet," Knock promised.

"Then you're coming over?" Zoe asked.

"Promise," Jinxy said.

I just laughed. "As if he'd turn down that offer, Zoe. Yeah, let us eat real fast and we'll be there in half an hour?"

"Should be just about right," Knock decided. "Ripper, you coming?"

"I fucking need pants," he grumbled, "but yeah. Is it even noon?"

"Nope," Cade said. "But it will be when you get here. Isn't this when we're supposed to cheer and say break or something?"

"Not jocks," Hottie reminded him. "And how about we hold the cheering until we see if this is really what we think it is?"

"Good plan," Ripper mumbled. "Fuck, this is not how I expected to wake up, but I'll take it."

Then, one by one, we all logged out. It felt surreal. The thing we'd been working towards for so long was done. We'd not only *found* the storage Alpha Team was using, but that Dylan had used the same username and password as all his other accounts?

Well, then again, that kinda made sense. A lot of people did that. It made it easier to remember. Besides, he shouldn't have a clue there was a keylogger on his computer. We wouldn't be able to guess his account credentials without it. Maybe with a script to work out the password, but only if we had the proper username to start with!

But it had happened. This had really, actually happened! We'd managed to *finally* get the information we needed! We were winning, and yet I was a little scared to see what we'd find in that hellhole. Was it nothing but his private porn stash? Knock already knew Dylan was addicted to the hard stuff. The real-life rapes that were snuck onto Pornhub and things like that. Maybe it was just pirated movies, or possibly even cheats for homework or tests at school?

In other words, this could be a really big letdown, but I didn't think so.

Yet after scarfing back the breakfast I'd made earlier, the three of us climbed into Hottie's car and headed across town. Jinxy laughed at that description, making a few jokes about how small Sanger was, but that just helped to pass the time. Then we pulled into Knock's place.

"Holy shit..." Jinxy breathed, looking out the window at the property.

"Welcome to Andrews Shires," Hottie told him. "While this looks like a horse farm, it's really the home of the best gamers in the world."

"This year," I added.

"In a while," Jinxy assured me. "Fuck, I don't know what I expected, but this was not it."

"Just wait until you get inside," Hottie told him as we parked.

We piled out of the car, gesturing to the landmarks around us as we made our way into the back yard. Looking a little confused, Jinxy followed, but we barely had the gate closed behind us before the loud - and vicious sounding - barks made the poor guy freeze in place.

"Quake!" I called, crouching down just as the big grey mongrel came around the corner.

"Fuck," Jinxy hissed, ready to bolt for the gate.

"He's a chicken," Hottie assured him even as he caught Jinxy's arm. "Dude, chill. The poor dog was abused. He's just announcing company."

"C'mere, you big tough guy," I baby-talked to the dog.

Quake's eyes darted between me and Jinxy, clearly aware there was a stranger in his yard, but he came. Once I started petting him, the big baby relaxed, and then Hottie made his way over to do the same.

"Just pet him once?" I asked. "He's a good boy, but he isn't sure if strangers will hurt him or love him."

"Yeah?" Jinxy asked, holding out his hand for Quake to sniff. "So like the rest of Ruin, huh?"

"Pretty much," I agreed.

Then Jinxy rubbed the dog's head. That was all Quake needed. Clearly, anyone who gave him pets was a friend. With that little obstacle handled, he was more than happy to trot beside us as we headed to the house and walked right in.

"We're here!" I called out.

Which made Riley rush out of the kitchen. "I heard we have..." She paused as her eyes went up, and then up a little more. "Damn. You must be Jinxy."

"Riley 'QQ' Andrews," Hottie introduced. "And yes, he is."

"Shawn," Jinxy told her, offering his hand. "You're a badass in the tournaments. I think Void's the only one who can even come close."

"Nope," the man in question replied as he jogged up the stairs. "My only chance is to catch her off-guard. It's why I seduced her, you know. So I could figure out all her womanly ways."

"Asshole," Riley tossed at him. Then, "Coffee? I heard there was a break."

"A break?" came a female voice from the other end of the house.

"Ruin did something this morning!" Riley yelled.

"Jinxy?" And that was a guy's voice. Knock's, I thought.

Within seconds, Knock and Cade tromped up the stairs. Kitty came out of her room, waddling with her hand under her belly like she was holding the weight of the baby up. We'd barely even made it inside the house, but the crew encircled us, all talking at the same time.

"I can't believe we got it."

"This one's Zoe's, right?"

"I need to know how he likes his coffee."

"You play shooters?"

"Enough!" I snapped, waving them all down. "Holy shit, guys. Isn't this fangirling supposed to go the other way?"

"Kinda what I thought," Jinxy mumbled.

Which made Kitty laugh. "Yeah, but we're used to us. You're the shiny new thing we've heard so much about." Then she shooed Riley out of the way. "Go make coffee. If Jericho's here, that means the rest are coming."

"Ripper and Zoe are on their way," Cade agreed.

"I'll help," Logan told Riley before the pair turned for the kitchen.

Jinxy just pushed out a heavy breath. "So, this place is basically chaos?"

"Yes!" Riley yelled back from around the dividing wall.

"It really is," Knock told him, gesturing to the stairs. "The good kind, though. And if you didn't figure it out, the one with a beach ball under her shirt is Kitty. Riley has the neon dreads. Logan's the one without tits."

Then Cade thrust out his hand. "And I'm Cade, he's Knock, and you're real."

"Make yourself at home," Kitty told him. "Like, literally. We're a house of gamers, so the profanity, tech jargon, and feet on tables is all pretty normal."

"Like this place already," Jinxy told her.

"Just wait until you see the basement," I said, heading that way. "And is the tablet still online?"

"It just went off," Knock said. "Maybe three minutes before you walked in? Quake, downstairs!"

The dog rushed again, looking thrilled with the excitement in his house, and the rest of us followed. Jinxy trailed at the back, but when he reached the bottom of the stairs, he couldn't help but chuckle. The setup was completely gamer-chic, functional, and exactly what we needed.

Knock was in the middle of giving him the basic directions - mostly for the bathroom - when Zoe and Ripper slipped down the stairs. It was Zoe's little gasp that gave them away.

"Your tattoos!" she breathed.

Because today, Jinxy was in a t-shirt. His arms were visible, with their full sleeve tattoos that resembled the circuitry on a motherboard. His left was black, with the lines left un-inked. The right was mostly skin with the lines in black. The overall effect was impressive, and from the look on Zoe's face, kinda sexy.

But Ripper just pushed his way forward, holding out his hand. "I'm Ripper, you're Jinxy, and I'm pretty sure I'm supposed to make it clear you need to be cool with my best friend, right?"

Jinxy laughed, accepted his hand, and then pulled Ripper in for a hug. "Bro, it's Jeri I'm scared of, but I'll take it. You can delete my hard drive if I cross a line, deal?"

"Works for me," Ripper said with a laugh.

But I realized Jinxy wasn't that much taller than Ripper. Oh, a few inches, definitely, although I wasn't sure when that had happened. Back when I'd first met him, Ripper had been a pretty average-sized guy. Maybe six foot on a good day. Now he was a bit taller than Hottie.

"Ripper, are you still growing taller?" I asked.

He immediately tugged at the legs of his jeans. "Maybe."

"You *just* realized that?" Zoe asked.

"Well, he's always been taller than me," I admitted, "and I kinda see him every day."

"She also doesn't look at my clothes," Ripper grumbled.

"Yeah, but the whole ankle thing went out in like the forties!" Zoe insisted. "I mean, I was just trying to..." She let her protest trail off. "If she didn't notice, then I helped, right?"

"You did," he assured her, even if it sounded like he didn't mean it. "Definitely helped, Zoe. Kept me from looking like a nerd or something."

"Nerd power," Jinxy said, offering his hand for a fist-bump.

Yet all of us responded. Seven different fists pressed in spontaneously, almost like that jock-like "break" thing Cade had joked about earlier. And, of course, we all laughed when we realized what we'd done.

"And that," Zoe said, "proves it. We're definitely all nerds, now can we see what we found? Because if this is it..."

"What if it's not?" I asked.

Zoe gave me a rather impressive dirty look. "Stop being so negative."

"But what if it's not?" I repeated. "What if this is nothing?"

"Then we ruled something out," Cade said as he claimed his chair in front of his computer. "It's still progress, Jeri."

"The bigger question," Jinxy pointed out, "is what if it is?"

All seven of us, in the same place for the first time, shared a look. Eyes jumped from person to person as the reality of what he was saying began to sink in.

"I think I need to tell my parents I'm spending the night," Zoe breathed.

"Yeah," Ripper agreed. "Same."

Because if this was Alpha Team's depository of evil, we might finally be able to crack this case wide open. We could remove the videos that had been used as blackmail against Tiffany's friends. If we played our cards right, we might even be able to convince the cops that those assholes needed to spend the rest of their lives rotting in jail.

Or, more likely, we were going to need to make this shit go viral. Because if the Kings of Gaming wanted to have a fight online, then I was more than willing to do that. This was *our* internet, after all. I'd be damned before I let their hatred, abuse, and misogyny take it over.

CHAPTER 56

RIPPER

Jinxy wasn't at all what I'd expected, and yet everything. The guy carried this cool vibe about him that made me feel a little jealous, and yet he not only sounded, but also acted, just like the guy we knew online. And from the way Cade and Knock kept glancing at him, I had a feeling he would be described as "hot" by most of my friends.

The best part about him, however, was that he took this shit seriously. With Dylan's tablet turned off, the odds were good that no one was looking at their cloud storage. Still, we took all the necessary precautions to hide our presence even as we began downloading the data en masse.

"There has to be over a hundred videos in here," Jinxy mumbled. "I don't like what that implies."

"On the tablet, a lot were duplicates," I assured him. "Well, the edited and unedited versions. Different cuts, and things like that."

"How many girls?" Jinxy asked, his eyes darting over to Zoe.

"Twelve," she answered for me. "A girl at school, Tiffany,

identified them before Ripper could show me headshots, but yeah."

"And there were around forty videos on the tablet," I told him. "If this drive is the same, that means we don't have hundreds of victims."

"Or it could," Hottie grumbled. "Guys, don't count that out."

"I'd rather go with Ripper's theory," Jinxy said. "Little less horrifying."

"Won't know until we sort it all out," Jeri said. "And how are we on the KoG site? Because this shit isn't going to fall together without the posts there."

And just like that, we were at work. Jinxy had his own laptop, which helped. He parked out on the couch, throwing those stupidly long legs out in front of him, but that worked out. Zoe, wanting to get to know him better, kept taking breaks to sit beside him.

So I did my best to sort the massive amounts of data being dropped onto the Squirrel, promising her it was ok. Bit by bit, we extracted, copied, chased, and recorded every act of evil these fuckers had done for who knew how long.

The light coming through the windows at the top of the wall turned golden. Sometime after that, Kitty, Riley, and Logan came down carrying plates of food that they handed out. We all ate at our computers, shoveling the meal in without really tasting it.

When it got too dark, someone flipped on the lights. After that, Riley rounded up coffee mugs and refilled them. When the Squirrel started to lag, Logan said he'd take care of it, and extra storage space magically appeared. The whole time, the hours slipped away.

No one wanted to stop. Knock's family seemed to accept that and didn't even try to tell us to take a break. There was a moment of Cade saying he had to clean the barn, but Riley just pointed back at his chair and told him he *was working*. She'd handle the rest, and Logan would help.

When Kitty wandered in wearing what was obviously pajamas, I realized it was well past midnight. The pillows and blankets in her arms made it clear why she was here. Without a word, she set the pile in the corner. Ten minutes later, Riley dropped a rolled-up and deflated air mattress beside it.

"Noise!" she warned, before turning on a little air pump and filling the thing.

Once it was full, she sorted the mess of pillows and blankets onto it, then shoved it against what counted as an empty spot on the wall. But just as she finished, Logan appeared carrying even more.

"They're not going to stop, you know," he said softly, his words for Riley.

"I know," she assured him. "I also know that if there's a soft spot, someone might take a little break. Even a ten-minute nap might be what it takes to refresh their minds."

"I hear you!" Knock grumbled.

"And you know as well as I do how hard you can push yourself," she said. "I'm just making sure comfort isn't why you miss something."

But I spun my chair to face her. "Yeah, um..."

"What, Ripper?" she asked gently.

I gestured to the murder board. "I have a feeling we're going to run out of room."

"Use the next wall," Logan replied before Riley could. "I'll take down the pictures."

"Not the horses!" Zoe gasped, because that section of wall had a few dozen little frames of old horse pictures.

"I promise I don't mind having them in my room," Riley assured us. "I also know this case isn't going away until it's done.

The day we get to repaint all of this will be a celebration, right? Then all of you can help me hang the pictures back up."

"Promise," Cade said.

"We'll make a day of it," Hottie assured her. "Maybe even cookout and go riding?"

"Any time," she agreed, heading for one picture and gently lifting it down. "Logan?"

"On it," he said.

While we worked, they changed the room around us and kept us going. It was two a.m. when Jinxy announced he'd reached the end of the KoG posts. Knock immediately started sorting through those. Cade made notes on the murder board.

By three-thirty, we had all the data. I was running on a little too much caffeine, feeling like I was vibrating, so I opened the folder on the Squirrel that had the videos. Without a word, Cade passed me a set of headphones, jerking his chin to make it clear I should use them. Then he gestured back to the couch.

Zoe had melted against Jinxy's side. The guy had shifted his laptop to the arm of the couch so she could use his lap, but was still going. He also kept smiling down at the redheaded mess curled up against him.

"Don't wake her," Cade told me.

I nodded to show I understood. "No, not with this."

An hour later, Jeri tapped out, claiming she was going to check on that air mattress. I leaned far enough to tap Hot, then tilted my head that way. He looked confused for a second, then just chuckled.

"Fine," he said. "Unless you need a break?"

"Not gonna sleep with this much caffeine," I explained. "Take a break. I'll wake you in an hour?"

"You'd better," he said, clasping my shoulder as he headed towards the air mattress Jeri had claimed.

But I didn't. I just clicked on the next video, changing the file name to reflect the girl who was victimized in it. Most of these, I'd seen before. That made it easier, even if I wasn't sure I liked it. Nothing about this should be easy. Seeing this should be horrifying, and yet someone had to watch. Someone had to sort this out, make it useful, and then use it as a weapon to destroy these fuckers once and for all.

Eventually, I came across girls we didn't know about. With each of those videos, I found a safe place to grab a screenshot, then carefully cropped it down to just the girl's head. That image got saved in a new folder that I titled "For Zoe to ID." Thankfully, there weren't too many of those.

Bit by bit, I was making progress. Cade printed out the new girls, got the dates of their videos, and added them to the murder wall. Every so often, Jinxy would speak up, reading from a post that had information for Cade to copy down.

I didn't even notice when Knock vanished. The open door to his bedroom explained where he'd gone, though. So did the bare feet hanging off the end of his bed. It seemed he hadn't even made it under the covers.

I didn't know when Riley passed out, but eventually I reached the bottom of my coffee cup. I thought about going to make myself another, but a glance over my shoulder showed that Cade had joined Jeri and Hot on that little air mattress. Jeri was in the middle, but that didn't mean it was any less cute.

"Just you and me," Jinxy said. "Or we can wake them up and let you tap out?"

"Let 'em sleep," I mumbled. "If I try, this crap will give me nightmares."

"Same," he said. "No idea how anyone can be this sick. I'm just trying to note the stuff that needs to be added to the board."

"Make a new folder," I suggested. "We've got room."

"Nice," he breathed.

Then we were back at it. I stumbled across another new face.

This time, the video wasn't taken in John's room like the rest, so it might be older. I was too tired to check, so just got the headshot and kept going. It was the video after that when everything changed.

Outside. That was the first thing that struck me as odd. With nothing but darkness behind them, I couldn't tell where the guys were, but it was clearly outside. The girl, however, was drugged. Ok, so probably not an old video, but this added a whole new layer to our theory!

Horrified, I kept watching as she tried to fight back even as her body was giving out. I'd seen Jericho and Tiffany in the same state, and it made my stomach turn. The guys didn't care, though. They just kept shoving at her, ripping at her clothes, and laughing. Always fucking *laughing*.

Then Wade's voice spoke up. "She doesn't have enough!"

"Give her more," Landon cackled.

"Shoulda just played nice," John taunted the terrified woman.

And from behind the camera, Dylan said, "No, not with a needle."

"Fuck off," Wade said as he entered the screen, burying a shot into the girl's arm.

I watched as he pushed the plunger, manhandling this poor girl so she couldn't pull her arm away. The look of fear on her face was more than I could take. I couldn't make my eyes watch that. Instead, I scanned the periphery, looking for clues, evidence, and all that shit.

The truck they had her pressed up against was Dylan's. As the woman struggled to push the guys off her, I caught clear shots of their faces. Landon, Parker, Wade, and John were all surrounding her. Then, as the injection began to take effect and the girl went limp, I saw a reflection in the truck's window. It clearly showed Dylan recording this mess on his tablet.

I was pretty sure this was the raw copy. If they kept to their typical habits, there would be at least three - if not more - versions of this cropped in different ways. Probably for these sick fucks to jack off to. Damn, I hated them, but I needed to know this girl's face. If we came across more people we didn't have names for, I had to be sure which ones we'd already discovered and which we hadn't.

My eyes hesitated, preferring to look at the details in the shot instead of the "action" that was so horrific. But when I finally forced them to her face, I realized it was slack. Not lax the way so many others had been. There was something wrong about this.

Had they knocked her out cold? Fuck, how much ketamine had they given her?

Then Dylan started laughing. "Dude, Wade. Check on her?"

"Busy!" Wade laughed.

"Fuck," Parker hissed as he pawed at her neck.

"Slap her a bit," Landon suggested, putting his words into action.

The girl's head just flopped.

Which made John and Wade both chuckle, but they didn't stop. It was like watching wolves trying to get their share of a kill. The group was clustered around this poor girl, doing unspeakable things, but thrilled with themselves for it. Fuckers, all of them.

And then Wade let her go. "Yeah, that's how it's done."

"Guys," Parker said.

"Your turn," Wade told him.

"She's fucking dead!" Parker snapped.

And I hit pause. My finger just twitched, clicking the mouse button like a flinch, but I'd heard that. I felt like my lungs couldn't get any air in them. Dead? No. We would've heard about that, wouldn't we?

Scrambling, I opened up the folder where the file was located and scrolled until I found the one I'd highlighted. There, I read the name, trying to make my brain decode the numbers into a date and time. It didn't want to. I felt like there was a short-circuit or something, because I'd heard them, but this video was new. Too new.

"Jinxy?" I breathed, daring to look back.

He lifted his head and clearly saw something wrong on my face. "Fuck, what happened?" he asked.

"I think I found the file they just uploaded," I breathed. "It's from Saturday night."

"Another victim?"

I nodded slowly. "Yeah, but I think she's dead."

"Dead?"

"Dead," I said again.

Which made him jump up, all but evicting Zoe from his lap. She made a little noise before rubbing at her eyes, yet Jinxy was rushing across the room to look over my shoulder.

"Show me," he demanded.

So I backed up the video a bit and pressed play, pulling off the headset so he could hear. He didn't bother putting on the headphones though, just held them up beside his head. But I'd forgotten all about Zoe.

"Oh shit," she breathed, scrambling off the couch to join us - completely ignoring the triggering shit on my screen. "That's her! Y'all, that's the girl from Denton!"

"Which girl from Denton?" I asked.

But Zoe was just pointing at her face. "Oh shit. Is she dead? She looks dead."

And that was when I closed the screen, refusing to traumatize her anymore. "What girl from Denton?" I asked again.

"The one on the news," she said. "Dad watches it when he gets home from work, and all week long, they've been putting her face up, asking for anyone with information to contact the cops. I guess she was killed at a campsite or something."

The pieces fell into place with a crash hard enough to stop my heart. "Fuck," I said.

"Wake up!" Jinxy bellowed. "All hands on deck. People, we got something, and this shit is bad. I don't care how good your dreams are. Up!"

Yet I couldn't tear my eyes away from my computer screen. There might be nothing on it right now, but that didn't matter. I could still see her face. I could still remember her expression. Most likely, I would never forget it, because I'd never seen a dead person before.

CHAPTER 57

KNOCK

Jinxy's voice jerked me out of sleep, but from the sounds of it, I wasn't the only one. Staggering back into the computer room, I found him, Ripper, and Zoe all clustered around the computer Ripper was using. Cade, Jeri, and Hottie looked lost. Then again, that was how I felt.

"What's going on?" I asked.

"They made a video last weekend," Zoe said.

"You," Hottie said, "need to go away so we can see what's going on."

Zoe huffed but actually obeyed, which made Jinxy glance after her with confusion on his face. Hottie just clasped the man's shoulder as he took Zoe's place behind Ripper's chair. I moved to his side. Cade pressed in behind me. Jeri squirmed her way in front of Jinxy.

Then Ripper pressed play.

We all stared in horror as the scene played out before us. There was no audible sound, yet I could hear something mumbling in the headphones Ripper had left on the desk. Yeah, that was probably for the best. Then Jinxy pointed.

"Is that the drug?"

"Ketamine," I clarified, "and probably. It works via injection in horses."

"They use it for ambulance stuff too," Cade added. "Some EMT overdosed a black guy a while back. You can Google it."

"Don't want to," Jinxy said. "But that's what did it."

"They killed her," Jeri breathed.

"Pretty sure it was an accident," I assured her. "Not that it makes anything better, but I don't think they were trying to."

"They were just trying to get her to stop," she snapped. "And that's how it goes. If a woman dares to fight back, she gets hurt worse. This! Don't you guys see? This is what fucking happens to us!"

"Which is why we're trying to bust them," Hottie reminded her.

"And they still killed someone!" she barked back, her voice much too loud.

Yet the sound of Riley's door opening still made all of us jump and spin. "What the fuck?" Logan asked. "At each other's throats already?"

"They killed someone," Jeri explained.

Jinxy just dropped his head. "Jeri, don't drag him - "

"I'm the attorney, Shawn," Logan said, cutting him off. "You're all my clients, so I need to know what I'm really working with here."

Which made Jeri gesture wildly at Ripper's screen with both arms. "Look!"

"Riley!" Logan snapped, leaning back through his door as he did so. Then, "Ripper, move. You need to sit somewhere else for a minute. Zoe, coffee all around? Cade?" He paused to look at the clock on the wall. "I think the donut shop is open by now."

My eyes dropped to the bottom of the screen, to that spot

where Windows showed the date and time. It was now Thursday morning, just after six a.m. Yeah, the donut shop should be open. It also meant Ripper was about to drop.

"Sleep," I told Ripper. "Use my bed?"

"No, I'm good," he said.

I tugged at his arm, all but evicting him from the seat. "You need to get some fucking sleep."

He let me guide him up, but when we were chest to chest, he shook his head. "I won't. Don't you get that? I've been looking at that all night. I won't fucking sleep."

"Riley!" Logan snapped again. "Tequila!"

"It's barely fucking dawn, who the fuck thinks this is the right time for..." She stumbled out of her bedroom with her dreads in wild disarray. "...drinking." Then she stopped hard. "Oh." Ducking back a bit, she returned with a half-full bottle in her hand. "Who's this for?"

Everyone pointed at Ripper.

"Big gulp," she told him, unscrewing the top. "Don't taste it, just suck it back and then breathe for the count of five hundred. If you're still awake, I'll make you take another."

"Fingers crossed," he muttered before sucking a long, deep gulp of the stuff. After making a face, swallowing, and gasping loudly, he gave her the bottle back. "Just let me know what happens?"

"Promise," I told him.

And then Logan took his place, adjusted the sound to come out of the speakers, and we all watched it again. Then one more time. Things were pointed at. My friends flinched, grunted in disgust, and looked away when they had to. But when Riley lifted the bottle and took a drink herself, I realized how bad this really was.

"Zoe said that's the girl from the news," Jinxy told us. "I don't know what she's talking about, but maybe one of you does?"

"Oh, fuck..." Jeri breathed before heading to another computer. Waking it up, she quickly opened a browser and pulled up a search. A few more clicks had a young girl's face on her screen with a banner below it for the Denton Combined Task Force tip line. "Is it her?"

"Looks like," Hottie said.

"And they were going camping," Cade grumbled. "Fuck! We should've seen this coming!"

"Not how it works," Riley assured him. "Before you start blaming yourself, go grab breakfast for all of us, ok? My credit card is - "

"Kitchen drawer," he finished for her. "I know. Kitty too?"

"Yep, because I have a feeling she'll hear us and want to see what's going on. Enough for everyone, Cade. We need brain food. Sugar and carbs count right now."

"Check on Zoe before you leave," I reminded him. "Make sure she's really ok?"

"On it," he said before leaving.

But none of this changed anything. The video was still right here, still in front of us. It wasn't going away, and the number of victims wasn't going down.

"Is that enough yet?" Jeri asked. "I mean, should we call this tip line?"

"No," Logan told her. "You most certainly should not call law enforcement like that."

"We have to tell someone," I reminded him.

"And we will, Knock," he promised, shoving a hand through his hair. "I'm just thinking. We have to do this right, and a few minutes isn't going to change anything. I'd much rather have the lot of you covered than considered suspects."

"But we have a video," Jeri reminded him.

"It has their faces," Jinxy added.

"And this is a fucking mess!" Logan snapped. "Just..."

"He needs a minute," I told the rest, waving them back. "It's been a while since he studied things outside of virtual law, ok? If Cyn was here, this would be so much - "

"That's it!" Logan said as he shoved to his feet.

"What is?" I asked, yet he didn't bother responding. He just jogged up the stairs like a man on a mission.

"Ok," Hottie said, claiming a chair just to lean over his knees. "We have most of a timeline. We have a video of a rape that ends in murder. Guys, we can't sit on this shit anymore. I mean, there's a pretty big difference between the cops saying she consented and the girl fucking dying, right? I'm not crazy here?"

"Nope," Jinxy said. "The problem is how we got it. I mean, this is how I got busted the first time. Tried to do the right fucking thing and it bit me in the ass."

"Ok," I said, thinking hard. "So I'll say I was pranking Dylan? I mean, he's a gamer. I'm a gamer. A little harmless fun online over Spring Break. It should track, right?"

"You sure about that, Knock?" Jinxy asked.

"What about the rest of us?" Jeri wanted to know.

"No rest of us," I said. "Logan can represent me. I'll say I did this on my own because I was pissed about him calling me queer or something. I just didn't expect to find this. I mean, I should get a slap on the wrist. Probably a fine, and I should be able to afford that."

"Don't like it," Jinxy grumbled. "What if they - "

"Got it!" Logan interrupted as he hurried back down the stairs holding a business card in his hand.

"Got what?" I asked.

He just flashed the card at me. I barely had the chance to see the familiar logo of the FBI on it before he answered. "Agent Bradley Matthews left this with me after the shooting. I think it's time for him to deal with Cyn's disappearance."

Immediately, I was on my feet. Before my half-awake big

brother could react, I'd snatched the card out of his hand and was headed to my desk for my phone. I'd left the thing charging there before passing out for my short little nap.

"This time," I told him, "I get to be the asshole." And I dialed.

It rang, then rang some more. Listening to my phone, I ducked my head and paced towards the murder board, trying to think of how I'd explain this. Unfortunately, after the fourth ring, it went to voicemail. Yeah, well, too bad for him.

I quickly disconnected and called again. I would stay at this for the next hour, if I had to. I didn't care what time zone this guy was in. Cynister was gone, no one was going to help us, and he was the only contact we had. He also knew enough about our house to back me up in this. He had to!

Of course, it went to voicemail again, so I called one more time. This time, after the first ring, a pissed-off man answered, "What?!"

"Agent Matthews?" I asked.

He grunted, clearly having been woken up. "Yeah, this is Agent Matthews. Who's this?"

"My name is Jeff Andrews," I told him. "You might know me as Knock from a shooting at our place last fall."

"Knock?" he repeated, sounding more confused about why I was calling than who I was.

"Yes, sir," I said. "Look, I have a problem and I think the FBI needs to know about it."

"What kind of problem?"

"Well, you remember the group who attacked us? The Kings of Gaming? Yeah, one of the members goes to school with me, and while I was fucking around with him online - you know, kinda hacking him - I stumbled across something."

"What kind of something?"

"About fifteen rape videos and one where a girl dies."

There was silence on the line for much too long. Finally, he asked, "What?"

"You heard me," I told him. "This asshole has been recording videos of him and his friends raping girls. Man, there's a lot of them too. And when I was trying to figure out what they were, since I thought it was just porn, um, I kinda watched one, and it's not ok. The girl is on the news. I guess she was killed last weekend or something, and there's a video of them raping her where she *dies* in it."

"Rape."

"Yes, sir," I said. "It's definitely rape, and since you helped us before, well, I was hoping you'd help with this."

"It is six-thirty in the morning," he shot back.

"And I just found it, so I thought I should say something," I countered. "Isn't that what the rule is? See something, say something?"

"No clue," he grumbled. "But I can't help you. Mr. Andrews, I work for the Federal Bureau of Investigation. What you need to do is turn this over to the police. Rape is not something I investigate. Nor is murder. Those fall under your local jurisdiction."

"There are something like fifteen victims here!" I snapped.

"So do your tech thing, put it on one of those little animal-looking drives all you gamers keep, and take it up to the Sanger Police Department."

"When?" I asked.

"Now sounds good," he told me. "Or in about two hours when most of the world is awake. Your call on that. But this is a state crime, not a federal one. I can't do anything."

"But they're in the Kings of Gaming!" I spat. "They're with the same fuckers who tried to shoot up our damned house!"

"And it's a completely different crime," he told me. "I'm not arguing with you. Go to the local cops. Drive your behind up there and make a report - and do not call me again!"

The line went dead.

I had to pull the phone away from my ear to look at it, but he'd hung up on me. That fucking asshole was supposed to help us. Cyn worked with him, so he should have enough background on these assholes to know just how bad they were!

For a little too long, I sat there staring at my blank phone screen. This wasn't how it was supposed to go. This was supposed to work out! Fuck. When I'd seen that card, I'd dared to hope that maybe, just *maybe*, we'd fix this without the worst happening.

And now I was going to go to jail.

"Knock?" Jeri asked, snapping me out of it.

I turned back to her, shoving my phone into my pocket. "Yeah, um... Seems the FBI can't help."

"Was that Cyn?" Hottie asked.

I shook my head. "No, it's the prick he works with. Cyn's cool. This guy?"

"Total fed," Logan grumbled. "So what did he say?"

"To take it to the cops."

Logan just nodded slowly. "Ok. Then let's put this together as well as we can. Coffee and donuts while we work." As he spoke, he was pulling out his phone. "And I'm going to call my dad."

"Your dad?" Cade asked.

Logan gave him a weary smile. "He's been an attorney a lot longer than I have. Yeah, I take advice from my dad."

"So," I said, speaking to everyone in the room. "Let's make this case into something presentable in the next hour. Logan can come up with a decent defense for me. And once we have that, I'm taking this shit to the cops."

"We are," Jeri said.

"No, baby girl," Hottie told her. "I think Knock's right."

"I am," I promised. "It's easier for me to explain this away than to explain, well, *all* of this."

"But no one sacrifices themselves for Ruin," she snapped.

God, I loved her for that. I loved how she was willing to walk at my side even into hell - or jail, in this case. I fucking loved that this woman simply would not quit, even when everyone else was trying to convince her to take the easy way out.

"I'm not sacrificing," I lied. "This is a tactical decision, Jeri. I'm the one with the best chance here."

"He's telling the truth," Logan said.

"For once," Jinxy told her, "you don't get to rush in first, Jericho. Suck it up."

She didn't look happy about it, but she nodded. "Fine."

Yeah, but I knew that word was not the good kind. Nope, when a woman said fine like that, it meant shit was about to hit the fan. I just hoped she'd forgive me when all this was said and done.

CHAPTER 58

JERICHO

Once Zoe and Riley finished the coffee and Cade was back with those donuts, it was all hands on deck. Our time had just run out. We already knew the cops wouldn't take this seriously, so if we wanted a chance, we needed to make it clear this wasn't a "little" crime.

No, this was a big fucking catastrophe!

So we worked. Cade continued to make notes on the murder wall. Hottie did his best to convert all of that to a spreadsheet the cops could follow. Zoe copied and renamed the necessary files and organized them in yet another folder. One she intended to copy to a USB drive for Knock to take with him.

The rest of us waded through the rest of the videos. In consideration of Zoe, we pulled on headphones. Then, Riley and Kitty came down to help. Logan, however, was upstairs, pacing loudly enough that we all heard his footsteps as he talked to his father.

By nine in the morning, we had it. No, it wasn't the best case we could make, but it was good enough. We had videos, the posted comments proving intent, and others showing how to make it look as if the girls had consented. We showed the escalation of abuse, the bragging on the KoG forums, and more.

There was just one problem with all of this. I had no clue how Knock would convince the police this was all just a joke gone wrong. There was too much here. Clearly, he'd been in places he had no business in. He'd broken the law. From what I'd seen of the cops in this town, they wouldn't let that go.

And still, he and Logan claimed the USB drive we'd made and left. All of us - including Riley and Kitty - watched them go. Silence hung in the room while we listened to a car start outside and the sound of gravel under its tires as it left.

Then I turned back to my computer. If Knock was going to go down, then I'd be damned if I let him do it alone. *That* was the rule with Ruin, after all. Hottie had demanded a few simple things. Somewhere along the way, we'd veered away from that, but not sacrificing one for the greater good was the thing that stuck in my mind. It didn't matter if it was ourselves or someone else. If we were doing this, then we were doing it together.

And I was going to make damned sure this shit stuck.

If I'd learned anything in the time I'd been in Texas, it was that law enforcement liked plain, simple evidence. If it wasn't biting them in the face, then they could overlook it, right? So what would make this work? Well, making sure these assholes all had the evidence of their crimes in a place that was *theirs*.

"Jeri?" Hottie asked as my fingers flew across the keys.

"Busy," I told him.

"With?" Jinxy asked.

"Can I help?" Cade wanted to know.

I turned to see as much worry on his face as I was feeling. For a split second, I almost told him no, but that was breaking my own rule, wasn't it? No, if we were doing this, then we needed to do it *together*.

"I want to make sure there's a copy of this shit on all of their hard drives," I explained. "None of those pricks will be awake at this time of morning on Spring Break. There's no reason we can't get in, dump the evidence in the back of their systems, and leave it for the cops to find."

"Do cops even look at that shit?" Zoe asked as she claimed her own chair.

"No idea," I admitted, "but they always do forensic somethings on television shows. I just don't want this to be for nothing."

"I got John," Jinxy said.

"Parker," Zoe announced.

"Landon," Ripper decided, sounding still groggy after his much too-short nap.

"I'll take Wade," Cade told me, "so you can hit Dylan."

"Orders, green leader?" Jinxy asked.

Which made me smile. "Nah, I'm pink leader now, Jinxy. And I want every single one of those videos - including all the edits - on every machine."

"Too much," he countered. "That's a massive amount of data."

"So what's option two?" I asked. "How do we make sure they all get blamed for these crimes?" And I turned to gesture at the murder wall.

Twenty-three women. That was how many it ended up being. In less than a year, those six assholes - because I was counting Evan among them - had derailed the lives of twenty-three different women. And fucking killed two of them - Amber and this new girl! It didn't matter if that had been through manipulation or force. They'd done it, they'd been proud of it, and I wanted to make sure they fucking *paid* for it.

"Making a new folder," Zoe announced. "I'm grabbing the raw

for every girl. That's still a lot of data, but I bet their hard drives are big enough to handle it."

"Check for secondary drives," Jinxy said. "Maybe not the C designation. Often D."

"Which would be storage for most people," I said. "Good plan. Even if we have to break it all up, I want it on there. I want the cops to find this shit."

"What about the save date?" Ripper asked. "Won't that give us away?"

"Fuck!" I snapped.

"We can spoof that," Jinxy promised. "The easiest way is to turn it all back to Monday. That way it'll look like they pulled it from the damned storage before we ever got involved."

"How?" Cade asked.

So Zoe leaned over and started talking him through it. Around the room, keys were clicking and drives were whirling. It was the sound of work being done, but it didn't kill the anxiety inside me. I kept waiting for the bad news to hit. I knew it would take a while, but what would we do when Logan came home without Knock at his side?

And did my friends realize that was what would likely happen?

Of course not. We were the "good guys." We were supposed to win, right? Sadly, we were just as much criminals as the Alpha Team, at least in the eyes of the police. That didn't mean we were as evil, but sometimes a little civil disobedience was a good thing. Vigilantism might be a better word.

I preferred to call it vicious.

Because if Knock was going down, I was going to burn these motherfuckers' world to make up for it. I was going to destroy them. If I had my way, neither Dylan nor his friends would ever see the light of day again. I wanted them to worry about bending over in showers. I wanted them to feel that fear in the darkness, not knowing if someone bigger, meaner, and more selfish was going to do whatever they wanted - at their expense.

I just wanted to make these rapists understand what it felt like for once. Men didn't get it. There was nothing in their world that could compare except to become a victim themselves. Normally, I wouldn't wish that on someone, but these guys had fucking asked for it. They'd all but brought it on themselves.

And I seriously hoped it hurt.

Mentally, emotionally, physically, and every other way they could feel pain, I wanted them to. I was just so fucking *done* with all of this. And to think, when I'd heard about that girl's death on the news, I'd assumed it was just some random crime. I'd become so used to the idea that we women would be made into victims that it had never occurred to me it could be related. Well, fuck them.

Fuck all of them! Fuck men who thought women were here for their taking. Fuck women who made excuses for them. Fuck the fear society drilled into us that made it impossible to speak up without ruining our own lives. Most of all, fuck the justice system that all but made excuses for them.

I was done with "boys will be boys." I was sick and tired of hearing about how there was yet another goddamned video out there! Most of all, I was pissed, and this rage needed to be put somewhere, so I used it to dive deep into Dylan's computer and bury proof of his crimes somewhere he wouldn't think to look for days.

Hopefully, it would be enough.

"Done," I said, closing the windows and leaning back.

"Almost," Jinxy assured me.

But Zoe slammed her finger down on the mouse. "And I'm out, so done too."

"Double-check me?" Cade begged.

"You're downloading," she assured him. "Just let that work through, and you should be fine."

"And the file placement?" he asked.

The pair leaned closer as she helped him. Beside me, Hottie closed his windows and reached over to rub my shoulder. Pushing my chair a bit, I scooted close enough to rest my head on his shoulder.

"This is going to work," he promised. "It has to."

"Yeah, but - "

Ripper hissed, the sound cutting me off. "Jeri." He looked over at Cade pointedly. "How about we keep a positive outlook for a few more hours, hm?"

"Positive?" I asked. "Ripper, you weren't there when that asshole told Zoe this would be too much work for him."

"That's not what he said," Zoe replied, proving she could hear us. "He simply told me the truth. No, it wasn't a pretty truth, but it was what I needed to hear, ok?"

"And it made you not report it," I reminded her.

"She's got a point," Ripper said. "Zoe, if he just wanted to tell you the truth, he would've promised to help. He would've said it'd be hard, might get ugly, but that he was on your side or such. He would've encouraged you to get justice. Instead, he shut you down."

"Yeah, but look at the number of women who recant," Jinxy pointed out. "Now, I'm *not* taking that cop's side, but I'm playing the devil's advocate here. Accusing someone of rape *is* hard. A lot of women change their minds and drop the charges. The cops bust their asses for days, or maybe weeks, and then nothing? It has to be demoralizing to them too."

"And rapists always get away with it," Cade said. "Fuck, even when they get busted, it's still worse for the women. I mean, look at the celebrities. A dozen women can speak up, they'll all get death threats, doxxed, or worse, and the guy gets a fine?

Probation? Maybe a tiny little slap on the wrist? It's not fucking fair."

"Which is why we're doing this," Jinxy said.

"Which part of this?" I asked, since that was a little vague.

Shifting his glasses higher up his nose, he smiled. "Planting evidence. Making sure there's no way for them to get away with it. Fucking them over, Jeri."

"Yeah, that part of this," I said, nodding. "It seems to be what Ruin's good at, right?"

"So let's not give up hope yet," Hottie told me. "I've heard rumors that Logan is one hell of an attorney. I mean, he got you out of fighting at school, didn't he?"

"Not even in the same category," I countered.

"Was to me," he promised.

"Knock will be fine," Ripper promised. "He has to be."

"He will be," Cade said, even though it sounded a little forced. "He'll make this stick. That fucker's smart. It's why he's a sponsored gamer. He's keeping up with the big names who have a decade more experience. He'll make this work."

So why was I so nervous? Why was I feeling guilty?

It took far too long for me to figure out the answer. I hadn't thanked him. I hadn't told him how much he meant to me. I hadn't taken the chance to whisper those words that might be the last I ever said to him. Jinxy had said it himself. It was easier if we knew the end was coming.

I'd never had that luxury before, and what if I'd just let it slip between my fingers? What if Knock went to jail for *years*? What if I'd been so worried about which words I used, closing this case, and everything else that I forgot to make it clear I did have feelings? That I didn't want to lose him - or any of them?

What if I'd fucked it up bad this time?

CHAPTER 59

KNOCK

On the drive to the police station, Logan gave me the rundown of what I needed to say, not say, and his plan for how to keep me out of jail. I nodded, doing my best to memorize all of it, but I was nervous. What if Jeri was right and they did limit me from using the internet? I'd heard of that punishment before. Shit, Jinxy said he'd had to deal with it as a kid.

I could handle almost anything else. Community service, sure. I could think of a million ways to work that off. Fines? Easy. Probation? Well, it would suck, but I'd figure it out. Jail? Yeah, that was the part that made my leg bounce in the passenger seat.

"Knock?" Logan asked.

Pulling in a little breath, I jerked my head over to him, realizing we were here. "Yeah?"

"Confident," he reminded me. "I need Jeff *Andrews* right now, not Beasley. I need every bit of the smartass you inherited from your sister, ok? Put on your game face, and let's win this shit."

It was a pretty shitty pre-game pep talk, but it still worked. Tossing him a smile, I opened the car door and climbed out. The police station in our little town was just a boring brick building a few blocks off the square. Once, it had probably been some small store or something. The only door had to be the entrance we were supposed to use.

Side by side, we headed that way. Logan was wearing a suit. It was his power move to make people take him seriously. Considering his suits were not the type that came off the rack, it usually worked.

I was in my normal gamer gear. My shirt was black today, with a blue logo for my Eternal Combat outfit. My jeans were old and faded. There was a rip over my left knee. And as we walked, I reached up, pulling my nearly shoulder-length blue hair back into a ponytail. That would make it easier to see the ring on my lip. Punk. My goal was to be a cyber deviant, and I was pretty sure I had that down pat.

Inside the police station, the waiting area was small. The walls were cream, too dark to even be off-white. The floor was some ugly brown and orange pattern that wanted to be cool and retro but missed the cool part. And there, at the far end of the narrow space, was a sliding window like at most doctor's offices. We headed straight for it.

Then we waited. There was no bell, no buzzer, or any other way to let them know someone had arrived. The front door didn't even have a set of bells on it. Yeah, I turned back to check. It was as if this little space was some kind of dead zone no one seemed to care about.

Letting out a sigh, Logan reached up to rub at the bridge of his nose. "You've got to be kidding me," he grumbled.

But his words caught someone's attention. "One second!" a man called from whatever was on the other side.

"We like small towns," I joked. "Calm, quiet places, right?"

"Perfect to raise a family," Logan replied, tossing me a devious look. "And I mean Kitty's, so don't even start worrying."

I chuckled just as the glass slid open. "Sorry about that," the officer said, and then he paused. "Logan Weiss?"

"Officer Sanders," Logan greeted the man. "Yeah, you helped with Riley's horses, and I think you were at our place when the shooting happened?"

"*Everyone* was at your place that night," Officer Sanders assured him. "What can we help you with today?"

"Well, my client has evidence of a crime that he wants to report."

The cop nodded slowly. "Client. That means you're working." Then he looked at me. "Jeff, right? Riley's adopted brother?"

"Yes, sir," I agreed, being polite and proper like Logan had told me.

Officer Sanders smiled. "Ok. So what's going on?"

"Murder," Logan said. "Serial rape to go along with it."

The cop's eyes jumped over to me for a second before returning to Logan. "Ok? And, um, you know this because..."

"My client stumbled upon proof of it."

Which was my cue to hold up the thumb drive. Officer Sanders nodded, held up a finger, and leaned back. His head was turned as if he was checking on something, and then he was back.

"Let me get the detective. It'll be a moment."

"Always is," Logan said, gesturing for me to find a chair.

Ok, so our little town didn't exactly have the biggest police force, but I would've expected a little more excitement over this. It almost made me feel like all of my own anxiety had been for nothing. Still, we waited in silence, glancing at each other occasionally, but not daring to say a thing. Never knew who might be listening, after all, and overheard information could still be used against me.

Finally, the door at the side opened and a middle-aged man in a polo shirt stepped through. "Would you two like to come to my office to talk about this?" he asked.

"Certainly," Logan said, gesturing for me to go first.

I wanted to smart off, but I was supposed to let Logan do all the talking. I was supposed to be pulling the tough gamer guy persona, but that was hard when I couldn't say shit. In truth, I almost felt like I didn't need to be here at all, but I knew that wasn't how this worked. If I wanted to keep Jeri, Cade, and my friends safe, then I had to be the one to do this. It *had* to be me.

The detective led us to one of two wooden doors, then opened it to reveal an office on the other side. Letting us enter first, he waved us to the pair of chairs before the desk, then moved around to claim the fancy leather chair behind it.

This place was the stereotypical "man's" office, though. Behind the guy was a shelf filled with leather-bound books. There were framed pictures on the desk - facing him, of course. On the side wall was a photo of this man with someone who was clearly supposed to be important. They were shaking hands, so maybe proof of an award?

Then the detective leaned forward and offered his hand. Naturally, it was to Logan first. "I'm Detective Durham," he said. "Can I get your names?"

"Logan Weiss, attorney at law," Logan said as he accepted the man's grip. "And this is my client, Jeff Andrews."

"Mr. Andrews." Detective Durham offered me his hand next.

"Detective," I replied as I took it.

"Brian Sanders said you have proof of a crime?"

Once again, I held up the drive, but it was Logan who spoke. "My client came across evidence of a murder. A video, to be exact. He feels confident that both the victim and perpetrators can be identified from it." Then Logan smiled. "However, before he'll turn over this evidence, I'll need a waiver for any potential criminal cyber trespassing that may or may not have occurred."

"Hacking," the detective said, rephrasing that.

Logan merely leaned back in his chair. "Such a vulgar - and not very legal - term. Now, regardless of what you decide, I will need a record of our attempt to discuss this with you, to make it clear my client has done everything expected of someone who comes across evidence such as this."

"Uh-huh," Detective Durham murmured. "And why do you think I'd be interested in this?"

"You mean besides the fact that my client has evidence of a murder?" he asked before turning to me. "Tell him who you think the victim is, Jeff."

"That girl on the news," I said, refusing to look away from the cop's eyes.

"And where did you get this supposed evidence?" he asked.

Logan lifted a hand. "We will need immunity from any potential legal recourse before answering that."

"And I can't offer you that without knowing what I'm buying with that immunity," Detective Durham countered. "Mr. Weiss, give me something here?"

"I already did," Logan said. "My client is offering definitive proof of the murder of that girl on the news."

"And why should I trust that his so-called evidence is worth anything?"

Logan chuckled in the smuggest way I'd ever heard. "Well, I can say that my client is one of the top gamers in the Professional League of Gamers. His technical skills are well known across the country."

"And we're right back to hacking," the man grumbled. "Illegally gained material does me no good in a criminal trial, so why would I ignore Mr. Andrews' hacking?"

"But that's not true, is it?" Logan asked instead. "Evidence gained unexpectedly in the course of any other activity, when turned over voluntarily, can be used in the prosecution of said crime. It's law enforcement who can't illegally obtain such things. That's a violation of the search and seizure clause."

The detective closed his eyes in a long - and very frustrated looking - blink. "Mr. Weiss..."

"You can try to talk your way around me," Logan told him. "We'll sit here and listen - if for no other reason than because it makes my client look even better when it comes right down to it. You can do your best to manipulate us into taking a bad deal. I promise that won't work, though. You see, I'm the top attorney in the nation for virtual law. I'm not bad with a few other things." Then he leaned forward. "Detective Durham, we both know that you - and the State of Texas - wants what this young man found. He wants to give it to you. All I'm asking is that you agree to ignore any civil disobedience that may have occurred in the process."

"And potentially grant immunity for identity theft?" Detective Durham asked. "Or maybe those scams we hear about?"

"Not how that works," I grumbled.

Logan shot me a warning look, reminding me he was supposed to be the one talking. "All I'll say is that if you won't accept the deal, we will gladly go to the news next. Once the evidence is in their hands, however, the Sanger Police might become a laughingstock. I'm sure that's not what any of our fine officers would want, right?"

"If the victim is the girl on the news," Detective Durham countered, "then it'll be the Denton PD who gets laughed at."

"Not this time," Logan said. "Trust me, sir. I've seen the evidence."

For a little too long, Logan and this cop stared at each other. It was some kind of standoff, but I couldn't tell if it was a power move sort of thing. I did recognize the detective's name, though. Granted, we might only have one in town, which would explain things. Still, this was the guy who'd talked to Zoe. The one Jeri was adamant had all but chased her off, and listening to him now, I could understand why she felt that way.

Maybe it was just his nature. Possibly he was one of those men who thought being a cop put him above the rest of the peons in the world. I wasn't sure which, and I didn't care. All I knew was that if he wouldn't work with us, then I had no idea how we were supposed to bust those assholes!

They'd killed a girl. I'd watched while Dylan and his flunkies not only raped her, but overdosed her to death. Letting them get away with that? No, I'd rather take a lesser crime than see that fucker skate yet again.

But outside the office, voices were getting louder. Not yelling or anything. Just more talk, and it was enough to be noticeable. Confused, I glanced back towards the door, straining my ears to see if I could tell what was going on. From the corner of my eye, I saw Logan look over, proving he was paying attention.

Then a fist rapped on the door. A moment later, it cracked open. "Detective Durham?" Officer Sanders asked as he peeked his head in.

"I'm in the middle of something," the detective replied.

"Yes, sir," Officer Sanders said. Then he stepped back and opened the door wider. "I think this is the person you're looking for, sir."

A Black man in a suit stepped in, looking at me first, then Logan. Finally, he turned his attention to Detective Durham. With a smile, the man reached into his suit coat and pulled out a slim wallet-looking thing. When he flipped it open, my mouth damned near hit the floor.

"Detective, I'm Special Agent Carver with the FBI, working with the Denton combined task force. I was told you have a witness to our crime?"

Beside me, Logan began to chuckle. "We do, Agent. I simply

need immunity for my client for any minor cybercrimes that may have been committed by accident or intent in the process."

The FBI agent began to smile. "I see." Then he turned back to the detective. "Sir, do you happen to have a room we can use? I have a feeling these men are about to break my case wide open."

CHAPTER 60

KNOCK

"What's going on?" I asked Logan, because right about now, my brain was breaking.

They had a tip? What the fuck? He had a feeling we could help? He was willing to grant me fucking immunity?! All of this was just a little too good to be true, so what the actual fuck? How would this guy know any of that? But Logan simply shook his head, reminding me to keep my damned mouth shut.

The agent and detective quickly made arrangements. Then, "Brian!" the detective yelled.

"Yeah?" Officer Sanders replied from just around the door, his face appearing only a second later.

"Put Mr. Weiss and Mr. Andrews in the second interrogation room?"

"Yes, sir," Officer Sanders said, gesturing for us to follow.

Logan stood first, which meant this was ok, so I did too. Quietly, we followed Officer Sanders, but that man wasn't exactly worried about incriminating himself. As we wound our way through the office space that made up the bulk of the police station, he glanced back and began explaining.

"So, the murder case down in Denton has become a big deal," he said. "They called in the feds. I guess it had to do with the other assaults. No idea. Anyway, while you two were in there, these three showed up, saying they'd been told we had witnesses for them." He paused to turn back. "He even knew your names."

"But how?" I asked Logan just as we reached what must be the interrogation room.

From the side, a woman responded. "Agent Matthews said we might want to hear what you have." Then she waved for me to enter first. "Gentlemen, I'm Special Agent Abril Palencia."

"Logan Weiss, attorney at law, and my client, Jeff Andrews."

She nodded. "My partners will probably join us in a moment, but can you tell me what is so interesting that we were told to make a trip this way?"

"Not until we have immunity for any cybercrimes that may have occurred," Logan told her. "In writing, ma'am."

She just nodded and pulled out her phone, tapping at it with both thumbs. "Do I get a hint of what I'm bargaining for?" she asked.

"A video," Logan said. "Or a few."

That made her eyes snap up. "I see." Then her thumbs began to move faster.

She was still typing frantically when the door opened and the Black man walked in. "You getting their immunity?" he asked.

"Mhm," the woman agreed.

"Ok, so can we see what is so interesting?" Agent Carver asked as he lowered himself into the last chair in the room.

"Not until the papers are signed," Logan said. "Legal reasons, you understand."

Which made Agent Carver laugh. "Well, I had to try. It's going to be a moment, though. They have to fill in the blanks and print it up. So, why don't you two tell me about yourselves?"

Logan's hand gently touched my arm in a silent warning. "I'm a specialist in virtual law, studied corporate law as well, and have some experience in defense. I've been in practice a few years now, but grew up with an attorney for a father. It's almost like law is in my blood or something."

"And gaming, I hear." He glanced down at his own phone. "There's something called the Professional League of Gamers?"

"There is," Logan agreed. "I work for the corporation. I also work for the law firm that represents them, so I'm basically a glorified show piece at some highly-incentivized tournaments. My client also is involved with the group. He's a sponsored gamer, earning his income through product endorsements."

"And you're what, seventeen?" Agent Carver asked me.

"Eighteen," Logan answered for me, a little smile twisting one side of his mouth. "His birthday party was when we had the shooting."

The agent nodded. "Yes, I have notes about that, although the intended victim was a Riley Andrews, not Jeff here."

"Mr. Weiss's girlfriend," Agent Palencia said, speaking up finally.

Which was when the door opened and yet another woman in a suit walked in. This one was middle aged, white, and grumpy looking. "Ok, I have the immunity agreement," she said, dropping a stack of papers on the table.

Logan immediately reached for them, but Agent Carver gestured to the woman. "So you both know, this is Special Agent Ibbott. She's also with the Denton task force." Then he looked at Logan. "Do you need a pen?"

Logan simply pulled one from his inside breast pocket. "No. I just need to read this."

I swore I could hear all three of the feds groan. Not that they did, but the looks on their faces made me want to laugh. Instead, I simply leaned back in my chair, lacing my fingers behind my head, and allowed myself to smirk a little.

The clock in the room ticked loudly with each second. The three agents shifted. Two were sitting, and the last woman paced, her shoes an arrhythmical counterpoint to the steady second hand. Logan ignored it all, reading each and every word. Hell, even I wanted to shift uncomfortably, but I knew this was necessary. This was how he was going to keep me from taking too big of a hit for this.

Finally, Logan pushed the papers at me, making an X where I needed to sign my name. "It's good, man."

So I signed. I dated. Hell, I even initialed in a few spots, just to show I'd been through every page. When all of that was done, Logan pushed the papers back at the woman sitting across from him.

"You're going to need a laptop," he said.

"Why?" Agent Palencia asked.

"Because we have video proof of twenty-three rapes and the murder of that girl on the news. Those videos show a pattern of behavior. My client has put together a timeline of events, showing the escalation of the group's behavior, their bragging about it online, as well as their *faces* in quite a few of these videos. The ones without faces are edits of the originals."

"Why?" Agent Carver asked.

At Logan's nod, I answered honestly. "Because they raped my friend."

"So she - " He paused. "I assume your friend is a she?"

"She is."

Nodding, he started again. "So she is among the twenty-three?"

"Technically, yes," I explained, "but the guy who raped her was already arrested for distributing her video. She was seventeen, you see."

"Child porn," Logan clarified.

"Here?" Agent Palencia asked.

I nodded. "The other five simply laughed at her, but I had reason to believe they weren't innocent, so I went hunting."

"And you made a timeline?" the second woman, Agent Ibbott, asked.

"I'll get a laptop," Agent Palencia offered, standing.

"And another chair," Agent Carver suggested. "I'm getting the feeling that our friends are going to be cooperative now that they got what they wanted."

"I simply wanted to make sure my little brother didn't go to jail," Logan admitted.

"Mm," Agent Ibbott murmured. "And why would he be worried about that?"

"You'll see," Logan promised. "Remember, that agreement covers all cybercrimes."

In mere minutes, Agent Palencia was back with a chair in one hand and a laptop under her other arm. When she paused to struggle with the door, Agent Carver hopped up to help, and then there was a moment of confusion as we got ourselves all sorted out around the table again.

Then I passed them the USB drive.

Without a word, Agent Palencia inserted it into the side of her computer and tapped. On the other side, Agent Ibbott leaned in. I could see the reflection of the videos on Agent Carver's glasses, giving me a hint as to what they were looking at.

They didn't seem to watch the videos all the way through. Then again, they really didn't need to. This was more like a cursory glance, making sure they had everything they needed. But when they came to the video of the girl from the news, all of their postures changed.

"That's her," Ibbott breathed.

"The last guy's face can be seen in the truck window at three minutes and twenty-four seconds," I told them.

Carver nodded, but they didn't look away. The lights played on his glasses. Thankfully, there was no sound, but they'd get that later. Then, once the video was finally over, the trio paused to look between each other as if trying to figure out what to say.

"And," I added, hoping Logan wasn't about to kill me, "there's more. Edits, more posts on a website where they talk about it, and things like that. I couldn't fit it all on a USB drive."

Ibbott lifted her chin at me. "What do we need to do to get that?"

"Think they'd agree?" I asked Logan, hoping he knew what I was talking about.

Pulling out his phone, he typed something under the table, then tilted the screen so I could see.

> **Logan:**
> Not sure about Jinxy, but the rest of Ruin will. Immunity for all in exchange for all?

I nodded.

So he dimmed his screen and put his phone away. "Are you willing to offer immunity again?"

"For what this time?" Agent Carver asked.

"Same thing," Logan assured him. "I just need a few more copies. Six, to be exact. I can guarantee that five of them will gladly take the witness stand."

"But not the sixth?" Agent Palencia asked.

"The sixth is the one I can't guarantee," Logan agreed. "Doesn't mean they won't. Just doesn't mean they will."

I flicked a finger at the laptop. "Check the file called timeline.xls and then let us know." Because I hadn't seen the reflection of that one yet.

Agent Ibbott gave me a confused look. "How do you know we haven't?"

"Agent Carver's wearing glasses," I explained. "No other trick to it."

But Agent Palencia was already opening the spreadsheet and scrolling through it. "Make the deal," she said softly. "If they have the evidence to back this up, they just made our case for us." Then she looked up. "Make the damned deal."

Agent Carver turned to Logan. "What will it take to get these six other people here?"

"A phone call," Logan said. "Then about ten minutes."

"We'll have the papers printed by then," he promised. "Same contract, although you can read all of them if you want."

Agent Ibbott simply stood and headed for the door. "I'll get us another room," she said.

"Or just more chairs," Logan suggested. "After all, I am representing all of them, and not a single one will talk without me in the room."

"Then chairs it is," she agreed.

But Agent Carver was now looking at the timeline we'd hastily made. "Can I ask how you have information from this KoG site?"

"Mr. Andrews may have come into possession of Dylan Marshall's account details," Logan explained.

Which made the two remaining FBI agents look at each other. Then Agent Palencia turned to Logan. "Does KoG stand for Kings of Gaming?"

"It does," he agreed. "I also happen to know that Agent Bradley Matthews might be interested in that."

"He would be," she agreed. "In fact, when he called to let us know about potential evidence, he said to keep an eye out for anything that might tie back to this site for his own case."

"Deviant Games," Logan said. "Yeah, I've worked with the

owners of that company. Friends, actually. That's why we called Agent Matthews first, but he said he couldn't help."

"Because he couldn't," Agent Carver explained. "Our murder investigation has nothing at all to do with anything in his division."

"So he punted it to someone who could help," Logan realized, looking at me. "Interesting. I guess that call this morning wasn't wasted after all."

"No, sir," Agent Carver agreed. "It certainly wasn't. If this pans out, you just closed one case and may have made a serious dent in another. I'm just curious how a young man could do it when the Bureau couldn't."

"Because I didn't play by the rules," I told him. "Hacking, Agent Carver. Hence the little immunity deal I just got. So you know, I'm pretty good at it."

"From the sounds of it," he said, "you had some good help too - although I don't expect you to confirm that until six more forms are signed, right?"

"Exactly," I agreed. "Looks like we both know how this game is played."

Which made the man do the last thing I would've expected. Reaching over the table, he offered me his hand. "And I'm glad to be working with you, Mr. Andrews. All of you. Very glad."

CHAPTER 61

CADE

It had been quiet for too long. Knock had been at the police station for well over an hour, but we hadn't heard anything. The donuts I'd picked up were now sitting heavily in my stomach, but at least we'd put the evidence on all of Alpha Team's computers.

Although, considering I wasn't handling this well, Jeri was even worse. Snappish was the nicest way I had to explain her attitude, yet I understood. Fuck, I felt the same way. I couldn't even count the number of crimes we'd committed to put this case together, and now Knock was sitting down with the cops?

If this went bad, it was going to ruin the rest of his life.

I was just about to push away from my desk when my phone rang. My head snapped over to it, but when I saw Logan's name on the screen, I was swiping to answer as fast as humanly possible.

"Please tell me he's ok?" I greeted him.

"He's fine, and he has immunity," Logan promised. "I also have six more offers of immunity for anyone who'd like to come down and share information."

Slowly, I turned my chair to see the rest of my friends scattered around the room. "All of us?" I asked.

"Mhm," Logan agreed. "And where I'm at isn't exactly private, although our conversation is covered by privilege, so I want to be careful. Just know the FBI is here. They're with a task force from Denton, and they want every single thing we have so they can put these guys behind bars for good."

"And what do we have to do for that?" I asked.

Logan chuckled, the sound making my insides relax a little. "Well, we're not giving them the Squirrel, so get everything on my old laptop. If they decide to confiscate that, they can have it."

"And it's yours," I realized. "Attorney privilege thing?"

"That's why you're my little brother," he praised. "Think you can do that in ten minutes and bring the crew here?"

"Make it fifteen," I told him, "but yes. I just hope your old laptop has some serious disk space."

"It has enough. See you then."

I disconnected the call, sighed, and then realized that all eyes were on me. "Knock has immunity," I explained. "They want *all* the data, and Logan says to put it on his old laptop."

"I know the one," Riley promised as she hopped up to handle that.

So I kept going. "He also has immunity for the rest of us. Sounds like everyone in Ruin."

My eyes weren't the only ones that turned to Jinxy. He'd been the most vocal about not trusting law enforcement. He was the one with the history to make him a bit gun-shy. But instead of shaking his head, the guy simply looked over at Zoe, smiled, and then began to nod slowly.

"If Logan fucking Weiss says it's safe, then I'll stick my neck out."

"So we're doing this?" I asked.

It was Jeri who answered. "Of course we are. Immunity for hacking? Why the fuck not? It'll put Dylan and his punk-ass pals in jail!"

"Just like they deserve," Zoe said.

It took eleven minutes to copy everything from the Squirrel onto Logan's spare laptop. It took three minutes to drive across town. We had to take two cars to fit all of us, leaving Riley and Kitty at home alone. I was in charge of the laptop, but Jeri took over the rest. And when we parked in front of the Sanger police station, she was the first one through the door, not stopping until she reached the sliding window on the far side.

Then she rapped her knuckles on it. "I was requested!" she called out.

A police officer opened the door at the side with a big grin on his face. "Let me guess, you're all with Logan Weiss, right?"

"We are," I agreed.

"This way," he said, gesturing for us to come in. "He and his other client are already in a room with the agents." He waited until we were all through the door, then turned to guide us in the right direction, talking as he walked. "Took a bit to find enough chairs, but this will give all of you the privacy you'll need. Can I get you water, soda, or anything else?"

"We're good," Jeri assured him just as we reached a door on the far side of this place.

The officer nodded, knocked, and then poked his head in. "I have six people here for Mr. Weiss."

"Bring them in," a man's voice replied. It wasn't Logan.

"Everyone," the officer said as he pulled the door open as wide as possible. "And let us know if you need anything, agents."

Stepping into the room, I got my first look at the feds who were sitting across from Logan and Knock. Closest to the door was a middle-aged white woman with short graying hair. Beside her was a tall, somewhat intellectual-looking Black man with glasses and a laptop in front of him. I was willing to bet he was the agent in charge of this. And on his other side was a younger woman, Latina, with what looked like a tattoo peeking out from the edge of her sleeve.

"This is Agent Ibbott, Carver, and Palencia," Logan said, gesturing at them from the door side to the far wall. "And before any of you say a word, I need your signatures on these papers." He held up a pen in a clear invitation.

I set the laptop I was carrying down in front of him and took the pen. "Where?"

Logan pointed. I scribbled, then passed the pen to Jeri when I was done. She repeated the process, giving it to Ripper next. Zoe came after him, with Hot and Jinxy signing last. After each of us signed, we claimed one of the many plastic and metal chairs, making a little cluster beside and around Knock and Logan's side of the table.

"Agents," Logan said once we were done, "these are my clients: Cade Bradford, Jericho Williams, Zoe Townsend, Elliot Kerrington, Grayson Harlan, and Shawn Paxton. You already know Jeff Andrews. Together, they make up the hacktivist group known as Ruin."

"Ruin?" Agent Palencia asked.

Jeri huffed, clearly not impressed. "Yeah, as in we ruin the ones who harm women."

"To do that," Logan explained, "they have a habit of finding virtual proof of things those men don't want seen. In this case, their target was a group who calls themselves the 'Alpha Team.' It's made up of five young men who attend Sanger High. There was a sixth, but as I mentioned earlier, he was arrested already for the distribution of underaged sexual materials."

"But he also raped some of these girls," Jeri snapped.

Turning back, I shot her a warning look. "Let Logan do his job, Jeri."

Zoe just mimed zipping her lips, locking them, and dropping the key down her shirt. Jeri rolled her eyes and sighed, but it seemed to be enough. Across from us, however, the FBI agents didn't seem annoyed. Oddly, they also weren't giving me the impression they were trying to fuck us over. Nope, all three of them were hanging on our every word.

"The immunity is already granted," Agent Ibbott promised. "We can't use any cybercrimes against you. However, due to the tragic nature of this case, we would like an agreement for the..." She paused, her eyes jumping across us. "...seven of you to testify when this case comes to trial."

"Shawn?" Logan asked, turning to look at him.

"Fuck, man," Jinxy grumbled. "Is this going to fuck me up?"

"Nope, you got immunity," Logan promised. "I mean, your record might be a point of contention in a trial, but it also proves you have a history of helping instead of sabotaging. Will you testify?"

Jinxy looked at Zoe, then nodded. "Yeah. If it means it'll get these guys off the street, I'll do it."

"And the rest of you?" Agent Carver asked.

All of us mumbled some variant of yes, even going so far as to nod. Granted, I didn't really want to. Hell, who wanted to be shoved into a stiff suit in a hot room and grilled by an aggressive attorney? Then again, Logan wasn't like the lawyers on TV, so maybe court wasn't either? And since this was for a good cause, we kinda had to.

"So what do we have?" Agent Carver asked, gesturing to the laptop.

But I knew more than what was even loaded onto there. Since Logan said we could talk, I decided to answer that honestly. "There's a group that started out made up of six guys," I explained.

"Dylan Marshall, John Markham, Parker Burque, Landon Venne, Wade Udall, and Evan Payne. I was friends with Dylan since like kindergarten."

"But you aren't now?" Agent Ibbott asked.

"No, ma'am," I assured her. "When I found out Evan had raped a friend of mine, I wanted nothing to do with that. In the process of trying to get someone to care about his crimes - and he was arrested last semester for it - I found out about the rest. These guys are drugging girls with ketamine."

"Like Special K?" Agent Palencia asked.

"Like a horse tranquilizer," I clarified. "Dylan's dad is a vet. Supposedly it's a regulated drug, but Dylan has it. At one point, he drugged my girlfriend's and ex-girlfriend's drinks at a party. We noticed they were acting odd, so we got them out before they could be victimized, but that's how easily he's using it."

"Wait," Ibbott said. "Two women?"

"Two," Jeri answered for me. "One was me. One was his ex. She and I are friends."

"Ok," the woman said, nodding to show she was keeping up.

"And that ex," Jeri went on, "had friends who'd been put in a compromising position. See, these girls drank too much. It's possible they were drugged as well. All of it was at a party, and when they went to make out with the guy they were into, his friends showed up, turned it into an orgy they really couldn't refuse, and then used the videos of the event - videos the girls didn't know were being made - to blackmail them later."

"These guys sound like real pieces of work," Agent Carver grumbled.

"You have no idea," Logan said. "There are currently five of them. Five young men, all eighteen years old, with wealthy and socially-respected families. They think they're untouchable. My clients here saw inconsistencies and poked. What started as those boys bullying my clients ended with my clients finding evidence of far too many crimes."

"Twenty-three," Jeri said softly.

"What?" Agent Palencia asked, not having heard her.

"Fucking twenty-three!" Jeri yelled. "That's twenty-three girls who have had their lives turned inside out because these guys were just being boys. Twenty-three people who didn't ask for any of this. Twenty-fucking-three victims - and *two* are now dead - all because one boy's dad is a cop, because a detective didn't want to do the hard work, and because no one listened when we tried to report it the first fucking time!"

"Jeri - " Logan tried.

"No," Agent Carver said. "She's right." Then he pushed to his feet. "Which officer?"

"Evan Payne's dad," Zoe muttered.

"Payne," Carver said as he headed for the door. "And the Detective?"

"The same one we spoke with," Knock told him.

Then Agent Carver stuck his head out of the room. "Can I have Officer Payne and Detective Durham?"

There was a reply, but I couldn't hear it. The agent returned to claim his seat, but before I could pick up the story again, the door opened. Detective Durham stepped in.

"Officer Payne won't be in until this evening," he explained. "He works second shift."

"Well, you're going to need to call him in," Agent Carver told him. "According to these witnesses, his son has been implicated. You will need to put him on leave while this investigation is being conducted."

Detective Durham's jaw visibly clenched. "I will get in touch with him."

He turned to leave, but Agent Carver wasn't done. "And I want you to explain to me about the initial report you ignored?"

The detective's eyes jumped straight to Zoe. "Sir..."

"I didn't make a report," Zoe said softly.

"You should've," Jeri countered. "Zoe, you *tried*."

"But?" Agent Carver asked the detective. "I'm waiting to hear what happened with that."

"The young woman wasn't a legal adult," the detective explained. "I simply made her aware of the complications that come with an accusation like this. When I pointed out that I would need to contact her parents before I could take her report, she changed her mind."

"You didn't try to help!" Jeri roared, shoving to her feet. "You were thinking about how much work this would be, how ugly it would get, and never mind the number of times you insinuated that it was because she regretted something consensual! You may have used all the right words, *Detective*, but you made it very clear that her abuse wasn't really high on your list of concerns. Not a real crime, right?"

"That's not - "

"No!" I snapped, jumping to my own feet. Zoe was my friend too, and I'd be damned if I made Jeri take all of this onto her own shoulders again. "You know Officer Payne. The pair of you are friendly enough that you knew Zoe was dating Evan at the start of the school year. You fucking well *knew*, and you were protecting your fellow cop, weren't ya?"

"Son..." the detective tried.

I just waved him off. "She tried to tell you. Zoe risked everything to report something so horrific you can't even wrap your damned mind around it, but you refused to listen. You thought of your friends, probably told yourself it was already over, or some other bullshit, but it didn't just stop with her! If you'd caught them back then, there'd be half as many victims. This girl wouldn't be dead!"

"Never mind Amber!" Jeri snapped. "I told you it wouldn't

stop. I told you there would be other victims, but you didn't listen. You think rape is no big deal, right? I mean, it's not like the valedictorian of our grade would kill herself over it! It's not like a group of serial rapists might think it's fucking *funny* when they kill a girl by giving her too much ketamine. It's not like any of this fucking *matters* to most people - but now look where we are!"

"This is on you," Jinxy growled softly.

"Easy there," Hot muttered at him.

"No," Jinxy said. "Cade's right. Jeri's right. We all know about the thin blue line, don't we? And even if they don't intend to, it's natural to protect our friends. Fuck, that's why we got caught up in this. But they're cops. They're supposed to be the ones on our side, helping the victims - not each other. They're supposed to protect and fucking serve, but who are they serving?"

"Enough!" Logan bellowed, slamming his hand down on the desk.

The room stilled. Most of us flinched at the sound. Everyone except Jericho.

She simply lifted her chin to look at Detective Durham. "*I warned you*," she told him. "But you didn't listen. You didn't care, because prosecuting rape is a little bit inconvenient or something. You probably forgot all about it the moment we walked out the door, because no one gives a shit about violence against women, but you know what? It didn't stop and women are dead. So many others will never be the same. Think about *that* when you tell your friends what crazy shits we are, hm?"

Agent Carver just cleared his throat, subtly trying to regain control of the situation. "Detective Durham? I'm about to put in a request for a few warrants. Will your officers be unbiased enough to serve those, or will I need to call in a few more agents?"

"For what?" Detective Durham asked.

Agent Palencia smiled, but it was Agent Carver who answered. "For the arrest of these five young men. Five serial rapists who have been operating in Sanger, Texas, since..." He paused to look at the laptop in front of him. "Looks like the end of May, last year."

"We'll be glad to help," Detective Durham promised.

Logan simply murmured, drawing all eyes to him. "I've also learned that we use the Denton County SWAT. Agents, I'm pretty sure they're part of your task force, right?"

"They are," Agent Carver agreed. "If you'd make arrangements for that, Detective? I want to get the last of this evidence, but we already have more than enough to get those warrants signed. The last thing any of us want are monsters like these on the street for one minute longer than necessary, don't you agree?"

"Yes, sir," Detective Durham said.

But I felt like my mouth was about to flop open. Dylan and his friends were getting arrested? This was happening? We'd...won?

Yeah, there was no way it was going to be that easy.

CHAPTER 62

JERICHO

The cops wanted to talk to us for a few more hours. They looked at everything on the laptop, asked if they could put the entire device into evidence - which Logan agreed to - and then we were done. Of course, there were all the standard reminders that they'd contact us with more questions, we'd be expected to testify at a trial if one happened, and all of that.

But it was happening. This was real.

The whole drive back to Knock's place, I was smiling. It felt like I was high on something, as if I could touch the clouds, and my shoulders hadn't been this light in my entire life! Little laughs kept slipping out, but no one picked on me for it. Hell, I wasn't the only one doing it!

And when I pulled into Knock's place to park, the guy was standing in front of Cade's car with his hands in the air, whooping at the top of his lungs. Climbing out, I joined him, letting out one hell of a banshee like scream!

All that rage. All the frustration. So many years of darkness and despair all came out in that sound. I screamed so hard my body bent at the waist, and fuck did it feel good. Then Zoe joined me. Ripper, Cade, and even Jinxy did as well, with Hottie giving in and offering an awkward whoop so he wouldn't be left out. The seven of us converged, hugging each other in some kind of wobbly-looking circle, and all of us were smiling so big that our eyes squinted.

"And we owe it all to Logan!" Cade called out, pointing at the guy trying to casually slip back into the house.

"No," he said, reaching for the backyard gate. "I just did my day job. You seven are the heroes. You're the ones who stopped the bad guys."

"Vigilantes," I corrected. "We're not the good guys, Logan. We're the villains' nightmares!"

"Nightmares!" Zoe squealed excitedly, bouncing in place as she did so.

Which led to another round of hugging and cheering. Out here, there weren't neighbors to get pissed about the sound. There were no worries about a cop showing up because they thought someone was being murdered. Only the horses could hear us, and from the looks of it, they were all out in the far back pasture.

"Ok!" Cade said. "I don't know about the rest of y'all, but I'm starving and it's got to be past lunchtime."

"Normal people lunch," Zoe teased, grabbing Jinxy's hand to haul him towards the backyard.

But I caught Knock's wrist, holding him back as our group slowly - and loudly - meandered towards the house. "Hey," I said.

He shifted his hand so his fingers were laced with mine. "Hey," he replied.

"Um, you know how you kinda went to take the fall?"

"Jeri..."

"No," I begged. "Knock, just, let me get this out, ok?"

He nodded.

"We both know you thought you were going to jail. I mean, this shit? Maybe Zoe, Cade, and Ripper don't get it, but I know exactly how illegal it is. I know what Jinxy went through as a kid. Hottie made sure of it, teaching me how to be safe - but you were going to throw all that away? I mean, your fucking job as a gamer?"

"And it would be easier to convince them it was just me because of that job," he said.

"But I didn't get to say anything to you before you left," I said, refusing to let him sidetrack me. "Knock, we both know you weren't expecting to come back. We were all so damned focused on this case we were making, and how it could help those girls, and I should've said something. I wanted to, but it didn't even dawn on me until it was too late."

"Which something did you want to say?" he asked, stepping closer until we were chest to chest.

I looked up into his beautiful dark brown eyes. My hand found his chest and my tongue darted out to moisten my lips. "I like you, Knock." Fuck. No. That was not what I meant. "I mean, I'm trying to say that you're so much more than a friend, and I know I have four boyfriends and all, but you're..."

"Special?" he offered.

"Yeah," I breathed. "I mean all of you are, but in different ways, and it makes me feel this thing..." I gestured to my chest. "I dunno. I mean, you and Cade are so cute, so don't get me wrong, but I like this. I like us. I..." My breath puffed out. "Fuck. Like isn't the right word."

"Partners," he said softly, lifting his free hand to cup my face. "Polycule. Jericho, we came up with those terms because you have triggers."

"But we won."

"And winning doesn't erase the trauma of the past," he reminded me before looking up. "Cade?"

"Yeah?" the guy called back from the steps to the porch.

"A second?"

"Yep!"

So Knock pulled me that way. I wasn't sure if my friends figured out that we needed a second, or if they were all just too excited about what had gone down. Either way, the rest made their way inside until only the three of us remained outside. Cade gave Knock a confused look as we joined him, but Knock simply moved me to Cade's side, then shifted to stand before us both.

"Look," he said, reaching up to shove his hair back. "I'm just going to do this all at once. Yeah, I did think I was going to get arrested. And yes, I was hoping like fuck that Logan would get me out of it with probation or community service. I also knew it might not happen."

"Yeah, kinda figured," Cade said.

"But," Knock went on, "I did it for one reason and one reason only."

"Because it was the easiest way to keep the rest of us from getting busted," I muttered, repeating what he'd said a moment ago.

"Well, that," he admitted, "but mostly because I didn't want the people I'm falling in love with to suffer." He paused to pull in a breath. "Yes, I mean both of you, and I'm telling you at the same time so you can't say I have a favorite, because I don't."

"Me either," Cade said, glancing at me, then back to Knock. "But are you serious?"

"Yeah," Knock said, his face getting just a little brighter, maybe even pinker.

"Me fucking too," Cade told him, grabbing the side of Knock's face to plant a hard kiss on him.

It made me smile. Damn, the pair of them were so cute. Not

just sexy, but adorable, sweet, and so damned good together that it was amazing. But Cade quickly broke the kiss and turned to me.

"And I like you, Jeri. I mean, really care about you. I want to use other words, but I won't because I'm not fucking this up."

"I..." My throat clenched, so I nodded. "Care. Care's a good word," I managed to get out.

"Fuck, she's cute," Cade said as he and Knock both stepped in to hug me hard. "Our bond is strong, Jeri."

"And like is also a four-letter word," Knock told me. "But I know. I can tell how both of you feel." He glanced at Cade, smiled, then leaned in to kiss my temple. "I like all of this. I love our polycule, Jeri, even if you shy away from that word."

"Is it ok that, um..." I quickly looked at each of them, feeling my pulse hammering me harder than it had even when Dylan had shoved me against my car. "I know how I feel," I tried next, feeling my palms getting clammy. "It's just..."

"We know," Cade assured me.

But that wasn't good enough. This chickening out at the last minute wasn't either. How could I face down all the other shit I'd been through but I choked up here? No. Of all the things that needed to be said, why was the bad stuff always easier? Why did it make me less *terrified* to tell someone off, potentially getting myself in shit in the process, then it did to put myself out there like this?

So I pulled in a deep breath and forced all the words out. "I think I'm in love with all of you, and I've never been in love before, so I'm hoping this is really real, but I don't want to lose any of you and I'm scared to fucking death, but we won. We finally fucking won, so maybe that means the curse is over now? Maybe it's ok? Maybe, just fucking *maybe*, I can love you without making it worse?"

"Fuck," Cade breathed.

"I love you too, Jeri," Knock said, hugging me hard.

Cade wrapped his arms around my other side, catching Knock up in his embrace. "So we're there now? We're actually in love?"

"Yeah," Knock said. "I think we are."

"And the others?" Cade pressed.

My reply came back in an embarrassed mumble. "I kinda already said something to them."

Which made Cade laugh. Not at all the response I'd expected. "Ok," he said, clearing his throat to halt his chuckles. "I'm going to guess it was just about as eloquent, hm?"

"Yeah."

Laughing, Knock stepped back and turned me towards the door. "I think this is definitely something that deserves to be celebrated." Then he fell in on my right. Cade took his place on my left, and the three of us headed in to join the rest of our crew.

No, our family.

Because that was what we really were. The seven of us had become so much more. We weren't mere friends. Our experiences had gone so far past that. We were a team, we were partners in literal crimes, and we were the support each other needed most. This was what I'd always wanted and had never imagined was possible in real life.

Inside, the crew had all stalled out in the living room. Riley was yelling about the table. Logan was saying he had to change out of his suit. Kitty was asking about lunch options and how hungry we all were. And there, at the side, Zoe had her phone in front of her, looking up at Jinxy as if checking something.

"She deserves to know," Jinxy said. "I think it's safe to give her an update."

"Ok."

Knock and Cade heard too, so they peeled away from me to see what was going on. Ripper immediately shifted in to take their place. I glanced over with a smile, then leaned into him, loving how easily he wrapped his arm around my back.

"You were amazing, you know," he said.

"Me?"

"Mhm," he agreed. "When you lost your shit on that detective? When you made it clear how he let Zoe down? I wanted to stand up and brag that you were my girlfriend. Mine, Jeri, and ours, but it's the mine part that keeps surprising me."

"Definitely yours," I told him.

He hugged, pulling me against his side. "Damn, you're amazing."

But that was when Zoe's phone call connected. "Hello?" a woman answered, making the entire room fall silent.

"Tiffany?" Zoe asked.

"Yeah?"

"Hey, it's Zoe and the gang," she said. "Um, we wanted to give you an update."

"Ok?"

A smile spread across Zoe's face. "We got 'em, Tiff. Dylan, Landon, Parker, Wade, and even John. All five of them are going down, because we found where they're storing everything. We have your videos and we can delete them now. Well, the girls' I mean. I just don't know if they're going to want to know."

"Why?" she asked, sounding suspicious.

So I called over, "Because we just got back from the police station and talking to the FBI!"

"What?!" Tiffany gasped.

"Yes!" Zoe squealed. Then she quickly sobered. "Although it's not all good news. Tiff, they killed a girl. We found the storage because Dylan uploaded another video - or a few. Um, and in that..."

"The girl from the news," Jinxy said.

"Who's that?" Tiffany asked.

"My boyfriend," Zoe bragged, "but he's right. That girl who died in Denton? The one who's been all over the news? Dylan and his friends did it. They raped her, Tiff, and we found the video, so we turned it in."

"And you're not in trouble?" Tiffany asked. "I mean, I know some of what you're doing is a little shady."

"Very shady," Zoe agreed, "but we got immunity, and we gave them the whole damned timeline."

"And," I added, letting go of Ripper so I could move closer to the phone. "It's possible that all of their computers have a collection of videos on them now. You know, the sort of thing that will not look good in court."

"Speaking of court," Zoe cut in. "That's the best part. The cops are going to arrest them today, it sounds like. I mean, this is it!"

"Uh..." Tiffany sounded confused. "Yeah, but according to TikTok, Dylan and the guys are all out mudding on four-wheelers. They aren't at home to get arrested."

"They'll get arrested," Hottie assured her. "The cops know their names. Let those fuckers have their one last day of fun, because their reign of terror is over!"

"Over!" Cade agreed. "It's done, Tiff. They're going away for murder, not assault, and I'm pretty sure we gave the feds enough to make a serial rape charge stick. They're done. They're going to fucking pay for what they've done. This is the last Spring Break those assholes will ever get!"

"Holy shit," Tiffany breathed. "Holy fucking shit! You're all serious?"

"Completely," Zoe promised. "Tiff, they fucked with the wrong girls. Together, we took them down."

Tiffany just laughed, the sound all breathy and relieved. "The bitch squad is going to be so relieved. Thank you! All of you. Shit, no. I mean thank you, *Ruin*."

We all called back that she was welcome, then Zoe ended the call. That led to another round of laughing and celebrating, but Riley and Kitty were in full-on caretaker mode. The pair of women called for us to head to the table if we wanted to eat, and they were already setting out quite the selection of snack foods to pick through.

"And more coffee for anyone who's fading," Riley promised. "At least drink enough to make sure you can drive home when done, or crash here."

"Here," Cade said as he claimed his seat.

I moved that way, but Hottie fell in at my side, wrapping his arm around my shoulders. "This?" he asked as he guided me to a seat. "This is how we need to end all of our missions, baby girl." Then he reached over to turn my face towards his. "If for no other reason than because I want to remember this look on you."

"Which?" I asked.

"Victory," he told me. "It makes you even more beautiful than I could've imagined."

CHAPTER 63

JERICHO

Food was good, but the lack of sleep was taking its toll. One by one, we all made our excuses and headed home.

Hottie, Jinxy and I were among the last. The high of winning helped, but the lack of sleep had Jinxy's head bobbing.

A long nap at home helped. Hottie curled up with me. Jinxy fell face first onto Hottie's bed and simply didn't move for a few hours. I half expected us all to sleep through the night, but it didn't work that way. Nope, two hours later, my mind called it enough, and I was up.

One long, hot shower later, and I was actually feeling like a person again. Surprisingly, Jinxy was moving around too. The moment I vacated the bathroom, he claimed it, and I heard the water running again. Hottie slept a little longer, but even he could only last so long. I was pretty sure it was the hunger driving us.

Because none of us had enjoyed a real meal since the one I'd been making when the alert went off. Donuts, snacks, and finger foods just didn't stick the same way. My tummy was growling, demanding I do something about it, and I had a fridge full of groceries and a little celebration of my own to enjoy.

"Jeri?" Jinxy called as he left the bathroom. "Flawed night?"

"Yes!" I called back. "I'm also making chicken fajitas. You good with that?"

"I heard food?" Hottie asked.

"Shower," I called up the stairs at him. "Then you both can organize one hell of a raid, because I think we've fucking earned a full-on PvP-fest!"

I heard feet on the stairs and turned to see Hottie making his way down. "Gonna let me spoil you?" he asked.

"Definitely," I agreed.

He made his way closer just to wrap his arms around my waist, tugging me up against his chest. "Because if you don't stop me, I'm going to officially announce you as the pink team leader, and I'm putting all your boyfriends on your team, plus Zoe."

"No, put Zoe on Jinxy's," I decided. "And make his the teal team."

"Can do," he agreed. "I actually like that. The downside is I'm going to move Dingo to green leader, though."

"But he's such a good backup," I whined.

"Or I could leave him on yours," he quickly backtracked.

I just laughed. "No, give Dingo his own team. I just want us to be a strike force, if you're good with that?"

"Pink, you mean?"

I nodded. "It's what we're good at, Hottie. Hit hard, hit fast, and do a shit-ton of damage."

"Mm, because you found the Flawed that work with you."

"And thus I'm not alone," I agreed. "Now turn the TV to some dance music for me, and go set all that up? Dinner should be ready in about forty-five minutes."

"Damn, I love you," he said, bending to steal a quick kiss.

But when he tried to pull away, I caught the waist of his pants.

"Hey, um..." I looked up into those jewel-like blue eyes of his. "I may have said that to the other guys too. Is that ok?"

"Why are you asking me?"

"Because you're my best fucking friend!" I hissed. "I need someone to tell me I'm not fucking up or something."

A little smile took over his mouth. "Not because you think you need my permission, though, right?"

"No," I huffed. "I just... I mean... Hottie, is it too fast? Am I rushing into this? Do I even have a fucking clue what - "

He kissed me again, cutting off my rambling. "Baby girl, if you feel it, you should say it. Life is far too short to hold back, so yeah. Love them. Tell them you love them, even if you aren't sure. If you think you do, then lean into it and let go. Fall, Jericho. Fall hard, because I swear to you all of us are here to catch you."

"And each other," I said.

"Yeah," he agreed. "That's why this works." Then he turned me towards the stove. "And I'll cook the rest of the week, because you're going overboard, I think."

"You," I told him, "only make healthy meals. I like some grease and cheese to go with my protein, thank you very much." I grabbed the knife off the counter, then flicked my other hand, shooing him towards the stairs. "Big raid, HotShot. Jinxy's here, and this is the first time the three of us will get to play in the same place, so make it impressive."

"Yes, ma'am," he teased before heading back upstairs, pausing at the living room to give me the music I'd requested.

It was modern pop, so I supposed that counted as dance music. Not quite what I'd been expecting, but good enough to cook by. Pulling out the chicken, I set that to defrost, then began gathering up the rest of my supplies. The pan went on the burner. I found the oil. The whole time, my butt was bouncing in some bastardization of a dance and a twerk-like thing.

Yeah, I probably looked stupid, but I didn't care. Today was the best day I could remember in far too long. This smile was simply stuck on my face. Hell, it had probably been there the whole time I'd been sleeping.

I loved my guys. Knock, Cade, Ripper, and Hottie. All of them were different, but each one mattered so much to me. I didn't have a first or last. There was no better or worse. They just were, and together we made something bigger than all of us. More importantly, something that actually worked - and which I was daring to hope might even last.

Because this was high school. Sure, the semester was passing quickly, but that didn't matter. It was the end of my "childhood," or so people had said, and I was more than ready for it. College was going to be my fresh start, yet I didn't want to lose my guys. Not just my boyfriends, but Jinxy and Zoe too! All of us!

We were Ruin. I chuckled at that, pulling out the chicken to start slicing it into thin strips. I'd met those people because of Flawed. The game that promised I wasn't alone had made sure of it. There was irony in that somewhere, I was sure. It also felt a lot like a miracle.

Upstairs, Hottie and Jinxy were doing something that had bursts of laughter coming down the stairs, loud enough to be heard over my music. This was how my life was supposed to have been. Happiness wasn't something a person should have to fight for. It should come easily, and I felt like even with all the shit we'd been through, Ruin had taught me that one thing.

I could be happy.

Me, the broken girl whose life was a tragedy on steroids. Me, the misfit gamer girl who didn't play well with others. Shit, me, the wild and crazy girl who was always ready to throw down or start shit. My friends - my fucking *family* - had somehow managed to show me a better way, and I really liked how it felt.

Because victory was one of those things that tasted so damned sweet.

I was dancing in place, smiling at that thought while trying to figure out how much chicken all of us would need. Jinxy was probably a garbage disposal. Those tall and lean types could usually put the food away. Besides, leftovers would be nice tomorrow. So, I pulled over another chicken breast and decided I'd rather make too much than not enough - when something creaked.

The air pressure changed. A second later, the front door thunked as it closed, causing me to spin in place, but what I saw did not want to compute. Dylan and Wade stood there, paused just inside the door, looking over - right at me.

"Well, that was easy," Wade chuckled.

Dylan cracked his knuckles and made his way closer. "So, Jericho. You wanna tell us what you did?"

"Huh?" I asked.

"Parker said there's SWAT at his place," Dylan snapped. "Fucking SWAT!"

My eyes were jumping all over the place, trying to find an escape route. "Why are you here?" I asked, the words coming out in a voice too high to really be mine.

"I thought we had a fucking truce," Wade told me as he followed behind Dylan. "That was the fucking deal and you broke it, now you're going to pay for that, bitch!"

And the pair rushed in.

The kitchen didn't have an exit. It was just an L shaped area, enclosed by the walls on two sides and the bar on the other. The only way I could get out was by going through these two, so in desperation, I decided to try.

Charging forward, I did my best to evade them, but of course it didn't work. Wade grabbed my hair, slinging me to the ground. Dylan followed up with a kick to my ribs.

I gasped as the air rushed from my lungs, but I wasn't about to lie here and take it. As I scrambled to my feet, Dylan got another kick in, but that only propelled me upwards, encouraging me to stand the fuck up, and to do it now.

Then I swung. My fist hit one of them. I wasn't sure which, because the other hit me back. A hard jab to my side made my eyes blur. That was where I'd been kicked only a moment ago! Pain had my head spinning, and yet I couldn't give up.

"Fuck you!" I yelled, trying to pick a target to focus on.

Because that was how it worked in game. Focus fire, right? I had a bad feeling the theory wouldn't apply to real life, but fuck it. I was now in desperation mode. Fight or flight had kicked in, but these guys had left me only fight as an option, so I doubled down.

Grabbing a bowl off the counter, I threw it at the closest guy: Dylan. He batted it away, and the bowl clattered to the ground loudly, spilling all of the bell peppers I'd just prepared. Yeah, well, fuck that. Let them have onions.

Grabbing a handful of those, I aimed for Wade's eyes. The guy just ducked his head, so I ran one more time, hoping this time I'd make it past, but Dylan was ready. At two against one, and both of them bigger than me, I didn't have much of a chance.

Dylan grabbed me by the arms and pushed, forcing me not only off my feet, but back. The tile floor was slick and hard. A grunt burst out as I hit it, but I didn't stop moving until I was even further back in that isolated kitchen area.

And Wade was moving in, reducing the room I had to move. Dodging was pretty much out of the question. My cooking supplies were now out of reach. All I had for weapons was the pantry, but maybe that would work? Pulling open the door, I looked for anything that might help, but it was a mistake.

In the split-second I was distracted, Wade grabbed me, dragging me to my feet and shoving his fist into my face while holding me still with a hand in my hair. Again, then again. I cried out at the pain, trying to block his hands with mine, but it wasn't working.

Then I heard a roar. There was no other word for it. Right after, Wade vanished, giving me a chance to see the rest of the area. Hottie was there, and the fury on his face may have been the most terrifying thing I'd ever seen.

"Not her!" he bellowed, throwing Wade into the wall.

But Dylan simply took his place. That was ok, though. One on one, I had a chance. With my right arm, I punched. My left was raised to block. Dylan leaned back, making me miss, then surged in to grab both of my arms, using his weight to shove me into the wall.

So I slammed my head forward, crashing into his nose with my forehead. Fuck, but that hurt, yet it was enough to make Dylan let go - and that was the lucky break I needed, because it seemed Hottie was not alone. Jinxy loomed over Dylan's back, grabbing the guy around the chest to drag him away from me.

And over by the front door, Hottie had gone feral. The man was roaring, letting out one long, continuous sound as his fists pummeled Wade. Over and over, I could see his arms move, but I couldn't see Wade. I also didn't care, because while Jinxy might be taller, he wasn't a fighter. Sadly, Dylan was.

He broke free, spinning to see the new threat only long enough to take a swing. That put his back to me, so I took my chance. Two hard jabs to the kidney made Dylan not only groan in pain, but turn back. Immediately, Jinxy was on him, grabbing Dylan by the arms, then struggling to get his elbows locked behind his back.

"Stop!" Jinxy demanded. "Fucking quit, you stupid piece of shit!"

Dylan didn't stop. He kept struggling, but Jinxy had finally gotten a good hold. I wasn't sure what it was called, but it was the sort of thing a cop used. With his arms trapped behind his back, Dylan couldn't do much more than thrash, which was good, because my head was pounding.

"What the fuck, Dylan?" I demanded even as Jinxy dragged him backwards, clearly trying to get the guy out of my kitchen.

"You fucked us, Jeri," Dylan snarled, spittle flying from his lips. "They're getting arrested. I know they're coming for me, so I'll be damned if I go down alone."

"Oh?" A strange calm came over me.

"Murder!" he screamed. "That's what Evan's dad said when he texted me. They're coming at us for fucking murder, so if I'm going to do the time, I'm going to do the fucking crime." Then he spit in my direction. "And no one will even miss your freak-ass."

Following him and Jinxy, I passed the food I'd been so happy to be making a moment ago. Calmly, almost with a mind of its own, my hand found the knife: the large blade I'd been using for consistently sized strips of chicken. Wrapping my fingers around it, I finally realized exactly how this was supposed to end.

"Because it's all about you?" I asked as I closed the distance between us. "Jinxy, stop."

"Jeri..." Jinxy said, clearly confused.

But I didn't slow down. I also no longer cared. Rules? Fuck that. This, right here, was vengeance. It was the payment I'd said those girls deserved. It was cold and brutal and exactly the sort of thing that could remove nightmares. This might not change the past, but fuck if it wouldn't make me feel a whole lot better about my own mistakes.

The moment I was close enough, I thrust. Jinxy yelped, jerking in place but not letting go. Dylan gasped, his eyes going wide as the eight inches of stainless steel slipped in below his ribs.

"You like that?" I asked.

"Fuck you!" Dylan groaned, struggling to get the words out around the pain.

I simply leaned in. "Nod, pretty boy."

"No."

So I slowly twisted the blade. "Nod, Dylan. Tell me you want it. Let me stick it wherever I desire. After all, my needs are all that matter. You're just my little bitch."

"Jericho!" Jinxy begged.

I ignored him, refusing to look away from Dylan's eyes. "You were asking for it, you know. Hell, you came here looking for it. Clearly you want me inside you." I pressed the blade even deeper. "Nod, Dylan. Nod like a good boy."

"Ok!" he panted, jiggling his head in a weak but panicked nod.

"And always remember what it feels like when your consent is taken away," I growled, giving the knife another good, hard twist. "Now fucking die."

I jerked the knife out and tossed it as far behind me as possible. Jinxy let go as if in shock. Behind him, Hottie was on his knees, planted over Wade's unconscious body, but his head was turned our way.

"What the fuck?" Hottie asked, slowly pushing himself to his feet.

"Call 9-1-1," Jinxy told him. "She fucking stabbed him, man. In cold blood!"

"In revenge!" I snapped.

"Fuck," Hottie was muttering over and over. "Fuck, fuck. Ok..." He paused to pull his phone out of his pocket, but didn't dial. "Jinxy, listen to me."

Jinxy just waved him off. "Dylan charged Jeri. She was in the kitchen, cooking. The knife was in her hand so she used it in self-defense. No, I got it."

"Ok." And Hottie finally dialed.

I just staggered back until my ass found the counter, giving me something to lean against. At Jinxy's feet, Dylan was moaning, clearly still alive. Blood was seeping from his gut, making a pool on the floor that I knew I'd have to clean later, but I didn't care.

Because fuck him. Fuck both of them. Fuck all of this!

"It was supposed to be over," I breathed, lifting my hands before me to see them both shaking.

The right one was partially covered in blood. Splattered was probably a better word. The left had raw knuckles. My head was pounding, and I knew my entire body was going to hurt so bad in a moment.

"What are we going to tell Mom?" I asked.

But there was no one to answer. Jinxy had bent to press both hands over Dylan's wound. Hottie was rambling on about breaking in and attacking. Likely, that was him telling the dispatcher why we needed the cops here.

The strange thing was that it all felt so calm. Not them, and not the situation, but me. The adrenaline might still be pumping through my body, but my mind had found the quiet it had always longed for. It was done. Payment had been made.

A tired smile found my lips. "You picked on the wrong girl this time, Dylan," I said, pushing myself off the counter to walk back over to him. "Do you hear me?"

"I'm dying," he panted, his eyes on Jinxy.

So I kicked his foot just hard enough to get his attention. "Do you hear me, Dylan?"

"Yes!" the asshole whimpered.

So I leaned in. "Women are no longer here to amuse you, asshole. I'm going to change that. I don't care how long it takes or what I have to do, but I *will* make sure all you men learn one thing. We. Are. Vicious. And we will never have to fight alone."

With a chuckle, Jinxy leaned in, pressing harder against Dylan's wound until the man cried out. "Death over Dishonor, Jericho. You might scare the shit out of me, but I will follow you through hell and back."

"Goes both ways, brother," I told him just as my knees gave out and I staggered down to the floor.

It wasn't pretty, and it certainly wasn't graceful, but I was so far beyond caring. Instead, I pushed myself back until I found something to lean against, and then I sighed. My head tilted back, my eyes closed, and I stopped trying to fight the agony in my body.

"I will take revenge; I will pay them back. In due time their feet will slip. Their day of disaster will arrive, and their destiny will overtake them," I breathed.

"Ruin 32:35," Hottie said as he moved to check on me. "The cops are coming, baby girl. Hold on just a little bit longer, ok?"

"I'm fine," I promised. "Tired, but fine." Then I huffed out a laugh. "But I think we might be ordering pizza tonight."

Hottie just palmed both sides of my face and kissed my brow. "Anything," he swore before kissing below each eye. "Just don't ever scare me like that again, ok?"

"Wasn't leaving," I promised, looking up to meet his eyes. "I was doing my best to send them to hell instead."

CHAPTER 64

JERICHO

I was still sitting on the floor near Dylan's feet when the police rushed through the door with their guns drawn. The first officer inside was actually a face I recognized. He'd been the smiling, happy guy from this morning.

Even better, Logan, Riley, Knock, and Cade weren't far behind. I wasn't sure when Hottie had told them, but clearly he'd whipped off a text in the middle of all that insanity. Me? I just sat there and panted, wishing I could go grab an Advil for my headache, but all too aware the cops wouldn't want me to leave.

"What's going on?" Logan demanded.

Knock didn't care. He pushed through the chaos until he was at my side. "Jeri?" he asked.

"Check her for a concussion!" Riley snapped.

"Ambulance will be here any second," the officer told her.

"Thanks, Brian," Riley said. "You should also know I have two more on the way."

"Everyone from this morning?" he asked.

She nodded. "Yeah, now can I get the victims out of your way and into the living room?"

"No blood on the couches!" I said quickly. "Mom would freak!"

"Stairs," Riley said instead, pointing that way. "Knock, get her up. Cade, help Jinxy. Hottie?"

"I'm good," he promised.

Yet while she was organizing us, the police were handling the guys. A pair was now standing over Wade's limp body. One of them had their hand on his throat like he was checking the guy's pulse. Part of me hoped he was dead, and yet I knew that would be even worse.

Another cop pulled on those funny purple gloves and gestured for Jinxy to move. There wasn't a lot of space to get around him, but Knock managed to guide me easily. Then again, I had a feeling he'd scoop me up into his arms if I staggered too much.

And then all of us converged at the stairs. I flopped down with a groan. Hottie sat behind me, but close enough he could wrap his arms around me. Knock was hovering beside me, next to the wall. Jinxy was on the other side, a couple of steps down with his feet on the actual floor.

"Ok, I need to get upstairs and find something to clean all of you up with," Riley said, weaving her way between us.

"Not yet!" that officer called. "They'll want pictures, Riley."

"Can you at least have the EMTs look at Jericho then?" she shot back.

"Can do," he promised.

I just waved in the direction of the guy. "What the actual hell?"

"He's a good cop," Riley said, sitting down where she'd been standing above all of us. "His name is Brian Sanders, and he helped out with a horse thing that ended up with Kitty and Quake in the attic while crazies ransacked the house."

"But that doesn't mean you talk to him," Logan said. "Not to anyone. Your job is to remain silent, and mine is to represent you, but to do that, I need to know what happened."

So Hottie took over. "Jinxy and I were upstairs in Flawed, planning a big raid. We heard some noise and rushed down to find those two beating the shit out of Jeri."

"What happened before that?" he asked, turning to me.

"I was making fajitas," I said. "The music was playing, and then I heard something, but I didn't figure out what it was until the door closed. When I turned, the pair of them were there, and they said Evan's dad let them know the cops were after them for murder, so if they - well, it was Dylan. He said if he was going down for that, he'd basically take me with him."

"Then they were on you?"

I nodded.

"And the wound?" Logan pressed.

I licked my lips, but before I could answer, Hottie did. "Dylan rushed her, man. She was in the kitchen, cooking. The knife was in her hand, so it was self-defense."

But Logan never looked away from me. "The best representation is the one you're honest with," he said.

I just looked up and smiled. "He deserved a little unasked-for penetration. I gave it to him."

"Good." He reached down to clasp my shoulder. "Just make sure Hottie tells the story, and you make a big deal about the bruises all over your head and how much it hurts."

"Fuck, does it ever," I agreed. "Just tell me someone knows how to get blood out of the grout?"

"Hydrogen peroxide," Riley said. "Bleaches things a bit, and Logan hates that I want to use it on everything, but we'll handle it, Jeri."

"I can scrub," Cade promised, moving to sit by my feet. "But are you honestly ok?"

For a little too long, I stared at the movement of the police and paramedics in my house. Wade had woken up at some point, and now had a woman shining a light in his eyes. Dylan's shirt had been cut open and a bandage was being taped over his wound. More people with long orange boards - for transporting patients, I was pretty sure - and others with stretchers were making their way in.

And that was when the officer who knew Riley made his way over. "Jericho Williams?" he asked. "This is your home, I believe."

"And Hottie's," I said, gesturing to him.

"Grayson," Hottie corrected. "I moved in around Christmas, since her mother's always away for work."

"Gotcha," the man said. "Well, I'm Officer Sanders, but my friends call me Brian. I'm going to need to get a statement, but I think the scene gives a pretty clear indication that this was self-defense. I mean, unless you invited those guys into your house after going through all that crap this morning to get the FBI to arrest them."

"Nope," I said. "I've never invited them in. I also need to learn to lock the front door."

"It's probably never going to be a problem again," Brian told me. "Then again, it seems the group of you does have a way of finding trouble, hm?"

Riley just chuckled. "It's an acquired skill. So who's taking pictures? Seriously, Brian, these kids are all covered in blood. Not like the house is going anywhere, but sticky hands? Not pleasant."

"I'll get them over here," he swore.

I was in the middle of having my face, arms, and hands photographed when Ripper and Zoe burst through the door. Ripper gasped, wanting to rush straight for me, but Zoe stopped him with a hug. Keeping her arm around his waist, she let him walk that way, but the key word was walk.

And then we answered more questions. After that came more. Hottie and Jinxy both got the same photo treatment, as did the rest of my house. At one point, I heard the ambulance take off with the sirens going. And the whole time, the front windows of my house were lit up with flashing red and blue lights.

Then it was done. One by one, the people left. Logan stopped Brian to ask a few more questions over by the door. It was too soft for me to hear, but I didn't care. Riley was busy wiping blood and dirt from my face - my hands were already clean, and the guys had been told to go wash their own hands.

"Knock?" she said. "There's a bottle of pills in the center console of the truck."

"Do you keep drugs everywhere?" he asked.

She just gave him a tired look. "I got kicked in the gut at a horse show once by a two-year-old draft horse. So, yeah. I do."

"I'll get 'em," Knock said.

"Cade, get her a glass of water," she ordered next.

"On it."

Which was when Zoe was finally able to slide in beside me and press her head against my shoulder gently. "Jeri, are you honestly ok? I mean, that had to be terrifying!"

"How bad are you hurt?" Ripper wanted to know.

"The kind of bad that makes me want to lay in bed all day tomorrow," I admitted.

"Playing Flawed," Zoe added. "You know that's what she's thinking."

"Mm..." I said. "Yeah, and maybe, just for a little bit, we can pretend to be normal? I'm thinking until Monday, maybe?"

"And then?" Jinxy asked as he made his way down the stairs to join us.

"Then," I told them, "we have the rest of a website to go through. The Alpha Team aren't the only assholes out there, and we can do this, guys."

"You've already done it," Riley countered. "When do you stop?"

I chuckled, meeting her gaze. "Why stop? I have six people

who I can work with. I have four men I'm in love with. I have everything I never thought was possible, and I found it all because I was finally doing the right thing, Riley. Why would I ever fucking stop?"

"Because this shit is hard for you too," she reminded me.

"So we take a break," Zoe said. "Tonight, Ripper and I can clean up the floor so that doesn't get worse. Tomorrow, we can all come over and fix any damage to the house, right?"

"Mm, food," I mumbled.

"And sleep," Logan said. "All of you are running on empty."

Which was when Hottie finally returned. "We're young. We're used to it. We're also smart enough to know our own limits."

"And speaking of limits," I said, not sure where the idea came from. "Can we please go to the tournament with Knock? Please? Like, maybe a little safe killing and bloodshed? Some relaxation? You know, as a team?"

"Mom won't let me," Zoe said.

Jinxy just murmured. "I'll try, but no promises."

"I'll go," Hottie promised. "Hell, I'll convince the rest, because yeah. We need some fun. Some good, wholesome fun." Which was when my stomach decided to growl - loudly enough for him to hear. "Ok, that's clearly a sign. So how about someone drive me someplace I can pick up food, because I have a feeling the kitchen might get the cops called on us by a delivery driver."

"Burgers?" Logan offered.

"Anything," Hottie said, pausing to bend down and kiss the top of my hair. "Be good for your boyfriends, baby girl. Ripper, take care of her."

"Always," he promised. "And Knock's getting her some pain pills."

"Which is why I have water," Cade said as he made his way out of the kitchen, stepping carefully. "You know, all of this would be a lot easier if we had one place, right? Less running across town for panic calls."

Logan chucked and turned around to catch Riley's eye. "Think the seven of you could keep from killing each other?"

Knock walked into the house just in time to hear that question. "Bro," he said, "haven't you figured it out yet? Teamwork is fucking overpowered. This? They're my team. We're like one big billboard for everything Deviant Games has been doing. I mean, we're flawed, but we're not alone. Levels won't stop us, just grab a gun and go. Doesn't matter which of their game taglines you use, from the popular to the handful that didn't do so good, it pretty much applies to us."

"Because we're perfect," I said, leaning back to rest my weight on my elbows one step above my butt. "All of you." I looked at Zoe. "And yes you."

"I kinda started this," she teased.

"Think I've learned how to be a girl yet?" I asked.

She laughed. "Kinda. I mean your own version, but I'll take it." Then she looked around at the guys hovering all around me. "Think I made you fall in love yet?"

"Yeah," I breathed, accepting the pills Knock was offering. "I think that maybe you actually managed to make it happen. Thanks, Zoe."

"It's what best friends do," she swore.

EPILOGUE

JERICHO

Well, we did end up going to the Dallas gamer's tournament. It had some special name, but damned if I could remember it. But it had been... fun? Interesting might be a better word. Naturally, I'd died in the first round. That part wasn't surprising.

Meeting Cynister, however, was.

The week after that whirlwind of an event, Ruin decided we had one final task to close out our big case. On a Saturday morning - ok, it was eleven, so that counted! - we all converged on Knock's place in our worst clothes. The kill streaks could wait a bit. The death matches weren't going to make or break someone's career. Most importantly, that Sharpie marker needed to go.

It was a case of all hands on deck. Jinxy only got out of it because he was back up in Colorado, working on his final exams. The rest of us unplugged everything, pulled all the furniture away from the walls, taped off stuff in a rather messy sort of way, and then we busted out the rollers.

"I think," Cade said, gesturing to the space over what was normally the charging area, "that Zoe gets the first roll."

"Oh, I'm taking it," she agreed, dipping her extended-pole roller into the paint tray and then smearing a little too much paint over the spot that had her name. "And now it's a free-for-all," she declared.

We laughed. Ok, we also made one hell of a mess, but bit by bit, the stories of twenty-three victims faded, but they were not forgotten. Their recovery would be their own. There was no way to change that. Their vengeance, however, had been ours.

"Did you hear?" Cade asked. "Sounds like Dylan took a plea deal."

"Which is why I gave his account info to Cyn," Knock explained. "It was part of his deal, but it also means Cyn can get in and do what he needs."

"Finally," Hottie grumbled. "What about the rest?"

"Well," Cade said, "Dr. Marshall is under investigation for his drug security. He's probably going to lose his license, at the very least. He might go to jail at the worst."

"Like father, like son," I said.

"And," Cade went on, "the other four asshats in Alpha Team are trying to say they're innocent. Damn, they're going to fucking fry. Oh yeah, speaking of cops... Evan's dad got fired. Sounds like that family is moving out of state. I mean, he'll probably just become a cop somewhere else, but still."

"And the detective?" I asked.

Cade shook his head. "Reprimanded, but that's it."

"And how do you know all of this?" Zoe asked. "I'm supposed to be the one living on social media."

"TeamSpeak," Cade admitted. "Our resident spook was around to make sure we had some good news. He said it was the least he could do for helping him get the girl of his dreams."

"And?" Zoe pressed. "How's that going?"

"It's going," Knock assured us. "Zara's a mess. Cyn's a mess. Figure that means they're perfect for each other."

And as we talked, the wall returned to the pristine state it had been when I'd first seen this room. I'd half expected something about this to feel sad, almost like nostalgia. Instead, it was one of the best feelings I could imagine.

"Guys..." I said when the conversation fell into a lull. "We did it. We actually fucking did it!"

"And we're not going to stop," Zoe declared.

"So," Hottie asked, "who are we going after next?"

"Soul Reaper?" Knock suggested.

"I think we should hit another lower group," Ripper said. "Look, the feds are already chasing the top, right? I mean, nothing says we can't help Cyn if he needs it - "

"I can't," Zoe grumbled.

"Don't worry, you're getting a deal too," Knock promised. "And Jinxy. We didn't forget you two, and he won't either."

"But!" Ripper said, proving he'd gained quite a bit of confidence lately. "Y'all, who helps the helpless? Who else but us would've listened to Tiffany and her friends and taken that seriously? I think we need to focus on the nobodies. The women who are getting hurt and considered to be asking for it, or whatever shit these people say."

"I like it," I agreed.

"I'm with Ripper," Cade said. Then he groaned. "But I also think we should help Cyn."

"Any time," Zoe said. "But I don't see why we can't do both. Look, he saved me. He was the one who got Evan arrested! We also know that sometimes his hands are tied."

"But ours aren't," Hottie agreed. "Granted, we don't know if - "

The trilling of my phone was loud enough to make not only him pause, but also forced everyone else to look at me. Apologizing, I pulled the thing out of my pocket and swiped. That was my email. Nervously, I swiped, opened the app, and then wanted to groan in disappointment.

"Fuck," I grumbled. "College application."

"You didn't get in?" Hottie asked.

I waved him off. "Of course I got in. No, I was just..." My words trailed off as another message loaded on my screen right before my eyes.

Letting out a little squeak of excitement, I tapped at it. My eyes sped through the words, but around me, everyone else's phones were beeping and buzzing as well. This was what I'd been hoping for. *This* was the big deal.

"We got the confidential informant contracts!" I cheered, and I wasn't the only one.

"What?" Logan asked, thundering down the stairs and skipping a few in his haste. "They came in?"

"Got mine too," Knock said.

"Same," Hottie agreed.

"As pretty as I could've hoped for," Cade announced.

But Zoe was busy texting. Ripper glanced at her, then told Logan. "I got one too."

"Zoe?" Logan asked.

She looked up. "Hm?"

"Did you get one?" he asked just as her phone dinged.

A smile immediately took over her face. "Yes!" Then she paused. "Uh, I mean I did, and it seems Jinxy just got his too!"

"And now," I said, "we are hacking for the government. So, Mr. Weiss, does that mean we're covered?"

"I'll make sure of it," he promised.

"Um..." Zoe said, dragging out the word. "If we're now working for the FBI, kinda, and we won't get in trouble for hacking KoG..."

"What are you thinking?" Knock asked when she paused for a little too long.

"Well, it's just that Jinxy was going through the KoG site as a mental break, you know? He was making sure we didn't miss anything or anyone, and looking for some other stuff we might tackle. And, um..."

"What?" I begged.

Scrunching up her face, she put down her roller and made her way over to one of the laptops then lifted the lid. "So, um, I think all of you might want to read this."

There wasn't a lot of space to put the long-handled rollers, but we managed. With the wall about half done, it wouldn't hurt for the paint to dry a little so we could do another coat over the worst bits. Then, once we were all watching, Zoe opened up the Squirrel and pulled up a saved image.

"This is from the day after Evan was arrested," she warned us.

DEATHADDER: New hard drives. Delete shit, clone it, then destroy the old ones. Dump them someplace you don't usually go. Another town is even better. Move everything to the dark web, man. Here's a [link] for a site I like. There's no need for you to lose your goodies. Just gotta keep the computers, phones, tablets, etc at home clean, right?

And you're doing good work. Two gamer girls? That's actually impressive! Can't wait to meet you next year at UNT. Inbox me if you need any more tips. I've been at this for four years now and no one suspects a thing.
Fuck those bitches. If they didn't want it, they wouldn't come begging.

The air rushed from my lungs. "He's at UNT?"

"Yeah," Zoe muttered. "We also don't have a damned clue who this guy is, what he's done, or any of it, but four years?"

Knock just chuckled. "Yeah, by the time we graduate, we'll know him, Zoe."

"So can we maybe make him fry?" she asked.

I just dropped down into the closest chair. "Ruin 32:35, right?"

"Ruin 32:35," Cade agreed. "We are the vengeance. We are their disaster and their fate."

"We will overtake them all," Knock agreed.

"We don't even need their feet to slip anymore," Ripper added. "We'll *make* them fall."

"And fuck whoever tries to get in our way," Hottie said. "Fuck KoG. Fuck men who think they can hurt women without consequences. It's time for someone to step up, so I say we ruin this fucker."

And around the circle, everyone slowly began to nod. We didn't need to call an official vote. This? It was enough. It was focus and determination. Most of all, it was our purpose.

"I do believe this means we have a new assignment," I said. "This fool has no idea his friends won't be showing up. No, I think we need to let him meet *us*, instead."

BOOKS BY AURYN HADLEY

Contemporary Romance: *Standalone Book*

One More Day

End of Days - Auryn Hadley & Kitty Cox writing as Cerise Cole **(Paranormal RH):** *Completed Series*

Still of the Night

Tainted Love

Enter Sandman

Highway to Hell

A Flawed Series - co-written w/ Kitty Cox **(Contemporary Poly):** *In Progress*

Ruin

Brutal

Vicious

Cruel

Savage

Wicked

Deviant

Gamer Girls - co-written w/ Kitty Cox **(Contemporary Romance):** *Completed Series*

Flawed

Challenge Accepted

Virtual Reality

Fragged

Collateral Damage

For The Win

Game Over

The Dark Orchid (Fantasy Poly):

Completed Series

Power of Lies

Magic of Lust

Spell of Love

The Demons' Muse (Paranormal Poly):

Completed Series

The Kiss of Death

For Love of Evil

The Sins of Desire

The Lure of the Devil

The Wrath of Angels

The Path of Temptation (Fantasy Poly):

Completed Series

The Price We Pay

The Paths We Lay

The Games We Play

The Ways We Betray

The Prayers We Pray

The Gods We Obey

Where the Wild Things Grow (Paranormal Poly):

Completed Series

Magic In The Moonlight

Spell In The Summertime

Witchcraft In The Woods

Wolves Next Door (Paranormal RH / Poly):

Completed Series

Wolf's Bane

Wolf's Call

Wolf's Pack

ABOUT AURYN HADLEY

Auryn Hadley is happily married with three canine children and a herd of feral cats that her husband keeps feeding. Between her love for animals, video games, and a good book, she has enough ideas to spend the rest of her life trying to get them out. They all live in Texas, land of the blistering sun, where she spends her days feeding her addictions – including drinking way too much coffee.

For a complete list of books and to receive notices for new releases by Auryn Hadley follow me:

Amazon Author Page -
amazon.com/author/aurynhadley

Visit our Patreon site
www.patreon.com/Auryn_Kitty

You can also join the fun on Discord -
https://discord.gg/Auryn-Kitty

Facebook readers group -
www.facebook.com/groups/TheLiteraryArmy/

Merchandise is available from -
Etsy Shop (signed books) - The Book Muse -
www.etsy.com/shop/TheBookMuse

Threadless (clothes, etc) - The Book Muse -
https://thebookmuse.threadless.com/

Also visit any of the other sites below:

My website -
aurynhadley.com

Books2Read Reading List -
books2read.com/rl/AurynHadley

facebook.com/AurynHadleyAuthor
amazon.com/author/aurynhadley
goodreads.com/AurynHadley
bookbub.com/profile/auryn-hadley
patreon.com/Auryn_Kitty

BOOKS BY KITTY COX

A **Flawed** Series - co-written w/Auryn Hadley
(Contemporary Poly): *In Progress*

End of Days - Auryn Hadley & Kitty Cox writing as Cerise Cole
(Paranormal RH): *Completed Series*

Falling For The Bull Riders (Contemporary Poly Romance):
In Process

Gamer Girls - co-written w/Auryn Hadley
(Contemporary Romance): *Completed Series*

Shades of Trouble - (Contemporary Poly Romance):
Completed Series

Ménage Contemporary Romance: *Standalone Book*
When it Rains

ABOUT KITTY COX

As you would expect, Kitty Cox has a love of cats, but also dogs, horses, and pretty much any animal. She's always enjoyed a good love story. A chance meeting involving a martini, a margarita, and some laughs with another author convinced her to finally put words to paper - and now she can't seem to stop.

From the sweet and tender idea of second chance romances, to the hot and dirty thrill of stories intended for adult audiences, the wonders of falling in love are where her imagination goes. She likes to blame it on the hot and spicy climate of her home town in Texas. Then again, it could just be a result of growing up on stolen romance novels hidden under her pillow at night.

For a complete list of books and to receive notices for new releases by Kitty Cox follow me:

Amazon Author Page -
amazon.com/author/kittycox

You can also join the fun on Discord -
https://discord.gg/Auryn-Kitty

Visit our Patreon site -
www.patreon.com/Auryn_Kitty

Facebook readers group -
The Literary Army
www.facebook.com/groups/TheLiteraryArmy/

Merchandise is available from -
Etsy Shop (signed books) - The Book Muse -
www.etsy.com/shop/TheBookMuse

Threadless (clothes, etc) - The Book Muse -
https://thebookmuse.threadless.com/

Also visit any of the other sites below:

My website -
kittycoxauthor.com

Books2Read Reading List -
books2read.com/rl/KittyCox

- facebook.com/KittyCoxAuthor
- amazon.com/author/kittycox
- goodreads.com/KittyCox
- bookbub.com/authors/kitty-cox
- patreon.com/Auryn_Kitty

Printed in Great Britain
by Amazon